T0165481

GREEN TANGO

LEV AMUSIN

iUniverse, Inc.
Bloomington

Green Tango

iUniverse books may be ordered through booksellers or by contacting:

iUniverse
1663 Liberty Drive
Bloomington, IN 47403
www.iuniverse.com
1-800-Authors (1-800-288-4677)

ISBN: 978-1-4620-2099-7 (sc)
ISBN: 978-1-4620-2102-4 (hc)
ISBN: 978-1-4620-2101-7 (ebook)

Printed in the United States of America

iUniverse rev. date: 06/19/2011

INTRODUCTION

In 1988, the economy of the USSR and then Russia began to promptly worsen. The government's desperate attempts at recovery were unsuccessful, however. Add to this the occurrence of several natural disasters and technological accidents, such as Chernobyl, as well as a wave of civil unrest and bloodshed that swept the country. The apotheosis of the long chain of negative events was an attempt to overthrow Gorbachev's regime by military force on August 19, 1991.

By that time, the country was also overflowing with an unprecedented amount of gangsterism. So in 1992, in Moscow and other cities, the curfew law was ordered. On the periphery of the area, the situation was worse still. For example, in the industrial city of Togliatti, fourteen gangster groups were operating, and the fifteenth was the SWAT team. Masked men routinely stopped vehicles and asked for ID, aiming guns into drivers' stomachs, but it was never clear who they were—police officers or gangsters.

At the same time, without government involvement, the country's economic conditions had been noticeably corrected by small operators called "shuttles." Like ants on their backs, thousands hauled from abroad back home consumer goods and foodstuff. On their treks, they were approached by gangsters offering protection, and attacked by government officials and customs officers. With the persistence of Arctic lemmings, however, they continued their work. With their earnings, they bought apartments and cars, and invested in savings for future business.

Many Russians considered living abroad, and for hundreds of thousands of officials, engineers, doctors, scientists, and others, that dream became reality. Many sent their kids to foreign colleges, participated in seminars abroad, and even formed fictitious marriages and divorces for the sake of obtaining permanent status in developed countries. More self-confident individuals tried to obtain dual-citizenship, allowing them to leave Russia to Germany, Spain, the United States, and who knows where else, on a moment's notice.

As a result, the head office of Microsoft now employs no fewer than two thousand skilled programmers from the former USSR. In every US university, there are Russian professors. And, according to one evaluation by real estate brokers in Orange County, California, two to three hundred thousand of its residents are Russian-speaking people, most of them professionals.

Back in Russia, former semi slaves, used to subsisting on miniscule salaries, understood that for a nice life, money was a necessary attribute. And so it began. People tried to steal and sell everything they could get their hands on: scrap metal, plywood, nickel alloy, fertilizers, even humans for trafficking. It was worse than an epidemic; it was a uniform orgy in the realization of a popular idea—to steal big money and escape.

Such activity slowed down sometime after the year 2000, when the political and economical climate in Russia noticeably stabilized. However, a recent study conducted and published on April 24–27, 2009, by the Yuri Levada Analytical Center questioned sixteen hundred Russian citizens from forty-six regions of the Russian Federation. It showed the 13 percent of Russians interviewed would like to emigrate. Among youth, that number rises to 29 percent, and among people with advanced educations, 18 percent.

In truth, however, the idea to "steal big money and escape" was far from being new. This practice has often surfaced in times of uncertainty and economic crisis. After all, where can you go and how can you survive without money?

It was perfectly described in Russian classical literature. Recollect the main character Tchichikov from *Dead Soul* by Nicholas Gogol. Tchichikov suddenly began to go around and buy the already dead but still registered as live souls of slaves from their masters. For what reason would he do that? The answer is simple: to use them as collateral on a loan from the bank, take the money and then to leave. Abroad, of course!

Despite this novel's authentic descriptions of some historical events, the characters and stories herein are the sole product of the author's imagination, and not to be taken as documentary. This includes the descriptions of companies, which have never existed and do not exist now. In short, this novel is purely fictional, with the sole purpose of providing entertainment to the reader.

PROLOGUE

This novel is a logical continuation of my previous book, *Bloody Oil,* a summary of which follows:

Far from Moscow, in the Siberian city of Tyumen, mobsters were trying to take over the oil-extracting enterprise the Tyumen Oil & Gas Production Association. Management was resisting, but the forces were unequal.

At the same time, there was a shortage of foodstuff and consumer goods in the region. In order to feed the association workers and supply the city, association management made the decision to sell crude oil abroad. The oil in reference was collected in storage and became the property of the enterprise—but as these stores were unrecorded, mobsters were unaware of them.

Management had already directed a reputable member of its Board of Directors, the young and beautiful Ms. Lydia Selina, to be its representative in the sale of this crude oil. So in the spring of 1993, she went to Moscow, and in a short time, executed a contract for the sale of five hundred thousand tons of crude oil to the company Agroprom.

Agroprom's representative in the dealings was the president of Agroprom-USA and a US citizen, Mr. Boris Goryanin. Goryanin made contact with one of the States' oil giants, Global Oil Research and Sales Corporation, only to find that Agroprom had neither license or quotas for trading crude oil, nor the finances to pay for it.

Using its connections in the FSB (the former KGB), Agroprom obtained a license for the sale of the oil and readied itself for negotiations with Global. They appointed an officer of the Service of External Intelligence, Lieutenant Colonel Yakubovsky, as a member of the delegation in Washington for the meeting. Yakubovsky was to meet his agent, receive the necessary information, and pay him money in return.

What the people of Agroprom didn't know was that the representative of Tyumen Oil & Gas had already executed a similar contract—also for the sale of five hundred thousand tons of crude oil—with another Moscow firm called Solvaig.

Solvaig had problems, but, unlike Agroprom, Solvaig had the financial resources to carry out the contract. Solvaig's owner, Mr. Arkady Fedorov, decided to find out what was really going on with Tyumen Oil & Gas, and to conduct an investigation of Selina, so that he could deal directly with whoever had sent her to Moscow. He charged his employee, Mr. Veresaev, with this investigation.

By this time, the Solvaig chief of security and colonel of Special Operation Forces, Vladimir Shkolnikov, and Ms. Selina have fallen in love. They have tried to hide their relationship from everyone at Solvaig, but the employees see through their façade.

By the summer of 1993, negotiations between Agroprom and Global Oil have taken place in Washington. The parties have agreed upon a fair formula for evaluating the Ural blend of crude oil and organized delivery of the oil for supposed processing at Global's refineries (an arrangement that was only possible using a loophole in Russian legislation). Global has taken the risk, agreeing to provide an advance payment on and transportation of the crude oil.

During negotiations, Boris Goryanin, a mature, married man, has fallen under the charm of the young British aristocrat Lady Melissa Spenser, the fiancée of the Global Oil representative in Switzerland, Mr. Eddy Pennington. Boris and Lady Melissa developed special relations, but have managed to keep their mutual feelings from colleagues.

During negotiations, Yakubovsky had met with his agent, with the consent of Agroprom leader Gavrila Kravchuk and in collaboration with a member of the delegation, Mr. Alexander Popov. When the agent had arrived at the meeting, Yakubovsky had observed that the agent was under surveillance. Despite that, he contacted the agent, received the needed information, and transferred the money. Yakubovsky understood it was their last meeting, and consequently appropriated the percentage due to his agent.

By the summer of 1993, Agroprom, using its employees' personal connections, has executed all of the necessary contracts for delivering crude oil by pipeline to the Baltic Sea harbor, Ventspils; converting US dollars into Russian rubles to pay for the oil; and coordinating the loading of the oil aboard tankers.

Boris Goryanin went back to Switzerland to open accounts that would allow for the accumulation of profit, and there, met with Lady Melissa. He remained there with her alone for several days. They couldn't keep their feelings from each other, but he was compelled to leave.

At the same time, in Moscow, the chief of Solvaig security, Vladimir

Shkolnikov, has married Lydia Selina, and she has become pregnant. It seemed that under these circumstances, all was ready to get back to normal, until Arkady Fedorov learned from Veresaev that Tyumen Oil & Gas had made an agreement with local gangsters. The mobster takeover of the association would happen in the winter of 1994. On the balance sheet, the assets of the association totaled three million dollars, but there were one million tons of crude oil in storage, which, in those days, would have made over a hundred million dollars. Local mobsters didn't know about it, but Fedorov did.

After his return from Washington, Agroprom leader Gavrila Kravchuk, by accident, ordered his chief of security, the retired officer of the Ninth Division of the KGB, Lieutenant Colonel Dmitry Cherkizov, to look after Lydia Selina. Thus he found out that she was cooperating with Solvaig. Having hesitated for some time, Kravchuk called a meeting with Arkady Fedorov, not realizing that Fedorov had been hired to liquidate geologist Veresaev for Veresaev's knowledge about the hundred million dollars. Fedorov already had made time to go to Tyumen, where he managed to force the director general of Tyumen Oil & Gas, Mr. Sviblov, to sell to him control of the association for three million dollars. Thus, Sviblov got his hands on Lydia Selina, not to mention on his long-time friend Joseph Kozitsky, with whom he had worked twenty-six years.

During Fedorov's meeting with Kravchuk, Kravchuk told him that Shkolnikov and Selina had been married and that she was pregnant with his child. Fedorov instructed Shkolnikov to go to Tanzania at the end of September, where Solvaig had developed a diamond quarry. Fedorov's son had supervision over the project, along with this father's instruction to kill Shkolnikov.

The political situation in Russia, by then, had been sharply aggravated, and in the autumn of 1993, the confrontation between Russian President Yeltsin and the Russian Supreme Council achieved apogee. Kravchuk knew that the presidential decree regarding the dissolution of the Supreme Council was ready and could lead to civil war.

By the end of September, Boris Goryanin had arrived in Moscow. Yakubovsky's accomplice, Popov, had been found dead on the roof of his apartment. Boris was waiting for Eddy Pennington to arrive with one million dollars cash as the prepayment for pumping crude oil through a pipeline from Siberia to the Baltic Sea. However, Kravchuk, understanding that Fedorov wouldn't let Tyumen Oil & Gas execute delivery of oil under the contract between Agroprom and Global, decided not to make this payment. Instead, he charged his chief of security, Cherkizov, to kill both Goryanin and Pennington, and to take the money. He knew that civil war seemed inevitable, to which he could write off everything. Unexpectedly, however, instead of Pennington, Lady Melissa arrived in Moscow, and she had brought the money.

That evening, Lady Melissa and Boris went for a walk. They stopped in a store that sold musical instruments, where Boris masterly played the violin, letting Lady Melissa know about his feelings for her.

The next morning, they took off for Samara, where everything was ready for the killing of two men. The arrival of the young woman broke the gangsters' plans. They took the two guests to an empty house in the village, and confiscated Melissa's travel bag with the one million dollars in cash. There, they plan to gang rape Melissa in front of Boris and then kill the both of them. But first, Cherkizov sent two gangsters to the grocery store to get booze and snacks, and then went to a telephone station to report on their performance of the task. He left Boris and Melissa locked in the bathroom, with one gangster to stand guard over the house.

Boris, taking advantage of the several minutes left to them, found a solution: on the bathroom floor were several wires, which he strung from the door handle to the electric socket. When the remaining gangster came to the bathroom for Boris, he grabbed the handle to open the door and was killed by the electric current.

Boris took the gangster's handgun and used it to shoot Cherkizov upon his return. Then he removed Melissa from the scene, made a trail of gasoline throughout the house, switched on the kitchen stove, and stuck the bathroom wires back into electric socket. The remaining two gangsters, upon returning from the store, entered the house just as it exploded.

Boris and Lady Melissa left in Cherkizov's car, in which they found Melissa's travel bag with the money. Knowing the car could be under surveillance Boris drove them to a nearby hospital, and hired an ambulance driver to take them to Togliatti, where Boris's old friend worked as the chief of security of Diamond Bank. With the help of this friend, Boris and Melissa were hidden the bank's private hotel, which was under the constant protection of bank security.

For Boris and Melissa, this time became a honeymoon, and Lady Melissa began to insist on using the money to start a business in the United States, which would be used for their future child.

Lydia Selina, under Fedorov's order, experienced a martyr death, and as the result of his delayed flight to Tanzania, Shkolnikov returned home too late. He found his wife torn to pieces by his subordinates.

His revenge was without limits. He burned the Solvaig building to the ground, and killed Fedorov, along with his son, his family, and his bodyguards. Then he committed suicide. Sviblov and Kozitsky had killed each other.

In Moscow, tanks had fired shots on the Russian White House. Boris and Melissa had taken off for Frankfurt.

1

Moscow, July 23, 1993

After negotiations conducted in Washington over the contract between Agroprom and Global Oil for the delivery of crude oil, Mr. Gavrila Petrovich Kravchuk and Mr. Vladislav Ivanovich Yakubovsky returned to Moscow. The next morning, Vladislav, or Vlad, awoke at 4:00 a.m. Besides having jet lag, he couldn't sleep because it felt as if his small bedroom was closing in on him. To boot, it was hot and humid. After having wandered around the apartment, he woke his wife and suggested they visit her parents, who live in a village about 160 kilometers from Moscow. His wife was surprised to hear such a request. Vlad normally didn't like to go to the village.

It was about six o'clock when they hailed a cab near the Kazansky Railroad Station, after which such a thing happened that was impossible to explain. The old gypsy approached them, her colorful, world-wise skirt touching the ground, covering what were no doubt her dirty, bare feet. Her faded, worn jacket concealed old, shriveled breasts, and her gray hair was tousled into a heap. But her deep black eyes looked straight into Yakubovsky's, and seemed to him to radiate with a strange luminescence. The gypsy touched the sleeve of his shirt with her long-unwashed hand, and spoke in a deep, guttural voice: "Stop, oh, you young and beautiful! I shall tell you your entire destiny."

"I do not believe in guessing," the lieutenant colonel said.

"Be gone from here!" Natalie, Vladislav's wife, roared at her. "Don't bother good people."

"Do not to shout at me," the gypsy growled back. "Be on your way. You don't belong here."

Then, in her magic, howling voice, she addressed Yakubovsky. "You will go far away, and you will leave with another wife. Not with her. You will be with a young and beautiful wife. You will be in love with her, and she with you, and she will have your children."

Yakubovsky, without understanding why, stopped. For the first time in his life, he stopped to listen to the old hag speak. Something in her words rang true. He didn't love his wife, indeed. Moreover, he hated her with all his guts, but how did the gypsy know?

The gypsy continued to broadcast. "Through the blood of fornicating with an innocent soul, a disgusting snake will come out from your heart, and you will change. But you will be better. You will quit working for the government, and through your grief, you will clear your soul.

"Now, give me a little money. You have a lot of it now, but it is not clean."

He didn't believe she really knew the truth, but reached into his pocket and withdrew a ten-dollar bill.

She took the money and continued: "You will become a merchant of different goods. And you will become daring with a lot of money, deceiving thieves.

"Your promised bride now prepares to meet you, but you will not realize your love for her in the beginning. First, you will undergo many trials and be hurt. Heavy grief will be upon you, but through this grief, you will incorporate your love. Under the thunder's roar, you will learn that she is your wife. Under the thunder's roar, you will conceive your child together. And when it is over, you will leave with your wife together far away."

With this, the gypsy's breathing became visibly labored, and it became apparent that she was expending much energy. She lifted both hands upward, and it seemed to Yakubovsky that electric sparks were slipping between her widely spread fingers, which were covered in golden rings.

"I expect no more money, as you have none left in your pocket, but the next time we meet, you shall be generous. Now, go. Go. Follow your destiny."

And with those words, the old gypsy disappeared, seeming almost, to Yakubovsky, to dissolve in thin air.

"So you have found someone you trust now!" Natalie snapped from her position behind Vladislav, but then she stepped back and held her tongue, afraid the old hag might exact revenge. Then Natalie shook her head. "It's nonsense! There is nothing to believe. Come on, let's move! We shall be late for the train."

Yakubovsky, who hadn't yet returned to his senses, obediently followed his wife, pensively dragging behind her. He didn't want to go to the village anymore. After all, he was still exhausted after the long flight.

As soon as they boarded the train, they took seats on a rigid bench, and he fell fast asleep.

They spent all day long in the village, and Vlad, having inhaled the rural air, fell asleep again after lunch. The rest of the afternoon, he was running so low on gas; they decided to stay in the village overnight. Natalie's father even asked his daughter whether her husband was ill.

He spent the night in a barn, sleeping on stacks of hay prepared for the family's goat. When he awoke the next morning, he felt like a newborn. The fresh air and the smell of the hay had made for a good night's sleep, and all day, Vlad was in a pleasant mood, horsing around. By evening, however, he was in a hurry to get home. He needed to be in the office the next day.

The train arrived in Moscow at about six o'clock. While waiting to board, Yakubovsky noticed that on the platform and the approach to the station, hordes of people were lugging around huge bales. In turn, porters, quickly moving through the crowds, were boarding the bales, instead of suitcases and packages. Further, there were hardly any folks being seen off. What was this diverse crowd of humans acting like ants? It was the first time Yakubovsky had seen anything like it.

"What is going on here?" he asked Natalie. "Who are these people and what are they carrying?"

"What's wrong with you?" she said. "Those are shuttles. They are carrying goods from abroad and are making tons of money. You know, we could do that."

Natalie was lost in a dream world, her husband thought. "But we don't have any money to start up a business." Of course, he hadn't told her about his concealed eight and a half thousand dollars from the agent, whom he contacted in Washington.

"Listen, Vlad," his wife continued. "Nina, from apartment fifteen, is in her second year of the business, and things are coming around for her already. She makes a good living and just doesn't blow it on junk. And the next-door neighbor! She is old and is pulling it off too. I don't know what she makes, but she doesn't complain, and she just bought a new apartment for her daughter. I'm telling you—we could do that too!" Natalie repeated in her dream-like voice.

"I wonder how much money I'd have to get together," Yakubovsky offered thoughtfully. "Hey, Nat, let's get together with Nina tonight and find out what is going on."

That evening, over tea and homemade pie, Nina told the Yakubovskys what they must do to make a "shuttle trip" abroad. She told them what and where to buy, and how to carry it all.

Nina's own story inspired Vlad, and after their meeting, he promised Natalie he'd borrow a little money from some friends. By the following Friday, Vlad, Natalie, and Nina were taking seats on a huge charter flight to Istanbul.

Was the old gypsy's prophecy beginning to come true?

2

Moscow, August 30, 1993

A month passed by after Yakubovsky returned from Washington. By then, he and his wife had gone on two shuttle trips to Turkey.

The "short-legged, clumsy creature," as Vlad had once endearingly called his spouse, understood nothing about business, however, and it was annoying. All of the merchandise they had brought from Turkey, she had sold to neighbors. After paying travel expenses, they had trebled of their seed funds.

From this money Vladislav was able to earn, he gave to his son Igor five thousand dollars to buy a used car.

But Igor, Vladislav's son from his first marriage, used the money to make his own shuttle trip to Poland, with a friend. Within a week, the two young men had been to Poland twice, and, unlike Natalie, didn't push their acquired goods on neighbors. Instead, they handed the goods over to stall-keepers. In ten days' time, Igor had returned the five thousand dollars to his father and given his mother two thousand—and for another three thousand, he purchased a used car. The remaining five thousand dollars he saved as working capital.

The rest of the summer indulged them in pleasantly warm weather rather than the usual intense heat. On those days when Igor didn't make shuttle trips, he'd go to the Plaza of Three Stations, to work as a taxi-cab driver. He liked transporting the passengers who had arrived on the morning trains, but more so, he was impressed by the Kazansky Station, which accommodated trains from Siberia, Central Asia, and Kazakhstan. Many people passed through Moscow on vacation, or on shuttle trips to purchase merchandise from wholesalers. As cab clients, shuttles were preferable; they required more work, but they paid much better.

By now, the whole area in front of the station had been hammered with private kiosks. They blocked passages to trains and exits from the station. The kiosks were open twenty-four-seven, and piles of garbage accumulated behind them. The garbage was only removed at the requests of police, who, in turn, only pretended to enforce the order. In reality, the cops protected all kinds of swindlers—gypsies openly trading drugs and prostitutes.

Periodically, some performance was given at the station. During one such routine, a train had arrived at the platform, and one of the "actors," an old man, imperceptibly alit onto of a stream of people with suitcases, bales, and boxes. As he went, he pulled a napkin from his pocket, ostensibly wiping sweat from his forehead, and as he did so, some change and small bills slipped out "accidentally" from the same pocket. The old man pretended he hadn't noticed, and disappeared from the scene.

Then, some of newly arrived provincial people noticed the money. In order to pick the money up, some person laid on the ground his suitcase and began to collect his earning. At this time, another "actor" from "show" slightly pushed the money collector from behind, ostensibly stumbling on him, leaning on him, and finally separating him from the suitcase. Simultaneously, there appeared a quick young man who grabbed the suitcase and with skillful extraction, instantly dissolved into the crowd.

As soon as the collector came back to reality, he began screaming for help. Instantly, a policeman arrived, pretending to try to understand what had happened, all the while enabling the young man with the suitcase to escape to a nearby van. Finally, the policeman had received his share of the profit.

On this particular morning, however, Igor, while waiting for passengers at the station, was noticing a girl standing alone on the sidewalk. She didn't appear to be a shuttler or prostitute, and was apparently dumbfounded. Nobody was there to meet her, and she seemed to be trying to determine what direction to go.

The girl appeared slightly Asian. She had slanting eyes, but, unlike the Chinese, they were large and deep set. Her long, dark hair had been thrown over one shoulder, and her dress fell over her, emphasizing her figure. Her lithe, muscular arms and long legs gave the impression that she was engaged in ballet or gymnastics. Only a scarf winding around her neck brought out the provincial in her.

In one hand, she held a travel bag, and in the other a pile of books tied by a cord. A handbag was thrown over her shoulder. Most likely she was a student, Igor thought. The girl irresolutely looked around and back, indicating that this was her first time in Moscow.

Igor pulled up to her, stopped his car, and got out. "Excuse me, please," he said, approaching her. "Would you mind looking after my car for a minute?"

"Certainly," she agreed at once.

Igor rushed to a flower booth and bought a bouquet of red roses. Having returned, he gallantly stretched it out to her. "Welcome to Moscow!"

The girl was confused, awarding his effort with a smile, but then resolutely refusing the flowers.

Then Igor said, "I see that you are in Moscow for the first time. If you will, I am ready to give you a ride wherever you need to go."

"Thank you, but I will go on my own," she said, trying to get rid of the annoying gentleman.

"My name is Igor Yakubovsky." Then, to confirm his words, he retrieved his passport and driver's license from his pocket. "Here it is. You may write down my name and license plate number and give it to the cop, if you have any doubts. If something happened to you, they would find me."

Finally convinced that he was an honest man, the girl accepted his offer. Igor opened the trunk, and took her bag and textbooks. Once they were in the car, she accepted the bouquet.

Igor learned that the girl had arrived from Tobolsk and that her name was Anna Wagner. She was a third-year student at Tobolsk Polytechnic University, but she wanted to transfer to the Moscow Textile University to become a fashion designer. As they continued talking, Igor grew to like Anna more and more.

Finally, he pulled up to the university and stayed to wait while she attempted to resolve the problems with her transfer in the dean's office.

After a lengthy wait, he saw Anna leaving the building. Her expression made it clear that all did not go well.

"Well, how are you doing?" Igor asked her. "What did they tell you?"

"They told me that I could be accepted as a full-time student with a loss of one year. But, the main thing is, they cannot give me a hostel. They have suggested I rent living accommodations from a private party, but I haven't enough money. And I do not know where to earn money in Moscow."

"Well, that can be taken care of," Igor said with confidence. "In the house where I live, there is an old lady. She has a three-bedroom apartment. She has one room for rent for a hundred dollars a month. I can lend you two hundred dollars to start, and then we could go together as shuttles to Poland or Turkey, and you can pay me back and begin earning your own money.

"Please, let me take you to meet my neighbor lady, and afterward, we can have a bite somewhere. Or, we can eat first and then go ask about renting the apartment."

"Really?" said Ann (as Igor had already begun to call her in his head). "That would be great!"

Igor Yakubovsky had once lived with his mother and father in a two-bedroom apartment in a five-story building not too far from the metro station, Autozavodskaya. This was the municipal apartment that then Lieutenant Yakubovsky Sr. had received after graduating from military school, when he was appointed to the External Intelligence Service Division of the KGB.

At that time, Igor had been young, and Mrs. Yakubovsky had been pregnant with a second child. Her pregnancy had enabled them to receive an apartment before those on the regular waiting list. From complications during the pregnancy, she lost the child, but the apartment remained theirs.

Later, when Yakubovsky Sr. was forced by circumstances and pressure from his superiors to leave the family, he left the apartment to his ex-wife and son. He and his new wife rented a single room for a long time, before receiving another municipal apartment.

Hastily, Igor and Anna grabbed a bite at a fast-food kiosk, and then went to see the old lady, who rented them a furnished room on the second floor in the apartment where Igor lived.

Anna and "Grandmother" liked each other right away, and as soon as Anna moved in, she was accepted to the Textile University.

Igor and Anna saw each other every day. Even when Anna was totally occupied with her studies or stayed late at the library preparing for exams, Igor would drive her to and from the university. He was falling in love with Ann without even realizing it. With each new meeting, he liked her more and more. And, to him, it seemed as if she felt the same.

After a mere two months, Igor proposed to her and Anna accepted. They decided that she would graduate first, and then Igor would apply for admission to some university. In the meantime, they would continue earning money with their shuttle business.

3

Moscow, August 30, 1993

Anna Wagner was of rather noble origin. Her paternal great-grandmother, Baroness Maria Pavlovna Wagner, came from a long line of Russianized Germans. Young baroness was a maid of honor for Her Majesty Empress Maria Fedorovna the wife of Russian Emperor (Tsar) Alexander III. The empress in her girlhood was Her Royal Highness the Danish Princess Dagmar and she was a relative of almost all European royalty.

Maria Wagner was born in 1875. Her mother had died at Maria's birth, and her father, the colonel, had been lost in 1878 in the Balkans, during the Russian-Turkish War. The girl was taken in by her unmarried aunt, her father's sibling. The aunt gave the little baroness a decent education, expecting that, in due course, the child would be accepted at the emperor's court where a worthy groom could fend for her.

The aunt's efforts ended in success in St. Petersburg, at an institution for noble maidens. Upon graduation from this prestigious institution, after taking numerous examinations and having her references checked, the nineteen-year-old baroness was accepted at the emperor's court. Maria Wagner was appointed to service the empress.

After serving for only a year, the baroness found herself in a situation with one of a young grand prince, who was regularly there at the court. Their amorous story together was terminated, however, when the baroness became pregnant. Emperor Alexander III was known for his religiousness and strict customs. He was never unfaithful to his wife and didn't encourage easy behavior in his court; further, suspecting even a hint of frivolity would exact punishment.

Despite the empress's request that the emperor indulge the unfortunate woman, he called the baroness into his office and lectured her. However, taking her word of honor that she would remain silent about the affair, he granted her a generous gift of seventy-five thousand rubles. He then requested that she get out of his sight and down to Odessa, the city on the Black Sea that fell under the guardianship of the general-governor.

Thus, Baroness Wagner was escorted to the railroad station. The grenadier brought her suitcases to the sleeping compartment, and then, ensuring that nobody could see him, handed her a cardboard gift box. In the box there were her favorite French pastries, a small Chinese lacquer box containing a man's gold ring with a miniature cameo of her, twenty-five thousand golden rubles, and a letter. She didn't read the letter, but burnt it on a candle and ate the French pastries, while examining the gold ring. On the ring's underside was an engraving: "Forgive and Pardon, A. M., 1893." After eating, she tucked the money, lacquer box, and gold ring away for safekeeping.

In Odessa, the baroness rented an apartment on Sofievskaya Street. At that time, it was one of the best buildings in the city, known as "Prince Urusov's Apartment." The building adjoined a magnificent garden that belonged to the archbishop of Odessa. Poorly adapted to real life, the naïve baroness, as soon as she saw the garden, planned to walk there with her future baby.

From her apartment on the top floor, Maria had an unobstructed view of Odessa's harbor. In addition to three bedrooms, there was a large kitchen, a toilet, and a separate bathroom with a big white iron tub connected to a water heater. She could wash baby diapers there, and then dry them in the attic, which was connected to her apartment by some stairs in the back. The apartment was well suited for the unlucky baroness, given her present situation.

A romantic person, she often dreamed that her son (and she didn't doubt she would have a son!) would become a naval officer and go to distant countries. She imagined that she would watch the harbor outside her window to wait for his return.

… And his father? Oh, he would suffer by not knowing his son.

Well… The window overlooking the harbor was from the toilet, but all the rest—with money she had—was manageable.

Maria Wagner was starting to grow her roots down into this new place. At the institution for noble maidens, she had mastered some trades. Among some other things she had learned was to create custom dresses. So she purchased the best sewing machine available, a Singer, with a foot drive, a set of sewing accessories, scissors, an iron, and an ironing table. Then having made friends with the owner of a shop that sold patterns and supplies for milliners, she began, with their help, to tailor and sew items for people out of her home. She didn't earn a lot of money, but enough to help her buy the essentials in life.

Andrew Wagner was born in 1894. The loving mother had prepared for everything so that her child would never feel fatherless. To help her care for the baby, she employed a rural fourteen-year-old-girl called Margery, who performed all the heavy work around the house. When the water pressure was low, and didn't reach the fourth floor, Margery drug full buckets of water up the stairs, warmed them using the water heater, and then washed and ironed diapers, bathed the baby, and washed the baroness. In a word, life proceeded.

Time flew quickly, and the baroness finally lost hope that a miracle might happen—that she might be reaccepted into the emperor's court. Maria tried her best to give her son the best education possible. She placed him in First Odessa's Classical Grammar School, located not too far from their apartment at the end of Princely Street. At this school, he studied divine Bible studies, languages, history, geography, and mathematics.

Soon enough, Andrew Wagner had grown to be a tall, nice-looking young man with good manners, and after graduating in 1912, he was accepted into the Odessa University to study jurisprudence. The young baron was planning to become an attorney or even judge.

Then World War I ignited in 1914, and Baron Andrew Wagner quit the university and joined the army. Mother was in despair, but what she could do? This was his destiny.

Upon his departure, she gave her son the gold ring that she had received as a gift from his father, for him to remember her by. The ring still held the cameo of Maria and was engraved with "Forgive and Pardon. A. M. 1893." She then wished on him blessings — feats of arms in the name of the tsar and the fatherland.

At the end of February 1915, Lieutenant Andrew Wagner appeared in Galicia in the reserve regiment. On the third day of his stay at the front, his regiment was thrown under the city of Perimyshel, which had been surrounded by the Russian army for six months. The Austro-Hungarian armies had resisted desperately.

In one of many counterattacks, the company's commander was wounded, though not killed, so Lieutenant Wagner led the company in attack. The regiment commander noticed the bravery of young man. After the battle, the regiment commander submitted a written request that Lieutenant Andrew Wagner receive a military award for his bravery.

By March 15, the company's new commander had been assigned, and on March 21, the Russian army invaded Perimyshel's suburbs. During the fight for the city, the company sustained heavy losses, so Andrew was ordered to deliver a report to the regiment's commander. On his way, Lieutenant Wagner received a chest wound, and though no important organs were damaged, the bleeding hardly managed to stop. Despite his wound, the lieutenant found the regiment's commander and delivered the report to him. Having recognized the young lieutenant as Wagner, the colonel submitted a second request for Lieutenant Andrew Wagner to receive yet another award for bravery. The wounded lieutenant was sent to the hospital.

After the capture of Perimyshel, the Russian Tsar Nicholas II cousin's the Grand Prince Alexander Mihailovich arrived. Among other things, he visited the hospital. Tied in bandages, Lieutenant Wagner rose to salute the grand prince as he walked by, and the grand prince stopped and rested his gaze on the gold ring with the tiny cameo, which was on the lieutenant's finger.

The prince thanked the young officer for his service to the homeland, and then, after learning his name, asked him about his parents. The Andrew's answer was simple: "The Mother name is Baroness Maria Pavlovna Wagner and the father name is unknown to me."

After leaving the hospital, the grand prince ordered the camp's officer on duty to pull up the young lieutenant's file. The officer brought the grand prince a folder with information regarding Andrew Wagner. Inside, among the many documents, the prince noted both requests by the regiment's commander to award Lieutenant Baron Wagner for bravery.

The grand prince had planned to leave Perimyshel, but the next evening, having postponed all other business, he returned to the hospital. He went to the hospital chief's office, ordered him to call Lieutenant Wagner, and then the chief to leave them alone.

Having set the young man on a chair, the prince then had a long conversation with him, which started with an inquiry about Andrew's parents. Andrew answered that he had never seen his father, but that he know from his mother, Baroness Maria Pavlovna Wagner, who resided in Odessa, that his father was a fighting officer and carried out the special orders of the sovereignty. Andrew also told him that, before joining the army, he was a student at Odessa University, and that his specialty was jurisprudence.

Attentively having listened to lieutenant, the grand prince wrote what seemed to be a letter to someone on a sheet of paper, and enclosed it in an envelope. Then he fastened it with his personal seal, and gave Baron Wagner the oral order: after his recovery and release from the hospital, Andrew would go to the city of Yekaterinburg for training in officer school.

The young man looked puzzled as the grand prince handed him the envelope and then pinned on Andrew's chest the Sacred George Officer's Award. The prince then gave him a small box that was locked and heavy for its size. Finally, the grand prince hung around the young man's neck a chain with a key to the box's lock, requesting that the lieutenant wait until his arrival at Yekaterinburg to use it. At the end of their meeting, the prince kissed the lieutenant three times, thanked him for his service, and blessed him and released him to go. They never met again. And in 1918, Grand Prince Alexander Mihailovich and his brother Sergey Mihailovich were executed by communists, their bodies dumped in a mineshaft.

In mid-summer of that year, having been discharged from the hospital, Andrew went to the officer's school in city of Yekaterinburg. There, he went to the commander's office, taking with him the envelope that he had received from the prince.

The commander opened the envelope in the lieutenant's presence to find a letter of personal recommendation, written on stationary with the grand prince's personal monogram and signature. Along with the letter, there was an order to assign Baron Wagner to the military rank of captain. As such, the fighting officer and the gentlemen of Sacred George's Order, Baron Wagner, enlisted in officer's school with a specialty of military jurisprudence.

After finding his separate room in the school barrack, Andrew Wagner, at last, dared to open the heavy box. Inside were one thousand gold ten-ruble coins and a gold chain dangling a golden cross stuffed with diamonds.

He hung the cross around his neck, understanding that this was not simply a gift, but what was it? Andrew Wagner connected the initials engraved on the ring "A.M." with Grand Prince Alexander Mihailovich full name. Perhaps this was the key to some secret?

Andrew wrote his mother, detailing all of the events that he'd been through the past several weeks. In the reciprocal letter, although she remembered the promise given to the emperor, Baroness Maria didn't explain anything. She wrote only that she was happy for her son and that she wished him good health and many years. He couldn't help but notice, however, that here and there, the ink was slightly smudged, as if by water drops … or tears.

To hide the gold coins, Andrew bought three vests. On one vest, he cut out pockets and then, using thick thread, he stitched it together with another vest. All of the coins he sewed up into stitched pockets. To hide the pockets, he sewed the third vest over the first two, so the last vest became the only one visible. Light gray with black stripes, this vest would go with any suit. Andrew took the resulting vest stuffed with the coins to the bank, and stored it in a safe.

At school, Captain Wagner became deeply engaged in the study of the Chinese language as well as in oriental combat sports. He also took private lessons from a Chinese teacher and even visited the Chinese speech pathologist to learn correct pronunciation. His persistent work yielded results, as Andrew eventually possessed a firm grasp on both Mandarin and Cantonese dialects, and an average proficiency on using Chinese weapons and self-defense methods.

According to his transcripts, some of the subjects that Andrew successfully passed at Odessa University could be credited by the military school; therefore, he was able to finish the three-year program in just a year and a half. So on December 31, 1916, Baron Wagner graduated from military school and received an order to prepare for the assignment of counterintelligence officer at the Russian embassy to China, in Beijing.

Before his departure, Andrew went to the bank and, ensuring he was out of sight, withdrew his vest from the safe. From then on, Andrew always wore his vest.

In the beginning of January 1917, Baron Wagner, along with the one hundred Daurian Cossacks under his command, was charged to accompany the Chinese ambassador on a trip with his family to St. Petersburg. By early February, Andrew's group met the ambassador and his entourage at the border of China. The ambassador, his family, and his entourage, including servants, Cossacks, horses, and so on, had taken a special train and have directed to Saint-Petersburg.

Baron Wagner, nice-looking, tall, gentle-mannered, and always ideally dressed, made an immediate impression upon the daughter of one of the officers in the entourage—eighteen-year-old beauty Ciao Lin. The girl's father, Officer Chang Ball San, was the expert on Russia, and her mother belonged to the Russian nobility.

Ciao Lin had a mutual affection for Andrew, and so the young couple began spending as much time together as etiquette allowed. Soon enamored, Baron Wagner proposed his hand and heart to the young beauty, and, having received her consent, asked for her father's blessing. Chang Ball San agreed on the condition that their engagement be announced only after their arrival in St. Petersburg.

But the revolution changed their destinies. Before clearing a situation in Russia, the ambassador made the decision to send the families of diplomats back to China. The families of Japanese and Siamese diplomats joined them.

Baron Wagner, with his hundred Daurian Cossacks, received the order to accompany them to the Chinese border. And since Chang Ball San had agreed to the union between his daughter and Andrew, the two married before the baron's departure. Andrew and Ciao Lin would not have to be separated.

The entourage trekked across Russia, caught up in the revolution. There was only chaos, disorder, and ruin. Gangs had ransacked the roads, and upon receiving an operative report that Siberia was unsafe, Andrew reinforced their steam locomotive with iron sheets. Then he ordered the Cossacks to install machine guns in the train cars' windows and small cannons on platforms between each car.

Having reached Yekaterinburg, where Andrew had been in officer's school, he left Ciao Lin with the family of his Chinese teacher, and being true to his oath and order, continued to escort the train. After the diplomats' families were delivered to Harbin, Baron Wagner directed his Cossacks back to Yekaterinburg.

In Russia, civil war had not started yet, but there was unrest. Soldiers met on a daily basis, and the authority in the city passed from hand to hand. Andrew and his wife miraculously avoided arrest, and after some fluctuation, they decided to make their way to Harbin.

When they got to Tobolsk, Captain Wagner was assigned to the army of Admiral Kolchak as the officer of counterintelligence.

But in the beginning of 1919, together with group of officers, he was directed to Harbin to receive emigrants from Russia. At that point, his correspondence with his mother was interrupted, and they never heard from each other again.

Likewise, in Odessa, authority changed hands nearly every day, sometimes twice a day, among the Bolsheviks, the General Denikin supporters, the Ukrainian warlord Petlura followers, the whites, reds, and gangs, and the anarchists. All was plundered, and everybody was ready to kill or be killed.

Maria Wagner gave five rubles to the custodian to move her furniture into an apartment on the ground floor. It would be easier on Margery, who was already forty, so that she wouldn't have to drag buckets of water up to the fourth floor.

By now, the forty-five-year-old baroness had completely forgotten about her life at the emperor's court.

Then in the summer of 1919, during a rare moment of calm, Maria Wagner made a trip to the store where she bought sewing accessories. This ended up being a lucky day for her, as the store had been plundered. Entering through the open door, the baroness began to collect sewing machine needles that had rolled off the shelves onto the floor. She resolved that even if they did not fit her sewing machine, she would be able to sell them on the market.

Creeping along the floor and collecting needles, among other things, she came across a box covered in cloth. Obviously, the thieves had not noticed it. Inside were whole spools of thread in all different colors. Maria didn't understand how she managed to get all the way home with the heavy box, but it enabled her to survive through the civil war and for many years after.

In 1921, Andrew and Ciao Lin moved to a Chinese village near Shanghai, but after two years, rural life became intolerable, so they moved to the city.

At that time, Shanghai had a large Russian community. There was Russian social life, and there were Russian stores and newspapers. Andrew Wagner got a job with the local law firm. His specialty was to settle legal problems related to Russian emigrants. His wife meanwhile, spent time managing the household.

Andrew and his wife were very much in love with each other. They lived economically but comfortably, still supported by the grand prince's gift. Once a month, they would sell one gold coin.

In 1927, their first son Nicholas was born. Then a daughter, Elisabeth, and in 1934, the youngest son Michael was born. Ciao Lin was engaged with the children. She read them books in Russian, Chinese, and English. When the children were older, they went to Russian grammar school. They lived silently despite the fact that Ciao Lin's father, Chang Ball San, had become the Chinese marshal—the highest military rank in the Chinese army.

Then in 1939, World War II broke out, and Japan had taken hold of a part of China. A couple years later, German armies had begun moving deep into Russia, and by September 16, 1941, occupied the city of Odessa.

In the first weeks of Odessa's occupation, the Germans evacuated the general population and executed any Jews, freeing several apartments. Then they left, and Romanian soldiers took over, but the Romanians didn't oppress local residents as the Germans had.

Still, war is war. People were executed and plundered. And a Romanian officer had occupied the largest room of Maria Wagner's apartment. By this time, she was sixty-six years old. He brought food to the house, though, from which the old baroness prepared him dinner, while Margery cleaned his room and washed his clothes. War is war!

Back in Russian Shanghai, people were separated into two camps. One camp wanted victory for the Red Army and the other for Nazi Germany. The Wagners were in the first camp.

When the war was over, the idea of returning back to Russia had begun to extend to the Russian emigrant community in China. Moreover, a Chinese civil war had begun. So in 1946, trains left with Russian repatriates who were told that the motherland was waiting for them.

In the spring of 1946, a fire broke out in the passenger ship *Victory* as it steamed across the Black Sea. Chinese Marshal Chang Ball San was among those burned to death. The scorched *Victory,* along with the bodies of the fire victims, was towed to Odessa.

Maria Wagner stood at a vista platform at the top of Market Street, among others of Odessa, to watch the arrival of the crippled ship. She could not know that she would be meeting, if it could be called a meeting, the father of her son's wife. What thoughts the seventy-one-year-old former baroness had, however, were hard to tell. She smoked her cigarettes and kept silent. She was accustomed to silence.

Her son Andrew, with his wife and youngest son, now twelve, had gone to Russia. The older children remained in China. Nicholas already had a family, and was well situated. Elisabeth had married a rich Chinese businessman from Hong Kong.

The motherland met its repatriates in her own "special" way. At the border, emigrants were told to hand over all of their valuables. Andrew didn't include the cameo ring and gold coins in his customs declaration, however.

Upon his family's arrival in Tobolsk, from the railroad station, they were sent to a barrack, where they'd been allocated a hundred-square-foot room without a kitchen, and with the toilet at the end of a hallway. Their son Michael had been separated from them and sent to a military school for youth. The next night, a KGB squad came to their room with a search warrant, and found the gold coins. And so, Andrew and Ciao Lin were arrested.

The questioning began. Someone had given them the information that Baron Wagner was the counterintelligence officer in Kolchak's army, and that the gold coins were a part of the Russian tsar's missing gold reserve.

Three days later, fifty-two-year-old Andrew Wagner and forty-seven-year-old Ciao Lin, together with group of unfortunate others, were taken outside the city and executed. The confiscated cameo ring and gold coins were gone.

Michael Wagner was in the Russian military school for four years, where he learned Chinese and English. He sent letters to his parents in Tobolsk, but it was in vain. He never received a reply. At the beginning of the Korean War, there was a shortage of military experts who knew the Asian languages, so sixteen-year-old Michael, as an exception, was directed to attend Moscow's Institute of Military Translators.

In 1954, the twenty-year-old Lieutenant Michael Wagner, who looked like a full-blooded Chinese, was then appointed to a group of military advisers in China. So, by the will of destiny, he again appeared in Shanghai, the city of his childhood.

Among other advisers, there was one KGB major, called Van-U Lee. To be exact, major's name was Feodor Kalinin. On Kalinin's finger, Lieutenant Wagner saw the ring that his father had used to wear. It was unmistakable, for on the cameo was engraved the profile of his grandmother.

During a party a few days later, Michael Wagner asked a fairly drunk major to look for his ring. When he finally had it in hand, he looked on its underside, to find the engraving: "Forgive and Pardon, A. M., 1893." It wasn't clear exactly what the forty-year-old major and the twenty-year-old lieutenant had in common, but since then, they became fast friends.

Almost six months later, on a hot, dark evening, Major Kalinin and Lieutenant Wagner had finished their work in the office early. The major had suggested a walk to the hotel. Nobody knows precisely what happened, but later that evening, the profusely bleeding lieutenant arrived back at the office, dragging the major behind him. The major had died of severe wounds.

The lieutenant told the investigator that they were attacked by group of gangsters on the street and that, among other things, the major's ring was missing.

That same year, in 1954, the Ponce-Brooks Comet was to be visible from Earth. The first time the comet had been observed was in July 1812, the year the war with Napoleon began. Seventy years later, in August 1883, the then eight-year-old baroness, together with her aunt, had searched the sky for this ominous comet. The aunt had told her: "The next time this comet will come back is in seventy years. God willing, you could see this comet one more time."

Now, Baroness Wagner could meet this comet again. On May 22, 1954, Maria scanned Odessa's sky with her weak eyes, searching for the Ponce-Brooks Comet once again. She smoked her cigarettes and kept silent.

The former baroness, now nicknamed "Cat Mother," lived until she was eighty-nine. Cats were her only joy by then. She bred them in great quantities, such that from the courtyard where they stayed, a loathsome stink arose. She became the local whimsical and disgusting old witch. She drove young boys nuts, calling them fleeciers and rascals. Then in the summer of 1962, she silently died, some said from insufficient intimacy. Her small corpse lay on the floor of her room for about two weeks before the door cracked open, and there had arrived some who looked like hospital attendants. With mittens on their hands, they thrust her shriveled little body into a plastic bag, fastened it from the above by a cord, and before the eyes of her neighbors, on a command of "One, two, three!" heaved it into the open back of a pickup truck.

The Korean conflict ended with the execution of a truth agreement between North and South, but by then, relations between the Soviet Union and communist China were spoiled, and the army no longer needed translators. So in 1957, twenty-three-year-old Captain Michael Wagner left the armed forces.

Still young and knowledgeable of several languages, however, he was quickly accepted into postgraduate school at the Tobolsk University of Foreign Languages. In 1962, he defended his PhD thesis, and thereafter, Professor

Wagner worked for the university, where he met and married Tatiana Tishina.

Tatiana came from long line of Russian nobility, but one of her ancestors had been banished at the tsar's order upon the settlement of Tobolsk. After his sentence ended, however, he remained there. Tatiana was twenty years younger than her husband, but that did not prevent their happiness. In 1973, their daughter Anna was born.

The Wagner family lived amicably, as the daughter grew and they continued to work, until 1991, when fifty-seven-year-old Michael bought a used car. He had not driven before then. And one evening, while driving with his wife as a passenger, they were involved in a fatal accident. As a result, eighteen-year-old Anna Wagner, the student, became an orphan.

Upon hearing her family history, Igor now understood from where she had gotten her Asian features—her slightly slanting eyes, high cheekbones, thin nose, short stature, and the most velvety looking skin.

In late October 1993, Yakubovsky Jr. introduced his girlfriend to his father. Upon his first look at this prospective daughter-in-law, Yakubovsky Sr. was shocked, as if struck by lightning. In his bloodstream rushed such powerful dose of testosterone that he was literally driven from within. This professional intelligence officer, a lieutenant colonel of the Federal Service of External Intelligence, had to restrain himself with great effort. It was the strongest attack of passion that Yakubovsky had ever experienced. Though he knew this young girl was the bride of his son, the poor man couldn't even look at Anna without becoming excited, so he rolled himself into a ball. To return himself to his senses, he began to think about his wife. The idea of this short-legged, clumsy creature sobered him, even if just slightly.

More surprising, however, is that Anna, upon this first meeting with Vladislav, experienced the same feelings for him. She felt a physical passion for her prospective father-in-law. There wasn't any logical explanation for it. After all, she was truly in love with Igor, and she loved him easily and loyally. But the feeling she experienced upon meeting the father of her groom to be, a man twenty-two years older than she, could be referred to as nothing less than love at first sight.

Yes, it is impossible to call such a feeling healthy. But once in a while, it flares up between people—and when it does, then how should they proceed?

4

Moscow, November 1, 1993,

On Monday morning, Vladislav Yakubovsky as usual, arrived at his office by nine o'clock. As usual, he took off his overcoat, and hung up it on a hanger. Then as usual, he sat behind his desk. He took a freshly sharpened pencil and, not having anything more to do, started to play with it, glancing over the office that he has occupied for three years—the wall panels, the window, the curtains. All was in order. As usual.

But this morning was unusual in that Vladislav smiled. He just sat in his chair, slightly reclined, and smiled. It was simple because Mr. Vladislav Yakubovsky had fallen in love. And he had not simply fallen in love; the mad passion had possessed his entire existence upon his first look at her, even to the point that he now had butterflies in his stomach just thinking about it. The most mad part, however, was that he had fallen in love with the girlfriend of his own son.

Last night, Vladislav's son Igor had invited his father to meet his girlfriend. They had agreed to meet at the new Indian restaurant, and Vladislav had come early. Because it was Sunday, no seats were available, until Yakubovsky flashed his KGB ID. Then the manager organized a table for three. Vladislav took a seat at the table and out of professional habit, sat with his back against the wall and lit a cigarette.

The moment Vladislav saw Igor and his girlfriend, he felt his heart hammering. The sensation was as if being carried away inside an avalanche. He wanted to love this girl passionately and gently, as one loves in youth.

Through the evening, all three were in a good mood. They joked, and drank. Actually, only Vladislav drank. His son was the designated driver, and Ann had never drunk in general, though she would socially sip her red wine every now and then. An Indian musician was sitting on a landing and, on some exotic string instrument resembling a guitar, strummed strange melodies. It was so unusual that he served as an occasion to make jokes. Then the Hindu man left, and some popular musicians came. They began to perform the songs that were well-known for the day.

Toward the middle of the evening, the maestro announced, "The green tango!" swinging a dollar bill, calling customers to order music. Some guy approached the stage and handed him five dollars. The maestro then announced, "The 'Argentinean Tango!' "

Memories gushed over Yakubovsky. He recollected how in high school, one evening in the disco, the boys crowded along the wall, while the girls danced with each other. When they had held the "white dance," where the girls invite the boys to dance, one of his classmates, Irene, had approached him. At that time, Vlad didn't know how to dance, so Irene showed him how to waltz. It didn't work. So Irene invited him to her place for a dancing lesson. He came. And the next day, he came again. Once he started getting the hang of the waltz, they moved onto the tango. When, at last, he had mastered the tango's simple steps in time with the music, Irene began making more complicated moves. Once, during the dance, Irene embraced Vlad's leg with her leg, and then she bent back in his arms. Being intoxicated by the sounds of the tango music and sensations of presence a girl who liked him, Vlad's caught his breath and kissed Irene. Three years later, they were married… Irene was Igor's mother…

The musicians had started singing. The lyrics were uncommonly trite:

As a beer bar was opened in the Rostov city,
The criminals used to gather there.
There were some girls Maria, Rose, Raja … [1]

Vladislav invited Ann up to tango. They danced, ignoring the stupid words to the song. A lot of things were trite. It was such a trite time. But they were dancing the tango—the dance of love.

Vladislav touched Anna, and from his affinity for her, the gentle aroma of her, and the sounds of the music, he felt his legs give way under him, just the way they had when he had learned to dance with his ex-wife Irene… Then

1 From a well-known Russian pop song; author unknown. The lyrics were translated by the author of this novel.

Vladislav and Anna quit really dancing; instead, they were nearly trembling. Then, having stumbled, they broke apart and returned to the table.

Afterward, Igor took his father home, but he and Anna didn't go up. Igor didn't favor his father's second wife. At his parting, Vladislav gallantly applied his lips to Anna's fingers, and as soon as his hand had touched her, his body began to shake treacherously. It was good that Igor hadn't noticed that.

Once in his apartment, and having seen his hated "the best half," Yakubovsky argued over a trifle, pretending that he was offended, and then went to sleep on the sofa. All night long, the tango music echoed in his ears and he dreamed about Anna.

The next morning, after a sleepless night, Vladislav Yakubovsky came to work pensively smiling, as if he were a boy. The lieutenant colonel of the External Intelligence Service of the Russian Federation was sitting in his office, but he was not thinking about how to recruit new spies for the motherland. He was thinking about how he should handle his love.

His specially trained analytical mind allowed him to objectively evaluate the situation. That this was not really love was clearly to him. Rather, passion had taken possession of him. Powerful passion. And passion was a devilish feeling. Streams of testosterone uncontrollably spread through his veins, causing a burning desire.

Passion did not demand reciprocity. Passion was feeling restless, nervous, and mad. But if the passion was mutual, it could transform into real love for life.

Love was a quiet feeling, in which sexual inclination was present, but on the same level as a feeling of care for the person one favored. Love was daily work, founded on reciprocity of feelings. Enamored people, as a rule, were quiet and assured. And so it was with his first wife. They were friends from school—classmates. Their relationship was well, easy, and reliable. And had it not been for the trip to the collective farm, they would continue to live peacefully together...

Yakubovsky sincerely loved his son. Even after the divorce, Vlad spent all his free time with his son, whenever he was not on trips or occupied by urgent work. He used to do homework with him, take him to Pioneer's Palace, visit all the local exhibitions, and make trips into the country.

Vlad sighed. How time flies! "Igor is grown up already. And now, after all of our history together, I manage to fall in love with Igor's girlfriend? I do not understand!"

Again and again, Vladislav repeated to himself, "I must see Ann as little as necessary. Then all will be settled."

Finally, Yakubovsky calmed himself down. Still, he thought, "I have to do something with my own private life. I have to. I cannot take this anymore. I cannot be with this short-legged, clumsy creature any longer. I am done. I am beyond done."

Then, as the lieutenant colonel of the Federal Security Service continued sitting in his office, thinking about his life, suddenly, something lifted him from his chair, and he began to silently sing last night's tango, dancing, imagining that was submerged in the tango with the darling Ann.

5

Bavaria, Germany, November 3, 1993

Convinced the flight to Los Angeles was finished boarding and that Boris would not show, Lady Melissa and her companion Frau Gartvig came out of hiding.

"Warum mussen wir uns von diesem Mann verstecken?"[2] Asked Frau Gartvig. "Ist er der Gangster?"[3]

"Nein."[4] Melissa could not give more of an answer.

"Deshalb. Was ist mit ihm falsch?" Frau Gartvig continued. "Haben Sie Angst vor ihm? Warum laufen wir immer von diesem Mann weg? "[5]

But what could Melissa tell her? That she madly loved this elderly man and was pregnant with his child?

So, with their luggage, they proceeded to the elevator in Terminal A, Frau pushing the wheelchair with Melissa into the elevator. Melissa's handbag with the money and documents was in her lap. They rode down to the parking garage and then walked through a parking garage and an underground tunnel to the railway station, where they purchased two tickets to Munich. Melissa and Frau then left Frankfurt.

Having spent the night in Munich, they took taxi the next morning to the boarding house located in mountains. Melissa's attending physician, Dr. Krauss, recommended she go there, as the "curative air, silence, and special diet" would ensure her a speedy recovery.

About forty kilometers from Munich, they reached the wonderful forested farm surrounded by high mountains and majestic pines. It was a small farm that specialized in providing rehabilitation services for patients

---

2 Why we are hiding from this man? (German.)

3 Is he a gangster? (German.)

4 No. (German.)

5 Are you afraid of him? Why are we always running from this man? (German.)

from German and Swiss clinics. Mountain air, natural spring water, and all-organic food—goat's milk and cheese, eggs, sausage, beer, and huge loaves of homemade bread with all-natural ingredients—were added bonuses that helped bring healing.

Melissa's room was very small, but exceptionally clean, hardly able to fit its narrow bed, nightstand, lamp, and wardrobe. The TV was hung on the wall. The bathroom, with a sink, toilet, and small shower, was the only convenience. But the view from the window onto the mountains was like that of ancient German fairytales. Upon taking it in, Melissa immediately imagined how beautiful it would be to live here with Boris. They would live together, drink fat cream, play cards, and walk hand-in-hand. But, she knew this was impractical.

Frau Gartvig, finally convinced that Melissa was in reliable, caring hands, under the supervision of Frau Martha—a woman who wore traditional Bavarian-style dress, with an apron and cap—left for Munich. Melissa remained on the farm where she could breathe in the mountain air, eat and sleep well, regain her strength, and learn to get around without the wheelchair.

If only Boris were next to her in this paradise! Melissa thought about him constantly—when she fed the goats grass; when she drank the pure goat's milk (which smelled terrible at first) and the beer mixed with sour cream; and when she greedily ate a good piece of rough bread. She felt lonely without his love, his care, and his jokes. At the time, she was the only patient at the farm, so nobody disturbed her. Still, she felt bad being alone. But gradually, having become accustomed to her new surroundings, she got used to the loneliness, and weaned herself from thinking constantly of Boris.

Meanwhile, she began looking at the positive side of things. She enjoyed the nice weather with sunny days, and rain pouring almost every night. She had gotten so used to the London climate that it pleased her. The healthy food was good, too, and restored her energy.

Every day before the formal breakfast, she would drink a mixture of goat's milk and carrot juice. An hour after that, she ate a thick chunk of fresh, tasty-smelling homemade multigrain bread smeared with butter made from goat's milk, along with a decent-sized piece of goat's cheese. She washed this "power sandwich" down with a good-sized glass of hot goat's milk. After such a breakfast, Melissa didn't feel hungry until the middle of a day.

It was only a week's time before Melissa was able to walk. At first, she just walked from one building to the next, but very soon she was able to go farther. Eventually, Melissa put on rubber boots and a raincoat with a cape, and tried to leave the farm, taking pleasure in the surprisingly clean air, fragrant with mountain grasses and autumn flowers.

After her walk, she, as a rule, ate the full dinner, consisting of vegetable salad, vegetable soup with a dollop of sour cream, and chicken or pork schnitzel with a glass of the house beer mixed with sour cream. Choking from such gluttony, Melissa then would lie down for a little rest. After a nap, she would leave again, walking increasingly more each day. Then for supper, her stomach had a celebration, with a big piece of homemade pie, stuffed with apples or black currants, and fragrant tea extracted from mountain grasses, dog-rose, and leaves of wild strawberry.

Soon Melissa felt as if her health had been restored. She started going into the woods and doing physical exercise. Everything that had recently happened to her began to fade in her mind, replaced by thoughts of the future. Now Melissa fully enjoyed the beauty of Bavarian nature and the forested farm; for her, it had become an island, a sanctuary away from the daily vanity of the modern world.

In addition to Frau Martha, her husband, her growing, clumsy daughter, and her two sons, two more German families lived on the farm—recent immigrants from Northern Kazakhstan. All of them were constantly working, doing everyday farm work, and weren't interested in the external world at all. Among themselves, they spoke a mixture of German and Russian.

One of the women, Frieda, had worked as a nurse in a rural hospital in Kazakhstan. The first time Melissa had seen Frieda, she'd felt that they had met before, but she knew it hadn't been possible. In the evenings, sitting at the house under a canopy, Frieda would tell Melissa about her life in the Kazakh village and about her daughter Victoria, who was a little older than Melissa and lived in Russia. Frieda's other daughter was unmarried and worked at the airport in Moscow. For some reason, she hadn't been able to come to Germany with the rest of the family.

Melissa, in turn, told Frieda about her adventures in Russia. Once, when Melissa mentioned Boris by his full name, Frieda suddenly looked strained, apparently trying to recollect something, but then as remembering nothing, returned quickly to the conversation.

A few days later, however, Frieda asked Melissa if she had Boris's photo. Melissa showed Frieda the small picture that Boris had left in her purse. Frau Frieda examined the photo for a long time, wiped it with her hand, and silently returned it to Melissa. After that, Frieda never spoke about Boris again.

After a month, nearly fully recovered, with a healthy complexion and almost chubby cheeks, Lady Melissa paid her bill and thanked the owners for their wonderful reception and care. On Sunday, December 5, she left the farm for Munich. On the way to the airport, the smile didn't leave Melissa's face. It was a pity to her to leave this farm with it primitive, but healthy life. It was a pity to leave those lovely people who accepted her so, particularly Frau Frieda, who, by age, was suited to be Melissa's mother.

But Melissa needed to plunge again into an ordinary life in the big city. After a short flight over the mountain ridges dividing Germany and Switzerland, her plane landed at the Geneva's airport. On Wednesday, in the Geneva Canton Court, would begin the hearing Lady Melissa Spencer vs. Mr. Eddy Pennington.

6

California, Autumn 1993

In California and across the United States, the economy was in a deep recession. Real estate had lost more than half of its value in 1990. It was the time to buy. Boris decided to use Melissa's money to buy several construction lots with ocean views. He then planned to design and build custom homes on those lots, and to sell them for a profit. The full cycle, from the purchase of the lots through the sale of the homes, could take a few years, and by then, he figured, the economy might turn around. Besides, good homes with ocean views were always in demand.

And so, Boris became acquainted with a real estate agent named Robert Hobbs. Robert was the virtuoso of his business. He knew all about houses and sites in the coastal zone south of Laguna Beach. One October day, Robert took Boris to a community named Ocean Ranch. When they arrived, there were many construction sites up for sale.

Boris had a strange feeling that he had been here before. And after a minute, he understood why. It was the smell of the air. A smell he would never be able to forget. It was the exact smell of the shore town by the Black Sea where he'd grown up: seaweed mixed with dry hay.

Two days later, he came back with his wife Ruslana, and she recognized the smell too.

The lots were just what Boris had been looking for. He made an offer for five half-acre lots, for the construction of custom homes that ranged anywhere from fifty-five hundred to eighty-five hundred square feet each.

Boris had no construction experience, but he'd had formal engineering education, he could read and make drawings, and he had life experience, and, most important, the desire to work hard and fair.

With his ambition and enthusiasm, Boris was able to convince another fellow Russian to invest in his project. They formed a legal partnership and, together, purchased five more sites.

In the community where they bought, the average custom home ran at a retail cost of about a hundred and sixty-five dollars per square foot. To increase that price, they decided to build their first house on the best lot, which had an unobstructed ocean view. Then, when a higher price per square foot was established, they would continue to build and sell other homes. Boris's new Russian partner was engaged in another business of his own, so he entrusted Boris with managing all of their new projects.

Hobbs started by introducing Boris to some important contacts, at which point the overall picture started to appear. So, it happens in life. When you are facing a new project, it looks like a polished wall in the heights of heaven. In the course of its development, however, you get closer to this wall, and it begins to appear less smooth than before. You notice cracks big enough to put a foot into. But there are also ledges to grip onto, and then, as you look harder, you notice some steps to climb. Little by little, you make your way up the wall—but only if you continue to work, and to work hard.

And so it was that, after becoming acquainted with several architects, Boris selected one. A middle-aged man with operational experience in coastal zones, Charles Haber had formulated resolutions to a variety of problems related to the construction of custom homes. He knew, for example, that such homes should satisfy several major goals. As buildings, they should meet the requirements of local authorities. Their elevation and floor plans should also satisfy the architectural standards set by the homeowner's association. In addition, its design should be unique and attractive to the majority of potential buyers. And no complex would be the landscaping around these houses.

Gradually, Boris and Charles reached an agreement: Mediterranean-style homes, at the present, were the most popular. A majestic front porch, elevated by symmetrical Corinthian columns, a tall and wide wrought-iron entry doors, large windows, high ceilings, and spacious rooms. The kitchen would have granite countertops, full backsplashes, and a bar made of marble. And custom fireplaces would not turn away people with the means to pay for the pleasure of living in such a home.

A target start-date was determined: construction of the first home would begin no later than early March 1994.

Before that point, however, routine work began, and Boris met people from the planning, engineering, and building departments. He spent the morning talking to the Fire Department inspector, and the evenings attending City Council meetings.

By the end of 1993, Boris called Arnold Isaev to Moscow. Arnold had left Agroprom, and had never received back the twenty thousand dollars he had lent Kravchuk. Now, he was looking for a job. There were some possibilities, but none that he particularly liked.

Boris didn't discuss his last trip to Russia with Isaev in detail. He and Melissa had reserved themselves for each other, and that was enough. Boris learned from Isaev, however, that Kravchuk had been in the hospital after a drinking binge, but that he was now good as new and had returned to work.

At Christmastime, Boris called his friend Kislov in Togliatti. He was glad to learn that Leonid and his wife Tatiana were planning to come to see them in Orange County in the spring. At the end of their conversation, Leo told Boris that he had an excellent gift for him, but that for now, it was a secret.

"You will see what it is when I bring it to you," Leo said.

All this time, Boris kept thinking about Melissa. How is she? What is she doing? But he didn't make any attempt to find her.

7

Moscow, November 9, 1993

More than six weeks had passed since Ivan Filimonov had started as the assistant to the Attorney General of the Russian Federation. He'd managed to escape the investigation being conducted on associates of the speaker of the Supreme Council of Russia, Mr. Ruslan Khazbulatov, and Vice President Alexander Rutskoy. With his new responsibilities and new coworkers to meet, he didn't have time to do anything with the information he'd received from Goryanin. But now, he made the time to begin investigating the death of Mr. Popov.

For the first step of the investigation, on Tuesday, November 9, Filimonov made an official inquiry to the Federal Service of External Intelligence concerning the meeting with the agent, in which Lieutenant Colonel Vladislav Yakubovsky was directed to Washington.

The inquiry from the office of the attorney general was delivered the same day. The inquiry was received by the deputy chief of the Personnel Department at the Federal Service of External Intelligence. The deputy chief of the Personnel Department Lieutenant Colonel Stanislav Ivanovich Terekhin was responsible for working with the staff of the Federal Service of External Intelligence—the same division Lieutenant Colonel Vladislav Yakubovsky was assigned to. Coincidently, Stanislav Terekhin and Vladislav Yakubovsky were friends from military school.

Having received the inquiry, Terekhin glanced into Yakubovsky's office and beckoned his friend out into the hallway. They agreed to meet after work on Friday, November 12, for a walk around the city.

November 10 was Police Day, which meant the day off at most establishments. And despite the fact that the Federal Security Service (former KGB) and the police competed on nearly every issue, both observed professional holidays. This holiday, by tradition, was celebrated not only at work, but also at an obligatory celebratory concert for the heads of departments, their assistants, and select employees, all fully dressed in uniforms complete with awards and medals. And exception was made only for officers of the Department of Internal Investigation, for the Federal Service of External Intelligence, and for officers of the Ninth Division, who were responsible for protecting the country's leaders and their families. Officers of these departments were forbidden to appear in public anyway, as they might be recognized, whether in uniform or in plain clothes. But in the workplace, all of them celebrated this holiday duly. So, by tradition, after the party, all of the tipsy officers were driven home in official cars, and accompanied to their entryway doors by the drivers.

The day after the party, Yakubovsky couldn't go to the office due to a hangover. He always suffered after a rough feast. On Friday, November 12, he continued to suffer, but at his office. By the end of day, he was sober and met his old friend Terekhin in the hallway. Then, together they left to walk the streets.

It was frosty and slippery, not suitable weather for a walk. The snow, as usual, had fallen nearly a week before but still had not melted. Here and there, the wind inopportunely rose and shook the random lantern, projecting freakish shadows onto buildings and the eternally hurrying crowds.

Yakubovsky and Terekhin went to eat at Field Camp, a restaurant on the corner of Kuznetsky Bridge Street and Neglinaya. The hostess escorted them to a table, where the men studied the menu.

"Stas," Yakubovsky addressed his friend. "Let's each start with a triple shot, a couple of bottles of beer, and a snack. Shall we also order a borsch?"

"Sure," Terekhin quickly agreed.

While waiting for their drinks, Yakubovsky kept silent, understanding that this meeting had not been scheduled without a purpose. But Terekhin remained silent too.

The waitress brought vodka and potato salad. The two friends poured the vodka into glasses, but the beer they left in bottles, toasting with them "to those in the sea."

Terekhin then began with, "Vlad. An inquiry has come about you. From the Office of the Attorney General. They are wondering why the hell you went to Washington. And I have to answer them."

Terekhin broke off, but Yakubovsky stayed silent, understanding that this was still not all. Yakubovsky, perfectly remembering how he had flirted with money in Washington, thought, someone has played me as the pawn. But who? All right. I can handle that accusation. But what if they know about my last meeting and phone conversation with Cherkizov? Then it would be not so simple.

They poured more vodka, and drank it while finishing off the potato salad. The waitress then brought the borsch. They poured vodka a third time and drank it silently.

Then Terekhin started back in. "Well, you were there … generally speaking. Don't worry. I will delay my answer a little. And you? If you have messed up somewhere, you know what to do. Clean up. How much time do you need?

"I think three weeks will be enough," Yakubovsky said, and then choked. He realized that he said too much and just handed himself over.

"Vlad, I am telling you—don't worry about it. We do not hand over good people so simply." Terekhin tried to encourage his friend. "We have handed over too many already."

"Thanks, pal," Vlad said, having calmed down already. Then with gratitude in his voice, he said, "Let's have some more vodka."

"Sure, sure ... And more beer, too," Stanislav quickly agreed. "As they say, vodka without beer is like money blowing in the wind!"

Yakubovsky called the waitress. He knew now that he would have to pay for dinner and for a taxicab too. He should have brought a gift for Terekhin.

Ever since Yakubovsky had misappropriated the eighty-five hundred dollars, he and his wife had gone to Turkey twice a month for shuttles. Tomorrow, they would board a charter flight to the Turkish city of Antalya, and would not be back until Sunday. And they already had tickets for the same shuttle flight on November 27.

So, if I have to return the money, I shall return it, he thought. I have made money on the interest-free credit already. And if they do not ask for the money, even better. But, I do need to bring a gift for Stanislav from Turkey.

They didn't discuss the matter more. As old friends, they just drank vodka and talked about life.

8

Moscow, November 13, 1993

Early Saturday morning, among 150 other shuttles aboard the charter plane Yakubovsky and his wife Natalie departed to Turkey for their shuttle expedition. It was clear that such shuttles trips had changed life not only for the Yakubovskys.

In fact, due to the shockingly poor economic conditions, about 20 percent of the population now drug around huge bales with all kinds of items from Poland, Turkey, Germany, Finland, and elsewhere. People carried everything from consumer goods and foodstuff to motor vehicles. And the country had begun to breathe again. Goods had started to fill up kiosks and stores. People had begun to accumulate working capital, which multiplied. For obvious reasons, however, none hurried to put their money in the bank or to use it to pay taxes.

As soon as they buckled up, Yakubovsky told his wife that he was tired and was going to take a nap. He closed his eyes, but he didn't sleep. On the contrary, he began to analyze the situation that he had gotten himself into.

Yakubovsky didn't fully believe Terekhin that the inquiry was related only to his last trip to Washington. Not because he didn't trust Terekhin, but because Filimonov's signature was on the inquiry from the Office of the Attorney General. The question, then, was not about how many dollars Yakubovsky had concealed, but about whatever information Filimonov had on Yakubovsky. Filimonov didn't care about eight and a half thousand dollars. Rather, it seemed that something in relation to Cherkizov's disappearance had sent up a red flag for him or in relation to both Cherkizov and Popov.

"Okay. So what do I know about Cherkizov?" Yakubovsky thought. "First, on September 23, Cherkizov took off with Goryanin and the British girl from Moscow to Samara's Kuromich Airport at nine fifteen in the morning. That meant he was in Samara at ten fifteen. But that was Moscow time. Between

Moscow and Samara, there was a time difference of one hour, so in Samara the time was eleven fifteen. By the time they left the airport, it would have been about noon, Samara time.

Cherkizov had called Yakubovsky at one thirty, Moscow time, which, in Samara, would have been two thirty. That meant that Cherikizov was approximately between one and one-and-a-half hours' driving time from Kuromich. That equaled a distance of about forty to one hundred kilometers.

So … when had Anisimov been shot in Novokuybyshevsk? Between eight and eight thirty in the morning, Samara time. That would have given them enough time to reach Kuromich.

Second, Anisimov's BMW had been missing. Then … when was it found? At six p.m. And where?

Third, he would need to inquire about all incidents, without exception, that occurred on September 23 between noon and six p.m., Samara time, in the area from forty-kilometer to one-hundred-kilometer radius around Kuromich.

Fourth, from where had Cherkizov called him?

Once he knew the answers to those questions, he could start to unwind the ball. It still was not clear, however, how in the world Goryanin was able to compete with Cherkizov, the lieutenant colonel of the Ninth Division, and three Caucasians? Who could believe it? That could only mean that there was someone else or something else involved. It just wasn't clear what…

Yakubovsky found himself leaning against Natalie, when she said, "Well, what are you muttering there, Vlad? Did you have a dream? We shall sit down soon."

"We shall sit down. We shall sit down," Yakubovsky answered, frightening her. "What are you croaking about? 'We shall sit down.' Don't sit down. It is the prosecutor that sits down,[6] but an airplane touches down." And with those words, he three times spat over his left shoulder[7] and, for extra good measure, also crossed himself.

Yakubovsky hated his wife's guts. Her very existence irritated him. This thirty-four-year-old woman, from an aerial view, looked similar to a frog. Moreover, her facial profile resembled a fish. Every moment she was around, she made Vladislav's life a misery.

Ever since her moving to the huge city of Moscow, Natalie had dreamed about that she and Vlad are moving back to the village where she was from, where they would raise hens and plant potatoes. Whenever she brought it

6 In Russian mobster's slang, the "to be sat down" means "to be in prison."

7 This is a Russian superstitious custom to spit three times over the left shoulder. It is a protection from tricks of devil, which sits on left shoulder and provokes good people to make bad choices or to be involved in bad situations.

up, he would only grind his teeth. This was already his second marriage, and that wasn't really welcomed by the Federal Service of External Intelligence. A second divorce would not be forgiven; he would have to quit his job. And where he would go? What would he do? He knew his business well. And he was fluent in English, German, and Spanish. But he couldn't do anything other than interrogate and search. What could he possibly do outside of the Federal Service of External Intelligence? Again, Yakubovsky grinded his teeth and kept silent.

A long time ago, Vlad was married to his school sweetheart Irene. They were in love and used to live like other people. But once, in a course of charity, young KGB officers were sent to assist villagers in harvesting potatoes. Among them was twenty-six-year-old Second Lieutenant Yakubovsky. On one autumn day, when a torrential rain poured down, and there was no need to work, he remained in the house where he was assigned to stay. To kill the time, Vlad asked the owner's daughter, a young, rather lazy fat girl, to start a steam sauna. While the sauna heated up, she poured him some homemade moonshine. Vladislav drank the moonshine by wine glass, first one, then another, while having a snack of pickled cucumbers and crude eggs. The fat girl drank with him also. What happened next is not known, but when the owner of the house returned home, he found his seventeen-year-old daughter and the tenant in the sauna. Everything that happened next was simple. The teenager, Natalie Ponamarev, submitted a written complaint to the Federal Service of External Intelligence. In the complaint, she claimed the Second Lieutenant Yakubovsky deprived her of her virginity. And notwithstanding the fact that Yakubovsky was married, and had a five-year-old son, Igor, whom Vlad loved very much, he was forced by his superiors to divorce his wife and marry Natalie Ponamarev. If he didn't do so, he would have to say good-bye to KGB and go for work as a police patrolman.

Fifteen years had passed since then. The fat girl had turned into "a short-legged clumsy creature," but for Yakubovsky, who had become a lieutenant colonel already, the price of working for the police, still would not be worth the joy of getting rid of her.

At the Antalya airport, a line of buses were already waiting, as most shuttles went shopping before they even checked in at the hotel.

When Vlad and Natalie arrived at the trading quarter, it was already swarming with people and merchandise. Trade went briskly amid a multilingual cacophony. Most of the Turkish wheeler-dealers had mastered

Russian enough to understand their buyers and lure them into their stores, promising the lowest prices for the best goods.

"Natasha! Natasha!" the dealers shouted, dragging the Yakubovskys into their shops. And then as soon as the couple was inside, the dealers would change their tune, both about exchange rate and the quality of their goods. The first opportunity these dealers had to steal something, they would do so without hesitation or remorse.

The Yakubovskys were surprised, however. How did the dealers all know Natasha's[8] name? Finally, they understood that Turks called all Russian women Natasha, and had a good laugh.

By midday, after having run several times to their bus to unload merchandize, the Yakubovskys had purchased all that they'd planned on. The buses then delivered the shoppers at the hotel. After check-in, they spent time examining, sorting, and packing their goods. Then on Sunday, until lunch, they were at the pool. After lunch, the same buses took them to the airport. The Yakubovskys have arrived back home late, carrying six huge bales hammered up with Turkish leather.

The next day, the lieutenant colonel called the Samara region's FSB office. After introducing himself, he asked to be connected to the Counter-Espionage Division's officer on duty. He then requested a brief run-down of all of the incidents that occurred on September 23, 1993, between noon and 18:00 hours, Samara time, in a 40- to 110-kilometer radius around Kuromich airport.

In two hours, the fax machine was ringing in his office. It was a list of all such incidents. From the one hundred and seventy-four items listed, including domestic violence, only eighteen attracted his attention.

Yakubovsky called Samara again and asked for detailed information surrounding the selected incidents. In addition, he requested a completed investigation report related to the murder of the chief of the Novokuybyshevsky oil pipeline-dispatching unit, Mr. Peter Anisimov, which should have been filed the morning of September 23, 1993.

When Yakubovsky returned from lunch, he found all of the information on his fax machine. Now that his circle of search had narrowed, Yakubovsky paid attention to trifles. He spread out the information on his desk, and then started to make notes, writing out whatever general details he knew about each incident. After a careful analysis, he was able to zero in on three particular incidents: Anisimov's murder, the robbery of a general store in a small village called Novomatushkino, and a fire in the same village.

Anisimov's murder took place between eight ten and eight twenty-five

8 In Russia the nickname for Natalie is Natasha.

a.m. Witnesses had reported seeing two or three Caucasians driving away from the scene of the crime in two cars: a red, Russian-made Zhiguli and a 540 BMW.

The robbery of the general store was committed at two thirty p.m. The saleswoman of the store gave a deposition, saying that the robbers were two Caucasians, and that they drove away from the store in red Zhiguli.

Later, the same car was found at the burned down summer cottage. Keys from both suspect cars had been laying on the driver's seat, but all documents were missing.

It was possible to assume that the store was being plundered at the very time that Cherkizov had called Moscow. It was also possible that inside the remains of the summer cottage, there was only one Caucasian, with Goryanin and the British girl being the other two unidentified bodies. If that was the case, it changed the whole picture. Cherkizov's name had already been added to the Most Wanted list, but it was still possible to add Goryanin's name.

And there was still one unresolved question: what happened to the money the girl had brought to Anisimov, which Cherkizov had told him about? How had Cherkizov even learned about the money? What did Kravchuk know?

Yakubovsky decided to use three of his paid holidays and left the same evening to Samara. He took the "Zhiguli"[9] train from the Kazansky Railroad Station. There were too many questions and ambiguities remaining to be resolved by phone and fax.

9 Zhiguli is the name of the mountains on the right side of the Volga River, north of Samara. Thus, it was adopted as a brand name for nearly everything in the region, from hotels and cars, to trains and beer and more.

9

Moscow/Togliatti, November 16, 1993

The next morning, the train came to the small town of Syzran. Yakubovsky had only a briefcase in which, in addition to a photo camera, pens, and paper, he had a shaving set, some toothpaste, and a toothbrush. Before his departure, he had called the Federal Security regional office and ordered an off-road vehicle, an assistant officer, and two soldiers with machine guns to meet him upon his arrival.

At the Syzran station, there wasn't a platform. So, Yakubovsky jumped from the bottom step of the railroad car to the ground, which was completely covered in snow. It was a calm, frosty morning, almost negative twenty degrees Celsius, without any wind. All of the trees, rooftop, and streets were covered in a thick layer of white, which made them look like sugar pies with whipped cream. The bright sun was separated from the intense blue sky by a rather turbid nimbus. The unbelievably pure air denied every forecast. The Russian winter had stepped into Syzran.

Yakubovsky promptly found his entourage and they drove off, rushing toward the town of Zhiguliovsk. Along both sides of the road were all kinds of motor vehicles that looked either beaten up or burned, and were interspersed with an amazing number of wooden crosses.

"I feel like we're in a cemetery," Yakubovsky said. Up to that point, he had been silent.

"Yes, Sir, you are right. It is a cemetery," answered the assistant officer. "On this road, emergencies happen every day. There are either car accidents, or gangsters killing each other. Nobody pays attention to the police anymore. Only SWAT teams are still able to somehow influence the situation."

The conversation broke off. Yakubovsky was about to start speaking again, when they passed a sign that said "Village Novomatushkino." He then ordered the driver to take him to the local post office, where the telephone station was located, before going to the burned down cottage.

At the post office, Yakubovsky and the assistant officer asked to see the manager of the telephone station. Having flashed his pocket ID—the blood-red bi-fold FSB certificate with the Russian state insignia embossed on the front—Lieutenant Colonel Yakubovsky ordered him to show them the book with all of the registered telephone calls. Then, opening to the page with records for September 23, he at once found two requests by Cherkizov for telephone calls, with receivers in Moscow. The first call was made to his direct telephone number. The conversation took place at two twenty-six p.m. and lasted three minutes. The next order was made to Kravchuk's number at Agroprom; this phone number Yakubovsky knew by heart. The conversation between Cherkizov and Kravchuk lasted for five minutes.

This final listing was the answer to the one-million-dollar question: whether Kravchuk was involved in Cherkizov's business. Yakubovsky's previous assumptions appeared to be true. Cherkizov had called from this village. Any answers that remained now could only be found at the summer cottage. So Yakubovsky ordered to telephone station manager to show them how to get there.

Winter days were short, so while they had been in the post office, the sun had started to set. By the time they arrived at the cottage site, it was nearly evening. The remains of the once quaint vacation home were covered in snow. Only the brick chimney flue stuck out, straight into the sky. Yakubovsky ordered the assistant officer to have ten soldiers, a criminologist, and the photographer there by morning. He also ordered they bring an army tent, to protect the burned remains from the wind, along with an electric generator with lights and heaters for inside the tent.

Suddenly, Yakubovsky remembered something. He opened his briefcase, took out a copy of the incidents reports, and read through the information regarding the fire. The red Zhiguli had been found near the burned down cottage, but Anisimov's BMW had been located near the local hospital. In both cases, the keys had been laying on the driver's seat, and in both cases, the cars' registration documents had been missing. So, somebody had first dropped off the BMW near the hospital, and then removed the documents. Who was it? Mr. Cherkizov or somebody else?

Yakubovsky requested the driver take him to the Old Town section of Togliatti, to the Zhiguli Hotel. But on their way, having seen a sign for the local hospital, Vlad ordered that he be driven there instead.

There were some ambulances in front of the hospital. Yakubovsky left the SUV and went through the emergency entrance. Seeing a group of drivers sitting and smoking, he greeted them, presented his FSB certificate, and introduced himself as the senior investigator. He asked the drivers if they could give a ride to some people. After receiving a negative answer, he came at them from a different angle.

"Guys, after your shift, on your way home, couldn't you just drop off some fellow travelers?"

"Are we bad people? Certainly, we would take along some fellow travelers," the drivers agreed.

"Now, please try to recollect that day when the summer residence in the village burned down. Did somebody transport some fellow travelers from the hospital then?"

"Yes," one of the drivers answered. "Gennady was the name of the driver. He took a man and his daughter to Syzran."

"And how do you remember that?" Yakubovsky asked.

"We've been asked this question a hundred times already," the driver said, smiling. "Gangsters asked us, and Caucasians. Everybody was looking for those people, but cops."

"And this man that the driver took was a mobster?" Yakubovsky continued.

"No! This was a civilian. And his daughter was legitimate. Clean."

"So, he took them to Syzran? To the railroad station?"

"Precisely."

"Did they have suitcases with them? Did you notice?"

"That's just the point. They went to the station, but didn't have any luggage. He had only a briefcase, like yours, and a travel bag. And she just had a handbag over her shoulder."

From his briefcase, Yakubovsky pulled the picture taken in Washington and showed it to the group. Among the many others in the photograph, the drivers at once picked out Boris and Melissa. This gave Yakubovsky no doubt that it was these two who had been transported by the ambulance. But what had happened to Cherkizov? And where was the money? Whoever took it would need to have either a suitcase or a large bag; it wasn't possible to stash a million dollars in your pockets. But according to the drivers, Boris and Melissa had had no luggage.

What if they took only a portion of the money? No way. It wouldn't happen. Nobody would leave the money behind. It was totally impossible.

He was guessing in vain. Tomorrow or the day after, things would be cleared up. Thanking the drivers, Yakubovsky returned to the off-road vehicle and requested they drive straight to Togliatti, to the Hotel Zhiguli.

They took the M-5 Road. The darkness was impenetrable. Only headlights from oncoming cars and trucks occasionally lit up the road. They passed the subdivision of Komsomolsk, and then Harbor Community, where the management of the largest Russian car manufacturer, AutoVaz, used to live in private homes. At last, they reached Old Town and pulled up to the gloomy hotel.

In the mid-sixties, Hotel Zhiguli had been built as a hostel for Italians working on the construction of AutoVaz. It was a large, nice building, made of brick, glass, and concrete. But after it became privatized, nobody was interested in doing the preventive maintenance—even when that meant something as small as changing a light bulb.

Yakubovsky flashed his ID at the security guards and walked straight to registration. Music and kitchen smells reached him from behind. There was a restaurant, and behind the registration desk, a bar. Further behind the bar hung the casino sign. Sitting around the bar at low tables and on a shabby sofa were teenage girls—prostitutes. In search for cars, buyers from all corners of the former Soviet Union traveled to Togliatti, so there was a sufficient amount of work for prostitutes. The decent-looking Yakubovsky had been noticed at once. While he filled out the guest card, one girl, having come nearer to him, looked down at the floor, patiently waiting for him to finish checking in, so that she could offer her services.

When Yakubovsky lifted his eyes to gaze upon her, he realized that in front of him was an exceptionally beautiful young woman. She looked like a top models. But she had her own destiny. This hungry, defenseless girl, who could shine at international fashion shows, was looking at him so pitifully that Yakubovsky had to ask her, "Are you hungry? Will you join me for a dinner?"

His heart was further impressed when he imagined Ann, who was about the same age, in her place. The girl didn't answer, but only swallowed and nodded. Yakubovsky took a room key.

"Well," said Yakubovsky, grabbing his room key off of the desk, "let's go up, darling."

And with that, they took the elevator up to his floor.

To tell the truth, Yakubovsky had no time for her, but having seen such expressive eyes on this unfortunate girl, he was moved to pity.

The room was warm, almost hot. Yakubovsky put his briefcase in the entryway closet, and took off his hat and overcoat. The girl wore only a thin dress.

"You know what? Why don't you go freshen up, and we will go down to eat. What is your name, darling?"

"Anastasia, but, please call me Nastia."

"My name is Vladislav Ivanovich."

"My grandfather's name is Ivan, too."

"And what is your father's name?"

"Basel."

"And how you have come to live such a life?"

"I am fulfilling my duty. My dad worked as driver in the village. Well, so, he and grandpa had gone to do some extra work there and, well, it seems they got drunk and collided with a car of Caucasians. So, neither my father nor grandfather had money to pay them off. So, they took me as payment. They will not let me go back home until their car is paid off with my services."

Anastasia spoke with the distinctive dialect of the Volga River region, diligently uttering "well" and often adding "so."

"Defile vile," Yakubovsky said maliciously, expressing his feelings about any individual who would take advantage of this helpless teenage girl. "Well, you are ready to eat?"

"Let's go, uncle," the girl responded, ready for anything.

As Yakubovsky marched into the restaurant with the girl-prostitute, all eyes were on them.

The host jumped up and declared, "It is against our policy to service prostitutes."

"Listen, flunky!" Yakubovsky bellowed. "Have you forgotten about the KGB already? It is up to the KGB to decide what is forbidden and what is not. Not you. Have you lost your sense?"

The host asked them to wait a moment and ran to the registration desk across the hall. He spoke with the desk attendant for a moment, and then returned silent. Then grabbing two menus, he led them to a table, saying to himself, "So what's the big deal? A gentleman can have dinner with a girl. Who knows—she could be his niece!"

After they were seated, one woman called the host over and declared loudly enough for all to hear that she would not stay in the same dining hall with a prostitute.

The host whispered into her ear, "If you left, I'm sure no one would cry." And with that, the scandal was exhausted.

Yakubovsky ordered two salads, two orders of borsch, two main dishes, and two bottles of water. He had hardly finished the salad and borsch, before Anastasia had gobbled down everything left on the table. Now properly fed, the girl flourished. Her eyes began to shine, though with her overloaded stomach, she could hardly breathe. Yakubovsky paid for dinner, and they left.

In his room, there were two narrow beds. Next to each bed, instead of nightstands, there were chairs. Anastasia began to undress in front of him.

"What are you doing?" Yakubovsky shouted. "You'd better go to the bathroom, take a hot shower, and lay down to rest. You probably were frozen the whole day."

The girl went to the bathroom. Vlad heard her filling the bathtub with water, and imagined how this long-legged girl with high, firm breasts might look, all while recollecting his short-legged, clumsy creature. With that, his masculine instincts took over triumphantly, and he quickly undressed and entered the bathroom.

During the night, he awoke Anastasia couple more times, and she, recollecting his kind attitude, executed her simple business with enthusiasm.

In the morning, they went down to the restaurant for breakfast, which the girl inhaled yet again. Yakubovsky then paid her twice what she required and asked Anastasia to stay in the room and have a good sleep.

"Also," Vlad added, "if you get hungry, you can go to the restaurant and buy as much food as you want. I will pay for it."

Then Vladislav asked her to stay with him as long as he was in Togliatti.

By the time Yakubovsky arrived in the parking lot, the assistant officer with two submachine gunners was already waiting. The assistant officer reported that all orders given yesterday had been executed, and they were ready to go.

Yakubovsky wanted to ask for a security guard to look after Anastasia, but then changed his mind. He figured she wouldn't leave the hotel anyway.

They reached Novomatushkino in forty minutes. Soldiers had already begun to clear the snow away and to set pieces of the scorched metal roof aside, out of the way of the search team.

Where the metal sheets had been, there was no snow, so the criminologists stepped in. Layer after layer, they habitually went about their work, photographing and gathering select material evidence. Meanwhile, soldiers, under the instruction of their superiors, carried away furniture remains.

Several hours had passed before one criminologist located a corpse, which was scorched and non-identifiable. The body had been located near the gas range. In a few minutes, three more charred corpses were revealed. On one corpse, which had been lying near what would have been the entrance to the former cottage, Yakubovsky saw a large metal seaman's belt clasp. This clasp, without a doubt, had belonged to Cherkizov. Yakubovsky perfectly remembered it.

He took a closer look at the scorched skull. The bullet aperture was distinctly visible. A similar bullet aperture had been found in the skull of the corpse in the kitchen.

No traces of bullets were detected in the remaining two bodies, but among the ashes and scorched rags where they lay, a criminologist found two Makarov pistols. This surprised Yakubovsky. A more likely place for the pistols to be located would have been near Cherkizov and the other body found in the kitchen.

However, Yakubovsky remembered that it was Cherkizov's habit to carry a knife in addition to his pistol. Indeed, a few minutes later, and on the body next to the entrance, a criminologist found a knife. Its plastic handle had been melted off. Now, Yakubovsky was totally convinced that those were Cherkizov's remains. Who the others were was of no interest to him, although the matching bullet apertures in Cherkizov's skull and the body from the kitchen still had his attention.

How in the world would Boris Goryanin, let alone with a Caucasian gangster, be able to take Cherkizov's weapon? Yakubovsky wondered. And how in the world would Goryanin then be able to kill Cherkizov, the lieutenant colonel of KGB's Ninth Division? And two more healthy, young, specially trained professional gangsters? It's impossible. Goryanin is a layman, quite possibly not even able to shoot. How he could cope with four men all by himself, or even serially, one right after another? It didn't fit the usual schematic.

It would be necessary to check up on the weapon that Anisimov had been killed with. Yakubovsky called over the assistant officer and ordered him to check the following: first, who had in possession the two pistols found near the bodies without bullet wounds; second, whether the bullet apertures in the two skulls coincided with that in Anisimov's skull; and third, where the fire had been first ignited.

It was a lucky coincidence that nobody from the local police tried to investigate the reasons for the fire, so that the material evidence remained untouched, Yakubovsky thought.

There was no reason for Yakubovsky to stay any longer. All of the facts were clear to him now, and any other material evidence could be collected without his participation—it would change nothing. Besides, he had better get back to hotel to check on Anastasia.

By the time they arrived at the hotel, it was absolutely dark, except for a cordoned-off square in front, which was surrounded by police cars shining their headlights. Some policemen were crowded around something, while a patrolman tried to push aside crowding civilians.

Yakubovsky left the car and headed toward the scene. The patrolman roughly stopped him, until seeing Yakubovsky's ID, at which point he saluted the senior officer and let him through.

Yakubovsky approached closely. Then he caught his breath. Under a tree, on the snow, Anastasia lay on her back. She was in the same thin dress she had worn that morning. Her throat had been cut from ear to ear. Yakubovsky knew what it meant. He had seen enough Russian soldiers' throats cut the same way, by mudjehadins in Afghanistan.

"What has happened here, captain?" Yakubovsky asked, hoarse with distress.

"And you would be?" The police captain politely inquired.

"I am the lieutenant colonel of the FSB. Here is my certificate." Yakubovsky extended the red bi-fold ID with the state insignia.

The captain saluted and unwillingly reported, "These Caucasians are at it again. They've killed a prostitute, the sons of bitches. Well! What have they not destroyed in our land? Every day, they do some killing. They are cruel without limit. In the city there are fourteen groups of gangsters, and in no way can we figure out … "

Yakubovsky had already turned and was heading back to the car. Suddenly, before him, was a vision of his meeting with the gypsy at Kazansky Station last summer. He remembered her every word: "Through the blood of fornicating with an innocent soul, a disgusting snake will come out from your heart, and you will change. But you will be better. You will quit working for the government, and through your grief, you will clear your soul."

Yakubovsky became terribly scared. Really? Had the gypsy predicted his future?

There was no reason to stay in Togliatti any longer. He didn't want to face the consequences of a potential meeting with the Caucasian gangsters who were pimping prostitutes.

"How soon could we get to Syzran?" he asked his assistant officer.

"Within an hour and a half," he answered wearily. He had already tired of taking care of the Moscow visitor, and wanted to get rid of him as soon as possible.

"Then, let's go. I just need to grab the shaving set from my room." Then fully understanding the assistant officer's situation, he continued, "Would you like me to go with you?"

"Yes. As they say, for the company."

Ten minutes later, they were driving from the hotel, and with the emergency lights and siren turned on, were rushing to Syzran.

"There are several trains to Moscow," Yakubovsky said, though he was mostly arguing with himself. "I'll be there by tomorrow morning."

All the way to Syzran they were silent. Only at the railroad station did Yakubovsky tell his assistant officer, "When the investigation report is complete, please send it to me by special delivery."

"Yes, Sir. The investigation report will be sent by the special delivery."

And with that, the two men saluted each other.

The next morning, Yakubovsky had arrived in Moscow and was headed toward the metro, when, suddenly, he stopped. Right before him there was the very gypsy that he had met last summer. Their eyes met.

"Do you recognize me?" the old woman asked.

"Yes, I do," Yakubovsky said with a dry mouth.

"The innocent soul with whom you fornicated has been sacrificed. Do you trust me, now? She has taken up your sins, and now you are clean. Follow your destiny. Don't be afraid. Go. All will be good with you."

Yakubovsky took a few hundred dollars bills from his pocket and extended them to the gypsy.

She accepted the money, saying, "Always be generous with those whom you are in love and with those who love you. I shall protect you.

"Divorce your wife. Run away from her. But now I shall say farewell. Don't look for me anymore. If it is necessary, I will find you." And with those parting words, the gypsy disappeared as she had at their first meeting, seemingly dissolving into the air.

10

Moscow, November 18, 1993

Yakubovsky stood for a few minutes, collecting his thoughts. Then he headed toward the metro station and found a payphone.

Gavrila Kravchuk greeted him.

"Working hard?" Vlad asked.

Kravchuk didn't answer. He was waiting to hear the reason for Yakubovsky's sudden call.

"Let's talk," Yakubovsky explained. "But not in the office."

"It is possible to meet in the dining room?"

"No," Yakubovsky quickly answered.

"Okay. Then, where?"

"Let's meet at the Bar-B-Q House in the glass building at the entry to Gorky Park. Do you know the place?"

"We will find it. When?" Kravchuk asked.

"In thirty minutes. Does that work?"

"It is understood. I shall be there."

Yakubovsky hadn't developed a strategy for their conversation yet, but to meet Kravchuk had become necessary.

Back in September, after Cherkizov had called Kravchuk from the village in Samara, Gavrila had suddenly felt in an excellent mood. He called for his car and left Agroprom to celebrate the good news. In fact, he celebrated the good news so diligently, that two of his most hefty security guard could hardly drag him home, where they undressed him and put him to bed.

The next morning, barely awake, he began to wait for Cherkizov. But Cherkizov didn't appear. In impatient expectation, Kravchuk passed the day. Then, a second day passed, and a third. Cherkizov had disappeared. Kravchuk decided not to make noise about it but realized that continuing to wait for

Cherkizov wasn't possible either. He didn't know what to do, but he couldn't sit and do nothing.

By the end of September, the political situation in Moscow was worsening by the hour, though on the periphery it was silent. Gavrila had decided to go to Samara himself. But where should he go? He called Peter Anisimov. The Novokuybyshevsk Oil Pipeline dispatch center seemed surprised to receive Kravchuk's call.

And so it was that Kravchuk found out that Anisimov was assassinated. Two bullets and a third control shot had been fired into his head, and his office had been set on fire. It was then that Kravchuk decided not to conduct an independent investigation. It was unsafe. Besides, that Goryanin and Melissa Spencer had been liquidated, he had no doubt. But where was Cherkizov? It became obvious to him that Cherkizov had appropriated the money and taken off.

Kravchuk, washed up under the pressure, participated in days of heavy drinking, after which the delirium tremens began. He awoke one night, ran into the walk-in closet, and started to involuntarily kick the wall. Then he began opening and closing the closet door, knocking it with his head. Hearing the commotion, his wife Alevtina sat up in bed and observed him in horror. When Gavrila, finally releasing the madness, had fallen on the floor, she called an ambulance. The diagnosis was simple: severe alcoholic poisoning. The ambulance took Kravchuk to a neurological hospital, where, the whole week he was connected to an IV. There, his entire system was cleaned, thus removing him from the condition to which he had driven himself.

Gavrila was discharged from the hospital in mid-October. When he returned to the office, he found over half of the employees gone. Isaev and Theodora had quit Agroprom without even receiving returns on the personal loans that they had made to Kravchuk. And Lydia Selina hadn't shown up in a long time. Only Kravchuk's secretary, young Valerie, was still there, sitting in the same chair and attracting the same attention from the young security guards.

Kravchuk sat silently in his office, waiting and thinking. Suddenly, he recollected that he still had the notebook that Cherkizov and Kuleshov had brought him. Gavrila then requested that Valerie find Kuleshov. He would investigate the situation for Kravchuk.

The next morning, Kuleshov was in Kravchuk's office. Still unemployed, he was delighted at an opportunity to earn money. Kravchuk handed Kuleshov the notebook with all of the names, addresses, and telephone numbers, and charged him to find out what had happened to Cherkizov. For this service, Kuleshov charged five hundred dollars.

Two weeks later, Kuleshov appeared at Kravchuk's office. It was Tuesday, November 8. What Kuleshov told him put Kravchuk in shock. But then how could he be surprised? Lydia Selina and her husband, Colonel Vladimir Shkolnikov, had disappeared, possibly having died in a fire near Fedorov's residence in the village. Fedorov, along with his wife, her sister, granddaughter, and a heap of security guards had been killed, and their cars had all been blown up. Moreover, the Solvaig building had burned to the ground.

But that was still not all. At the Tyumen Oil & Gas Production Association, the contract for the delivery of crude oil had been signed with, its general director, Mr. Sviblov, and Deputy Kozitsky had shot each other. Right after that, mobsters had taken over the Tyumen Oil & Gas Production Association.

Kuleshov still had not found Cherkizov, however. He had some ideas, but one way or another, Cherkizov was just gone.

Today, when Yakubovsky called, Kravchuk was delighted to hear his voice.

Yakubovsky stepped onto the escalator and rode down to the metro station. He walked down Circle Lane for about fifteen minutes, until he reached the Octyabrskaya Station. He then walked down the street toward Gorky Park. The image of the murdered Anastasia would not leave his mind. In the train, all night long, he dreamed about her. Nastia had attracted him. He could still feel the heat coming from her body. As memories gushed over him, Vladislav felt frost entering his stomach, and he began trembling.

Now, after his second meeting with the gypsy, Yakubovsky believed that the incident with the young prostitute was a sign from above. From now on, his life would change. Vladislav had quit dreaming about Ann. She was his son's girlfriend. Why should he think about her? Let Igor do that.

Yes, my life should change, he thought. But how? I shall divorce Natalie, but then what happens? Where would I go? Where will I live? I have a little money, but the service doesn't pay too much, and an appointment in the Office of the Attorney General doesn't look promising.

If Filimonov tries to put my back against the wall, I will find some way to talk back. Especially now, after learning that Goryanin was involved in Cherkizov's death. I shall bring everything down on him. It was Goryanin who killed everybody and embezzled all the money. Try to prove the opposite. And why should I get confused with Goryanin or Cherkizov? I must wait for the report from the criminologists. Aha. Here is Kravchuk.

Kravchuk and his entourage pulled up to the Bar-B-Q House in two cars: a Mercedes 600 often called by the nickname Gelding in Russia, and a Jeep. When they got out, Gavrila towered above the four bodyguards that accompanied him.

"Winter has come already," Kravchuk said in place of a greeting.

"It has," Yakubovsky agreed. "Where should we go?" Yakubovsky joked, opening the restaurant door and motioning theatrically with his right hand for Kravchuk to go in before him. "Go ahead, sir! Please."

"Oh, no sir!" Kravchuk objected, making the same theatrical gesture with his left hand. "Only after you, please."

Yakubovsky ceremoniously entered into the Bar-B-Q House. They walked to the end of a hall, took off their overcoats, and hung them on some nearby hangers. Then the men found a table. Kravchuk's bodyguards sat at a table nearby.

Both Kravchuk and Yakubovsky were silent. Neither of them seemed to know how to begin the conversation. Kravchuk waited, hoping that Yakubovsky would talk first, but Vlad couldn't collect his thoughts.

A fat waitress, wearing a thick jacket and a long-unwashed apron approached them.

"What do you wish to order, gentlemen?" she asked.

"You know what?" Kravchuk began. "Bring us a one liter of vodka, two bottles of mineral water …"

"We've run out of mineral water," the waitress interrupted. "There is beer."

"All right. Bring us two bottles of beer, pickled cucumbers, bread, butter, two orders of shish-kebabs, and take good care of my guys." Kravchuk nodded toward his security guards. "Feed them well. Let's bring the beer, vodka, bread, and mustard at once."

Kravchuk looked at Vladislav and explained. "I would like to cool down"

The fat waitress brought them two glasses, vodka, beer, rye bread, butter, and mustard. Yakubovsky then asked for another glass.

"What?" Kravchuk said. "Are we waiting for somebody else?"

"Not anymore," Yakubovsky answered.

"Then what do we need one more glass for?"

Yakubovsky was silent. As the waitress set down the third glass, he smeared a slice of bread with mustard. Kravchuk did the same. Then, Yakubovsky opened a bottle of vodka and poured it into the three glasses. He covered one glass with a piece of the bread.

"Who has died?" Kravchuk asked.

"I suggest we drink for the tranquil soul of the recently departed," Yakubovsky said not looking at Kravchuk. "God's slave,[10] divine Dmitry." Then he widely crossed himself.

"What are you talking about? Are you talking about Cherkizov? So, he has been added to the list of the Most Wanted."

Not getting a response, Kravchuk crossed himself, and both men drank their full eight-ounce glasses of vodka in a single sip.

Slightly frowning, Kravchuk then washed his down with beer. "So, come on. Please. Tell me what you know," Gavrila said, and then beckoning again the fat waitress, he ordered two more bottles of vodka and four more glasses.

When she had brought the vodka, Kravchuk called over his bodyguards. "Here, guys. Have a drink for the tranquility of Dmitry Cherkizov's soul. He has lost his life as the hero of Russia."

Then addressing Yakubovsky again, he repeated, "Tell me. Go on, tell me."

"What should I tell you? You know everything. After all, he called you from Novomatushkino."

Kravchuk understood immediately that Yakubovsky knew more, but he didn't let on. "Yes, Cherkizov called me. He told me that they had reached their destination."

"Where was their destination?"

"They went to Novokuybyshevsk to make a payment to Anisimov."

"Do you think I don't realize that you already knew that Anisimov was killed—two hours before Cherkizov, Goryanin, and Melissa Spencer even landed in Kuromich? And you … are it possible? … do you not know that the village Novomatushkino is located in the opposite direction from Kuromich airport that the city of Novokuybyshevsk?"

Kravchuk was silent, considering the complicated situation he was in. To delay answering, he poured vodka into his and Yakubovsky's glasses up to the rim.

"Why did you send Cherkizov to me?" Yakubovsky asked, looking directly into Kravchuk's eyes.

"So he could bring you photos from me."

"Photos, you say? You have recorded our meeting. You have set me up. This is what you did, didn't you?"

"What are you talking about, Vlad? Please, tell me more. What happened to Cherkizov there?"

10 In accordance to Russian tradition, all recently departed souls are called "God's slaves."

"It looks like he and three Caucasian gangsters were gunned down by friend of yours, Mr. Boris Goryanin. He has appropriated the money, too."

Kravchuk dropped his jaw. "Goryanin? He got Cherkizov? And three more Caucasian gangsters, as well?"

Kravchuk drank his full glass of vodka, and then silently snacked on a crust of bread with mustard. "Did you call me here to tell me jokes? I am telling you, Goryanin isn't capable of doing that, either morally or physically. He isn't capable of murder or theft. Can you imagine! This gentleman, instead of appropriating five and a half million dollars from Eddy Pennington, returned the money back to him. Would you return five and a half million dollars? I am asking you!"

"The point of our conversation isn't about that," Yakubovsky objected while chewing some bread with mustard. "I do not have proof that Goryanin took the money that he and Melissa were carrying for Anisimov. By the way, what did Cherkizov tell you about the money when he called from the village?"

"That the money was in the car," Kravchuk admitted, lowering his eyes.

"Yes. Yes. Yeees," Yakubovsky said, thoughtfully stretching out the word. "Goryanin may not have known the money was in the car. People saw him with a briefcase and a travel bag, and Melissa had only a small handbag. And if they did not know, that means the cops could have carried the money away. Our last hope is to find out whether they had luggage with them when they crossed the border. But … Goryanin offed them professionally. That's a fact. What if he is a CIA agent?"

"Are you okay?" Kravchuk gave him a stern look.

Yakubovsky ignored his question and asked another. "Do you know how Goryanin use to pass registration at the airport?"

"Through the VIP Service Center."

"Is that true?"

"If that's what I told you, it's true."

When the waitress brought their two orders of shish-kebabs, Kravchuk, after all that he had just gone through, ordered another bottle of vodka.

Yakubovsky again recollected young Anastasia. He called the waitress and ordered her to bring one more empty glass. The careless waitress walked away muttering something about how they were using up all her clean glasses, but brought another glass anyway and set it on the table. Yakubovsky poured vodka into his glass, into Kravchuk's, and then into the empty glass. He covered the forth glass with piece of bread too.

"I am suggesting we drink for the tranquil soul of the recently departed, God's slave, the divine Anastasia. She was the fornicator with an innocent soul, and because of that, I have found favor with the Lord." Yakubovsky widely crossed himself and drank.

Kravchuk did the same. The waitress then approached the table, about to lay into them for blocking the door to the restaurant without her permission. But upon seeing the glasses covered with bread, and the bread with mustard, she departed on tiptoe, shrinking her head down into her shoulders.

Right then, somebody knocked at the closed entryway door. Through the glass, it was visible that three men wished to enter. The waitress rushed to the door, opened it, and blocked the entrance with her fat body.

One of the visitors spoke up. "For what reason won't you let us enter the premises?"

"Shut up!" She hissed at him. "Silence, at once. Are you blind? Don't you see what is going on here? The Godfathers are having a funeral feast, remembering their dead. Don't you see what kind of cars they came in? You'd better get lost. You could get me in trouble." And with that, she resolutely closed the door in their faces.

Now drunk, Yakubovsky kept silent. And it dawned on him, though somewhat against his will, that he should tell Kravchuk the story of how he met the girl-prostitute in Togliatti, how he had grown fond of her, and how he had found her with her throat cut.

Kravchuk listened to Vladislav's story without interruption. When it was over, he was suddenly struck with grief. For Yakubovsky, for Cherkizov, and for this innocent girl.

With a slowly turning drunken tongue, he said, "Do you see, Vlad? It looks like it is necessary for us to bail out of here. And that Goryanin guy understood that initially. You and I should steal money and escape … as they say … to make big money. Understood?"

Yakubovsky, though totally drunk, understood that Kravchuk had precisely formulated a solution to their problem: "to steal money and escape." He reflected for an instant and suddenly, absolutely unexpectedly, started singing with a chest baritone:

… The lift-off roar isn't dreaming any longer,
And this stillness is not colored in ice blue!
Instead we dream of the grassy lawns of home,
The green grass lawn! The green, the greenest grass! …[11]

11 From the famous Russian song "Grass Lawn," by A. Poperechny. This quotation was translated from Russian into English by the author.

Yakubovsky diligently finished singing and shed a few tears. Continuing to cry, he asked Kravchuk, “Why we are like this? Why we are not like other people?”

“Because we are chosen by the Lord,” Gavrila explained.

“Are we? Instead of Jews?”

“No. We are!” Kravchuk announced, lifting his index finger, and then calming down.

“Please, take me back home, brother,” Yakubovsky uttered in a barely audible voice. “To the short-legged, clumsy creature.” His head dropped onto his chest, and he began to snore.

The bodyguards approached them right on time. They habitually pulled money out of Kravchuk’s pocket, paid the fat waitress, and put the men’s overcoats and hats on them. Then they ceremoniously carried both Yakubovsky and Kravchuk out of the restaurant and to their homes.

11

Moscow, November 19, 1993

Waking the next morning, Yakubovsky felt exactly like an individual should feel after drinking so heavily the night before; he suffered from the non-contentious social illness called a hangover. Therefore, having a drink of cold water, he decided to stay in bed and consider his present situation.

After an hour or so, he had determined that his next step was to go to the Sheremetyevo Airport. He needed to find out when Boris and Melissa had crossed the border and whether they'd had any luggage with them. If they had not crossed the border at Sheremetyevo, he would have to request the information from the FSB's Division of Border Security, and that would not be easy.

Then the sobering Yakubovsky made his second decision of the morning: to separate from his wife. But he should leave her easily, without causing any problems. Quietly. Without hurry, he should save some money, rent an apartment, and only then leave. That way, if his superiors should call him out, he would already have a place of his own and some money. And anyway, there was bedlam around, without limit. So his service to the FSB has ceased holding any value for him.

Finally, by midday, Yakubovsky got out of bed, shaved, took a hot shower, ate some oatmeal, and made a cup of instant coffee. Feeling much better, he decided to go to Sheremetyevo.

At the second-floor VIP Service Center, Yakubovsky approached the shift manager and presented her with his FSB certificate.

"I am listening," the senior person answered obsequiously. She was blonde and was well-clad in the dark blue Aeroflot uniform, with a white and red scarf around her neck.

"I need to know, when the US citizen, Mr. Boris Goryanin, and the British citizen, Lady Melissa Spencer, crossed the border."

"Do you know the approximate date of service?" she asked, getting the service registration book.

"Likely sometime between September twenty-third and October seventh."

"Let me have a look." The woman began to move her groomed finger down several pages of the book. "Well, here there are. Yes. On October second, both of them checked in on Flight Thirty-three Sixty-seven, which took off for Frankfurt on time, at fourteen twenty-five."

"And what about their luggage? What kind of luggage was with them?" Vlad asked.

Then, as the manager searched for the information, he thought, If they left Syzran on the evening of September twenty-third and didn't depart from Sheremetyevo until October second, where were they all that time?

But on the other hand, maybe that didn't make any difference.

"No. No check in luggage was registered," the woman finally said.

"Does that necessarily mean they didn't have any luggage?"

"Yes, it means they had no check in luggage," she confirmed.

"Did they declare any money at the exit?" Vlad pressed.

"It is recorded that Ms. Melissa Spencer declared one million dollars upon her entry in Russia on September twenty-second. There is a custom declaration's number. But there is no custom declaration's number upon her exit." The woman looked up at Yakubovsky. "She spent a million in a week. Some people have a good life!"

"Does that mean she had no money to declare?" Vlad said.

"It means she had less than fifteen hundred dollars upon crossing the border."

"And who served them?"

"Yes, here she is. Our Vicky. Victoria Koval served them," the manager said, and then whispered loudly to a beautiful young woman with blue, blue eyes. "Vicky, a comrade from the FSB wishes to ask you something."

Vicky walked up to the desk, not lowering her eyes from Yakubovsky's. It was apparent that she knew her worth. She approached the desk and awarded him with a charming smile, complete with snow-white teeth.

"What it is necessary for you to know, sir?" she asked him.

"The comrade lieutenant colonel wishes to specify something," the manager answered, instead of Yakubovsky.

"I am listening," Vicky sang, slightly tilting her head to the left.

Yakubovsky has showed her the same photo that he had shown the drivers at the hospital in Novomatushkino. "Do you recognize anybody?"

Victoria looked closely at the photo, and stuck out her long index finger with a well-groomed pink fingernail. Then she pointed to Goryanin. "This gentleman. He is a very pleasant man. His name is … his name is …" she looked in the service registration book. "His name is Boris Goryanin."

"Is there any place we can go to talk?" Yakubovsky asked.

It wasn't really necessary to repeat his question concerning their luggage, but he very much liked Vicky, and wished to extend the conversation with her as long as possible.

"Here. Let's proceed to this room," Vicky answered and went ahead of Yakubovsky, slightly rocking with her hips.

When they got inside, Yakubovsky shut the door. "Do you remember, Vicky," he began, "whether there was any luggage with them?"

"They had no luggage. He had a briefcase, and his companion had only a travel bag and a small handbag. It was just as it was recorded in the registration book."

"And that's all?"

"That's all."

"And why had you not informed us?"

"Not informed you of what?" Vicky looked at Yakubovsky, slightly squinting her sky-blue eyes.

"That they were taking off for Frankfurt," Yakubovsky continued, understanding that his words were nonsense.

"Because there was no inquiry on them. Unless they were under search?"

"No, they weren't under search. But this Mr. Goryanin is a suspect in a murder investigation. So you should have informed us, but you did not. That means you should pay a penalty." Yakubovsky knew he should stop carrying on like this, but he couldn't stop. The presence of this blue-eyed beauty totally confused him.

"What are you talking about?" she said. "He is a nice person. Affable. You have got to be kidding me."

"Well, I should tell you that he didn't kill four people for the purpose of robbing them. He had to protect his companion, and probably himself too."

"Ah, the British girl?" Vicky recollected. "Oh. He is the man! Well done!"

"Well, I don't know for sure. But there will still be a penalty."

"Are you trying to fine me by going out with you?" Vicky asked.

Yakubovsky felt his face getting red. "No. I am simply asking you to join me for a dinner. About the penalty … well, that was primitive and unsuccessful joke," he uttered in an apologetic near-whisper.

"I will be your date, but on several conditions: first, that you don't grab me with your hands; second, that you don't drag me around the streets; and, third, that—if we are attacked by hooligans—you will protect me."

"Do you have a specific proposal?"

"Would the Hotel Salute suit you? It's a restaurant where we can eat and dance."

"Vicky, you are perfection!" Vlad said. "When you will be available?"

"Tonight. After work. I am an unmarried girl," Vicky answered with affectionate modesty.

"Tonight. At eighteen hundred, in the lobby of the Hotel Salute?" Yakubovsky specified.

"Yes, sir. Tonight. At eighteen hundred in the lobby of the Hotel Salute!" Vicky playfully confirmed. "And please, consider, sir, that I don't like it when men are late and come without flowers."

Yakubovsky, instead of uttering a basic farewell, took Vicky's hand and, having felt its well-cared for but thin skin, brought it to his lips and gently kissed it.

Then as he was leaving the room, he turned at the doorway and said, "See you exactly at eighteen hundred. Remember that I know where you work and how to find you!"

"Yes," she replied with a big smile. "And remember the conditions you agreed upon!"

12

Moscow, November 19, 1993

Yakubovsky knew where, besides Aeroflot, Victoria Koval worked and how to find her, since all employees of the VIP Service Center, including Vicky, were informers of the FSB.

Victoria Schmidt was born in May 1964 in the village of Fedorovka to a family of Russianized Germans. In 1941, when Nazi Germany had begun the war with the Soviet Union, all Russianized Germans were relocated in Kazakhstan and Uzbekistan. So the Schmidt family was relocated from the large settlement of Gross Libental, in the Odessa region, to Northern Kazakhstan, in the Pavlodar region. Her family spoke German fluently.

Later, when Vicky went to school, she learned Russian and Kazakh. She was a good student. Though she wasn't an honor student, the languages she picked up easily. Villagers didn't have internal passports, and native, even Russianized Germans couldn't be accepted to universities. Therefore, shortly before graduation from high school, Vicky's father, having bribed the necessary person, received for Vicky a new birth certificate in which she was named Victoria Koval—a native of the Ukraine. Thus, her diploma was issued to her in her new last name.

In 1982, Victoria Koval was accepted into the Moscow University of Foreign Languages' Greek-Roman program. When her teachers asked where she had learned German so well, Vicky answered that near their Ukrainian village there was a German town, and that she'd had friend there. Having spent a year in the German program, she went into the English program, and as a secondary language, Victoria chose Spanish.

At the end of her third year, when Vicky was twenty-one, a young man, introduced as an employee of the Department of International Friendship, came to her university. His name was Alexander Pushkov. Really, he was the second lieutenant of the KGB's Ninth Division, which carried out the surveillance of foreigners. He gave a speech about the international youth movement, about international friendship, and the solidarity of working youth. By the end of the presentation, he suggested students prepare themselves for work in the youth organizations at USSR embassies. They could do this by frequently visiting hotels where they would have the chance to get acquainted with young people visiting the country. As hospitable Soviet citizens, they should show these visitors the capital of Moscow and tell them about the Soviet way of life. However, in order to avoid suspicion, Pushkov said, the students should write a proclamation stating their willingness to inform the police of any politically questionable behavior displayed by their new friends.

Some students, after referring to their textbooks, refused to write such statement, but Vicky and two other girls dreamed of working abroad, and so agreed. As such, Victoria Koval became an inadvertent non-staff informer for the KGB and began her "work" in this capacity at the Hotel Salute.

The saddest part of this story, however, is that this son of a bitch Pushkov ended up enticing her. Under the pretense of wanting a serious conversation with Victoria in official apartment, he gave her a drink contaminated with a "date rape" drug, and then deprived her of her virginity. After that, he photographed the unconscious naked girl. A few days passed before Vicky finally came to her senses. She easily overcame the physical pain, but every time she remembered what happened, she started to sob.

Pushkov called Victoria two weeks later and ordered her to come to the dean's office. When Pushkov showed her the photos he'd made of her, Victoria ran into him with her fists. But he stopped her by threatening to send the photos to the dean if she refused to carry out a special task for him. And so Victoria became a KGB prostitute. The two other girls were recruited as well.

Vicky didn't quit the university or even transfer to a new campus. On the contrary, she remained a full-time student, and even began to give more attention to her studies. However, she didn't have time to get acquainted with a normal guy.

Victoria did, however, feel it necessary to leave her dormitory, as she had become a shame before the other girls. Therefore, Victoria rented a room from an old lady. The apartment was located near the Voikovskaya Metro Station, which made it convenient for her to get to both the university and to the hotel for work.

The old woman was also a former political victim. In her youth, she had been sentenced to eighteen years in camps and afterward was sent to a settlement. But during Khrushev's time, she received amnesty. She, a daughter of the former "enemy of people," received a two-room apartment in Moscow in a large apartment complex constructed by captured German soldiers.

The old woman was lonely. She worked in the dressing room at some theater and was paid practically nothing. Therefore, the rent and the company were both beneficial for her. The old lady used to bring Victoria complimentary tickets to the theater. Thus Victoria, the humble village girl, became acquainted with theatrical Moscow.

Tatiana Pavlovna, Victoria's apartment owner, quickly understood what kind of "work" her tenant engaged in. Gradually, she was able to get Vicky to admit it to her. After that, Tatiana Pavlovna educated Victoria how to survive in her not-so-easy trade. As it turned out, Tatiana had received an advanced degree in the art of survival in the labor camps.

Taken away in the notorious event of 1937, just after graduating from high school, the innocent Tatiana was raped by two guards the very night of her arrest. After that, she was gang raped in all of the prisons and camps. And so it proceeded until one experienced female thief advised her to pretend that she was a lesbian.

"Think about it," the thief had told Tatiana. "It's not a big deal if women do you, and then you don't have every dirty stud always harassing you. Plus, you can't get pregnant that way. Besides, if you were to have an unsuccessful abortion, you could die."

The female thief also educated Tatiana on how to behave with both men and women during intimae. Her simple science allowed Tatiana to survive the nightmarish conditions created by main goal of the native communist party: to get rid of as many of their own people as possible.

Victoria, in turn, acquired these lessons from Tatiana, and put them into practice with success. Upon meeting a client, she would usually go to a restaurant with him. Victoria began watching what she ate, choosing only light or dietary dishes. She never accepted an alcoholic drink, but drank only mineral water and green tea. Then during dinner, she started engage into physical contact with the client making him to feel quasi physical pleasure. The client paid her additional money for her diligence, even after not receiving that for which he had originally bargained.

Victoria didn't remain a prostitute. Casually having been revealed as a KGB victim, she was finally released from her obligations. Then after graduating in 1988, due to her acquaintance with several middle-ranking KGB officers and her experience dialoguing with men, Vicky, under Tatiana's guidance, landed a job at the VIP Service Center at the Sheremetyevo Airport.

It was not a highly paid job, but every day, Victoria received gifts and tips from passengers. She sold those items to a neighbor, who was working in a beauty salon, who then resold them to her clients for even more. Vicky paid to the senior person on duty and the manager of VIP-service their share of all gifts and tips she received from passengers. Thus, by 1991 Victoria was receiving a decent income, and, together with Tatiana Pavlovna, managed to privatize their two-bedroom apartment. The title was vested as a joint tenancy. Obviously, Victoria paid for the privatization of the apartment with her own money.

In early 1992, Tatiana was diagnosed with Stage Four breast cancer. Doctors were rarely mistaken in such cases. Vicky looked after the old woman, but "Grandma" as she had become known to Victoria, didn't make it. So Victoria became the sole owner of the apartment.

All these years, Vicky had continued to financially help her family in Kazakhstan. Now her parents, as native Germans, were immigrating to unified Germany. Vicky couldn't go with them, however, since, per her modified birth certificate, she wasn't their daughter. And, in general, she was registered as a native Ukrainian, not a German.

Victoria's unpleasant experiences had an ill effect on her life. She took no satisfaction in dating, although several nice young men had taken an interest in her at one time or another. Passengers, who came through the VIP Service Center, though they noticed her, could not have guessed that she was just a poor young woman aspiring for simple happiness. As a result, she began to consider men not as potential grooms, but as merely a source of income. And though she was nice with everybody, she was actually colder with those men who tried to draw her attention.

Yet, for some reason, Victoria Koval had seen in Vladislav Yakubovsky the soul of an adventurer—and agreed to go out with him.

13

Moscow, November 19, 1993

Before his meeting with Vicky, Yakubovsky decided he should take himself up a notch, so from Sheremetyevo, he went straight to the hair salon. He had haircut and a shave, and then rushed back home. Fortunately, his wife wasn't there, or she'd have asked about his unusual grooming. Vladislav cleaned his shoes. Then he took a hot shower, brushed his teeth, and put on aftershave. He dressed in a rather good-quality, light gray suit that he'd recently purchased in Turkey. In the same place, he had also bought a coordinating dark-blue shirt and dark-gray tie. Now, his new outfit would go to good use. Out of habit, he put on an arm holster to hold his Makarov pistol.

Yakubovsky looked in the wardrobe mirror. The face looking back at him belonged to a youngish man, but it was beginning to grow old already. He massaged his face with both hands.

"Well," he told the image. "That's the best I can do. If I become involved with Vicky, however, I shall stop drinking."

He went to his hiding place in the bedroom and took out two hundred dollars and some Russian rubles. "For representation," he said to himself. "Though, eventually, I will spend this on myself."

It was time for him to go meet Vicky, but he stalled, thinking about something. After a short negotiation with himself, Vlad climbed in the wardrobe and got a box covered in dark blue velvet. In the box there was a decent-sized silver pendent attached to a twisted silver chain. He put the gift box with the pendent in the inside pocket of his coat.

Yakubovsky then put on a new black leather overcoat, with a black scarf. He took a final look in the mirror. In this new outfit, Vladislav looked sharp, even attractive. He crossed himself for success, and then, without a hat, run out to catch a taxi.

Mist was hanging in the air. It was a typical Moscow winter, with frost during the day, but warmer by the early evening. The snow had slightly melted, creating pools.

Finding a cab wasn't a problem. Before they arrived at the hotel, however, Yakubovsky requested a stop at the metro station, where he got out momentarily and, without hesitation, bought a bouquet of scarlet roses. He reached the Salute at five minutes to six.

Victoria, with her magnificent, shoulder-length, blonde hair, her sparkling snow-white teeth, and her healthy radiant pink cheeks, was still in her light blue Aeroflot uniform with the red and white scarf. He watched her proudly approach the hotel, entering the lobby at exactly six o'clock. She inspected the lobby and, not having seen Yakubovsky, took from her small handbag a pocket mirror. She looked at herself, wrinkled her nose, retrieved some pink lipstick, no doubt the same color as her well-groomed nails, and lightly freshened her full lips.

"Yes! She is a woman," Vlad murmured. "Just as the doctor ordered!"

Then as he walked up to her, he thought, *Such pleasant women become generals' wives. I shall be a general too!*

He quickly returned from his dreams of generalship to reality, approaching Victoria from the behind, and clicking his heels loudly as he'd learned in military school. She slightly shuddered at the sound and turned to see the smiling Vladislav, extending a bouquet of scarlet roses.

Having inspected Yakubovsky, Victoria smiled and coquettishly cooed, "You surprised me."

"And so I will always!" he replied.

Generally speaking, Yakubovsky was not a rascal in the usual sense of the word. He was a refined product of the KGB. As such, he was made by the system.

But in his private life, he was the usual forty-two-year-old man—slightly playful and well-read. In crowds, he was able to draw women's interest. Though, he was weighted down by his foolish second marriage, he continued recollecting his first wife, who hadn't remarried but was involved with someone. Still, on the order of "Take it!" he took it, and then he took it fiercely and without mercy.

Still holding out the bouquet, Yakubovsky looked into Vicky's sky-blue eyes. He had already closely examined the rest of her back at Sheremetyevo.

"This is for you, Frau-Madam," he said theatrically.

"Vielen dank," she returned, having bowed in a curtsey no less dramatically.

"Sprechen sie Deutsch?" Yakubovsky raised his eyebrows.

"Naturlich. I graduated from a foreign language university. I'm practically fluent in both English and Spanish, but German and Kazakh are native languages for me."

"Are you serious?" Yakubovsky was genuinely surprised.

"What? So for the KGB prostitute, knowing several languages is a plus, isn't it? You have looked at my private records already, haven't you?"

"I did not. No time. And I came here not to see a prostitute, but to be on a date with a beautiful woman who has given me the pleasure of joining me for dinner. Though, as for your special experience in bed, for us military people, that's necessary too, you know." With that, Yakubovsky offered his hand to Vicky and directed her to the restaurant, which was on the ground floor.

Having handed over their overcoats, they found a table. In those times, menus in Moscow restaurants were very poor, so Vicky and Vladislav ordered salads and Russian authentic meat mixed with pickle soup. Victoria refused a pork steak and wine, asking instead for a bottle of mineral water.

Further, she didn't allow Yakubovsky to order even a glass of wine, directly declaring, "I would like to have quality time with a sober man, instead of listening to his drunk babbling."

Yakubovsky recollected his recent desire to quit drinking. He liked Vicky more with each minute. He started looking for an opportunity to present his lady of the evening with his gift, but then resolved that it would be better to do it after dinner.

Inhaling the sweet aroma of her hair, he imagined putting the pendant around Vicky's neck, gently turning her by the shoulders toward him, and then kissing her on her full, pink lips.

Victoria, as if reading his mind, said, "Vlad—may I call you Vlad?—cool down! In your dreams you are doing me already. Please, come back to earth and tell me about yourself. It is more interesting than being thrilled all by yourself."

Right that minute, Yakubovsky knew that this woman was his destiny. "Vicky, I shall ask you a question with the frankness of a Roman. Do you like me as a man?"

"This is exactly what I am telling you. You've had sex with me already, and now you are asking whether it was pleasant to me. I like you. Yes, I like you. Otherwise, I would not go out with you. But calm down. I am not going anywhere."

"And let me tell you something. It is your organization that has made me look bad. But I am not that way. I am decent. I have not been engaged in that dirty, stinky business for a long time, and when I was, it was only at the compulsion of that rascal Pushkov. The son of a bitch enticed me into the official apartment, put drugs in my drink, and then raped me and photographed me naked. Me—an innocent girl from a small Kazakh village.

"After that, the villain threatened to send the photos to the dean's office, if I didn't watch some foreigners for him. What could I do? I was totally defenseless!

"This is how your KGB has crippled people. I would castrate that Pushkov guy personally, such a reptile! I was saving myself for my husband, for the first night of our long and happy marriage, and this is what he does to me. But, why I am crying to you? In fact, you are precisely the same."

"I am not," Yakubovsky objected. "I am the lieutenant colonel of the Federal Service of External Intelligence."

"You lie!"

"No. The truth. Do you want to see my certificate? I shall show you."

"All right. You will show me some other time. By then I will be … I will be …" she turned her head as though she had moved into a dream. "Then, I will be …" and, not finding anything more suitable, said, "your connection. Shall we dance now?"

Swinging a dollar bill above his head, the maestro announced, "The green tango!" and invited guests up to request specific songs. Directly thereafter, the maestro announced, "The 'Argentinean Tango!' "

And with that, the maiden-singer diligently produced the popular words: "As the beer bar opened in the Rostov city …"

Vicky easily moved in step to the music, silently repeating the awfully trite words.

When the tango finished, they returned to their table. After pulling out Vicky's chair for her and helping her be seated, Yakubovsky took her hand in his and brought his lips to it in a kind kiss. He liked this woman. He hoped the evening would not end for a long time.

But as soon as Yakubovsky sat, Victoria sighed and whispered,

"That son of a bitch Captain Pushkov is here. Hide me!"

But it was too late. Pushkov had already walked in accompanied by a friend who looked like a strong bull—obviously an athlete. Pushing back his blond, average-length hair, Pushkov had noticed Vicky too. Following the host, they went to their table, then, Pushkov, not sitting down, walked directly up to Vicky.

"How are you, sweetheart?" he asked with a foolish smile. "How's business? And where did you pick up this hillbilly?" He winked at Yakubovsky.

The lieutenant colonel held his breath. This piece of shit dared offend not only a lady, but also his most senior ranking official. After regaining his bearings, and without deliberation, Yakubovsky rose and thrust his fist into Pushkov's face. Blood ran from Pushkov's nose.

A woman at the next table cried, "They are killing each other!"

Pushkov, though, instead of punching Yakubovsky in retaliation, began to strangle Vicky. In fear, Vicky seized the bottle of mineral water and struck it on Pushkov's head. Pushkov's buddy rushed over to help him, but Yakubovsky had already retrieved his pistol, and had it pointed at the big bull.

"Stand up, don't move, hands behind the head!" Yakubovsky yelled.

The bull stopped and became as still as stone. But at that moment, there was an abrupt shout, and two security guards with rubber batons flew in. They did not notice Yakubovsky's pistol. One whacked the bull's head, and the other put his fist into Yakubovsky's face. Vlad dropped the pistol, and blood poured from his nose onto his new suit and shirt. His eye and lip instantly swelled.

The other security, having finished both Pushkov and his pal, was about to inflict his baton on Yakubovsky as well, when the police arrived. Roughly seizing the fighting, the cops dragged everyone into the security room, where they divided the men up and checked their documents. They also interrogated some witnesses and apologized to Yakubovsky, returning his pistol and documents to him. They returned Pushkov's documents as well. They wanted to take both Vicky and the bull away to the police department, but Yakubovsky defended Vicky, while Pushkov stood up for his friend.

The cops were just about to leave when Yakubovsky, having recollected that Boris Goryanin had offed four people at once, kicked Pushkov in the groin with such force, that he was doubled over.

"That's so you won't be able to spoil our girls again," Vladislav sneered, promising, "I'll see you in court!"

The cops, now realizing the men would kill each other if left alone, stayed and called an ambulance for Pushkov and Yakubovsky. Victoria suggested the police take her and Vladislav to her apartment, instead, but Yakubovsky undoubtedly required medical assistance. So, she asked them if they would instead escort Vlad and her to the emergency room at Airport Sheremetyevo.

The cops retrieved Vlad and Vicky's overcoats from the wardrobe, and seated them in the back of the police car. Vicky held a wet towel on Vladislav's face.

Victoria was obviously impressed by that fact that Vlad has risen to occasion to be her protector and had beaten the shit out of her hated offender. But she had been a victim of the ordeal too. Her neck was covered in bruises, from Pushkov's tightly wound fingers.

Vladislav held Victoria's hand all the way to the emergency room, meanwhile thinking, *I'll bury him in the ground!* Just in case, he gave Victoria his FSB certificate and the pistol.

Hardly able to move his broken face and swelled up lips, he whispered to her, "Please, save these for me. You can give them back to me when I ask.

Until then, you know nothing about them. You haven't seen them, and you know nothing about them."

Victoria bent forward and whispered back, "Why do you even need these?"

"I don't know," Yakubovsky answered. "Sometimes they can be useful."

In the emergency room, first aid was rendered to both Vladislav and Victoria, but they were ordered to check in to a polyclinic or hospital in the morning.

From the emergency room, they caught a taxicab, and Vicky suggested that Vlad not go home, but spend the night at her apartment, so that she could take care of him. He immediately agreed.

Once there and settled, he presented her with the silver pendant on a chain, but there was one small problem: the gift box had been broken in the fight. Still, Vicky was delighted to receive such a gift and wanted to kiss Yakubovsky, but couldn't find an unwounded spot on his face.

All night long, Victoria fussed over Vlad, changing wet towels and bandages. His new suit, shirt, and tie were ruined by bloodstains.

The next morning, she took him to the military hospital by taxi. The doctor, having examined Yakubovsky, checked him into the hospital for treatment.

Yakubovsky asked Vicky not to worry about visiting him in the hospital, but only to call. He promised to call her too. And he told her that, as soon as he recovered and was discharged from the hospital, he wanted to see her again. Vicky, understanding the complex developing situation he was in, agreed, and left to self-treat at home.

With two cracked ribs, trauma to the soft tissue in his face, damage to his skull, and a minor concussion, Yakubovsky was prescribed to stay in the hospital on bed rest for no less than two weeks.

14

Geneva, Switzerland, December 5, 1993

Melissa arrived in Geneva from Munich. As usual she had no luggage but only a travel bag. Frau Globke met her and took Melissa to her apartment. The rent had been paid up to the end of year, so it remained open for Melissa's use. On the way from the airport, they stopped at the grocery store, where Melissa purchased enough food for a few days.

Upon seeing her again, Frau Globke stated that she had only gotten prettier, and that was the truth. While driving, they chattered on without stop.

Frau Globke told Melissa about all of the changes in the company. She told her that they would replace the name Pennington International with Global Oil Research and Sales Corporation. She told her that Eddy Pennington had been discharged from the management team. She said that, despite its recent failure, managers were still considering trade not only with Russia, but with other partners as well. And finally, she said that she had changed her attitude toward Goryanin after finding out that that he'd returned the five and a half million dollars.

To that, Melissa asked, "And he saved our lives before that. Was that not enough?"

"But he made you pregnant."

"And where was I at the time? It was my desire to have his child. I am in love with him. And I am happy to know that I will be mother of his child."

Seeing her love for Boris, Frau Globke went on to tell Melissa that Boris had come to Geneva searching for her, and that he had spoken with Mr. Barker. But he didn't give him any details regarding what had happened.

"And it is good he doesn't know what I have gone through," Melissa declared.

Back at the apartment, after talking a little more, Frau Globke left. Melissa put way her groceries on the shelves and in the refrigerator. After hastily preparing supper, she found she still had time to begin preparing for her departure from Geneva.

Next morning, Melissa met her lawyer, Dr. Stainmayer. He told her that he had received the settlement from Leber & Associates, LLP, in New York, the law firm representing the interests of Pennington International and Global Oil. They offered to withdraw her complaint from the court, but to settle the case by providing her financial compensation for material, moral, and mental cruelty, as well as for physical pain and suffering. The criminal part of the complaint concerning Mr. Eddy Pennington's personal responsibility would still be heard by the court, and the attorneys had recommended he plead guilty to all charges, thus softening the court's verdict.

As Melissa listened to Dr. Stainmayer, she was once again convinced that her decision to study jurisprudence in California was the right one. Being particular by nature, she liked accurately formulating a course of action that would lead to a decisive conclusion.

She continued listening to the lawyer.

"The essence of Leber & Associate's offer is that Pennington International and Global Oil Corporation, first, will be responsible for any and all expenses related to your medical treatment, including, but not limited to, all medical bills from the hospital, the clinic, the sanatorium, and all related travel expenses to and from these locations."

Dr. Stainmayer continued. "Second, they will cover all charges connected to legal expenses, including, but not limited to, lawyer fees, the investigation, paralegal services, etc.

"Third, as restitution for mental cruelty, pain, and suffering they will pay you, Lady Melissa, three hundred thousand dollars. They will also resolve all outstanding financial matters with Mr. Pennington, such as calculating his fair share of the compensation. This offer does not include Mr. Pennington's personal financial responsibility and his restitution payment for the pain and suffering he caused you personally."

Dr. Stainmayer looked directly at Melissa. "If you consider legal recourse against Pennington International and Global Oil in the States, the amount of compensation could be considerably higher than in Switzerland, but then the American court system could take much longer."

Melissa had a thought. "Dr. Stainmayer, I would like to continue my education in the USA—to become a lawyer. Besides, as you know, I am pregnant. I'm not looking for any opportunity to demand more than would be considered fair from Global Oil. Therefore, my counteroffer would be as follows: first, Global Oil will pay for my medical and legal expenses. Second, they will pay me, up front, a lump sum of sixty thousand dollars. Third, Global Oil will sign an agreement with me that they will pay me these three hundred thousand dollars, but divided into five years, payable in a sixty-thousand-dollar amount annually. Also, during those five years, they will provide me and my child with medical insurance, including additional coverage for my pregnancy and the birth of my baby. Additionally, they will open for me a US H-1 working visa for five years, and pay for my education in law school in California, including books, a computer, and any miscellaneous expenses, not to exceed a thousand dollars a month."

"I will send the counteroffer to New York today," Dr. Stainmayer promised. "I hope to receive an answer by tomorrow morning, because the court will be in session the day after, and they don't like the idea of being involved in this unpleasant case."

Melissa thanked him and asked permission to make a phone call to Dr. Krauss. She had scheduled an appointment with him for tomorrow and needed to confirm it.

After making the call, Melissa went home and spent the rest of the day sorting her belongings. Finally, she packed into two suitcases everything that she wanted to take with her. Everything else, she would donate to the local church for distribution to the poor.

Next morning, Melissa checked back in at Dr. Stainmayer's.

"I have good news for you," he said, kissing her hand, without even greeting her first. "Leber & Associates has accepted all your conditions. Now you just need to sign a draft of the agreement, which I will send them by fax. The executed agreement will come back tomorrow, via overnight mail."

After Melissa signed off on all the pages, she handed the agreement back to Dr. Stainmayer, thanked him, and left for the clinic for her appointment with Dr. Krauss.

Grangettes hospital was not far, so she walked. *I have to walk as much as possible,* she thought, inhaling the fresh morning air.

Once in her room at the clinic, Melissa changed into the special dressing gown provided. The nurse drew blood and did other routine analyses. Then Dr. Krauss gave her a medical examination and performed an ultrasound. During the ultrasound, Dr. Krauss asked Melissa whether she was interested in knowing the sex of the child. Melissa said it made no difference to her; the main thing was known that the child would be healthy. Dr. Krauss assured her that both she and her baby were absolutely healthy, and that she didn't have any reason for anxiety.

By the end of the visit, Dr. Krauss, smiling, asked again whether Melissa wanted to know what she would be having—a boy or a girl. This time, she said yes. The doctor took Melissa's hand and answered, "It's a boy."

Melissa couldn't constrain her pleasure. She put her hand on her stomach and said, "My dear boy. Your name is George, and I am your mum. I love you very much."

Then she threw her arms around Dr. Krauss' neck and kissed his cheek as a token of gratitude.

Before Melissa left the doctor's office, the receptionist made copies of Melissa's medical records that she could take with her to the States. And then from Grangettes, the ecstatic Melissa went to the bank to learn how to transfer money from her account in Geneva to one in California.

At last, she was ready to move on.

15

Moscow, December 6, 1993

Yakubovsky's position at the Federal Service of External Intelligence allowed him to conduct investigations at his discretion, given only that he informs his superiors. Yakubovsky thus used his hospital stay to prepare a report of his service over the past few weeks, and addressed it to the commander of his unit.

Yakubovsky was finally feeling much better. The swelling had gone completely from his face, and he looked almost as he had before the incident.

His wife, Natalie, hadn't come to the hospital to see him once, but that didn't disturb him. He was happy to speak with Victoria over the phone. His son, Igor, visited him daily, however, except for the few days he was shuttling in Poland. Sometimes Igor brought Ann with him, as well, and though Vladislav was always glad to see them, he regretted being seen by Ann in such an unattractive condition.

About two weeks later, Yakubovsky was discharged on a Saturday. Igor picked him up from the hospital. On their way back to Yakubovsky's place, Vlad asked Igor to make a stop at the photo studio, where he could make photos for a new passport and FSB certificate. Just in case, he ordered ten complete sets. His FSB certificate and official firearm he gave Vicky to keep. But, in order to stress his case against Pushkov, Yakubovsky pretended that his FSB ID and pistol were lost during Pushkov's attack on him.

The next day, Yakubovsky tried to get back into his office without his FSB ID, but the security guards would not allow it. He'd assumed this would happen. Since Vlad didn't have any personal ID, for now, he would have to ask some fellow officer to request a temporary pass for him.

From the front office, he called to his friend Terekhin and told him what had happened to him in the restaurant.

"Do you understand, Stanislav? I am engaged in the investigation of the murder of four citizens, including the retired officer of the Ninth Division, Lieutenant Colonel Cherkizov and Alexander Popov, which was a person who rendered me invaluable help during my personal field contact with one of my agents in Washington. On Friday evening, on November 19, at eighteen hundred, I met the witness, also our informant. I invited her to the restaurant in the Hotel Salute for an informal interview, and as soon as we got there, this idiot, the serviceman of the Fifth Division, Captain Pushkov, asked to dance with my witness. He'd come in with his pal, some security guard for a private bank. When I protested, Pushkov began a fistfight, which ended with me being beaten by group of gangsters. This Pushkov guy ended up being their headman.

"So, my FSB ID and official firearm were stolen. I was picked up by the police and taken to the station. After all that, in the middle of the night, I was transferred to the emergency room at the Sheremetyevo Airport and then to the hospital for treatment. The doctors found two cracked ribs, trauma to the soft tissue in my face, damage to my skull, and a minor concussion."

Terekhin did not respond.

"So what kind of advice would you give me?" Vlad asked.

"You'll have to write up an official report addressed to the commander of your unit, with a request to begin a criminal investigation. On the report, attach a statement from the police and your medical records, and then send everything to me. Don't worry—we won't let it go. We will cut out this evil spirit with a red-hot iron. I'll bring you a new FSB ID by lunchtime."

Yakubovsky had actually known the procedure; the idea had been to get Lieutenant Colonel Stanislav Terekhin directly and immediately involved.

Vlad thanked his friend and hung up. While the receptionist prepared his temporary pass, Vladislav went outside and found a payphone. He called the airport VIP Service Center and was told that Victoria Koval had the day off. When he called her at home, Victoria answered the phone at once, as though she had been expecting his call.

"Vicky," Yakubovsky began. "How are you? I hope you have already totally recovered from our incident?"

"Vlad, I wish to see you very much."

"I wish to meet you too. Would you like to meet at the Salute again?" Yakubovsky joked.

Victoria laughed. "Oh, no dear! They already know us there, and I don't think they like us too much. You'd better come here. I'll fix you dinner. Do you remember where I live?"

"Due to the circumstances that night, I'm afraid I was too disoriented to notice."

"I believe you. Do you have a piece of paper?"

Victoria then dictated her address, and they agreed that he would come to her house after work at about seven.

In the hospital, Yakubovsky had had the time to develop a plan for separating from his wife and terminating his service at the FSB. His desire was to start living with Victoria.

During his hospital stay, Vladislav had called his wife and asked her to give Igor ten thousand dollars. With it, Igor and Ann had gone to Poland and purchased merchandise that they had passed on to local dealers. They made thirty thousand dollars profit.

Igor and Ann were planning to go to Poland again, but now were planning to bring back so much merchandise that they wouldn't be able to pass through the customs without paying customs duty. They would have to go through the VIP Service Center, where it wasn't necessary to go through customs control. Yakubovsky had plans to get Vicky involved.

16

Geneva, Switzerland, December 8, 1993

On Wednesday, ten minutes to nine, Lady Melissa Spencer appeared at the courthouse in Canton, Geneva. Dr. Stainmayer came in five minutes later and had her follow him to a meeting room. There, he informed her, on behalf of Mr. Vito Laviterri, Eddy's attorney, that Pennington was ready to plead guilty on all charges and pay restitution in exchange for the reduction of his prison term from twenty years to twelve, provided the case was settled out of court.

Knowing this meant that she would be relieved of listening to endless discussions and reliving the horror of what Eddy had done to her, Melissa agreed. She demanded only one condition: a special provision stating that, after his prison term, Eddy Pennington would be prohibited from coming closer than one hundred feet within her or her child, by penalty of returning to prison for the remainder of his twenty-year sentence.

Dr. Stainmayer asked Lady Melissa to come back in two hours, and then left to finalize negotiations with Mr. Vito Laviterri.

It was warm and sunny, so Melissa decided to take a little walk across Geneva. After all, when would she be able to return to this wonderful city? Suddenly, an idea dawned on her. She smiled and raised her hand to hail a taxi.

She asked the driver to take her to the small restaurant where she once went with Boris. She wanted to sit again at that table in front of the lake, to look at the water, and to plunge into memories of the wonderful time they had together.

In the restaurant, she walked straight to the table where she and Boris had sat. When the waiter approached her, Melissa, smiling out of sentiment, ordered a glass of vodka, a ham sandwich, and a potato salad. Then after thinking a moment, she added a pickled cucumber.

The waiter acted surprised and asked Melissa if she was Russian. After receiving her negative response, he explained that he'd wondered because only Russians usually made such an order, especially in the morning.

In a few minutes the waiter brought out the order, and with great pleasure, she drank the vodka and snacked on the pickled cucumber. She ate the salad and took another drink. Then she hungrily dove into the ham sandwich, becoming so occupied by it that, not only had she forgotten about Boris, she also didn't notice that Frau Globke was approaching her table.

"I knew you'd be here!" Frau said, clapping once. "I was at the courthouse, and when I found out the session was postponed, I guessed this might be where you'd come."

"Mu-gu," mooed Melissa, her mouth full of sandwich.

"Melissa?" Frau Globke exclaimed. "Have you learned to drink vodka just since this morning? You must have had a good teacher."

"Mu-gu," Melissa mooed again and joyfully nodded.

Frau Globke sat at the table opposite Melissa, as Melissa finished the sandwich and sighed with relief. Then having wiped her mouth with a napkin, she sighed again, and, smiling, told her friend, "You cannot imagine! It is so tasty to drink Russian vodka straight-up, especially with a pickled cucumber."

To Frau Globke's silence, Melissa continued with charming smile. "You wouldn't believe it, but I can drink cream straight-up too. I shall teach George to do it. I am sure that he will like cream. By the way, I am drinking vodka for the last time. It is too soon for George to start drinking vodka!"

"And who is George?" Frau Globke asked with a raised eyebrow.

Melissa pointed to her stomach. Frau Globke then realized that this was a different Melissa from the one she'd known three months ago. Here, before Frau Globke, in place of the young, unskilled, naive girl that she's always known, sat a mature, adult woman. A woman who had been through the hardest of tests and passed all of them.

Frau Globke congratulated Melissa on the great news. After that, the girlfriends ordered coffee and the kind of tasteful pastries that could be found only in Geneva. Then they left together for the meeting with Dr. Stainmayer.

The smiling attorney brought Lady Melissa the most recent draft of the agreement. Per this agreement, Eddy Pennington was accepting twelve years of imprisonment, instead of twenty. He agreed pay restitution in the amount of three hundred thousand dollars. And he had accepted the condition in which he would never come closer than a hundred feet within her or her child.

Dr. Stainmayer told her that she could pick up the check in the full amount, along with the signed agreement, in his office the next day. Dr. Stainmayer added that theoretically, within ten days of her signing the agreement, Mr. Vito Laviterri could file the motion for Pennington's reduced prison term. Melissa responded by saying the main thing she cared about was just not to see the monster again.

Having fluttered out of the meeting room, Melissa, joyful and full of energy, hastened to tell Frau Globke the results of their negotiations. Together, they left the building. They shared a taxi, which dropped Melissa at her apartment first, and then Frau Globke at the former office of Pennington International. They had agreed to meet that night and spend Melissa's final evening in Geneva together.

By the end of day, Melissa was completely ready for her departure. However, after deciding she shouldn't take anything that could remind her of Eddy Pennington, she had re-sorted her things, packing only what she was sure she would use in California. Thus, the culmination of her two years in Geneva barely filled her two suitcases.

Frau Globke arrived at six o'clock. Afraid that Melissa might drink again, she was not easily persuaded to return the small restaurant of that afternoon. Melissa assured her she would not drink any more vodka, but told her jokingly that the pickled cucumbers were so good, they had to be sacred.

It did not seem like a December evening in Geneva. Instead, it was temperate and relatively warm. At the restaurant, a young woman was playing an accordion and singing. When she played the Russian gypsy song "Ochi Chornie," Melissa recollected how Boris had played it for in Moscow, on the violin. She grew melancholy, but not for long, as the new life that waited her in California already had its grasp on her.

In bed that night, Melissa had trouble falling asleep. Her mind was overflowing with worry about her future and everything she'd have to do over the next few days before leaving.

I will figure out my finances when I get there, she finally resolved. For now, I just need to focus on getting out of the apartment in London, resolving things with Father, and getting ahold of my old friend, Sharon Smith, in California. Tomorrow, when I get my documents and checks from Dr. Stainmayer, it will be clear what I need to do with the working visa and the all rest.

She would also need to stop at the bank again to deposit the checks from Dr. Stainmayer and to confirm that her account was prepared for wiring to California.

But, most important, she needed to remember to stop in at Grangettes Hospital, to thank Dr. Krauss and Father Weiss for everything that they had done for her.

And with this final thought, Melissa fell asleep.

On Friday, at ten, Melissa was at Dr. Stainmayer's, being led to a meeting room. Upon her entrance, he shook her hand and then got down to business.

"FedEx just delivered the package from Leber & Associates. It had both the executed agreement and the check for the first payment of sixty thousand dollars. From this point on, it would be easier if you just stayed in direct contact with Mr. Barker. You already know each other, of course, and he is a decent person.

"If any complications arise, however, I will still be here, so please do not hesitate to approach me or Mr. Rubin from Leber & Associates in New York. You'll find their addresses and phone numbers on their cover letter."

Dr. Stainmayer handed Melissa the FedEx envelope. "Go ahead and familiarize yourself with the documents and then sign at all of noted places. I will return in fifteen minutes with papers from Mr. Vito Laviterri."

As he walked out, Melissa opened the envelope, browsed the documents, and signed the remittance copy of the agreement. She put the check in her purse.

Dr. Stainmayer returned, carrying the papers from Mr. Vito Laviterri's office, as well as a check for three hundred thousand dollars. Melissa closely looked them over. While reading through the agreement, however, she couldn't find the restraining order against Pennington. Melissa mentioned it to Dr. Stainmayer. He attentively listened, then left for a few minutes and returned again.

"Mr. Laviterri apologized for such a careless omission. He will quickly include the additional paragraph in another draft. I told him you are leaving Geneva today, but he has to go to the prison to get Mr. Pennington's signature approving the additional wording. So … I'm so sorry for the inconvenience, but … you will have to come back in a bit."

Melissa sighed. "Well, then, I will be back in a few hours. For now, with your permission, I will go deposit the check into my bank account.

"Yes, yes. I expect he will have all of the documents to me within that time."

Arriving at the bank with both checks, Melissa was greeted affably, as always, by Mr. de la Perie, who expressed regret at her misfortune. Having deposited the money, Melissa asked to exchange it into US dollars. Thus, her account balance came out to four hundred twenty-three thousand dollars. Melissa said good-bye to de la Perie, leaving instructions to wire all of money.

From the bank, Melissa went to Grangettes to see Dr. Krauss and Father Weiss. Both were in their offices, and both were happy that Melissa was in a good health and spirits. Father Weiss blessed her and her baby. It was always a pity to say good-bye to such nice people, she thought.

When Melissa arrived back at Dr. Stainmayer's office, the documents from Mr. Laviterri's were waiting for her. Dr. Stainmayer told Melissa that Mr. Pennington was categorically opposed to the inclusion of the request, but that Mr. Laviterri had told him that the court would be on Melissa's side in any case. Only after that did Eddy sign all the papers.

And so it was that Lady Melissa, with a fast stroke of a pen, finished this sad period of her life. She thanked Dr. Stainmayer for everything and said good-bye.

Back at her apartment, at the place that had been her home for more than two years, she grabbed her suitcases and rolled them to the door. Frau Globke knocked. Melissa, as Boris had once, stopped where she stood, mentally checked that everything was in place, and then left. On the way to the car, Melissa stopped at the concierge and left her keys. And with that, her life in Geneva had come to an end.

Melissa's flight for Frankfurt was scheduled at six ten p.m. Having arrived at the airport, the women said good-bye and shed a few tears. Who knew if they would meet again? Melissa checked in for the flight, and then embraced Frau Globke a final time.

In Frankfurt, Melissa went to the Hotel Astron. At the registration desk, a familiar clerk recognized her and offered her the very room in which she had stayed, first, with Boris in the autumn and a second time on her way to Munich. The clerk expressed an interest in Melissa's state of health and then asked whether Mr. Goryanin had found her at the airport. She shook her head. She wanted to avoid the memories.

Melissa then went to her room—to that room. She hung her dress in the closet, sat on the bed, and, after several seconds, burst out crying. In the beginning, she cried silently, but then escalated to an all-out sob. She had told herself that she should not recollect what had happened, but being here, she couldn't help letting the memories gush over her.

To help herself stop sobbing, she tried to blame Boris in her mind for everything that had happened. But it didn't help. She was in love with him still and would be always. And with that thought, she relaxed, and stopped crying. In fact, she actually felt better now than when she'd arrived. Her crying had given release to all of the internal pressure that had building over the weeks.

After a shower, Melissa lay down on the bed—that bed— embracing that pillow, and as soundly as a child, fell off to sleep.

17

Moscow, December 8, 1993

After returning back to Russia from the United States after doing several shuttle trips abroad, Yakubovsky had made, in addition to his normal salary, more than a hundred thousand dollars. The time had come to think about finding apartments for himself and his son. Igor was planning to marry Anna. Vlad deeply sighed thinking about it. The young people looked well together. He and his first wife had looked well together too. And who knows, she might still be his wife, if that demon hadn't have spoiled it all.

Yakubovsky called Kravchuk, and they agreed to meet on Monday. Yakubovsky would be at Agroprom by ten, and, as he'd told Kravchuk, "Except for tea, I shall drink nothing. I've quit."

After hanging up, Yakubovsky returned to his office, sat at his desk, and wrote the official report for his commander.

> *To: The Head of the Office of*
> *The Federal Service of External Intelligence.*
>
> *<u>The Report</u>*
>
> *At the present time, in addition to my official duties, I have been engaged in the investigation of the death of four citizens of the Russian Federation, including Lieutenant Colonel Cherkizov (Ret.) of the Ninth Division of the KGB. These individuals are suspected of being, directly or indirectly, involved in the disappearance and death of Alexander Popov, also a citizen of the Russian Federation.*

Citizen Popov provided invaluable help through contact with one of my agents (Private File #124/Case A.E./Security Level: Supreme/Region of activity: USA) in Washington, DC. Date of contact: July 19–21, 1993.

One suspect in the investigation is a citizen of the USA (and former citizen of the USSR), Boris Goryanin. His participation in this case is also subject to preliminary investigation.

In the course of the investigation, on Friday, November 19, 1993, at 18:00, I met a witness citizen Victoria Koval, who is an employee of the VIP Service Center at Airport Sheremetyevo, and a non-staff informant of the Fifth Division.

With the purpose of conducting a frank yet personable interview, I invited the witness to a restaurant at the Hotel Salute. I ordered the special, and drank mineral water only. During the interview, one of restaurant visitors (who I subsequently learned was the officer of the Fifth Division, Captain Pushkov), being intoxicated, approached us and invited Koval to dance with him. He was there with his friend, who is a security guard in a private bank. When I politely protested, Pushkov initiated a fistfight. As a result, I was beaten by a group of gangsters led by Captain Pushkov.

My money, official FSB ID, and official firearm (a Makarov pistol, which I did not use at this time) were stolen. Citizen Koval, Captain Pushkov and his companion, and I were detained by officers from the Ministry of Internal Affairs and were delivered to a regional department, where a report was made. Then, having determined my condition, police personnel provided transportation for my delivery to the emergency room at Airport Sheremetyevo, where first aid was rendered. With the diagnosis of trauma to the skull, two cracked ribs, and injury to the soft tissue of the face, I was then delivered to the departmental hospital, where I was prescribed with two weeks of bed rest and medical treatment.

With the facts as stated, I ask that the FSB initiate a service investigation and punish the guilty party.

Lieutenant Colonel V.I. Yakubovsky
December 8, 1993

Just as Yakubovsky finished the report, Terekhin arrived with Vlad's a new ID. The friends went to the cafeteria and had lunch, after which Yakubovsky requested the service car to take him to the police station, the emergency room, and the hospital. He received the necessary police reports and medical documents at each.

Then returning to work, he attached the copies to his report, and personally carried the packet of documents to the deputy chief of the Personnel Department.

18

Moscow, December 8, 1993

Victoria wasn't expecting Yakubovsky until seven, but he was knocking at her door just shortly after six. Unprepared for their date, she answered it in a dressing gown and slippers. A bouquet of red roses entered first, followed by her guest.

Having observed Victoria in her house clothes, Yakubovsky at once recollected his short-legged, clumsy creature, and thought, *Yes! The difference is enormous.* Feeling a little uneasy, however, he wasn't sure what to do. Then Victoria directed him to the kitchen, where something was boiling in a saucepan and something else was cooking in a frying pan. She put the bouquet in a vase and charged Yakubovsky with watching the stove, while she went to go change.

Vlad, having once been a professional scout, was skillful at nearly everything, including cooking. At the same time, being by nature lazy, he didn't like, and in every possible way avoided, such a sissy job. But now, aspiring to win Vicky, he thought he would prove himself worthy. He took off his coat, rolled up his shirtsleeves, and put on an apron. He lifted the cover from the frying pan and saw two pork schnitzels, simmering in onions and sauerkraut. After that, he surveyed the saucepan. There was boiling pea soup with a decent-sized smoked and meaty pork bone.

Instantly noting that both dishes were German, Yakubovsky recollected how Victoria had told him that German and Kazakh were her native languages. So, what was she, native Ukrainian? No, she didn't look Ukrainian. Something between Polish and German seemed more like it. He would need to check these facts!

He got a spoon and tasted the soup. He looked around the kitchen for a pepperbox, added a little pepper to the soup, and tasted it again. Now, it required some salt. However, before he could find the salt, he realized the schnitzels urgently needed turning over, as they were on the verge of burning.

He began to feel in a bit of a panic, when Victoria walked in and found him.

"Oh, dear! What is going on?"

Having turned and seen Vicky, Yakubovsky forgot about his cooking, and he could not keep his jaw from dropping for an instant. Before him, in a long, fitted red dress, with a diving neckline, was a young, gorgeous woman, looking full of vitality. On her high breast was the silver pendant that he had given her.

Their evening was superb. They chattered about nothing, joked, and danced a little, during which Yakubovsky gently kissed Vicky on the neck, the cheeks, and, at last, the lips. Victoria accepted his caresses, but then, a moment later, suddenly stopped.

"Vlad, if it's okay, I think you should leave soon. Otherwise, you will end up sleeping with me. Your advances are so pleasant. I will let you stay and make more advances, but just for a little while. No one has ever treated me so beautifully," she said, emphasizing the final word.

So, after a few minutes, they stopped and had tea and apple pie, during which they agreed that tomorrow night they would meet again. Yakubovsky then left, but not before kissing every finger on Victoria's beautiful hands.

19

London, December 11, 1993

After going through passport control in London, Melissa found the baggage claim, and cautiously, trying not to strain herself too much, lifted both her suitcases from the conveyor belt and put them onto a baggage cart. The suitcases were not too heavy, but she wanted to protect herself and George. Melissa had even told him that, and as if George had understood, he immediately calmed down.

She pushed the baggage cart out to the taxi line, and in her turn, Melissa took a cab and gave her address to the driver. They got into two traffic jams, which the driver, a native Hindu, blamed on "those damn Pakistanis," accusing the British government of allowing the damn Pakistanis to immigrate to the United Kingdom both legally and illegally. Melissa didn't listen to him. She had left her impression of London in her memories of the town, when she had lived there as a girl. Back then, London had really been different.

Soon enough, they reached her apartment, and the driver took up her suitcases. As soon as she got in, she switched on the heater and called her father. She asked him how he was feeling, but then realizing that he was a little out of it, asked him to give the phone to Ms. Doughty.

Melissa asked Ms. Doughty if they needed her to bring over any groceries, but Ms. Doughty icily told her that they had everything they needed, and Melissa shouldn't come just to catch a virus. Melissa agreed and then left for the supermarket, to buy herself enough food for the next few days.

The next morning, she went to the US Commerce Department office in London. There, she made a copy of the Law School Admission Test requirements. Then she went to the bookstore and purchased the self-preparation manual for the test.

The rest of the day, Melissa prepared for the LSAT. At first, she, as any normal person, felt slightly lazy, but after remembering her priorities, she finally became motivated.

That evening, when she knew it was about seven a.m., California time, Melissa called her school girlfriend, Sharon Smith. The last time they'd spoken had been right before Sharon had gotten married. Melissa had just started work in Geneva and couldn't take leave to attend the wedding. Sharon had been offended, but there was nothing Melissa could do. Now, however, upon hearing Melissa's voice, Sharon seemed glad to hear from her old friend.

Jumping from one topic to another and frequently interrupting each other, they told each other what had happened to them over all this time. Sharon now lived with her husband in Costa Mesa, in Orange County. The location was very convenient for her, as she worked as a flight attendant for United Airlines and flew all over the continental US from the Orange County airport. Sharon's husband managed a construction supply company also located in Costa Mesa. So far, they didn't have any children.

When Melissa told Sharon about her plan to study law in California, Sharon was delighted that her girlfriend would be so near. After all, she told Melissa, "In childhood, we were almost like sisters, weren't we?"

Sharon and Melissa were both touched and hung up happy.

Then Melissa called Mr. Barker. They had known each other for about two years, so they spoke as old friends. Jonathan never mentioned Eddy's name, and Melissa, in turn, didn't remind him of it. Jonathan did ask Melissa how she was doing, and accurately joked about her craving salty food and pickled cucumbers.

Their conversation ended with Melissa informing Mr. Barer that she was scheduled to arrive in Washington, DC, on January 3, 1994. While waiting for her H-1 visa, she could stay in Ritz Carlton and prepare for the LSAT. Mr. Barker responded, if Melissa preferred, she could go to work temporarily for Global Oil. Regardless, he promised to overnight her airplane tickets.

After the conversation with Mr. Barker, Melissa was filled with happiness for all that had successfully developed for her over the past weeks. She wished she could tell Boris about it. She thought for a few moments and then clapped her hands. She held her breath, and dialed Boris's phone number. The call went through, but nobody picked up.

"Oh well!" she said to herself, finally exhaling. "It's probably better this way."

The days ran into one another, and at her father's house, everyone had recovered from their illnesses. Melissa visited them daily by foot. On her first few walks there, however, she would be filled with the sensation that all of the streets in her old neighborhood had somehow changed. Nothing looked different; all the houses were the same. But things just weren't as they had been before. After a while, she realized that it was because the once deserted streets were now filled with people walking. That day, Melissa shared her epiphany with her father, who told her that there were new inhabitants in the area, buying up all the houses. Without negotiation, he said, they were paying asking prices.

"Basically, they are rich Arabs," he said. "And recently some Russians as well. Yes, times are changing."

Later that day, Melissa paid a visit to the old doctor who had delivered Melissa at her birth. He examined her, after which both were glad that everything looked to be in good order. He gave her some simple guidelines to follow: "Keep moving, avoid stress as much as possible, continue taking the prenatal vitamins, and if possible, stay in the sun."

"So, what do you think about California?" Melissa asked him.

"I wish I could go to California right now!" the old man answered.

Within two weeks, Melissa had completely worked through the LSAT self-preparation manual. She finished right before Christmas. She then spent the holiday at her father's house. They bought and decorated a Christmas tree, and went to church for the Christmas service. Melissa exchanged gifts with her father, Mr. Howard Wiggins, and Ms. Doughty. Opening the beautifully wrapped boxes, they all felt as happy as children. George behaved perfectly, and Melissa didn't overeat, so that George would grow normally. If he were to become overweight, it would be more difficult for his mum to deliver him.

After Christmas, Melissa prepared for her departure to Washington, DC, and on December 30, she spent the very last night in her apartment.

The next morning, she turned in her keys, and then went to her father's house, where they celebrated New Year's Eve and then spent the entire night talking.

The morning of January 3, Sir Spencer took Melissa to the airport, where Melissa checked in and proceeded to the terminal. At their parting, the two embraced and shed a few tears.

And so, Melissa's new life had begun. Life in the USA.

20

Moscow, December 13, 1993

On Monday morning, December 13, Yakubovsky was at Kravchuk's office at Agroprom. Gavrila had offered the visitor "a small shot" to start, but Yakubovsky's resolve was unshakable, having now resolutely declared, "That is it. I quit."

Gavrila poured a decent-sized glass of cognac for himself and emptied it into his throat. Then having snacked on a slice of lemon with sugar, he kept silent, feeling the warm drink move through his body. Finally, he nodded in satisfaction and turned his attention to Yakubovsky.

Vlad held up his right hand and made an ellipse in the air, asking with his eyes whether any listening devices were suspected.

Gavrila wrinkled his face, slightly reddened from the cognac, and waved his hands in front of him. "Not at all. All is clear."

"Then I suggest we continue our recent conversation regarding our need, as you specified, to steal large sum of money and escape."

"So we will," Kravchuk answered.

"Great. But we should start today for a brighter tomorrow. Preparations can take a year or more. We'll need to open accounts in different countries, at different banks, and in different names, which means making several trips to prepare documents. And all of this will require money. Do you have something saved for a rainy day?" Vladislav attentively looked into Kravchuk's eyes.

Gavrila fidgeted in his armchair and grimaced, seeming uncertain. "Well, I have something, but not a lot."

"Come on! Quit showing false modesty!"

"I am speaking the truth," Gavrila said, bringing his right hand to his chest, as if insulted.

"Look, I know you. You would eat dirt for money," Yakubovsky joked.

"Come on! Maybe you should go shuttling with my son, or send your wife to do it. Maybe, you can attach your son to a common cause."

"I don't have a son. Just a daughter. She is fourteen. It is too early for her."

"But you have to do something."

"I know," Kravchuk said and sighed. "I shall think of something."

Kravchuk had given up. He had already forgotten how to make a decision on his own.

"All right. So let's move to the next issue. Have you heard about any two-bedroom apartments for rent or sale?"

"The late Ms. Selina's apartment is still available, but locked up. You will need to talk to the local police about it. We could clean it up and even do some cosmetic repairs, and then it would be yours. Selina, as far as I know, doesn't have any successors."

"Sounds like a good deal. Do you have the address? I'll run over there right now."

Gavrila pressed the intercom button. "Valerie! Would you bring me the address of the apartment where the late Ms. Selina lived?"

Gavrila and Vlad were silent, thinking, until Valerie entered with a piece of paper.

"Thanks, Val," Kravchuk said, and then handed the paper to Vladimir. "This is for you, Mr. Yakubovsky."

Yakubovsky took the address. "Thank you. Thanks a million." Feeling they had covered everything for the time being, he then stood and said, "So, I'll be running."

As the men shook hands, Kravchuk replied, "So long. We'll be in touch."

And with that, Yakubovsky left to go see the apartment, and Kravchuk, having finished the bottle of cognac, left for home.

Yakubovsky found the building, in front of which, despite the cold, dank, typical winter weather, three elderly women sat on a bench, protecting themselves from the mist with pieces of cardboard.

Yakubovsky addressed them in a gallant voice. "Well, sitting out here can't be too good for your health, can it?"

The women amicably looked at Yakubovsky but kept silent, obviously uninterested in having a conversation with him. So he decided to approach them from another angle.

"Isn't it too cold to be sitting out here?" he asked, shrinking from the frost.

"Isn't it too cold for you to be walking out on the road?" One of the old ladies answered.

"You're right," Vlad said. "But the road brought me here, to Apartment Fifty-six."

"Oh!" The old women gasped and crossed themselves.

"What do you mean by 'Oh'?" Yakubovsky asked.

"That apartment is no good. It's haunted," the same woman said. "The former tenant died about a year ago, and her husband left somewhere. Then recently married young couple moved in. They both were decent people, but the gangsters killed her. That happened in October, on the exact day that the tanks scorched Moscow. The next day, three people came—an elderly man with two young guys. They locked the apartment, and left the keys with Mrs. Ukhov from Apartment 57. She gave the keys to the subdivision policeman. Later, the cop told her that the woman who had lived there actually had not been killed by gangsters, but had killed them, and now had gone missing. So the apartment is empty. Nobody lives there. But we are afraid to go there. Even the subdivision policeman never goes there—at least when he is sober. He goes only when he is intoxicated, as, he says, devils cannot stand the smell of alcohol."

"And where can I find the subdivision policeman?" Vlad asked.

"The next door down," said the woman, waving her hand to specify the direction he should go. "Ground floor. The police outpost is in his apartment. He maintains the order in the neighborhood from there."

"Well, girls. Stay alive. I need to go see this cop."

Despite the early hour, the subdivision policeman was already decently drunk, and now stood barefoot in his underwear. Yakubovsky handed him his FSB certificate.

Looking at the certificate with the state insignia, the man hiccupped, and then he saluted, the hand on his forehead still holding a book he'd apparently been reading.

"Sorry. I didn't recognize you, Comrade Chief. Please forgive me. I didn't have time to collect my thoughts."

"It's all right. You can make it up to me by taking me to Apartment 56."

"It is not possible," the policeman said. Then he had a second thought. "It is possible for you, but it is impossible for me. There is a seal on the door with the state insignia."

The neighborhood order-keeper radiated such a foul alcohol odor that Yakubovsky was sure that the devils had run away long ago. "You'd better make yourself decent before we go," he said.

"I am going already," the man said in an obedient tone, walking back into his apartment and then putting on the uniform shirt, pants, and cap, and shoving his feet into slippers. "Do you have keys?"

"Do you have keys?" Yakubovsky replied.

"I have my keys on me," the order-keeper answered.

"And I have my keys on me," Yakubovsky said, clapping his shirt pocket.

"Then, it is possible," the cop said and hiccupped.

With that, the two men walked down to the second entrance. They were being eyed by the resident retirees who were obviously trying to keep their distance, probably wondering how this stranger had been able to persuade the neighborhood order-keeper to go into the evil apartment. The policeman opened the broken door into the building, hung only by a hanger, and entered a hallway.

Just then, the cop, appearing as if he were trying to remember something, asked Yakubovsky, "And, excuse me, but for what reason are you here, and who are you?"

Yakubovsky held out his FSB certificate again, this time holding it right in front of the cop's nose, and barked, "KGB!"

The cop hiccupped again, then saluted, hardly uttering, "Excuse me. Then it is possible. It is possible for you, and it is impossible for them."

Yakubovsky was not clear whom the terrible neighborhood order-keeper had meant by they—the old women or the devils.

They rode an elevator up to the seventh floor, and when they found the apartment, the cop tried to get a key in the lock. He wasn't able to open it, however, even after a third attempt.

"It is impossible for you. It is impossible for me. It would be better if I guarded you from here," he explained.

Yakubovsky wasn't going to waste his energy trying to figure out what the cop meant by all of this being possible or impossible. Instead, he took the keys from policemen hand and opened the door. He was struck by a rotten stench. In the entryway were chalk outlines of three bodies. Not stepping on the chalk, he went to the kitchen and glanced into a bathroom. On the bathroom floor, there was a pool of dry blood. In one bedroom, everything had been overturned, and on the floor, rolled up linens had been lain intermittently with clothes. In the second bedroom everything was upside down too. He approached the door of the private balcony, which overlooked a large forest.

It's good, Yakubovsky decided. We will just need to clean everything and make repairs.

"So," Yakubovsky addressed the order-keeper, who was trying to keep his balance by leaning against the wall. "What is your rank?"

"Sergeant Makarchuk," the cop gallantly reported while saluting.

"And so, Comrade Sergeant Makarchuk, the country's leaders are charging you with a special assignment: to hold the order in the neighborhood and watch this apartment. It is not necessary for you to go in this apartment. I will retain the keys. But the naval order shall stand, and I will personally checkup. From now on, I shall be engaged in this apartment personally. It is possible for me."

"Sir! Yes, Sir! Exactly! It is possible for you. But for me it is impossible."

"I thank you officially and here is a monetary premium for you in the amount of ten … no … twenty dollars. From now on, you are responsible for the order personally."

"Sir! Yes, Sir! Yes! Serving the Soviet Union!" The guard of the order barked, accepting the money from Yakubovsky. "I shall let no one play with this money."

After Yakubovsky left, the subdivision cop, ensuring that the money would not be spent in vain, rushed to the grocery store. And then, during the next few days, the guard held control over the subdivision from his apartment.

So far, everything I am doing is going successfully, Yakubovsky thought, in a taxi on his way back to the office. It will still be necessary to submit all of the documents for the apartment to the notary, for registration, as soon as possible, however. Twenty dollars per week for a neighborhood cop will be enough. And then, we shall see!

At this moment Yakubovsky remembered his second meeting with old gypsy, and her words "Follow your destiny. Don't be afraid. Go. All will be good with you." … and the cold came upon lieutenant colonel.

Then from his office, Vladislav called several friends, asking whether it was possible to quickly re-register an empty apartment in his name. Having learned the name and phone number of a notary who could help him, Yakubovsky made an appointment for the next day at three o'clock.

Yakubovsky had grown less and less interested in his service for the FSB. In front of him, he saw new opportunities that didn't relate to his present job.

Vladislav left his office before four p.m. and went to Victoria's apartment. She, naturally, wasn't home yet. The day before, however, she had given him keys to the front door. Vladislav took of his overcoat and hung up it on a hanger in a hallway. Entering the living room he began to examine a wall unit. Among the books, he spotted a picture album, so he took it out and opened it. There, on the very first page, he saw a photo of little Vicky, probably with her parents. The photo had been taken in the front yard of a rural home, and all of people pictured appeared to be German. As confirmation of its origins, on the back of the photo was written in German:

Der Vater Johann, Die Mutter Frieda,
und Die Tochter Victoria—4 Jahren.
1968. Dorf: Fedorovka. [12]

Vlad put the album back on the shelf and lay on a sofa, with both hands under his head. He had a lot of things to think about. Yes, life had certainly opened up some opportunities, and to miss out of any of them, he knew, would not be desirable. Without realizing it, however, he fell asleep and did not hear Vicky silently enter.

Upon seeing the sleeping Vlad, Vicky left the room on tiptoe, closed the door, and, trying not to make much noise, started to fix them supper.

12 Father Johann, Mother Frieda, and daughter Victoria - 4 years old. 1968. Village Fedorovka. (German.)

21

That evening, after leaving Victoria's, Yakubovsky returned to an empty apartment. His wife was probably the neighbor's, discussing their problems as old hens. He called Igor and told him about the new apartment. Vladislav gave him the address and directions, and asked him to find a locksmith to replace the locks on the entryway door. Before handing up, they agreed to meet at the new apartment the next day at five p.m.

Next day, the hour hand had barely reached four when Yakubovsky was already rushing off in a taxi to the new apartment. When he arrived, Igor was already there with the locksmith, talking with the same three old women.

Once they were inside the apartment, while the locksmith puttered with the locks, Yakubovsky and Igor went shuffled through some of the items left by former residents, now scattered throughout the rooms. They stayed out of bathroom and kitchen, however, where terrible events had obviously occurred. When the locksmith had changed the locks, they paid him for his work and he left.

Yakubovsky then left to go find the old women. He wanted to ask them what exactly had happened in that apartment. They categorically refused to discuss anything, although they did advise him to invite over a priest to consecrate the evil place before they started cleaning it. Only then, they said, would it be possible to enter the apartment and grow new roots there. Needless to say, Yakubovsky became rather concerned, and asked the women where the closest church was. Vlad then called the church to set up a meeting with the priest, and asked Igor to take them there.

The Father Theofil appeared to be about seven years older than Igor. When he learned what Yakubovsky's visit was all about, he agreed and said he would be able to consecrate the apartment as soon as tomorrow. They planned for Igor to swing by and pick him up at four thirty the next afternoon.

The next day, during lunchtime, Yakubovsky drove to the notary public. After about ten minutes of waiting, he walked straight into the notary's office. Gray-haired, but not old, the notary closely listened to his story about the apartment and said that he could take the case. He would be able to complete the transfer within no more than three to four months. He would charge for his service about half of the market price of the apartment. When Yakubovsky objected, saying the price was arbitrary and trying to negotiate it down, the experienced notary public rather delicately pointed out that the act of self-capturing another's real estate property was also, in fact, arbitrary, and an act of violence, as well. Yakubovsky, understanding that he was actually getting off easy, didn't continued to negotiate, but instead asked what kind of documents would be required to register the apartment in his name. Having received the list of documents, Vladislav scheduled another meeting with notary in a week and returned to his office before the end of lunch. By now, Vladislav understood more than ever that he could not continue at this job, but quitting now would be too premature. He would need to continue at least until he secured the title to the apartment.

Shortly before the end of the working day, Stanislav Terekhin called Yakubovsky. Stanislav asked Vladislav whether he was ready for a meeting in the office of the Attorney General. Having heard an affirmative answer, Stanislav then told him that he would prepare an answer to the inquiry from the attorney general and would keep him informed.

This evening, Yakubovsky didn't go to Victoria's, but he called her to say that he would visit tomorrow. Tonight, he was going to be unusually lovely to his wife. He had bought her some flowers, and decided to take it easy on her for the time being. His wife was surprised and even shed a few tears, after which Vladislav told her that he had received a confidential assignment, and would be taking on a special undercover operation that would require them both to behave extremely cautiously in the coming weeks. It was possible, he told her, that he would be under external surveillance, and rather probable that he might sometimes disappear for two to three weeks.

She listened and then boiled some pelmeny,[13] Vlad's favorite authentic Russian food, all while sobbing. She poured vodka for him at dinner, but Yakubovsky only pretended to drink. He rinsed his mouth with the vodka and then spit it out when she wasn't looking. Then later he pretended he was drunk. With braided tongue, he told his wife that he would be in charge of training killers, and that she must keep silent.

"Look, Nat, if you spill the beans," he said, "not I, but others, will off you. And don't call me at work anymore. Out on the street, you should be attentive. You could be under surveillance, as well. But don't be afraid. I shall ask my

13 It is Russian authentic meal. Pelmeny looks like ravioli but larger.

bosses to allocate a pistol for you, in case you even would need to shoot back. The best thing for you, though, is just to go quietly from the apartment to work and back. Quietly watch the TV and quietly, without advertising, go on the shuttle trips. I shall ask Igor to help you."

"No, I shall handle the shuttling on my own," Natalie protested. She and Igor couldn't stand each other. "Better, I will get my nephew involved in the business … let him learn."

Natalie took another shot of vodka and stared at the table, thinking. Quite possibly, she wanted Yakubovsky to be killed so that she could receive his pension and move back to her village.

When Natalie finally got drunk, Vladislav, having pretended to be drunk too, lay down on the bed, turned away from his wife, and pretended to fall asleep. Instead, he was filling in the details of his forthcoming operation.

22

Moscow, December 14, 1993

Considering the constant competition between the FSB and the attorney general, Lieutenant Colonel Stanislav Terekhin had prepared an answer for the attorney general that was both brief and uncertain.

> *The Internal Memorandum*
> *To: The Office of the Attorney General of the Russian Federation,*
> *Attn.: Assistant of the Attorney General of RF,*
>
> *General Major I.F. Filimonov*
>
> *Regarding your inquiry on November 10, 1993, Lieutenant Colonel V.I.Yakubovsky was on an official business trip to the USA in July of this year. The results of this official business trip are classified as top secret and are not a subject to consideration by any other state offices of the Russian Federation outside of the Federal Service of External Intelligence of the FSB, Russian Federation.*
>
> *Upon reading this internal memorandum, this document is to be the subject of destruction. Instructions for its destruction are attached.*
>
> *The Deputy Chief, Personnel Department,*
> *The Federal Service of External Intelligence of the FSB of the RF,*
> *Lieutenant Colonel Terekhin S.I.*
> *December 14, 1993*

Terekhin signed and applied the department stamp to the internal memorandum. He then stuck it into a special delivery envelope with enclosed a special destruction package labeled "Instructions for Destruction." He sealed the envelope and transferred it to the secretary, with directions to send the whole package to the office of the Attorney General by special delivery.

The next day, Mr. Filimonov received a package from Lieutenant Colonel Terekhin. He immediately opened it and read through the internal memo, which didn't contain any useful information. He then enclosed the memo in the destruction package along with a capsule, which he squeezed to release some chemicals. After that, he sat in the armchair for several minutes, considering his next step. So far, he couldn't come up with any reasonable ideas and so decided to request that Yakubovsky come to his office for a serious conversation … but not right now.

Meanwhile, Yakubovsky was in his office suffering from idleness. His affiliation with the Federal Service of External Intelligence had ceased to be of any interest. He did nothing at work now. After accepting their strategic decision, he now spent all of his time contriving tactical steps and details of their personal plan. The main things he had to remember were not to rush and not to make any stupid mistakes.

That evening, Yakubovsky went to the new apartment. Igor and Ann had already brought in the priest. The Father, having served up a special prayer, consecrated the apartment, and then handing Igor a handout listing the church's special needs, was put in a taxicab and sent away. The three old women, convinced that the Father had consecrated the apartment, then started cleaning it under Anna's supervision.

In the elevator, on his way up to the unit, Yakubovsky heard the loud voice of the subdivision policeman, Makarchuk. He was supervising the old women also, trying to earn his next payment. It was impossible at first to tell whether he was drunk or sober, but then after listening to him a few minutes, it seemed that Sergeant Makarchuk was in his usual condition. He was drunk. Having seen Yakubovsky, he threw his hand up to his cap in a salute and loudly announced, "Serving the Soviet Union!"

Yakubovsky reached into his pocket and pulled out a mixture of rubles and dollars, which he handed to the cop. Makarchuk accepted it, saluting and again bellowing, "Serving the Soviet Union!" so loud that the old women amicably crossed themselves and advised the order-keeper to save both his voice and his money.

"It shall be a naval order," he said to them. "I shall not let anybody play with this money." Then he left somewhere, although likely not to the regional library.

While the women were packing dishes in boxes, washing shelves, cleaning off various stains, and changing linens and towels, Yakubovsky, together with Igor and Ann, was sorting the remaining things. In the wardrobe hung a plastic garment bag with the parade uniform of a paratrooper's colonel, complete with medals and awards. On the wardrobe shelf there was an officer's holster with a Makarov pistol. There were also various high-quality women's clothes hanging in the wardrobe. The most valuable among these items had been diligently stored inside plastic covers. Anna tried some of them on and they fit her marvelously. But most interesting was that, under the bottom shelf, wrapped in plastic and packing tape was a package of money. It held eight thousand dollars. It was clear that the police hadn't investigated the circumstances of the crime that had happened in this apartment on October 2, 1993.

Yakubovsky offered Anna to leave all of the female things to her. And this is when it dawned upon him what he should do…

"Do you know what, guys?" he declared. "I shall register this apartment in my name, but it will be yours."

Wide eyed, Igor and Ann alit from the sofa.

"We … you …" They couldn't find a single word to say.

Igor approached his father and embraced him. "Thanks, Dad." But Ann was more emotional, embracing Vladislav and Igor with both arms, hanging on their necks, and kissing them both. Having felt the touch of her lips, Yakubovsky, despite the fact that he had already taken a great interest in Vicky, again felt moved. He liked this girl very much.

Within three hours, the old women had cleaned the kitchen, the entryway, and the bathroom. Yakubovsky, Igor, and Anna combined all of the things from both bedrooms and then dusted everywhere. The old women then cleaned the bedroom floors. In an hour, the apartment was finished. Yakubovsky, in his generosity, gave twenty dollars to each of the women. Beside themselves with pleasure, the women were about to leave when Makarchuk showed up. In his hands was a plastic shopping bag.

"Happy housewarming to you!" he addressed Yakubovsky, pulling from the shopping bag, and then spreading out on a table, a bottle of vodka, two pies, a loaf of bread, a link of sausage, and a container of vegetable salad. The old women were in no hurry, so they covered a clean table with a paper tablecloth, and laid out glasses, plates, and forks.

And so the housewarming party started. The first toast was "for happiness in the new place." The second toast was offered by the perspicacious neighborhood cop, who winked at Igor and then lifted his glass, announcing, "For youth." Ann was embarrassed, but she and Igor kissed, and all have drunk again. By the third toast, because God loves a trinity, there was not enough vodka left for each to have a full glass.

23

California and Moscow, December 31, 1993

The Goryanin family celebrated the New Year in the company of friends. Their son Anton, called Tony, had come home for Christmas. At the time, he was involved in an internship program in a hospital in San Jose. As always, before their son's arrival, Boris's wife, Ruslana, made a visit to the local Russian grocery store to buy various delicacies. Boris, long before the approach of the holidays, had made some purchases at the local store specializing in the sale of alcohol, cigars, and coffee. They liked the sparkling wine with the taste of almonds. He had bought hard booze, as well.

New Year's Eve, they took it easy. Boris hardly made it to midnight before falling asleep, but Ruslana, along with Anton and two more couples, celebrated till morning.

In Moscow, Vladislav celebrated the New Year with Victoria, Igor, and Ann. By Russian tradition, they watched the special New Year's TV movie sitting around a table of delicacies, and then continued to sit glued to the TV until morning, when the city buses resumed their service, at which point they dashed into their separate rooms to sleep.

Yakubovsky continued to look "beautifully" after Vicky, continually presenting her with flowers, kissing her fingers, and taking her to nice restaurants. Still, they had not been intimate.

Every night, after taking Vicky back home, Yakubovsky, as malicious as a devil, would spend the night on the sofa in his new apartment. He continued telling Natalie that he was substituting as the officer on duty in his division. The obvious lie disturbed Natalie, but not much.

24

Moscow, December 31, 1993

A few days before New Year's Eve, Captain Alexander Pushkov had been fired from Fifth Division. The reason for his dishonorable discharge was the internal report from the chief of the Department of Internal Security of the FSB. The General Major had called Captain Alexander Pushkov to his office and ordered him to provide a written explanation of his uncivil behavior. But Pushkov, instead of confessing, described all of his achievements over the last ten years in recruiting non-staff agents for watching foreign citizens in Moscow.

The general looked at Pushkov and said only, "Get out." And with that, Pushkov's years of service were in the sewer.

New Year's Eve, Pushkov spent alone, drunk as a beast, spending the whole next day with a hangover. By January 2, early morning, he had recovered enough that he went to the Moscow subdivision, Sviblovo. He needed to tell his father everything.

Alexander's father, Pushkov Sr., a retired major in the police force, listened, without interruption, to his unlucky son's story about the fight with the senior officer in the restaurant, and the ensuring consequences. He silently poured vodka into his glass and drank all the while.

When Pushkov Jr. asked for vodka in his glass too, the senior put his hand on the bottle and said, "You have to learn how to drink first. Then I will pour for you, too. As you have dared offend the officer, and moreover the one of senior rank."

"So, I didn't know that he was a lieutenant colonel. There was just a guy with a prostitute. How I could know that he was from the FSB, moreover with the Federal Service of External Intelligence?"

"And who should know for you? You have to learn to feel these things in your gut—who to bark at and whose ass to kiss. As for me—"

"As for you ..." His wife, and Alexander's mother, interrupted. "Have you forgotten how, when you were Andropov's time, you and my brother were arrested in the bar? Well, you'd better stop and remember. And wasn't it me who then covered you up? Or, did you think that only you and your boss were able to do all of your tricks alone? Okay then, you are on your own."

Ivan Sidorovich Pushkov had worked for the police since 1956. After demobilization from the army, as a draftee who served as a sergeant, he was accepted into police school. After graduation, he was promoted to lieutenant and received an assignment as the neighborhood policeman in the Sviblovo subdivision, with temporary placement in a barrack. Shortly thereafter, he became acquainted with Maria, a kind young girl who worked in the local grocery store. They were meant for each other. Having dated for just a little while, the young people were married, and soon after, their daughter was born followed by a son. The barrack was demolished, then, and the Pushkov family moved into a three-room apartment.

Finally, the youngest son, Alexander, was born. For a few years, Maria stayed at home to care for the children. Then, she got a job in a nearby eatery. First working the floor, she eventually moved up to storage clerk. Owing to her new job, native wit, and sharpness, Pushkov Sr., by then promoted to captain, used to meet his wife after work by the car every evening. She never left work without two bags full of food to feed the family and to sell to the neighbors. On a rare day, the eatery manager would also hand Marie a fat pack of money, as he knew the storage clerk job wasn't easy; a lot of things could happen, such as shrinkages, spills, and even rodents.

One time, perhaps by mistake, some young cops from the local branch of the Division of Work-Crimes Investigations dropped by the eatery and made a control purchase. Maria called her husband. He met with the chief of the branch, and together they paid the visit to the eatery. After that, the criminal case was dropped, and nobody from the division ever had to make a control purchase there again. Well, naturally, though, it had been necessary for Pushkov to provide valuable gifts to all of the participants.

Pushkov had not only covered his wife and the eatery, but he was also a personal friend of everyone at his police station, as well as at the local branch of the Division of Work-Crimes Investigations.

The Pushkovs had a reputation as hospitable hosts. They did not forget to give gifts to all of the department and company chiefs on holidays. Further, the local gangsters respected the subdivision policeman and knew him as a fair cop.

And so these simple people with the right attitudes were building their life and earning the respect of their associates.

"By the way," Pushkov continued, now speaking to his wife, "your brother's son is the chief of security of Food Commerce Bank. Okay, so let's give them a call. And you, mother, get busy collecting some gifts. We shall visit and bid them a Happy New Year. Alex's situation isn't a joke."

The brother-in-law was at home, and so the Pushkovs announced that they would drop by tomorrow afternoon.

The next day, having loaded up the gifts and booze, they went to Pushkov Sr.'s brother-in-law's place. They sat with the family and discussed things with the brother-in-law's son until all of Sunday had passed.

The son had told them that Food Commerce Bank was looking for more people, because all of the banks are expanding. In particular, his bank, by the middle of the year, would open a few more branches, at which point he would need another assistant.

"So let Alexander work for a while as a security guard," he said. "In that time, he will gradually grow accustomed to what is going on, and in half a year, I shall promote him as my deputy."

Pushkov Jr. was the designated driver and took his parents back home.

On Monday, January 3, Pushkov, first thing in the morning, was at Food Commerce Bank.

There was no time even for a little vacation, he regretfully thought, sitting in the personnel department. Well, you, Yakubovsky, won't get the best of me! I shall finish you, so that all chiefs will cease to recognize you, he dreamed, as he signed the application.

For his new job, Pushkov would report on the January fifth.

25

Washington, January 3, 1994

On Monday, Melissa Spencer arrived in Washington. She had been here about a dozen times, but as the majority of business travelers, she would stay only for a couple of days and then depart. This time would be different. Now she would remain in this country. Melissa knew that it would be hard for her, but she was young, full of energy, financially well off, and had precisely determined what she should undertake.

From the baggage claim, she called the Ritz Carlton and asked them to send a car for her. Having received her luggage, Melissa loaded it onto a baggage cart and left the terminal. The driver was already waiting for her outside. He put her suitcases into the trunk, and within twenty minutes, they were pulling up to the hotel.

It all reminded her of Boris. There is where he helped me get into the minivan and compressed my hand so that nobody saw it. And there is where we walked after supper! How he is doing there, in California? Does he still remember me or has he already forgotten?

Melissa has proceeded into the hotel, having left her luggage under the care of the driver. She went to the registration desk, where the clerk checked her in.

"Do you wish to check into the same room in which you were the last time with Mr. Pennington?" he asked.

Melissa had kept silent for a moment, and then said, "If it is possible, I would like to check into the room where Mr. Goryanin was the last summer."

To her pleasure, the room was available.

Taking the carpeted hallway from the elevator to her room, Melissa looked at the familiar walls, covered in cherrywood. The same carpet! Suddenly, for an instant, it seemed that Boris would just walk around the corner. But he didn't. And he wouldn't.

I need to get over this idiocy, or I'll go mad! Melissa firmly decided.

The room was set up as always. Melissa removed her black cashmere coat, threw it on the back of an armchair, and then stopped, turned, and hung up it appropriately in the wall closet. She replaced her shoes with the hotel slippers, and, having approached the window, drew aside the curtain. The room became lighter and homier.

The porter with Melissa's luggage knocked on the door. After tipping him, she put her clothes away in the closet and drawers and sat her suitcases out of the way.

After making the room orderly, Melissa sat at the table and called the hotel operator, asking him for the telephone number to Kaplan's Test Preparation and Admissions Center. By luck, the nearest center was nearby. Melissa called there and made an appointment for the next morning. She then scheduled car service with the front desk, which she could use for the rest of her stay. After that, she dialed Jonathan Barker. He wasn't in his office, so Melissa left the message that she had arrived and was looking forward to meeting him.

In the lounge, as usual, the tables were bursting with delicacies. This time there were puff pies with various fillings, as well as a variety of cheeses, fruits, vegetables, and juices. After a decent lunch washed down with cranberry juice, she returned to her room and called Jonathan again. He wasn't back yet, so she left him a second message, asking him to call her back tomorrow, at seven thirty in the morning.

Taking a warm shower, Melissa washed off the weariness. She took a sleeping pill, set the alarm clock for six, and, having drawn the curtains, lay down in bed, blissfully taking to sleep.

The next morning, she awoke in an excellent mood, having decided this was the beginning of a new life. She did a few stretches, took a shower, and then went out for breakfast—a small bowl of porridge, a few slices of cheese, and a glass of warm milk.

When Melissa returned to her room, it was seven twenty. She had hardly finished her morning ritual as the phone rang. It was Jonathan Barker. He warmly greeted Melissa and asked her how she was feeling. Then receiving positive answers to all his questions, he asked when he might expect her at his office, to begin her registration for work. He suggested she begin work in the Crude Oil Sales and Acquisitions Department of Global Oil Sales and Research Corporation as a senior contract expert.

Then having found out that she needed to be at Kaplan's by eight o'clock, he asked, with forced surprise, "Do you not want to work for us?"

"Jonathan," she responded. "I hope that you remember the conditions of our contract?"

"I remember, but I'd like to have such a charming employee as you in our office!"

Melissa felt that Jonathan Barker was trying to flirt with her, and she had not included that, in any way, into her plans. She had made a firm decision to become a lawyer, and not just anywhere, but in California, near wherever Boris lived. At the same time, she didn't want to offend Jonathan, so she told him she would call him, or, better, she would come to Global Oil's office after finishing her business at Kaplan's. And on that, they said good-bye.

Melissa took the handbag with her documents, a little money, and took the elevator down, to find the car waiting for her at the entrance. Kaplan was less than two miles from the hotel, so they arrived in no more than five minutes. Melissa told the driver that she would call the hotel when she was done, at which point she'd need a lift to Global Oil.

At the registration office, Melissa filled out the necessary registration forms, paid seven hundred fifty dollars, received several brochures, and went into a classroom, as directed. The current test preparation session had begun two months earlier, and all of the students were graduates of local colleges, but Melissa would be doing her studies independently, and she had graduated from the London School of Economy and Political Sciences, one of the most prestigious educational institutions in the world.

Also in her favor was the fact that, for more than two years, she also worked as the contract expert in her company, engaged in international business. And, she was mature enough already. Melissa knew that she would quickly understand what to do. However, for now, she would listen to the teacher attentively.

The lectures, it turned out, would be conducted by a tall, somewhat bald man, approximately forty years old, wearing a sound but slightly shabby suit. He spoke with a slight Scottish accent.

During a break, Melissa approached the teacher and introduced herself. Robert MacDaget, having heard Melissa's obvious London dialect, immediately asked her why she wanted to become an American lawyer. So as not to get caught up in explanations, Melissa, with the most charming smile she was capable of, answered that she was simply bent for adventure. Robert MacDaget, throwing a cursory glance at her already expanding waistline answered that he would always be glad to help her catch up with the rest of the group, even if it meant staying after hours.

The afternoon flew by, after which, Melissa called the hotel and asked them to send a car for her. The weather was disgusting—not cold, but somehow uncomfortable. If it were better, Melissa would go on foot, but the damp wind and icy spots on the sidewalk didn't give her a great desire to walk. Melissa put her new books and computer discs into her strong Kaplan bag, and threw it over her shoulder.

While waiting for the car, her hands became frozen and her skin got tight and red. She regretted leaving her gloves at the hotel, but then remembered how Boris had told her once, "Those whose hands are cold have warm hearts."

Memories gushed over her. Melissa recollected how they had sealed the windows in that small apartment in Togliatti, and she suddenly wished she were there with him again, and that he would make her drink tea with a teaspoon again. The thought made her depressed and she wanted to cry, but the hotel car had come, bringing her back to reality.

Melissa called Jonathan Barker from the Global Oil reception hall upon her arrival. Jonathan had already requested a visitor pass for her, so she signed the visitor registration book, and went to the personnel department. Melissa asked the receptionist who she should address about documents, so the receptionist called over a huge woman, who smugly inspected Melissa and declared that she was not working on documents today and that Melissa should come back tomorrow for an interview. Melissa didn't take no for an answer. She asked the receptionist to speak to the department manager. The woman called someone over the phone.

Seconds later, the department manager, a man of average years, approached them, obviously dissatisfied that someone had distracted him. And having learned the problem, he asked the huge woman why she was forcing him to deal with her problems. The woman rolled her eyes and retrieved a folder from a filing cabinet, checked its contents, and handed it to Melissa.

Melissa walked back out into the hallway, looking for a place to sit and fill out the documents. She saw an empty room with the door open and immediately recognized it as the meeting room in which she and Boris had worked on the contract the previous summer. Apparently, she would never be able to get off those memories! Only time would help.

Melissa sighed and took a seat at the meeting table, noticing a phone. She decided to call Jonathan Barker. He answered at once, as if expecting her call.

She issued her complaint about the situation in the personnel department.

"Where are you now?" Jonathan asked. "I will be down in a few minutes."

When he arrived, Melissa stood, and they returned together to the personnel department. Having taken from Melissa the folder of paperwork, Mr. Barker excused himself and went directly to the department manager's office.

Returning a second later, he said, "You don't need to communicate with them anymore. They will make everything happen within the next several weeks. For now, you can concentrate on your studies. Keep your receipts from Kaplan. The company will pay for all your expenses within two months. By the way, have you had lunch already?

"I have decided to eat in the hotel. It is convenient and tasty."

"If you don't object, I would be happy to take you to your hotel."

"I'd be grateful," Melissa answered. Still having jet lag and now in her fourth month of pregnancy, she wanted nothing more than to sleep.

Jonathan assisted Melissa into the passenger seat, and as soon as the car got under way, she drifted off.

Approaching the hotel, Jonathan looked at the sleeping Melissa for a few minutes, unsure what to do, before he dared wake her. It was clear to him that, at least today, she needed a good rest.

Having said good-bye, Melissa went up to her room, washed her hands, and then went for something to eat. After her late lunch, she returned to her room and slept until five o'clock. After having resolutely risen, she slipped on a warm hotel dressing gown and arranged a work space on the desk.

Melissa connected the computer, and spread out her textbooks, manuals, and paper. Then she made a plan for her test preparation; at this point, that was priority. The admission test for schools in the American Bar Association consisted of five thirty-five-minute sessions. Four of them consisted of three groups of questions with set answers, while the answers given in a fourth part were considered by a selection committee at the educational institution chosen by the entrant.

The number of questions varied, but remained about a hundred. The maximum number of points was 180, with the lowest passing score ranging anywhere between 150 and 180, dependent upon factors such as the prestigiousness of the chose educational institution, the payment, and the number of students.

Besides her studies, Melissa would also need to, in an unfamiliar part of the world, determine a place to live and a mode of transportation; adjust to a new way of living; give birth to a child; and then be engaged with the baby. But, she was financially independent, self-motivated, and, most important, had the desire—the desire to become a lawyer, and the passionate desire to live near Boris. Someday, they would meet. She was sure of it. But for now, she needed to focus on her testing.

Next morning, before class, Melissa went to the office at Kaplan, where, having paid a hundred dollars, she filled out the registration form for the LSAT exam. She also learned from the registration clerk that in a bookstore located in the shopping center adjoining the Ritz Carlton she can buy additional textbooks. She was told the test would take place Friday, February 4, and that she should be prepared to the point that her score would be no less than 160.

And so Melissa has begun her routine test preparation. She studies thirteen hours a day, going to the hotel gym twice a day for thirty minutes each. One hour she left for meals, and what little time was left, she slept.

26

Washington, February 1, 1994

Almost one month had gone since Lady Melissa Spencer came to Washington. Today, when Melissa returned from Kaplan, the phone in her room was blinking. Jonathan Barker had left a message informing Melissa that Global Oil had received her H-1 working visa from Immigration and Naturalization as well as her Social Security card confirming that she had the right to be employed in United States. Further, he said, he had the Letter of Guarantee stating that Global Oil would take full financial responsibility for Melissa's studies in the educational institution of her choice. Further, he had a certificate for five years of medical insurance for Melissa and her future child, to be paid in full by Global Oil.

Melissa dialed Jonathan, thanked him for his care, and told him that she would come to his office to pick up the documents.

Jonathan answered that he would be happy to bring the documents to her at six o'clock that evening and invited Melissa to dinner.

With gratitude, she agreed. Melissa then called the Red Lion Hotel in Costa Mesa, California. Sharon Smith had recommended this hotel to Melissa, because it would be close to everywhere Melissa would need to be. Melissa made a reservation for a single room for forty-five days, which included breakfast and access to a gym. Now, being nobody's burden, Melissa could take care of business on her own.

At six o'clock, Melissa went down to the lobby dressed in a dark blue suit—a long skirt, a jacket, a light blue blouse, and black pumps. A thread of pearls around her neck and matching pearl earrings gave her face an additional freshness. Melissa was on the fifth month of pregnancy, and her suit couldn't hide her increasing waistline anymore. But she didn't care to hide her condition. On the contrary, she was happy to show it off. The pleasure of knowing that motherhood was impending only added shine to her radiant eyes, and softened her already beautiful features.

Melissa hadn't seen Jonathan for about a month, although he had occasionally called her, asking about her health and offering help. She always politely rejected his attempts at rapprochement.

Now, upon seeing Melissa in her new position, he was pleasantly surprised to witness her inherent tenderness.

Melissa suggested they go up the hotel's cafe, where they spent about an hour having general conversation and even joking a little. Jonathan then gave Melissa the folder of documents. By then, however, Melissa felt she needed to be getting back.

It was already nearly seven when she rose from her chair. "Dear Jonathan, I have to excuse myself. I need to continue preparation for the test, scheduled for Friday. Besides, I should start to put my stuff together. I purchased my airline ticket to California on Sunday."

Jonathan moved forward, as if wanting to object to something, but Melissa softly squeezed his hand and looked directly in Jonathan's eyes. "Please, don't say anything. I don't wish to be a burden on you. I am very grateful for everything that you have done for me, but I am not in a condition to give you what you deserve. If I accepted your offer, both of us would later regret it."

Jonathan's plans had failed. He had hoped for a serious conversation, in which he wished to admit his feelings to Melissa and suggest they become engaged, so that he could take on caring for her and her baby.

And with that, Melissa outstretched her hand, shook hands with her dinner companion, and walked away.

Early Friday morning, Melissa arrived totally prepared for the test and fully alert. In the first group of questions, she ran through the text, read the questions, and then referred back to the text to provide answers. She kept precisely kept on time. The second and third groups of questions presented no problems either, though she was running a little behind. The fourth part was an essay, in which Melissa had to discuss a hypothetical scenario. The scenario revolved around a contract for the delivery of copper pipes for a hotel's construction. She knew nothing about construction, but she had dealt with issues much more complex than this one before.

After the exam, Melissa went back to her room and wished only to sleep. To sleep and sleep and sleep. She changed into a sleeping gown, lay down in the bed, and did not open her eyes again until it was fifteen minutes to six. She smiled to herself, pleased that the test was behind her already, and she would no longer need to sit with her books. She arose from the warm bed and went to take a shower. In the nude, she examined herself in the mirror. Her breasts had increased one size and had become simply magnificent. Silently sighing, she wished that Boris could see her now. She examined her tummy, which, though slightly larger, was still defined. "So what do you think, kiddo," she addressed George, "does your daddy sometimes still remember us? We are so lonely!" But not receiving an answer, she slightly sobbed and stepped into the warm shower.

On February 6, Melissa departed from Dulles Airport bound for Chicago where she changed planes. A mere three hours later she was appearing in Irvine in Sharon Smith's embrace.

27

Moscow, February 1, 1994

Yakubovsky had rushed through the registration process for the apartment. He had tried to submit all of the necessary documents to the notary before the end of spring. He spent hardly any time at home anymore. He was either in his office, or with Igor or Victoria, continuing to look after her beautifully, as she had asked him. He brought her flowers and drove her to restaurants at every corner of city. Paying the bills in such expensive restaurants wasn't too much of a strain considering that Igor and Anna continued their shuttling trips, and Anna, as it turned out, had exquisite taste. After all, she was now a junior at the textile university, majoring in fashion design.

On February 1, Yakubovsky received the notice from Filimonov. He requested that Vlad report to the Office of the Attorney General on February 4 at ten a.m. The subject of discussion would be the official investigation of the death of the citizen Alexander Michilovich Popov.

The notice was strange. General Filimonov's position was the assistant to the attorney general. That meant that Mr. Filimonov simply could not be the investigator. But then that meant there could be no open investigation. So what was this request all about?

When Yakubovsky reported to Filimonov's receptionist, she immediately announced the lieutenant colonel's arrival. Yakubovsky entered into Filimonov's office, and upon seeing the general major in uniform, seated at his large desk, he habitually saluted and introduced himself. "Comrade General Major! Lieutenant Colonel Yakubovsky arrives on your order."

"Come in, Lieutenant Colonel," Filimonov said in an exclusively polite tone, but without a smile. "Please, take a seat."

Yakubovsky sat in a chair next to a meeting table, consumed with the two questions that had continued to disturb him: What did Filimonov know about him? And what did he have on him?

Filimonov's desk was spotless. There wasn't even a single piece of paper. Only three telephone sets, arranged in straight lines.

Filimonov was silent, but quickly ended the delay with a question: "I believe you can guess for what reason you are invited here, to the Office of Attorney General."

"According to the notice I received," Vlad said, "I am here as a witness for the official investigation of the death of citizen Popov."

"Yes. The investigator will contact you about that. But I had hoped that you would enable me to find out something concerning the disappearance of Lieutenant Colonel Cherkizov."

This statement didn't catch Yakubovsky unaware. He'd suspected that Filimonov had known something more. And because Filimonov knew, there was no sense in hiding that Vladislav had been in Togliatti and in Novomatushkino.

"Yes, I spent some time in the investigation of this matter. His scorched corpse was identified in the house where he was murdered."

"How did you find out what village and house he was murdered in?"

"Please, excuse me, Comrade General Major, but our External Intelligence Service been charged to keep all information confidential."

"Your service? Was it not from very this village that Cherkizov called you before he was killed? What did he tell you?"

This question caught Yakubovsky unaware. Now Vladislav understood that Filimonov knew everything—even more than Yakubovsky could know. But, from who had he received his information? From Kravchuk? No. He wouldn't. Though … who knew?

Yakubovsky was silent, not knowing how to answer.

Then Filimonov interceded. "Did Dmitry Cherkizov inform you that he kidnapped the US citizen Boris Goryanin and the citizen of Great Britain, Lady Melissa Spencer? And did Dmitry Cherkizov inform you that he was keeping them against their will? Did he inform you that he had prepared a terrible death for them and that he had one million dollars on his hands?"

Filimonov's tone, which had taken a one hundred and eighty degree turn from a minute ago, told Yakubovsky that Filimonov really knew all.

"Are you considering the idea that I might be involved in this crime?" Vladislav said.

"I don't know. You tell me."

Suddenly, it became clear to Yakubovsky that he had only one thing to say. "Really, I am not involved in this business. And actually, there is nothing to investigate. The gangsters received their due penalty, and the heroes were saved. Only one thing remains unknown: where is the money? And do you know who, then, executed all four villains?"

"Yes, I know how he rescued himself and rescued the fellow traveler as well. I know his name, too. He is Boris Goryanin. In fact, you had met him in Washington, correct?

"Goryanin? That intellectual egghead? But who helped him?"

"Probably, God helped him!"

"It cannot be. And the money?"

"I don't know. But I think you do know, don't you?"

"I know that Cherkizov and three gangsters were killed. But who killed them and where the money is, I do not know."

At that instant, the image of Anastasia lying in the snow with a sliced throat flashed before Yakubovsky's eyes. He felt terrible knowing that she had experienced her inevitable end, and knew that Boris Goryanin dare not let his courage break before such a face of death.

Vladislav asked Filimonov in almost a whisper, "Forgive me, Comrade General Major, but from whence did you receive your facts?"

"From Goryanin." Really, Filimonov had no evidence against Yakubovsky, except for the phone call. Yakubovsky's involvement was only a suspicion—not enough for a basis to press charges against him. Therefore, Filimonov pulled from a desk drawer Goryanin's statement and handed it to Yakubovsky.

Having read it through, Yakubovsky silently returned the papers to Filimonov. Goryanin was legally clean. What he did, he did in self-defense, and by all means, he had actually been the hero.

"Not everyone could do what this man did," Yakubovsky said to Filimonov.

"And so considering, what do you have to say now about Mr. Popov's death?"

"Being abroad, I carried out an important governmental task. For its success, I resorted to the help of a citizen of our country. He assisted me, and the task was executed successfully. After coming home, I completed a written report, specially noting Alexander Popov's merit. I don't know any more than that."

"As I already have noted, we do not have anything on you that would be the basis for pressing charges. But the management of the Office of the Attorney General of the Russian Federation holds the opinion that it would be better for everybody if you would resign. We are giving you six months. During this time, you should be able to hand over all of your responsibilities to your replacement and find another job. You can take a vacation. It's up to you. And your management will be informed at the appropriate time. I hope that you understand; I don't dare detain you any longer. Please, give me your temporary pass."

Filimonov silently signed Yakubovsky's pass and returned it to him.

Back outside, Yakubovsky felt awful. He walked on despite the frost, not feeling a bit cold. "Damn it all," he muttered. "I'm lucky I wasn't sent to that special prison for the police and KGB officers for seven years. Well, I had decided to leave anyway, and Kravchuk had formulated their future plan, to steal big money and escape, precisely."

28

California, February 1, 1994

The architectural and structural plans for the first project had been finished, and Goryanin had handed them over to the city's building department for approval. Now, he just needed to look for a bank that would provide him with a construction loan.

Boris visited several small banks providing commercial loans for the construction of single-family homes. After talking to various loan officers, Boris was convinced that the people were what make all the difference. One loan officer suggested that Boris put down as collateral the same amount of money he was asking for before the bank gave him a loan. Another lender showed more creativity. They suggested he sell them the properties with the approved plans at the price Goryanin had paid for the land. And they were surprised when he told them exactly what he was thinking about.

At a third bank, all was simple. They suggested Boris provide them with a construction cost breakdown, supported by quotes from subcontractors. The total amount of the construction loan, payable upon completion of construction and the issuance of a Certificate of Occupancy by local building authorities, would be sixty percent of the estimated price of the project on the open market. The cost of construction lot and all expenses, including those of development and design, property taxes, and fees, they considered as actual expenses. Such a reasonable approach quite suited Boris; in particular, it would allow him enough money for the development and design of the next house, on the second parcel of land.

By the end of March, when the rainy season had ended in California, the construction loan was signed. With Boris's consent, the bank would release funds for delivered materials and performed services, both of which had passed city and bank inspection. In turn, the loan department, every other week, would send an inspector out to the site to ensure all requirements were being met.

From that point on, Boris's routine work had begun: every day by seven, he was on the construction site until the end of the workday. And in the evenings, he did paperwork, checking and paying invoices, writing financial reports for the bank, organizing receipts for auditing, and studying for the general contractor's license exam.

Being totally involved in his business, Boris didn't think often about Melissa. Definitely, he remembered her, but as they agreed, he would wait and she would call him as it became necessary.

29

California, February 6, 1994

Melissa and her old schoolmate Sharon hadn't seen each other for six years. Looking at each other, they just now understood how much each of them had changed. Short telephone calls and greeting cards just hadn't allowed them to watch how much they had matured. From schoolgirls, they had turned into young women.

Together, the women went to get Melissa's baggage and then went to Sharon's car. From the airport, the girlfriends went to the Red Lion Hotel on Bristol Avenue. As before, they talked about their lives, often interrupting each other, until evening silently crept up on them. Sharon then left for home, and Melissa took a bath and laid down to rest.

On Monday morning, Sharon arrived at Melissa's and they had breakfast together and went to lease a car. The leasing company, Nickel, was on Adams Avenue and Harbor Boulevard. Melissa chose a simple Buick. On both sides of Harbor Boulevard there were car dealerships, but Melissa still wasn't ready to buy. First, she needed to open a bank account and transfer her money from Geneva.

Melissa was a good driver, but it had been awhile since she'd been behind the wheel, and she felt a little uncomfortable. In about ten minutes, though, she lost her nervousness. She followed Sharon to the nearest branch of the Bank of America. There, she opened a personal checking account and deposited into it practically all of the cash that she had brought from Washington, along with the two checks from Global Oil, having left her with only a handful of change. Still, she could use her credit cards from England and Switzerland.

Later, Sharon left Melissa alone to rest at the hotel. But after laying down for a half an hour and not having fallen asleep, Melissa went down to the hotel gift shop and purchased a detailed map of Orange County, where she was lodging and planning to live. The first thing she did was find the street where Boris lived. It was so close! Melissa was delighted, but then grew sad.

Then, so as not to postpone things any longer, she found the location of the law school on the map, and then went there directly. She walked into the admissions office, introduced herself, and said that she would like to discuss her admission as a new student with an advisor.

Mrs. Backinsale, the elderly affable woman behind the counter, also had a strong British accent, and after hearing Melissa speaks about her background and work experience, she instantly grew fond of her. The feeling appeared mutual. Mrs. Backinsale gave Melissa a package of forms to fill out and bring back the next Monday.

"You won't have any problems being admitted to our school," she told Melissa, "even if your LSAT score is less than perfect. Based on your education, skills, achievements, and experience with contracts, you certainly will be accepted for the autumn semester. In the meantime, I would advise you to take the test for the judicial translator license for German, French, and Italian in all of the courts in both Orange and Los Angeles counties.

Mrs. Backinsale then gave Melissa the phone numbers of the municipal and superior courts of Orange and Los Angeles counties' state and federal courts. Each of those courts required a separate license, but the test for each would be the same.

When they had ended their conversation, Melissa asked Mrs. Backinsale whether she knew of any Russian grocery stores nearby, but the elderly woman didn't have an answer. She told Melissa that Orange Coast College had a Russian program, however, and therefore might have someone who could help her.

Melissa returned to the hotel and did a little workout in the gym. Then she had dinner and talked to George before falling asleep as soundly as a righteous person in heaven.

In the morning, Melissa prepared two requests for wiring funds from London and Geneva to her account with Bank of America and sent them by fax. Then she decided to begin searching for a house. In the telephone directory, she found a real estate agency named Tarbell on Brookhurst Street, approximately five miles from the hotel.

Marsha Roberts, the real estate agent, listened attentively to Melissa. Having learned what she was looking for and hearing that her new client would be willing to make a purchase with cash, Marsha told her that, right behind their office, there was a community called Mariposa, which had a wonderful four-bedroom house, with a large kitchen and dining room, and a modest backyard. The house had been constructed ten years ago, but was in amazing condition and demanded little repair. Only the interior needed some paint work and the carpet would have to be replaced. The owner, she said, was asking three hundred and forty thousand, but might consider a smaller all-cash offer.

"If you would like," she said, "you can see this property now."

Melissa didn't want to waste time.

As they walked to the house, Marsha pointed out that, nearby, there were a hospital and a large grocery store, and Melissa had figured out on the map that the law school was within two miles. What else was necessary?

After walking through the house, Melissa made an offer for three hundred ten thousand, and offered deposit of ten thousand dollars.

Marsha called Melissa the next day. The owner's counteroffer was three hundred twenty-five, and it was upon that price that they settled.

So, within three days, Melissa had solved all of her problems. Now, she was just waiting for the wires from London and Geneva.

30

Moscow, February 14, 1994

A tradition adopted from the West, Valentine's Day, had become fashionable to celebrate in Russia. Today, Yakubovsky surpassed himself. In the central market, he purchased for Vicky and Ann bouquets of red roses. In addition, he bought two pounds of fresh strawberries, a can of whipped cream, a box of chocolates, and a bottle of real French champagne.

They celebrated the new holiday at Victoria's apartment, sitting silently and listening to good music. Yakubovsky received the traditional ration of delicacies from his office. At about one o'clock in the morning Igor and Anna left, and Yakubovsky, for the first time, stayed with Victoria.

The next morning, Vladislav awoke at daybreak next to Vicky, who lay on her right side, nestling into him. Heavy ringlets of her naturally blonde hair fell over his chest and pillow. Yakubovsky had been lying motionless with his left arm beneath her, and now his hand had become numb. Cautiously, trying to not wake her, Vladislav liberated his hand, but Vicky awoke for an instant, kissed Vlad, and then turned onto her left side and fell back to sleep. Her right hand was now above the blanket, and on her right arm, right above the elbow, Yakubovsky noticed a small birthmark with a form that reminded him of Australia.

Yakubovsky was a professional service man with a mind specially trained to hold long-term memory. Memory training, in fact, had been his instructor's specialty, and even hypnosis had been applied for this purpose. Now, using this skill of recollection, Vlad was absolutely confident that he had seen precisely such a birthmark before, but where and when he couldn't remember. And then, as sharp as a knife, the memory cut through him. It had been last summer in Washington. He had come to Goryanin's room, and Goryanin had answered the door wearing a T-shirt and holding a towel. On his right arm, above the elbow, had been the exact same birthmark. It couldn't be a mistake. But how could Vicky and Goryanin both have the same mark? It was impossible. Too much of a coincidence. Vicky had barely even remembered Goryanin until she'd seen the photo of him, and she hadn't seemed to be lying. But now, it was clear, everything was not so simple. Something definitely was being hidden from him.

"All right, I will not let her know I've seen it," he resolved. "But it will still be necessary to dig. I need all the information I can get from both of them—Victoria and Boris—but then what information would that be? What am I even looking for?"

Yakubovsky silently rose from bed and went to the bathroom to brush his teeth and wash his face. Then he walked to the kitchen, where the table was still a mess. He tidied up, collecting the dishes, and then poured water in the teapot, found some instant coffee, and filled two cups. Vladislav poured the hot water in the cups, put them on saucers, and went back to the bedroom.

Cautiously setting the cups on the floor, he quietly removed the blanket from Victoria. For the first time, he saw her totally naked. Before his eyes was a young beautiful woman with a fine body. Yakubovsky froze for a minute, admiring the image. Then he recovered her, knelt, and gently kissed her on the mouth. Vicky woke up, lifted both arms to embrace Yakubovsky, and having exposed her sexy C-sized breasts with erect nipples and emitting a pleasant fragrance, she made Vladislav dizzy. He removed the blanket from Vicky again.

"Vlad, why you aren't sleeping?" Vicky whispered returning his kisses.

"I have brought coffee for you, Vicky," he whispered back, knowing they would have to drink cold coffee.

"Coffee in bed?" Vicky asked.

"Or send it far away," Yakubovsky said, kissing Vicky passionately.

The coffee had its turn much later, after they had finally crept out of the bedroom into the kitchen. They ate the leftovers from their celebratory supper, drank coffee, and then rushed back to bed. They did not get out of bed till the next morning.

The next day, having arrived at his office, Vladislav Yakubovsky proceeded to write his chief a request for two weeks' vacation.

31

By the middle of February, Melissa's checking account had accumulated four hundred sixty-five thousand dollars. The purchase of the house had gone well, and now Melissa had begun shopping for a car. In view of the fact that she would need to accommodate a car seat and stroller in addition to shopping bags and other baby supplies, she decided to take the advice of Sharon's husband, Frank, and buy a minivan or SUV. Within two hours of arriving at the Toyota dealership, she had a brand new white 4-Runner, and had gone to AAA, to look into car insurance.

After returning to the hotel, the tireless Melissa then continued to prepare for the judicial translator tests. While doing so, she made up her mind that, soon, she needed to go test for her California driver's license and make an appointment with a local doctor, which she could do now that she had a permanent address.

Pregnancy proceeded easily, even making Melissa seem more feminine. She didn't suffer from toxicity, and had no discoloration on her face or body. She made sure not to overstuff herself, and ate by the book: vegetable juices, the right type of fish, poultry, fruit, vitamins, and whole grains. She had practically excluded from her diet all bleached flour products and white potatoes. Therefore, she carried her toned but growing belly with special grace.

Only one thing about her pregnancy was a pity: that Boris was not with her. She thought of him often, however, particularly at night whenever she awoke in loneliness.

32

For the next two weeks, Vladislav and Vicky took vacation together, seldom leaving the apartment or the bed except to get groceries. Yakubovsky didn't think about his wife once the entire time.

Then on March 1, Yakubovsky went back to work. At lunch, he met his old buddy Stanislav Terekhin in the dining hall and talked business with a few colleagues, before leaving with the distinct feeling that such dialogue was no longer interesting to him.

The next day, Yakubovsky called Kravchuk. Valerie answered and told him that Mr. Kravchuk, several days ago, had been admitted into a rehab center in a grave condition. She didn't know any of the details, except that he was constantly connected to an IV.

That's what vodka does, Yakubovsky thought. Then he called to his notary to find out how the registration for the apartment was progressing. The notary's secretary told him that the senior notary would be back in the office in three days.

At last, the time had come to make inquiries regarding Goryanin. Yakubovsky sent an inquiry to the Ministry of Internal Affairs regarding "former citizen Union Boris Georgievich Goryanin, year of birth, 1945."

Then, as there was nothing left to do in the office, Yakubovsky went home to discuss divorce with Natalie. When he opened the front door to his apartment, the first thing he noticed, to his silent pleasure, were men's boots sitting in the entry hall—and hung on a hanger above them, a man's coat.

The bedroom door was closed, and only the squeals of his "lovable" could be heard through it.

With that, Yakubovsky decided to act out a little performance. He drew his pistol from its holster and kicked open the bedroom door. On the bed, his short-legged, clumsy creature lay naked on her belly, and on top of her was a naked stud, going about his work.

"Don't move!" Yakubovsky ordered, pointing the weapon at them. "Stand and put your hands up!"

Seeing the pistol, the stud rose from the bed and lifted both hands. Natalie groaned and pulled a sheet over herself.

"So, young man," Yakubovsky addressed the stud, "why don't you finish what you've started? I'll wait for you in the kitchen." Then Yakubovsky left the bedroom.

Natalie, overcome the shame, and having turned back to her young lover said, "You really should get back to work and finish the job. I cannot stand waiting for a happy ending." But after a shock and presence of Natalie husband in the apartment, he wasn't able to get back to work. But he tried hard …

Meanwhile, Yakubovsky, laughing silently, went to retrieve his money from its hiding place in the bathroom. He had two hundred thousand dollars. He'd hoped the couple had heeded his advice, as he'd needed time to get the money out and then to store it in his pants pockets, his jacket and overcoat, and his briefcase. When the money was all gathered, Yakubovsky went to the kitchen and put a teapot on the stove. Then he had a seat at the table and began to laugh loudly. Who would think that he, having found his wife with a lover, would be sitting in the kitchen, waiting to enjoy some tea? But he didn't care now. Natalie could not even be compared with his Vicky, so young and beautiful.

And this way, I will receive the divorce without argument. And I will receive it today, so that I can have all the money with me, Yakubovsky thought, continuing to laugh to the point that his tears start coming.

The teapot began to whistle, so he took a cup out of the cabinet, rinsed it under the faucet, poured in the boiling water, and dropped in a tea bag. At last, the bedroom door opened, and the naked stud ran across the hall into the bathroom. Then, from the bedroom, with her long-unwashed naked body wrapped in a dressing gown, Natalie emerged. She opened her mouth and began to wail, but Yakubovsky interrupted her:

"Be silent, creature! I shall shoot you," he said. "Do you remember our last conversation? I am walking on a razor-sharp edge, carrying out a confidential task, and what do I come home to find you engaged in?"

Natalie again prepared to roar, but Yakubovsky continued. "Who is he? What he is here for? Where did you meet him? Is he following me? I shall kill both of you. I shall execute both of you right now."

"You … please … forgive me, and … and …" she silently sobbed. "He is my nephew." She tumbled to her knees before Yakubovsky:

"Be silent," Vlad whispered. "I told you to make it quiet. The apartment is bugged. I had it checked."

Natalie covered her mouth with her hand and shivered. The "nephew" then walked naked out of bathroom and back into the bedroom.

Yakubovsky continued his vigorous reproach. "I will not bear such shame. Either we get divorced or I shall execute both of you now. I don't need anything from you. Give me ten thousand dollars for this apartment, and I will disappear. The consent to divorce I will write now. This apartment is yours. Is that clear? I am asking you, is that clear?"

"Yes, but how I shall live without you?" Natalie sobbed. "And what about our love?"

"What are you, a nut? Has your top absolutely gone? You'd better bring me the money and a piece of paper. I will write the divorce statement."

Natalie, squealing a little, left the kitchen, and from the bedroom appeared the so-called nephew, now fully dressed.

"You are very understanding," he said, approaching Vlad. "I respect you—you did the right thing. I would do the same." Then turning, he yelled, "Natalie! Bring the money!"

Natalie brought out ten thousand dollars and handed it to Yakubovsky. "It's all here," she said. "It is not necessary to count. And it's the last of it. I don't know how I shall live now."

She made her final comment, however, in the mere spirit of the moment. In truth, she didn't need Yakubovsky. In fact, she hated him. They'd grown tired of each other, and Natalie was silently pleased to be handed such a simple resolution to the problem.

Yakubovsky took the clean sheet of paper, which had been pulled out of a notebook, together with the money Natalie handed to him, and within three minutes, he had written a statement to the court, saying that he didn't object to divorce with the citizen Natalie Yakubovsky. Then he signed it and went to collect his belongings.

Actually, there was not much left to collect—just his dress and parade uniforms, and some shirts, socks, and underwear. He didn't have photos or personal papers, and there was no sense in taking any books. His toiletries were already at Vicky's. He put his items in a suitcase, and said his final words to Natalie.

"Do you remember our conversation? If so, don't ever call me at work. If I need you, I shall find you." And with that, he left the apartment, and planned never to come back.

33

Moscow, March 1, 1994

In the morning on March 1, Melissa's real estate agent Marsha Roberts called and told her that all of the closing paperwork was ready. Now all that was left was for her to bring the check in the amount of three hundred fifteen thousand dollars, which included the ten-thousand-dollar deposit. Melissa went to the bank and withdrew a cashier's check for this sum, and took it to Marsha at the escrow company. Then Melissa signed all of the necessary documents, and the house became the future home of her and her baby. Marsha told Melissa that the former owners had already vacated the house, but had agreed to meet on Saturday at two o'clock to give her the keys. Melissa asked Marsha to go with her and help to choose furniture. She also asked Marsha whether she knew anybody who could paint the interior, lay carpet, and generally clean up the house. Marsha promised Melissa that, on Saturday, she would bring a guy who could do all of it.

On Saturday, March 5, at two o'clock, Marsha stood at the entrance of Melissa's new house with a tall young man who introduced himself as Stephen Carter. Melissa asked him to paint all of the doors, windows, and baseboards in an oil-based white, and all of walls in light, water-based beige. She also asked him to lay woolen carpets in a light tone, with speckles of darker color. He looked through the house, and told her that all of the work could be done within a week, and that, by tomorrow morning, he would fax Melissa the estimate.

When Carter left, the women walked through the house, and then left together to buy furniture, linens, and kitchen utensils.

In the Levitz Furniture store was everything to satisfy Melissa's simple tastes. For her bedroom, she purchased a narrow single bed, a mattress, a credenza, and a nightstand with a lamp. For the downstairs bedroom, she purchased a queen-sized bed, two nightstands with lamps, a mattress, and a credenza. For a small room that she had intended to make a study, she bought a computer desk, a printer stand, a bookcase, and a regular desk. The furniture for the living room was simple, too: a sofa, the loveseat, an armchair, and a coffee table. For the dining room, they decided to buy a sliding table for twelve people, with twelve chairs. Then Melissa purchased for the breakfast nook a table with eight chairs. The superstitious Melissa would not purchase anything for her little George, however. That would come later, after the birth. She scheduled delivery and installation of the furniture for March 11.

From the furniture store, Melissa and Marsha went to Sears, where Melissa bought a full set of kitchen utensils and dishes—a set of eight for the breakfast nook and a set of twelve for the dining room—coffee and tea cups for eight, two sets of sleeping accessories, a new washing machine and dryer, a vacuum cleaner, a large refrigerator, two TVs, and a video recorder. The delivery department scheduled her goods' arrival on Saturday, March 12.

34

Moscow, March 9, 1994

Yakubovsky received the answer to his inquiry concerning Boris Goryanin. Vladislav didn't have any interest in Goryanin's personal file, however. He was interested in one question only: where Boris Goryanin was the summer of 1963. From a copy of his work-records file, Yakubovsky gathered that from 1962 to 1963, Boris Goryanin was a full-time student of the Nikolayev branch of Odessa Polytechnic University, and from 1963 to 1966 he was a full-time student at Odessa Polytechnic University.

Yakubovsky called Nikolayev in the Ukraine. There, in the city's KGB office, worked his former fellow cadet Peter Grach. Due to his success, he continued to work in the same place, but the organization was now named something in the Ukrainian language that was impossible even to pronounce.

Yakubovsky found his old buddy in the office, upon which Peter Grach told him that the Nikolayev branch of Odessa Polytechnic hadn't existed for a long time, and therefore, there were few archives left.

"What information do you really need?" Grach asked Yakubovsky.

"Whether Goryanin was on a virgin soil in the summer of 1963. And, if so, where he was in particular."

"That would be part of the Komsomol program," Grach said. "That is not a problem. The city archives are in full order. Give me a couple of days, and I shall find out."

"Thanks, my friend," Vlad said. "I am your debtor."

35

California, March 9, 1994

When Melissa called the law school to get the results of her LSAT exam, Mrs. Bakinsale informed her that her score was 163, and congratulated Melissa on her acceptance as a full-time student for the autumn semester. She then invited Melissa to come to the office and choose classes on Monday, March 14, at ten o'clock.

Now, Melissa decided, was the time to get her California driver's license. She would need it to take the judicial translator test and to register at the Orange Coast College where she could take Russian language classes. She went to the Department of Motor Vehicles the very next morning.

During breakfast, Melissa noticed a man speaking on a cell phone in the hallway. She waited until he finished the conversation, and then asked him where she could buy such a phone. The man told her that the sales office of L.A. Cellular was located across the freeway on Bristol Street.

The joyful Melissa, hastily swallowing the rest of breakfast, rushed to the car and off to L.A. Cellular, only to be lightly disappointed. To register for this phone, she needed a valid California driver's license. She sighed, went to the Department of Motor Vehicles, and picked up the California driver's manual to help her prepare for the exam. Then she went to the college to sign up for Russian classes.

Melissa parked her car and went inside, but on her way to the admissions office, she casually glanced over and saw a hand-written advertisement on a bulletin board: "Professional Russian-language teacher seeks student. Reasonable price. Sorry, I have no car. Call (714) 133-2266." Melissa jotted down the telephone number and decided that individual lessons might suit her better than a college course.

Having returned to the hotel, she called the number. A woman who sounded about sixty answered. She spoke practically no English and could hardly dictate her address. They agreed that Melissa would go arrive there at four.

Having verified the address on her map, Melissa found the street, and at four o'clock was pulling into the parking lot of a twelve-story building for low-income residents. She took an elevator to the tenth floor and knocked on the teacher's door. The door opened, and there stood a small senior man dressed in a checkered shirt and precisely the same trousers as Boris had bought in Togliatti. Even the color of the trousers was the same—lilac ink. But this man wore them unusually, having pulled them up so that the elastic band was directly under his armpits. His shirt's sleeves were rolled up twice, just as Boris's had been in Togliatti.

The man kept looking at Melissa. It was clear that he didn't know how to tell her to come in. Melissa greeted him and introduced herself by name. Then a woman approached them, wearing the same type of dressing gown as the maid that had come to clean their apartment in Togliatti—the woman whom Boris had given money to and then asked to bring bread and cream. Her hair was pulled up by a very similar hairpin. Finally, the man, by gesture only, invited Melissa to come in.

The apartment was only one large room with a small kitchenette. Next to the kitchenette were an outdoor table and three collapsible chairs. A phone hung on the wall, and instead of a bed, a bare mattress lay on the floor. An old TV with a wire antenna sat on a floor. And that was all.

Melissa, recollecting the movie *Tarzan*, pointed to herself and slowly uttered the syllables, "Meh-lih-sah." Then she pointed to the woman, and carefully repeated the syllables given to her in reply: "Lee-yood-Mih-lah … Mih-lah … Mila!"

Mila was what she and Boris had called each other, and what Melissa had planned to name their baby had it been a girl. This was too much for her. Tears rained from her eyes.

The seniors could not understand what was happening—why this young, decent-looking woman had begun to cry after hearing her new teacher's name. Lyudmila Petrovna brought Melissa a cup with water.

Melissa spent the next three hours there, gradually learning that the man's name was Valentin, or easier, Valya. The couple had offered Melissa a cup of tea with homemade apple pie. When Melissa uttered "Pel-me-ny," Lyudmila, as best as she could, explained to Melissa that this meal would be possible to make at home.

The dialogue calmed Melissa down. She very much liked both of them, and somehow felt cozy and homey. In her position, alone and pregnant, it somehow seemed that their dialogue was necessary. She felt she needed someone like these two to look after her, to treat her with homemade pies and pelmeny. She didn't want to leave, and she felt as though they wanted her to stay as well. They even, somehow, started to communicate more easily.

Eventually, Melissa learned that there was a lady who could assist in their communication. She was a former teacher of English who now worked for Social Services. Her name was Elena. Melissa took down Elena's telephone number, and then, having returned to the hotel, dialed it. Elena appeared affable and sociable and told Melissa the seniors' story.

"Valentin and Lyudmila Trunovs came to the US from the Siberian city of Krasnoyarsk three years ago. Valentin was an engineer, and his wife was trained to teach Russian, although, upon the birth of their first daughter, she began to work in a children's day nursery. Then she gave birth to two more children. So she ended up working in a day care all her life.

"Their children have been grown for some time now. They are married and have their own families. The oldest daughter moved to her husband's apartment, and the second child, a son, and his wife are living with his in-laws. The youngest daughter, Svetlana, got married just before graduating from medical school. Her husband became a programmer. But the Svetlana could not find an apartment, so, with their two small children, they moved into a hostel, waiting for their turn in a municipal apartment.

"In 1990, Svetlana and her husband decided they should move to America. As they didn't have enough money, however, they arranged a fictitious divorce, so that Svetlana could become a mail-order bride for an American. She would settle down in a new place, and then call her husband and let him know where she was.

"Through the marriage agency, Svetlana became acquainted with a new American friend who was, it is easy to say, not very attractive. Besides, there was an error in translation. He had told her that he was a lifeguard at the beach, but the Russian interpreter, after consulting a dictionary, decided that he had said he was a member of the Coast Guard, meaning a navy officer on a sea vessel.

"So Svetlana married this idiot guard, whose mental capacities were suited only for work on a beach. In addition, he earned so little money that he had to share a one-bedroom apartment with two other blockheads. All three of them were waiting for inheritances from relatives. And on top of everything else, he took Svetlana's passport from her and threatened to sell her to a Mexican brothel. Having been married to this moron for almost a year, now, Svetlana understood more than ever that she had made a big mistake, but she didn't know what to do. She was afraid that anything she did would get her deported back to Russia. Plus, she didn't have any money.

"Somehow, she became acquainted with a group of illegal aliens that cleaned houses, but all the money she made cleaning, the lifeguard stripped from her."

Elena continued. "Somehow Svetlana got acquainted with Russian family living here in Orange County. Those people didn't have any knowledge and finances to help Svetlana. So they referred Svetlana to me. That's when Svetlana and I met, and I advised her to go to an organization that assisted abused women. At that point, Svetlana saw a chance to climb out of the hole she had fallen into, until more trouble came upon her.

"Back in Krasnoyarsk, Svetlana's husband Nikolay, who had instigated this adventure to begin with, became involved with that Russian interpreter woman who had effectively separated him from his wife. At least Svetlana's parents had managed to take the children from him. But at the same time, Svetlana's American husband had a policeman friend arrest her on the basis that she had no legal documents for her stay in America; even though he'd been the one to take her passport from her.

"When I learned what had happened to her, I called Valentin and Lyudmila with the news, and they immediately decided to go to America, to rescue Svetlana. But they had no money, so there was only one thing they could do: sell their two-bedroom apartment. They sold it to the very same interpreter who had effectively separated their daughter from her husband in error. She bought their apartment for pennies on the dollar, and then, to add insult to injury, moved in with their former son-in-law. What a weasel!

"The poor elderly couple left behind everything they had, managing only to transfer both of their retirement payments to the address of their oldest daughter. Then they rushed to America on the tourist visa. Fifteen hundred dollars they spent for tickets to the US. Five thousand more hired a lawyer who, within fifteen minutes, had pulled Svetlana out of jail, as her case had not even been started. They then paid a thousand for Svetlana's tickets to the Russian consulate in San Francisco, where she got a new Russian passport, and a ticket to Moscow, and from there, up to Krasnoyarsk, where her sister and brother would take care of her and her children. They also gave Svetlana another thousand dollars …

"She was rehired at the hospital where she had worked before moving to the US, but made pennies. Only one positive came out of the whole thing, and that was that she had taken back custody of her children. But now Svetlana and her two children are living in some slum.

"And at the end of the story, the seniors remained without anything. I helped them legalize their status in the US and helped them get on Medicare and welfare. They still managed to send Svetlana one hundred dollars a month, though, as they knew she and their two grandchildren were living in a single room in a community apartment, without a private toilet.

"Almost two years has passed since then, and there has been absolutely no place for the seniors to go, neither in America, or in Russia."

At the end of the conversation, Melissa asked Elena to let the seniors know that she would see them at five o'clock the next day. She took their story close to her heart. These people were old and absolutely alone. It was a pity for them to have to get involved in such an unpleasant ordeal. And consequently, she, too, was absolutely alone.

All night long, Melissa couldn't sleep. She was thinking about how she could help them and how they could help her. She could learn Russian from them, and they could help her with the baby and prepare her meals. And, most important, Melissa would not be alone. And they would not be not alone either. If they could just live together somehow, it would be the solution to all their problems.

So the next morning, Melissa tested for her driver's license. She'd had time to read through the manual only twice, but that had seemed good enough. She handed over the written exam and passed after the first time. The driving test wasn't necessary, considering her ten years' driving experience. She received a temporary driving document with the promise that a permanent driver's license would come by mail.

From the DMV, Melissa went to buy a cell phone, and then, proud and pleased with her new toy, she went to see how Stephen Carter was doing on the house. His crew had already pulled out the old carpet, and he was close to finishing the painting.

Having driven off from her new home, Melissa decided to stop at the local hospital. Less than six hundred feet from her house, the location was more than convenient. And she was pleasantly surprised to learn that, at the corner of Talbert and Brookhurst, there was a medical center. Melissa parked and went in. On the list of doctors was a pediatrician, Dr. Lerner, but she patted her belly and said, "It is still too early for us. But here is Dr. Rosen, an OB, who will be good for us now."

She walked up to the second floor and found Dr. Rosen's office. She asked the receptionist whether she could see the doctor and was informed that he was examining another patient, but that he could find time for Melissa when he was finished. Melissa provided her medical insurance card and her temporary driver's license, and then seated herself in the waiting room and began to fill out new patient forms. The doctor became available just as Melissa was finished answering the final question.

The doctor's assistant invited Melissa back, where she took Melissa's height and weight, and checked her temperature and blood pressure. By the time the doctor had arrived, Melissa had changed into a paper examination gown. Doctor was tall, affable, and attentive. He carefully examined Melissa, and asked in detail about her pregnancy, including why she had not come to see a doctor earlier. Then he performed an ultrasound. Finally, he asked Melissa to bring to him an extract of her medical records from her previous clinic.

In the end, he told Melissa that she was in magnificent shape, and that the boy was developing normally. He praised her for being engaged in physical activity, having a good diet, and consuming the correct vitamins. Then he suggested that he become acquainted with the kid's father. With Melissa's sad sigh, however, he understood that such an acquaintance would not take place. Now the doctor sighed, clapped Melissa's hand, and told her that if he were younger, he would consider it happiness to be with such woman as she.

"Keep doing what you're doing and come back in two weeks," he said. "And, most important, stay positive."

That evening, Melissa arrived at the Trunovs. They wrote, drew, gesticulated, and ultimately understood each other. Melissa invited them to eat with her at a Sizzler just a few blocks from her new home.

Though they had been in America for about two years, Valentin and Lyudmila, for the first time, were eating in a fantastic "all-you-can-eat" place, where you could eat as much you wanted. And they did. Fried shrimp disappeared at a speed incongruous to their age. Watching them, Melissa began to worry about their health. Later, Melissa would learn the Russian proverb "For free, even vinegar is sweet," but for now, she saw only that Valentin's belly was growing and that Lyudmila was beginning to choke.

In order to stop this gluttony, Melissa suggested she show them her house. And with that, the seniors, hardly able to move their legs, and unwilling to abandon this wonderful institution, were directed to the exit. They were at her place in less than five minutes.

It was almost eight, but Stephen was still working. The walls, doors, windows, and baseboards were all painted, and he was removing the masking tape. The three walked around the house, trying to not touch the newly painted surfaces. Melissa saw how much the Trunovs liked everything. By the tone of their voices, Melissa understood that they were sincerely congratulating her and wishing all the best. And then Melissa couldn't restrain her emotions any longer. She invited them to move in. They did not understand her, though. Melissa wanted to call Elena, but her cell phone still did not work, and the house phone wasn't connected either. So, she took the seniors home and went back to the hotel to call Elena.

Melissa explained to Elena that she had offered the seniors the chance to move in with her. They would have a separate furnished bedroom and a separate bathroom on the first floor. They would all eat together. In return, she asked that they do housework, cook, and help with the baby. In addition, she was willing to pay them one thousand dollars a month. Thus, they would keep their "financial aid" and be able to save up money to return to Russia.

After hanging up with Elena, Melissa waited twenty minutes and called the Trunovs. On the other end of the telephone, instead of an answer, sobbing was heard. And so, Melissa would have helpers and teachers, and George would have a good babysitters.

Melissa and her new friends moved into the readied house on Saturday, March 18. They arranged a housewarming party, inviting Sharon and Frank Smith, Marsha Roberts and her husband, Elena and her husband, and Mrs. Backinsale, all of whom came and brought gifts: a food processor and a wall clock.

Now, routine life had begun. Melissa purchased some sports equipment, which she put in the garage, and having support in cooking and homework, Melissa concentrated on preparing for the judicial translator's test. She passed the exam rather successfully, and thereafter, began in the study of the Russian language. Taking a complete plunge into the lessons, in a month, Melissa and her seniors had begun briskly communicating in a Russian-English mix.

Melissa looked perfectly. She visited Dr. Rosen, who was very happy with her, though owing to Lyudmila's efforts, she'd begun to gain a little more weight than was normal at her stage of pregnancy. It became necessary to reduce the amount of baked pies, pastries, and rolls, which were all very difficult to refuse.

Then, together with Mrs. Backinsale, Melissa chose classes for the autumn semester, developing a schedule that would allow her to take two hours of lessons, go back home to feed George and rest, and then return to school for two more hours. They decided that, instead of the regular two years of law school, Melissa would study for two and a half years. This timeframe was completely satisfactory to her.

36

Moscow, March 11, 1994

Peter Grach kept his word. He called Yakubovsky and told him that he had the member list for Nikolayev's construction brigade in the summer of 1963. Boris Goryanin's name was included. But, he said, there was also something very strange. In a folder, there was a request by Regiment Commander Major Lev Petrunin to award Boris Goryanin a medal.

Then Grach read Yakubovsky the following quotation from the request:

"I ask that Goryanin Boris Georgievick, for his demonstration of courage and heroism in the rescue of Second Lieutenant Kasatkin Ivan Vladimirovich, be awarded with a medal. Goryanin, in difficult conditions, delivered the severely wounded second lieutenant to the hospital in the village of Fedorovka, located fifty-five kilometers from the company, where he then remained with the wounded officer and repeatedly donated his blood to save the officer's life. Signed. The commander of the regiment, Major Lev Petrunin."

"So what happened?" Yakubovsky asked. "Was he awarded?"

"No. There is no resolution.... And why do you need this? After so many years have passed?"

"I am conducting an investigation in a case in which Goryanin is a main suspect," Yakubovsky thoughtfully lied. "Could you fax me copies of both the list and the request? The fax number is the same as the phone. I will switch from phone to fax mode as soon as I hang up. Just give me a couple minutes before you send it over."

In a few minutes, faxes of both documents were in Yakubovsky's hands. The circle had been completed. Vicky Koval had been born in May 1964, and Goryanin had been in the same village where she was born exactly nine months prior to her birth.

37

Nikolayev, Ukraine, July 2, 1963

Music rattled the sun-drenched platform of Nikolayev Railroad Station, as students boarded a groaning, steaming locomotive adorned with a huge banner that read, "Let's Go To Virgin Soil." The student construction brigade to Northern Kazakhstan for summer work was in progress.

At the entrance of each train car was a group leader verifying students' names on an approved list—only students who had passed all of their annual final exams could receive recommendation for this list from the Komsomol Committee, the young Communist organization that controlled all of the educational institutions in the USSR. Students were bunched in groups, childishly laughing at every occasion.

Among them, Boris Goryanin had just completed his first year at the Nikolayev branch of Odessa Polytechnic University. He had planned to transfer to Odessa Polytechnic, but the opportunity to make money in the construction brigade came up, and Boris, not hesitating, went for it. He went to see the Komsomol Committee and had his name added to the list of students wishing to go to Kazakhstan for summer work. There was but one condition: that he received good grades. After all, there were more than one thousand students who applied each year for the Nikolayev brigade, but only fifteen common cars were allocated for them.

Boris approached his car. In his backpack, he had only the most necessary things. In addition, the group leaders had ordered them to not bring along any warm clothes. When it was his turn, he presented his exam record to the group leader, who, convinced that Boris had passed all of his exams successfully, let him board. Boris decided to take the narrow shelf located on the third level. This was the worst place, which meant no one would disturb him. Finally, everybody was settled, and the locomotive howled and got underway.

The first day, the students received a chunk of bread and hot water twice.

The next day, the train arrived in the industrial Ukrainian city of Kharkov. There, the train was directed to a deadlock branch and the students were fed a hot dinner in an army kitchen: cabbage soup, barley gruel, and tasteless stewed fruits.

In Kharkov, two more cars with female students from Odessa's Economics College connected to their train. Among these bookkeeper colleagues who joined them, one skinny, long-legged girl with huge gray eyes and a ponytail caught Boris's eye. He walked by her two times but was too shy to approach. The third time, their eyes met, and they smiled at each other. But after that, they went their separate ways, and never got acquainted.

The next day, the train arrived in Syzran. Students were fed the same dinner as they'd received in Kharkov. Boris again saw the girl with the ponytail. He noticed her as soon as he left the car, and so, as they lined up for their cabbage soup, he appeared next to her, as though accidentally. Their eyes met and they exchanged smiles again. But then she was called by another girl, and walked away.

After dinner, Boris went and stood near her yet again, but this time he didn't lower his eyes. Having seen Boris, she approached him and said, "My name is Ruslana Anatolievna Katushkina. Come with us in the sixteenth car, will you? We shall play cards."

"Really?" Boris said.

"Really. For you. And your name is … "

"Boris."

"Boris, Boris. Come see us, all right?" she asked. "Will you?"

"I will. When?"

"When we get underway," she said and then escaped to her girls.

Not having shaved since their departure, Boris hastened into his car, got his shaving set, soap, and a towel, and locked himself in the restroom. He carefully shaved under a jet of cold water, and then removing his shirt, washed up. By then, the train was already underway, and people were knocking on the restroom door.

Boris walked out and then put his things back. Then he walked back several cars and found Ruslana. She was sitting on a lower shelf near another girl. Opposite them was a huge guy, and it looked as if they had been waiting for someone.

Boris shook everyone's hands and introduced himself. The guy, instead of giving his name, told Boris that everyone called him "the old man." When Boris had shook Ruslana's hand, he noticed that her hand was noticeably colder than his.

She immediately responded with, "If my hands are cold, it means my heart is hot!"

This Ruslana girl obviously had a quick tongue, Boris thought, smiling.

The four of them sat down to play cards, but Boris, being confused by Ruslana's affinity, constantly made mistakes and kept losing. When it was his turn to deal the cards, Ruslana's friend, Svetlana, encouraged him with, "Whoever loses the card game will win in love."

But eventually, after growing bored of teasing Boris about his obvious crush on Ruslana, they began to talk about other subjects of interest to second-year students. The "old man," whose name was actually Eugene, amazed Boris with the openness and boldness of his statements concerning the Communist party. He was obviously older than the others. And due to the fact that he was in love with Svetlana, Ruslana's friend, the guys easily made friends.

In the Ural city of Chelyabinsk, the train stopped, and stood all night long, letting other trains pass. Boris, by now completely enamored with Ruslana, dreamed that they would stay on this train together forever. But, from the West Siberian city of Omsk, they went to the Northern Kazakhstan city of Pavlodar, where canopied trucks equipped with benches for the transport of people, waited for them.

Boris was prepared to sit near to Ruslana, but right before loading into the truck, he caught a small frog. He approached Ruslana and outstretched it to her in his closed right hand.

"Guess what's in my hand?" he asked.

"Probably something awful," the suspicious girl answered. "Please, do not frighten me, all right?"

Boris opened his hand, and by accident, the small frog made a start with his long paws out of Boris's palm and jumped directly on Ruslana's chest. Ruslana screamed. Boris didn't know that she was deathly afraid of bugs, even butterflies, never mind mice and frogs.

"I told you not to frighten me!" she screamed. "You're crazy! Go away! And never speak to me again. I told you not to frighten me—you are a traitor!" She kept holding her heart.

And so Boris left to go sit in another truck.

The construction brigade had been divided among several farms. Boris and Ruslana, however, as fate would have it, appeared in the same farm. Ruslana remained in the central manor, together with the basic group. But Boris and twelve more guys, including Eugene, went five kilometers further up to a remote village.

There, they were taken to a huge, old barrack. Eugene noted that it was obviously a former labor-camp barrack. It turned out he was right. In front of the barrack, sitting on wooden benches, was a small group of young women, who examined the students without interest and then silently got up and walked away. Inside the barrack were three rooms. The first small room, they were told, was being used to house six prostitutes who had been sent here, from various cities, as part of their probation. The second room was small and empty. The third room was furnished with plank beds—this was to be the students' quarters. In the middle of each room, there was a free-standing cast-iron heater, with a chimney going out of a hole in the wall. At the barrack entrance, there was a huge water heater for portable water, called "Titan."

The village was terribly dirty. All of the houses were lopsided. The fences were uneven and bent. Later, the guys learned that the village had arisen in the middle of the last century. At this time, Ukrainian independent farmers had been arrested and deported into open fields by Stalin's regime. In the middle of winter, they'd been brought here to this very this barrack, and many of them didn't make it till spring.

Each student received a chunk of bread, and then everyone approached the "Titan" with his mug to get hot water. That was all they got for supper. It was late when the students finally spread out their old sleeping mats with identical pillows and, not even undressing, went straight to sleep.

Next morning, they piled into the truck and went to the central manor for orientation. In front of a village eatery, students were received by Communist party leaders and, in turn, welcomed and wished successful work and excellent rest. After that, each student received an old, shabby, cotton soldier's uniform, tarpaulin boots, and a pair of mittens, along with two pairs of socks and a cotton-padded jacket. On some soldiers' blouses, there were metal buttons with two-headed eagles, which made it clear that these regimentals had been in warehouses even before WWI.

This warm uniform, complete with boots, mittens, and a cotton-padded jacket, would not be necessary for those who worked in the kitchen, however, and so the young women, including Ruslana, were not given one.

Boris tried talking to Ruslana a few times, but each time she made it absolutely, categorically clear that she didn't wish to speak with the traitor ever again. Each time, he would respect her wishes and leave, but he never missed her from a distance. Several of these times, Boris noticed that she seemed to be searching for him, but then whenever their sights met, she turned away. Boris then turned away too.

And so the life of the student construction brigade began. They got up at six o'clock, had a half an hour for gathering, and a more-than-simple breakfast of a chunk of bread and hot water. Then they worked from seven to midday. For lunch, it was another swill of water, slop made of leftovers, and the remains of stewed fruits. Then they worked until six. For supper, it was the same chunk of bread with hot water. For teenagers such a lean diet was obviously insufficient. Everyone constantly felt famished.

The presence of the prostitutes rendered no influence over the students;

the students were not interested in them, and the feeling appeared to be mutual. However, the managers of the students' brigade, having found out about the prostitutes, moved into a small room in the barrack. Consequently, they didn't work, but instead constantly partied with the prostitutes, getting drunk and leaving with the girls. Such an environment did little to promote strengthening student morals.

38

Northern Kazakhstan, Summer of 1963

Goryanin's group had to build a granary. Actually, it was to be an impressive-sized concrete platform with walls and a roof. The students manually—with picks, pickaxes, and shovels—had to dig trenches for a seven-foot deep foundation, fill them with rebar and hard boulders, and prepared them for the pouring of concrete. To pour the concrete, they would have to prepare cement, sand, and gravel in a mixer with water. Then the concrete mixture would be carried by hand in vats and poured down into the trenches. Students with previous construction experience supervised the process.

Boris was ordered to bring powdered cement. The cement to be loaded on a three-axel rear-dump truck capable of transporting up to ten tons of loose material. The cement storage facility was in the village of Fedorovka, located approximately sixty kilometers from their village, and there wasn't a road between them. Therefore, a one-way trip through the virgin land took almost two hours.

In the cement storage facility, the truck backed up under a loading platform. From a cylindrical silo, cement powder seeped down onto a platform, and from there, the cement was loaded into the truck. The scale that normally measured the cement portions didn't work anymore, so the truck's driver, Vasily Ohryamkin, told Boris, "It has to be loaded by shovel—twelve hundred shovels is the right amount. I counted them personally." And so while Boris loaded cement powder, the driver peacefully lay under his truck and dozed.

Fedorovka amazed Boris. All of the streets were clean. The houses were bleached and their windows and doors painted. Children wore shoes, and even geese wandered down the streets with seeming advantage.

Boris asked the driver, "What's the deal?"

The answer was simple. "They are German. They are not like other people."

The afternoon was scorching. Boris had to undress down to his belt, and tried to fill the truck as soon as possible so they could leave—all twelve hundred shovels took a mere three hours. But by the time they returned to the central manor, dinner had already finished. The boilers stood empty, and nobody was in the dining room. Only Ruslana with some other girls washed dishes. Except for a few random pieces of bread, there wasn't anything else. Boris left the dining room, not saying good-bye to anyone. And though he was terribly hungry, he hadn't taken any bread.

The next day, Boris took with him to the job site a tape measure, a few pieces of paper, and a pencil. He drew a sketch of the platform onto which all of the cement fell, and then measured the distance from it up to the spout. While loading cement into the truck that afternoon, he was concentrating on something.

This day was even warmer than the previous, way over a hundred degrees, and after loading the truck, Boris was terribly thirsty. Right next to the cement storehouse was a hospital. He went in to ask for some water. Nobody was there, except a nurse. Boris liked the young, rather attractive blonde at once. He introduced himself and asked her name. The young woman, not much older than Boris, replied that her name was Frieda Nushke.

"Frieda Nushke?" Boris asked, noticing that she was reading the German newspaper *Der Welt.* Boris had taught German at school, and although he couldn't speak it fluently, he could read it well enough. He asked her for a glass of water, and while drinking it, he learned from the nurse that the Germans had appeared in the middle of this huge steppe in 1934. Frieda told him that her parents, her husband's parents, and all of their other relatives had been relocated here from the town of Gross Libentale, near Odessa. That's why the village now consisted of Germans, she said.

Boris thanked Frieda for the water and, saying good-bye as a gallant gentleman should, for the first time in his life, he kissed the woman's hand. Her hand was soft and supple, as she was. Frieda blushed and told Boris not to hesitate to come see her at any time.

When Boris returned to the barracks, Ruslana approached him in the dining room and told him that instead of pretending to be the prince of Spain, he should have for lunch what she had saved for him. Boris said nothing, but accepted a full tray of food. After lunch, he began to search for her. She was gone, and he had to leave to continue unloading cement.

That evening, Boris made some obscure construction sketches. He drew in details and counted meters. Next morning, he and driver Vasily loaded the truck with lumber, sheets of plywood, and galvanized steel. He took a saw, hammer, nails, and other carpenter's tools.

Then, when they arrived that morning, instead of loading cement into the truck, Boris and Vasily assembled a large inclined trench of sort, which they installed onto the platform right under the concrete silo. The top part of the trench was directly under the silo, and the bottom of the trench would cantilever onto two-thirds of the truck. The truck would back up under the bottom end of the trench, then someone on the platform would slightly open the silo hatch, and the cement would fall down onto the curved galvanized steel trench into the open truck. Passersby in the village attentively watched to see what Boris and Vasily were engaged in, and as a token of approval, many gave them a thumbs-up.

After constructing the trench, they had less than a half an hour left before lunch to fill the truck, but they were late anyway. As she had yesterday, however, Ruslana expected Boris to be back late, and when he finally arrived, she silently brought him a tray with his lunch. Now Boris didn't even to try to speak to her, having decided that she didn't like him at all.

The next day, they quickly filled the truck, after which the driver told Boris that he was going to take a short break. So Boris went to visit Frieda. There were no patients in the hospital, and the doctor was in his office, so Frieda was bored. For more than an hour, Boris chatted with the pretty woman. Frieda told him that she was married to Johann Schmidt, but that now he was in trade school learning to become a smith. Boris told her about his university, about the city of Nikolayev, and about his plans to go to Odessa Polytechnic University. It was interesting to both of them to learn about different lives.

After this, every day, Boris quickly loaded the truck with cement, and then, while the driver had a nap, he would go to see Frieda. He would talk about history and tell her stories. And, somehow, on one such visit, Boris and Frieda started to kiss. A week later, Frieda led Boris into a dark room and made him a man. All of his subsequent trips to Fedorovka ended in this same dark room.

His relationship with Frieda changed Boris's private world. He hadn't forgotten about Ruslana, but had ceased dreaming about her.

Ruslana, having noted that Boris wasn't trying to talk to her anymore, resolved that she had tormented him long enough, and began to search for an occasion to talk to him. But there was no occasion. And her pride wouldn't allow her to start speaking to Boris out of the blue.

By now, Vasily had taught Boris to drive the truck, so Boris had taken up driving from their village to Fedorovka and back, while the driver peacefully dozed beside him. All the while, Boris studied the path so that he eventually knew every hump and hollow. And once they arrived in Fedorovka, Boris continued to spend time with Frieda in their dark room.

Then about a month after the students had arrived, on August first, the students received their first salary. Having received his money, Boris went directly to the general store. He purchased a Chinese-made rabbit-fur hat, a pair of warm gloves, and a small green frog. Boris still hoped to reconcile with Ruslana. But, like Ruslana, Boris could not find an occasion to begin speaking to her, though he regularly ate the lunches that Ruslana saved for him.

A week after receiving their salaries, the students finished the slab. There was no need for more concrete and thus no need for Boris and his new buddy Vasily to drive to Fedorovka. Therefore, Boris had ceased to meet Frieda.

The granary walls were made from lumber reinforced with plywood and were erected in three days. For insulation, they used dry cane, and a carpentry crew was to construct triangular frames for the roof. But the plywood for the frames wasn't delivered in time, so Boris, officially recognized as the resident longshoreman, went with Vasily to Fedorovka. There, they learned that plywood wasn't necessary, as the roof was already made of iron, which would suffice. It contradicted common sense. Metal sheets nailed to plywood would be much stronger, especially considering the gusty winds and winter snowstorms of this area. So Boris and Vasily visited the local building authorities and within few minutes received approval to use plywood.

The two men loaded the plywood quickly, and then Vasily, as usual, lay down to nap. Boris rushed to Frieda. She told him that her husband would return tomorrow and that they wouldn't be able to meet anymore. The sentimental Frieda had a little cry, and then, after their love-making, not unnoticed by Boris, she simply remained in the bed—when before she had always run off to wash up.

Frieda just looked at him and said that her husband was still an unskilled boy, and that she wished that any child she had could, instead, be as clever as Boris.

"Do you want a child from me?" Boris was surprised. "And what about your husband?"

"He wouldn't know. He comes back tomorrow, so the baby could just as well be his."

Then Boris left Frieda feeling absolutely powerless and fell asleep in truck next to his comrade.

On August 8, soldiers arrived on huge trucks to help farmers transport grain from their fields to the granary, and, later, to a grain elevator. Right next to the unfinished granary, the soldiers installed large military tents, and by the next day had already started to carry grain. But then the weather deteriorated. Cold gusts ran through the steppe, and there was a harbinger of approaching heavy rain. So the soldiers joined with the students to bring in more hay, stacking up the sheaves as high and tight as possible to insulate the granary walls. Eugene advised them to install plywood on the walls before stocking the sheaves, but nobody listened.

It became really cold that evening, especially after sunset, and the students used the cast-iron heater in the barrack for the first time.

A couple days later, Boris noticed Ruslana running from the girls' barrack to the dining room, shivering from cold. Right then, he made a decision that only a person with pure feelings of interest could make: he had to help Ruslana. After lunch, he went to the general store and purchased a Chinese-made goose-down jacket, tall winter boots, a warm sports' suit, two pairs of socks, and warm mittens. He wished to buy Ruslana a fur hat, as well, but the store was out of stock. So instead, he bought her a woolen scarf and a large chocolate bar.

Boris packed his purchases into the cardboard box that the saleswoman gave him, and then carted it all to his barrack. He didn't show anybody what was in the box.

That evening, after work, he got a notebook, pulled out a sheet of paper, and, carefully considering each word, wrote a letter to Ruslana. He wrote that he was in love with her and could not live without her. Then Boris put his letter, together with the small plastic frog that he had purchased earlier and the chocolate bar, in an internal pocket of Ruslana's new jacket, where they weren't visible and couldn't be tampered with.

From the next room, had heard drunken shouts and loud laughter. The management had been partying with the prostitutes all day, but nobody did anything about it. They were all so used to this way of life by now.

Next day, when the students went to lunch, Boris carried the box of gifts to Ruslana's barrack. There was nobody. He put the box on her bed and left. But then, by some strange coincidence, he ran into Ruslana at the entrance to the dining hall. She was shivering from the cold. He greeted her, and this time, she didn't try to escape. On the contrary, she told him that she had been waiting for him and then asked him to come to see her that evening. Then she told him she would like to celebrate with him tomorrow on Builder's Day.

"Peace?" Ruslana asked, stretching out her cold hand.

He took it and agreed. "Peace."

He wanted to embrace Ruslana and kiss her, but he restrained himself. Instead, he only took her hands in his, warming them. Ruslana didn't oppose. He brought her hands to his mouth, breathed on them, and kissed them.

Ruslana, for an instant, nestled into Boris, but then whispered, "Please, not now. Later, darling, later!"

Boris kept silent about the gift he had purchased for her. Let it be a surprise, he thought. Tonight, he would tell her everything.

Ruslana found the box when she returned from kitchen duty, and asked the girls who had brought her the wonderful things. But they didn't know. Then a guy named Vadim, who was always following her around those days, told her that he had received them for her in the warehouse. Ruslana, a simple soul, believed him, and didn't think to look into the jacket's internal pocket.

The next day was considered Builder's Day, which meant contractors usually had the day off, but considering the unusually cold weather, and the expectation for heavy rains any day, Boris and many others would work anyway, as they needed to hurry to finish the granary. Nevertheless, that evening, Boris sacrificed a good night's sleep and went to see Ruslana. What did sleep mean when you were going to see your beloved girl?

Heading toward Ruslana's barrack, Boris saw her at a distance, among a group of people. She was dressed in the warm clothes that he had bought for her. Then, as he came closer, he saw a guy tried to embrace Ruslana. It was that disgusting Vadim. Boris was ready to kill the guy, but he turned around and walked back.

Ruslana, having noticed that Boris had seen it, pulled away from Vadim and ran for Boris, but Boris was not looking back. She called him, but Boris only picked up his pace and ran away from her as fast as he could.

At this moment, Boris hated himself for his weakness. But there was nothing else that he could bring himself to do.

39

Northern Kazakhstan, Summer 1963

It was dark when Boris returned. Approaching the barrack door, he heard a weak groan. Boris peered in and, on the right side of the entrance an officer lay in a pool of blood, the handle of a table knife sticking out of his chest. He could smell the strong scent of vodka.

Taking a closer look, Boris recognized him. It was the second lieutenant—the company commander. He had made friends with some of the Komsomol leaders and even drank with them. But now, it seemed, the party had ended.

There was no telephone in the barrack, or even in the village. So Boris ran into his barrack and found his friend Eugene on his plank bed reading a book.

"Eugene, there's a problem. The second lieutenant has been wounded. We have to save him."

"The hell with him!" Eugene snapped. "It's not our business. Let his buddies figure it out."

"What is wrong with you? He is human!"

"Yeah? And would this human have tried to save you?"

"Eugene, please help me to take him to the hospital. He will die!"

"Well, you are quite the hero, aren't you? Whatever. All right, let's go."

While Boris outside, Eugene stayed with the wounded man. Boris rushed to the truck, still loaded halfway with hay, and grabbed the key off of its usual spot on the driver's seat. He turned the engine. Fortunately, it had a full tank of gas. Then, without letting it warm up, Boris drove back to the barrack, where he and Eugene cautiously lifted the man and lay him on the hay. Eugene sat in the truck bed with him, and off they went to Fedorovka.

Boris tried to go as quickly as possible, but in the dark, the path was harder to see, and he wanted to make sure he was taking them the right way. Then Eugene began to knock on the cabin's roof. Boris stopped.

"I need a rope," Eugene said. "He's leg's bleeding badly, and I need to elevate it."

Boris reached behind the driver's seat, where there was virtually everything you could ever want, including a tick rope. Boris handed the rope back to Eugene, and then continued driving in total darkness. They reached Fedorovka in forty minutes.

The hospital was barely visible in the dark. Boris pulled up to the porch, stopped the truck, and ran in to awake the doctor. In five minutes, the three of them had retrieved a stretcher and brought the wounded officer into the hospital.

"Run for Frieda," the doctor told Boris, and he started to prepare for surgery.

Frieda lived nearby. She didn't expect to see Boris, but she understood the problem at once. They rushed together to the hospital, and by the time they arrived, the wounded man was already on the surgery table. Eugene was on the phone with the police.

The doctor administered a general anesthetic, and then, together with Frieda, started to operate. First, they had to remove the knife from his chest, but before that, the doctor took two photos of the chest with the knife in it. Then he carefully wrapped the handle in a sterile napkin to pull it to preserve the stabber's fingerprints.

The police officer arrived ten minutes later, recorded Boris's and Eugene's stories, and left to get the inspector.

The doctor came out of the surgery room and told Boris and Eugene that things didn't look good. The wound in the chest wasn't dangerous, as the kitchen knife had been ground off and, by sheer luck, hadn't harmed any of the body's vital organs. But the wound in his leg had cut an artery and led to the loss of a lot of blood, which meant the officer's heart could stop any minute. A blood transfusion was required immediately.

The doctor explained, however, that the officer's blood was Type O, while Frieda and Eugene both had Type A. Boris didn't know what type he had, but offered to have his blood drawn for analysis. Frieda let Boris in the surgery room, where the wounded man lay unconscious. His facial features were pointed, and the mask of death had already appeared. Frieda wiped Boris's hand with alcohol and searched for a vein. After a few minutes, the analysis showed that his blood was Type O.

The doctor decided to perform a direct transfusion from Boris's vein into the officer's. So Frieda searched for a vein on Boris's other hand, while simultaneously inserting a needle into the wounded man. By now, the doctor had cleaned and stitched the man's cut leg, and applied dressing. And within seconds, Boris's blood, drop by drop, flowed into the wounded man, turning his cheeks pink. Boris, on the contrary, began to turn pale. The doctor watched both men's pulse and blood pressure, until, at last, he said, "Enough." It had become impossible to take more blood from Boris.

He requested Boris drink a hot tea that they made him, and then Eugene stayed with Boris, while the doctor tended to the wounded man, and Frieda ran home to cook them all a good meal.

The police inspector arrived soon after. When he found out that the wounded man was the army officer, he called the military prosecutor's office, but nobody knew the second lieutenant's name.

Then the inspector interrogated Eugene. Eugene reported that in the barrack where they lived, drunkenness and easy behavior by the managers of the student construction brigade was a usual phenomenon. The Komsomol leaders, Eugene told him, never worked, but spent all their time with the prostitutes. This second lieutenant had joined their company just the evening before, so, in his opinion, they had fought over the women.

The inspector asked who found the wounded man first, and Eugene told him that Boris had come running into the barrack and had persuaded him to help him take the officer to the hospital. And he told the inspector that Boris had driven the truck with the wounded officer through the dark to get here. The doctor confirmed that the wounded man was highly intoxicated and that Boris was totally sober. So the inspector had a short discussion with Boris and then took his fingerprints in order to exclude Boris from being a suspect.

At dawn, the inspector called the police team and ordered them to detain all of the participants of last night's party. Then Eugene asked the inspector to give him a ride back to the farm, and they left.

Frieda came with a hot meal. She asked Boris to drink some hot chicken soup and beer with sour cream, and then had him eat raw eggs. In an hour, she gave him more beer with sour cream and a piece of bread with bacon. Boris washed it down with hot tea and, after the sleepless night, fell fast asleep. While he slept, Frieda sat near Boris, looking at him and whispering something in German.

The police arrested four Komsomol leaders, who were all still drunk and couldn't remember anything that had happened the night before. The prostitutes, however, confirmed that the men had been drinking so much that they had passed out on the table. All except for Ivan Vladimirovich Kasatkin (as the second lieutenant's name turned out to be), who'd had a fistfight with Paul Kuznetsov. The subject of the argument was: who could farthest take a leak from their spot on the porch. Eventually, the very drunk Paul seized a knife. Ivan was the one to hit first, but then Paul stuck him with the knife, first in the leg and then in the chest. To the question about why the girls hadn't tried to separate them and help the wounded man, the amicable answer was that this was cop's business, and they had already had their sentences.

The police hadn't found Paul Kuznetsov. His belongings had disappeared too. So Kuznetsov was added to the list of Most Wanted. Eventually, he would be located in Pavlodar, arrested, and sentenced to three years in camp.

The investigator from the military prosecutor's office arrived at the hospital by the end of the day. He interrogated Boris, Frieda, and the doctor Konstantin Murashov. Ivan Kasatkin had gradually come to his senses, after which the investigator spent almost an hour with him, recording his every word. The ensuing events of this interrogation were as follows: Ivan, nervous and stressed out, jerked out some of the stitches on his leg, sending blood gushing from the open wound. While the investigator called the doctor and the doctor tried to stop the bleeding, Ivan lost consciousness, and his blood pressure fell to critical levels. The doctor then made the unique decision to take Boris's blood again.

Boris was rushed into the surgery room, where, Frieda, trying to find a vein in a rush, made several punctures, until she found blood at last. By the time the transfusion had finished, Boris was also close to losing consciousness, but Ivan had been saved.

The inspector had to go to the farm to complete his inspection of Boris. He already knew that Boris had saved the officer's life, first, by finding him, and second, by driving him to the hospital in the dark, and finally, by giving him two blood transfusions. But the process of closing the case against Boris demanded a final element: Ruslana's interrogation—as Eugene had told him that Boris, before finding the wounded officer, had been with her.

When the inspector arrived at the kitchen workers' barrack, it was late. He found Ruslana in a group of people walking around the camp. The inspector introduced himself, took Ruslana aside, and asked her to go with him into the barrack, where they could talk in private. Ruslana knew nothing about what had happened to Boris.

Inside the barrack, the two sat at a table, and after formally announcing the interrogation, the inspector asked her about the nature of her relationship with Boris and about when she had seen him last. In the beginning, Ruslana didn't understand what was happening and just joked around, but finally she realized that something serious was going on. She told him that Boris had come to see her, but that she was with some guys at the time, and so Boris, possibly jealous, had left. The inspector asked Ruslana whether she thought Boris was capable of killing a person. Ruslana categorically answered no.

She then asked the inspector what had actually happened. The inspector told her that Boris had saved the life of an army officer, but that now he was in critical condition from giving a lot of blood to the wounded man. Ruslana reacted in fear, impulsively pressing her hands to her chest, and as she did, she felt something firm in her jacket pocket. She reached into the pocket and took out a chocolate bar, a small plastic frog, and a folded piece of notebook paper.

Having opened the paper, she scanned through the lines written by Boris. Now, she understood all. She understood that it had been Boris who had bought her the warm clothes and delivered them on her bed. She understood the depth of feeling that Boris felt for her. And so, she burst out crying. First, she began to cry silently, and then cried more loudly. The inspector took the letter from Ruslana's hands and read through it, and then offered to take Ruslana, if she wanted the hospital where Boris was.

"Frieda will not be able to take care of two patients by herself, anyway," he said.

Ruslana asked him to wait two minutes. She rushed to grab a suitcase, into which she put a dress, a change of linens, some socks, a toothbrush, and slippers. She only had time to tell Svetlana that Boris was in the hospital, that he had saved the life of an officer, and that he loved her. And then, not looking back, she ran out to find the military car.

At the exit of her barrack, she met Vadim, who blocked her way, and playfully, with both hands, seized her by the waist. Ruslana took her elbow to his solar plexus with such force that he lost interest in playing games. Then not explaining, she scurried off to the waiting car.

"What's the matter with her?" Vadim asked Svetlana. "Is she mad or what?"

"Her Boris is in trouble," she answered. "He is in the hospital. He has saved someone's life, but has suffered himself."

"So what's it to her?" Vadim asked with surprise.

"She doesn't have any interest in you. She loves him."

"What? I don't get it!"

"Well, Vadim, that's because you are stupid!" Svetlana summed up.

The military inspector and Ruslana arrived at the hospital at about midnight. They knocked on the door. Having seen Ruslana, Frieda understood everything. She had always felt that Boris was in love with another woman. But this was a girl. Then again, he wasn't much older than that.

The inspector asked Frieda's permission for Ruslana to spend the night in the hospital, as Ruslana rushed off to wash her hands and change into a dressing gown, silently sobbing.

"How is Boris?" she asked Frieda when she had returned.

"He'll be better tomorrow. Both his hands are swollen. He can't move them. He gave a lot of blood, and he needs to restore his energy. Tomorrow, he'll be better."

"Let me take care of him, please. I will help you. I can do anything you want," Ruslana said, wiping tears from her cheeks.

"You don't need to cry," the inspector told her. "Your guy is the hero. You should be proud!"

"Go to him," Frieda said, gently moving Ruslana toward the door of Boris's room.

Boris was on his back, semiconscious. In the twilight of the room, in the glow of a nightlight, Ruslana could make out Boris's thick hands covered in iodine.

"Let's give him tea," Frieda offered, as she came in. "He should drink a lot. And we will drink some with him."

"Is it possible for me to pass?" Ruslana objected.

"But he needs you to be healthy. He is absolutely weak."

"Well, all right. Is it possible for me to give him the tea then, first? And then when he is finished, I will have mine."

Frieda called the inspector to join them, and then poured hot water into three cups. Ruslana carried one cup to Boris and tried to wake silently him, but he just moaned.

"Sweetheart, you will recover, won't you?" she said sweetly. "I promise I will not abuse you anymore. From now on, I shall be with you always. I don't need anybody else. Only you. You. You are mine." Ruslana, after giving vent to her feelings, started to kiss Boris.

Boris, feeling someone kissing him, soon realized that it Ruslana. He opened his eyes. "Do the warm clothes I got fit you? Are they warm enough?"

"Please, drink the tea. I am warm. And I shall be with you always."

Boris drank his tea. "Ruslana, dear. Please call Frieda. I need to tell her something."

"You can tell me."

"No. Please, call Frieda. I cannot tell you," he whispered.

Ruslana called Frieda, who came at once and bent over Boris. "I understand," she said, before Boris had said a word. Then turning to Ruslana, she said, "He needs to go to restroom. He cannot do it on his own, as his hands are not working. His fingers do not bend."

Then Frieda did a small trick. She retrieved a night-pot from under the bed, raised Boris, and, having removed the blanket on him, in front of the girl, dexterously helped him relieve himself. Ruslana groaned quietly. She had never seen an exposed man in her life.

Boris sighed too. He became confused his nakedness.

Frieda then rolled in a hospital cot and arranged it next to Boris's bed. Ruslana lay on the cot, put her hand on Boris's shoulder, and fell asleep. During the night, she woke up several times and had him drink water. Meanwhile, Frieda ran between Ivan and Boris all night long.

By morning, Boris was worse. His hands had swelled to the point that it seemed the skin would burst. His temperature had risen to 104 degrees Fahrenheit. Frieda called the doctor.

The doctor said he would have to order an injection of penicillin, as there were only seven doses of five hundred thousand units each in this rural hospital. The doctor made an emergency telephone call to the military hospital and asked them to send him two courses of penicillin treatment: one for Second Lieutenant Ivan Kasatkin and another for Boris Goryanin.

The person on the other line refused to comply with the doctor's request, saying that all medicines from their stock were available exclusive for military patients. So the doctor awoke the inspector, who had stayed at the hospital, and declared that if he didn't receive the requested treatment, both Ivan and Boris could be lost to gangrene. The inspector called the military hospital. He introduced himself to the person on duty, and then promptly threatened to press criminal charges for negligence on all hospital management unless they immediately allocated the necessary medication for the rescue of two Soviet citizens. By midday, a special military messenger on a motorcycle had delivered a box of penicillin.

Ivan was now in better condition than Boris. Ivan's body had not been weakened by long weeks of starvation, and Boris had developed an abscess that could be terminal if it grew into either gangrene or a blood infection. The next forty-eight hours were critical.

Boris raved, constantly calling for Ruslana, even though she hadn't left his side for a minute. She patiently moistened napkins in cool water and put them on Boris's forehead. From fever, he continuously poured with sweat, and Ruslana kept removing his wet hospital gowns and replacing them with dry ones, no longer hesitating about his nakedness.

Frieda brought Ruslana and Ivan homemade pie and Boris raw eggs. But Ruslana refused to eat.

Frieda, senior in age and more experienced, shouted at her; it was necessary that Ruslana concede.

But Boris could not eat at all. He drank only warm, sweet water.

And so passed one more day. The doctor administered five hundred thousand units of penicillin to Boris every four hours, but his condition did not improve. That night, the doctor remained with Boris. He ordered Ruslana to sleep in another room and Frieda to look after Ivan.

That night, Boris was in crisis mode. He raved, shivering in fever, pouring with sweat. Then the illness receded. Completely weakened, he fell asleep by morning and slept almost twenty-four hours. He didn't wake up even when receiving injections.

Early the next morning, he awoke and saw Ruslana next to him. He looked at her with surprise. Her presence was the best medicine for him. Ruslana told him that Frieda had been working nonstop for days and that the doctor had released her for a day.

Ivan still could not get up, but his pain was now tolerable. The doctor's wife cooked a chicken for them, and Ruslana drank both Ivan's and Boris's broth. She had quickly grown accustomed to the hospital. She washed all of the hospital gowns and bed sheets, and cleaned the floors in every room. But every free minute she had, she went to see Boris. They had met only eight weeks ago, and though they did not talk for nearly a month, within the last few days they had become so close, it were as if they had known each other all their lives.

The regiment commander, Major Lev Ivanovich Petrunin, came to visit his second lieutenant, Ivan Kasatkin. Being a man of action, he brought three bottles of cognac and three bottles of vodka; a bag of onions, a bag of carrots, and a bag of potatoes; a large bottle of vegetable oil; two big loaves of bread, a box of apples, and a box of military-packaged stewed pork; and a box of condensed milk. The major, who had long abused Ivan, told him that since this was his first time he was forgiven, but that the next time he would send him to the military tribunal.

Lev then thanked Boris for saving the life of a Soviet officer. For such a feat during wartime, Boris would be decorated with a military award, the major told him. Having estimated Boris's condition, he promised to strive for a free voucher in a sanatorium; "for two vouchers, in fact," he said, winking at Ruslana. Then saying good-bye, he gallantly clicked his heels, kissed Ruslana's hand, and told them he would be back.

The next day, Ivan was taken for treatment in the military hospital. They suggested Boris go too, but he refused because he didn't want to go without Ruslana and, besides, this rural doctor had exceptional skill. He was honest and sincere, and his wife cooked tasty food, on which Boris and Ruslana both gained weight.

For Boris, returning to work wasn't even an option. His hands still hurt, and even the smallest weight on them caused him sharp pain.

On Sunday, Eugene and Svetlana came to visit and brought Boris's and Ruslana's belongings. Seeing how Ruslana stuck constantly to Boris, and how he hardly took his eyes off of her, Eugene and Svetlana understood all.

"Looks like a wedding is coming," Eugene whispered to Svetlana as they said their good-byes.

Not a week had passed when true autumn had come. Cold, gusty wind and heavy rain became a daily reality, and the students couldn't work outside anymore. So the leaders made the decision to send the construction brigades back home. The management issued disability money to Boris and paid Ruslana for patient care. Then they sent a car to pick up both of them.

Boris and Ruslana said warm good-byes to Frieda, the doctor, and his wife, at which point Frieda burst into tears and ordered Ruslana to look well after Boris and to take good care of him. That she was pregnant, Frieda never told Boris. And since that day, they never saw each other again.

Boris and Ruslana didn't leave each other for even one day after that. Together, they went from Odessa to Nikolayev, so that Ruslana could get acquainted with Boris's mother and sister.

Boris was transferred to Odessa Polytechnic University and simultaneously started work for a foundry. The couple married in December, and in August, their son Anton was born. But that, as they say, is another story.

40

California, April 4, 1994

Melissa was on her twenty-second week of pregnancy. At her next check-up she brought Dr. Rosen copies of her medical records from Grangettes Hospital. The doctor closely examined her and asked her pointed questions about her sexual life. Melissa frankly told the doctor about the circumstances around which she had lost her virginity and about the sadistic bents of her former groom, but clarified that, as a matter of fact she had only had one man in her life from whom she had received pleasure and love.

Based on her story, Dr. Rosen told Melissa that, in his opinion, it would be preferable that she deliver via a planned caesarean section. It would be hard for her to pursue natural childbirth, he said, as even under normal circumstances, there could be ruptures and the possibility of complications.

Melissa thought for a minute and asked, "Won't that be painful?"

"On the contrary. It will be much easier to you. The surgery will happen under anesthesia. You will not be able to feel any discomfort. It will allow us to eliminate any unexpected risks, and the day can be chosen in advance. Your current due date is somewhere between June 23 and 28, so we'd need to pick a date within that timeframe, and don't forget that July 4 is Independence Day, and the hospital is always overloaded on that day. So let's try to schedule the birth before then. Say, June 27. You will come in the morning and stay for about five days."

"Doctor, I am so scared!"

"Don't worry, dear," the doctor said in a calming tone. "For me, your birth will be …" Dr. Rosen looked in his calendar "… number two thousand eight hundred and seventeen."

"Is that true?" Melissa asked with surprise and admiration.

Now that George's birthday had been scheduled, the reality that, at last, she would see her baby became both scary and joyful to Melissa. It made her want to meet Boris awfully, as she had learned some time ago that they were no more than one and a half miles from each other … but then, they were just as far apart.

Having returned from the doctor, Melissa whispered with Lyudmila about her appointment. Her dialogue with the seniors had become easy, and she now felt their sincere care for her—and she always replied in kind. Melissa knew almost three hundred Russian words, had learned the alphabet, and fluently read a standard grammar school textbook. Every day, she intended to learn ten new words, and not just learn them, but diligently write them out several times.

Melissa spoke often by phone with Sharon, but they also met once a month. In addition, Melissa had taken upon herself a new rule: to call her father two times a week, on Tuesdays and Fridays, at eight o'clock in the evening, London's time. Sir Spencer grew used to this schedule and was always pleased to receive Melissa's calls. He waited with excitement for Melissa to give birth to her son, too. He had planned to come to see Melissa in California by autumn, when the baby would be a few months old. Then he would be able to communicate with his grandson.

41

Moscow, April 4, 1994

Yakubovsky checked into the municipal court for the decision on his divorce with Natalie and carried the official court document to the regional records office. There, he received the divorce certificate and rushed to the regional police office to get a divorce stamp on his internal passport.

Almost two months had passed since Yakubovsky had moved in with Victoria. And, as a matter of fact, it was the first time in his life that he really was in love with a woman.

Victoria, feeling this from Vlad, reciprocated. Together, they bought him nice clothes for the office, so that he always looked sharp and tasteful. Besides, Victoria regularly washed and ironed his clothes, so Yakubovsky always was looked a well groomed. His whole look and demeanor had changed so much that colleagues began to notice.

In general, through his relationship with Vicky, Yakubovsky had become a different person. First he quit drinking, and now Victoria had insisted he quit smoking. As a first step, he reduced his daily limit from two packs to five cigarettes. He also tried very hard to regularly purchase groceries for them, and even to cook and wash the dishes. In truth, he very much liked to love the young woman and to be loved by her.

Their apartment was always clean and cozy, and they tried to give their breakfasts and suppers together some class, preparing meals and table settings with soul and mood. And on their days off, when Igor and Ann came to see them, Victoria and Vladislav achieved near miracles of cooking. They looked every bit the ideal couple. Vladislav was, it seemed to him, happy… although, each time he saw Ann, he still got butterflies in his stomach.

Often enough, Yakubovsky met with Kravchuk, who always drank, but Yakubovsky, remembering his promise to Vicky, was never moved to temptation. Their conversations revolved around ways to realize their plan, for which purpose Yakubovsky also had met bankers, entrepreneurs, and traders, and the project gradually began to materialize.

Then, in the middle of February, Kravchuk introduced Yakubovsky to Alexey Semenov, an expert on export-import projects. After the break-up of the Soviet Union in August 1991, Alexey Semenov had conducted some successful commercial transactions and thus restored his self-confidence. Consequently, he had even begun to speak and walk very slowly and deliberately, with the quality of someone who looked like he knew what he was doing. Anyway, he was a person with connections.

Kravchuk told Alexey that he and Vladislav were considering the purchase of wheat, but could only buy twenty-five thousand tons of high-quality wheat for no more than two hundred dollars a ton. In other words, they were looking for a five-million-dollar contract.

"Two hundred dollars a ton?" declared Alexey. "That's tough, dear comrades. But the inquiry has been made, so we shall work on it. How you are planning to pay?"

Kravchuk made a gesture signifying that all had been arranged with the Ministry of Economic Development and the Central Bank.

"You only need worry about the price and guarantee of delivery," Semenov told them, concluding their conversation.

Thus, a loan amount of five and a half million dollars was determined. Now, one small thing remained: they needed to find a lender ready to participate in the transaction and start work on the contract.

On April 5, Yakubovsky left his office and rushed to a meeting with the manager of the commercial loan department of Food Commerce Bank. There was the usual April weather, cold, with penetrating gusts. The sun wasn't visible, shielded by heavy, dark clouds. Countless snowdrifts of dirty snow rose up on every horizon. The bank was on Zholtovsky Street, about a half an hour's drive.

Having parked his car with its fender sticking halfway into a snowdrift, Yakubovsky, dressed in a lamb parka, got out, and put on the big fur hat that would save his life. Coincidentally, Alexander Pushkov, fired from the FSB, had gotten a job as a security guard at Food Commerce Bank, and today was his shift as the outdoor watchman.

Now, Pushkov, recognizing Yakubovsky as soon as he had left his car, shouted, "I'll get you, you reptile!" and then swung his rubber baton directly onto Yakubovsky's head. Yakubovsky fell, and Pushkov continued to strike him nonstop. Finally, some other security guards, who had come running upon hearing the commotion, arrived on the scene and dragged Pushkov away. Meanwhile, a bank employee called an ambulance for the unconscious Yakubovsky.

Having found out that Yakubovsky was the senior officer of the Service of External Intelligence, the ambulance driver took him to the same military hospital he had been in right before New Year's. Alexander Pushkov was sent to jail in Moscow's Central District.

It wasn't until the next evening that Victoria managed to find out what had happened to him. Having been delivered to the hospital with numerous bruises, broken bones, and a concussion, Yakubovsky remained unconscious for a few days. Personnel at the military hospital reported to Yakubovsky's office what had happened. Not having been informed about his divorce, the office called and informed Natalie, who then called Igor and told him that his father was in the intensive care unit at the military hospital.

By that time, Victoria had already called the police, and all of the hospitals and morgues, but nobody knew anything. So after hearing from Igor, Vicky requested a leave from work and rushed off to the hospital. But the hospital personnel wouldn't let her in. At last, Victoria understood what they were looking for. She gave the paramedic on duty five dollars, then she immediately put on the clean white dressing gown he handed her and asked to see Yakubovsky.

Upon seeing Vladislav with a swollen face, wrapped in bandages, and connected to all sorts of medical devices, poor Victoria began to sob until, to her relief, Igor arrived with Ann. Since morning, they had been detained by the paramedic on duty, until they too had given him money. Somehow, Igor and Anna calmed her. But when she learned that it was Pushkov who had done the damage, she found no limit to her indignation. Again this ill-fated Pushkov had dare cross her path.

As the doctors in the hospital were virtually wrestling for Yakubovsky's life, news of the whole scandal burst out in the Central Administrative Board of the Service of External Intelligence. There, it had become known that, on February 21 at the Dulles Airport, during an attempt to board a flight to Europe, an invaluable agent had been arrested—and that, quite possibly, it had been that same agent whom Yakubovsky had contacted in the summer of 1993.

The director thus raised one simple question: who was the agent's curator? Yakubovsky? And where was he? The director's secretary started the search for their suspect and traced him to the military hospital. What was he doing there, and moreover, for the second time in the last half a year? What was he involved in? And why was he never in the office?

No one could come up with an intelligible answer, and so, in general, the director made an executive decision: Yakubovsky would be fired. It would be better, however, to release him from his duties based on his newfound physical inability.

For two weeks, Yakubovsky was in a coma, and after being fed only intravenously for so long, he lost twenty-seven pounds. Victoria took an extended leave of absence to look after him.

Finally, as he began returning to his senses and gradually eating on his own, Vicky went to the Central Farmer's Market to buy all the best for him. Then she made up an old German recipe that she had recollected hearing from her grandmother. She mixed honey with melted bear fat, and then pounded into it ground walnuts and cranberries. Victoria gave him this very nutritious mix six times a day by a teaspoon. He could hardly eat it, washing it down with hot cocoa. But soon he began to recover.

42

California, April 5, 1994

In March, Boris began the grading on his first construction site. By this time, the rainy season had ended, making it possible to work without any fear of water damage. Boris's construction experience being limited to Kazakh's virgin territory forty years ago. Therefore, for rather decent money, he hired a skilled general contractor, expecting to learn more about the business from him. Every day, Boris was at the construction site the first, and was the last one to leave. He worked with enthusiasm. After all, it was remarkable working all day long in the fresh air. Besides, he liked being with professional contractors. They were easy-going, down-to-earth guys, not afraid to tell rough men's jokes.

On April 1, Boris's long-time friend Leonid Kislov, with his wife Tatiana, arrived from Togliatti. They had come simply to see the Goryanins—to sit around a table reminiscing and to just have quality time together. They also brought the Goryanins an absolutely remarkable gift—a four-month-old puppy, a Central Asian shepherd dog. Shocked and nervous after his long flight, the puppy came out of his kennel slowly, walked around the room, and sniffed everything. Then he sat down in the middle of the living room and stuck out his tongue, panting, showing that he was thirsty. Ruslana brought him water in a bowl. The puppy stood up, bent over the bowl, and began to lick it up furiously. Then he sighed hard and lay down with his head in his paws.

"Look at him," Tatiana exclaimed. "He acts so spoiled! You'd think he's a true British lord."

"Oh, that's it. His name will be Lord," Ruslana declared. "A beautiful name for such a stately dog." Then looking at Boris, she said, "While Tatiana and I set the table, why don't you guys go and buy him a bed, and some food and toys." And so the Goryanins' new family member had appeared, and

Lord grew quickly accustomed to them, and behaved like a prince. He never had accidents in the house, always waiting until he could be walked outside. He didn't jump on strangers and practically never barked. He took under his protection Ruslana and Anton, but respected only Boris.

The Kislovs stayed for two weeks. During that time, they and the Goryanins went for a few days to Las Vegas. Luckily, Anton was working at an internship near the Goryanins' home, so he'd been able to stay with Lord.

The Kislovs had had to force the Goryanins to take some vacation, and all the while, time passed imperceptibly. Their two weeks flew by as if they'd been only a couple of days. And before they knew it, the Goryanins were taking their friends to the airport and heading back to routine life.

Now, however, their life was filled with caring for Lord. The Goryanins even took Lord with them when they went to see friends. And Lord grew so quickly that in six months, he was larger than most adult dogs of his kind.

In general, Lord was constantly with Boris, running around in his spacious Toyota 4-Runner. Every day, Boris took him to the construction site, and Lord knew all of the contractors. But, as a true lord, he never was the first to greet, and, most important, never ate from another's hands. He trusted only his family, and Ruslana in particular, who always opened the refrigerator for him. Boris hadn't forgotten about Melissa. He was often thinking about her, but had ceased dreaming about her.

43

Moscow, April 6, 1994

When Pushkov Sr. first learned what had befallen his youngest son, he was taken aback, but then he just became angry. That evening, he didn't tell his wife what had happened to Alexander until they returned home.

Maria Pushkov had bought a smoked hen, red caviar, salty cucumber, and a loaf of bread, and as was their family tradition, the kitchen table was set for supper early, while a full teapot simmered on the stove.

"Is it some holiday or what?" Maria asked her husband after seeing on the table a bottle of Stoli.

"You'd better sit down," Vasily Pushkov said, practically falling into the chair opposite his wife. "This isn't a holiday. It's a trouble day. We have to help Alexander. He is in jail. Our son, it seems, finished off that lieutenant colonel who he fought before. You, mother, had prayed that this Yakubovsky would be able to recover. But instead, now we just won't see our son anymore." A tear rolled out of Vasily's right eye. "Well, that's just the trouble!" Maria threw up her arms. "Why didn't you say anything to me before? What's wrong with you?"

"I just learned about it today. It only happened yesterday."

Pushkov poured vodka for both of them, and they silently served up the food. And for the rest of mealtime, they sat finishing off the Stoli and thinking about what they could do to rescue their son.

"It is necessary to pray that Yakubovsky doesn't die," resolved Vasily. "That's the main thing. I'll try to work something out with someone who Alex might have let out of jail in exchange for the promise not to leave town. And then, if Yakubovsky gets through this, I don't know how, and I don't care, but Alexander will become the lieutenant colonel's best friend. He is going to kiss Yakubovsky's ass."

He kept silent for a while. Maria, red from both the news and the vodka, just looked at her husband, enabling him to think.

Then Vasily, slowly, as though addressing himself, asked, "How could they have even run into each other again? Moscow is a large city. People don't meet so simply." He sighed. "Give me another hot tea, mother, and then let's go to bed. Tomorrow, I will go see him the jail and get his story. Then we will know what to do."

The next morning, Vasily woke up earlier than usual. He found yesterday's loaf of bread and cut off four thick chunks. He smeared each piece with butter and then put a few slices of cheese between two of the chunks and a few slices of sausage between the others. He poured some hot tea into a thermos, and put everything into a thick plastic bag. Then Vasily Pushkov put on his police uniform with the epaulets, took his wife to work, and drove to the jail, where, in the "red insulator"—the place where former police and KGB officers were detained—his son would be. Pushkov Sr. found the officer on duty. They knew each other. And when the officer found out on what business Major Pushkov was there, he called a guard, whom he ordered to escort Alexander Pushkov to his office.

When Alexander arrived with his escort, the officer on duty told Pushkov Sr. that he would be around, and stepped out. A silent Pushkov Sr. put the bag of sandwiches and tea on the desk.

"I brought lunch for you. Go ahead and eat, but talk to me. Tell me everything. That you are guilty, I have no doubt, so there's no sense in not telling me the truth. I will decide what to do with you later. But now, I will listen."

"Well, there isn't much to tell," Alexander said, shrugging. "Something just came over me. I regret it already. When I saw that Yakubovsky guy leaving his car near the bank, I just got my baton and began to beat the shit out of him. That's all there is to it."

"So you saw him at the bank?"

"I was working as the street guard outside." Alexander took another bite of sandwich and washed it down with the hot tea. The whole time he spoke, he had not looked once into his father's eyes.

"Why would Yakubovsky be at the bank?" Vasily asked.

"I don't know."

"People go to the bank to deposit money, withdraw money, or ask for a loan. Hmm. Tell me, who is your police investigator?"

"Vagan Grigorian. He was transferred from the Central District."

"I haven't heard of him."

"He's young. He just started."

"He's young? That's not good. And it is even worse that he has just begun to work there. He will still feel it necessary to prove himself to his superiors. Oh, son! It will be very expensive for us to help you, you know. Your mom and I have been trying to save money to buy you a car. We wanted it to be a gift. But now, that's all out the window."

"Forgive me, Dad. I do not know what came over me." Alex finished eating. He wiped his mouth and lowered his head. "Please don't leave me here. Don't disown me. I shall make you grandkids."

"We already have grandsons from your sister and brother. And now you, the fool, are the one we have to help."

Just then, the officer on duty walked in the door. "So, Vasily, are you finished with your discussion already?"

"Yes. Already. And, forgive me, but I'll be back again tomorrow." Pushkov Sr. rose and handed the officer a twenty-dollar bill.

The officer took the money and, not looking at it, put it in his pocket, while simultaneously shaking hands with Pushkov Sr. And after both Pushkovs left, the officer took the bill out and looked at it. Satisfied with himself, the officer nodded and thought, *You are welcome to visit every day, if each time bring me twenty dollars!*

Vasily was on the move the rest of the day. First he went to the military hospital, where he inquired about the status of Lieutenant Colonel Yakubovsky. Having learned that that he was in the intensive care unit, with heavy trauma his to head and face, he became overwhelmingly upset.

From the hospital, he went to the bank to meet with his brother-in-law's son. The head of security was not only available, but in the beginning of their conversation, also verbally lashed out at Vasily as though Pushkov had arranged the beating himself. But gradually, he calmed down, and they even went to McDonald's together for lunch.

This was Vasily's first time eating fast food, and he didn't like it. He said Maria could do much better. But then he didn't really care about hamburgers right now. He just needed to find out why Yakubovsky had been visiting the bank. Eventually, his brother-in-law's son gained enough trust in him that he told him that Yakubovsky had planned to see the manager of the Commercial Loan Department to get his credit preapproved; he had been interested in financing a purchase on wheat imported from the USA or Canada.

Vasily then took the guard back to the bank and went to the Central District Police Department. He was acquainted with a couple of guys there who would be able to prompt the management to help him.

His old friend, Senior Inspector Lieutenant Colonel Javorsky, supervised the homicide division, but it appeared they weren't involved in his son's case. Alexander Pushkov's case, it turned out, fell under the jurisdiction of the criminal division and had been classified as "attempted murder with the motive of revenge." Those charges were serious enough. Even if Yakubovsky recovered completely and without consequences, Alexander Pushkov still faced three to five years in the red zone.

Inspector Javorsky took Pushkov to the chief of the criminal division Lieutenant Colonel Vlasov. The three men had a long conversation behind closed doors, and then Javorsky left Vlasov and Pushkov alone. In about half an hour, Pushkov left Vlasov's office and returned to Javorsky's office. They agreed that Javorsky and Vlasov, along with their spouses, would come to the Pushkovs' home on Sunday, at two o'clock.

Lieutenant Colonel Vlasov called his subordinate, Inspector Vagan Grigorian, and ordered him to report on the results of all of the investigations that he was in charge of. Attentively having listened to Grigorian's reports, Vlasov asked whether he needed help in any of the investigations. The young officer was confused, but didn't refuse the help.

And with that, Lieutenant Colonel Vlasov suddenly offered: "Would you like to take me as your assistant, inspector?"

Absolutely taken aback, Grigorian couldn't find anything better to do than smile and say that he would more than welcome the opportunity to have such an experienced assistant. Then Vlasov spread out the eight case folders, and pretended to randomly selected three; among them, of course, was the folder with Pushkov's case.

Vlasov looked through all three folders, and then returned the two that did not matter to him to Grigorian.

"I'll take over this one for you," he said, and then wished the young officer success with the rest of the cases before dismissing him.

Vlasov opened the folder to find only a few pieces of information. Lieutenant Grigorian still hadn't had time to meet with Pushkov for a personal interview.

Just as day turned into evening, Pushkov Sr. reached his apartment. He had hardly gotten out of his uniform when he collapsed on the sofa, and, as soon as his head touched the pillow, he fell asleep. He awoke around seven. The room was dark. The wind shook a lantern behind a window, and the shadows projected by light of a street lamp moved around the room. Vasily lay on the sofa, thinking about the unfairness of the relationship between parent and child.

When children are small, parents must help them when they get sick or are too lazy to study. And now, even after their son Alex had become adult, he was in trouble. So, who else but his daddy would help him?

He got up and, as usual, set the table for supper, and then left to pick up his wife from work. On their way home, Vasily told Maria that, tomorrow,

Alex would be home, and that on Sunday, at two o'clock, they would have company.

"And we must keep the meeting with our company completely confidential," he told his wife.

To that, Maria shortly answered, "That's obvious. We will keep it a secret as never before."

"Alexander is going to have to creep on his belly before Yakubovsky and kiss his ass," Vasily said. "I just hope it's enough to convince Yakubovsky not to submit a complaint to the prosecutor's office."

44

Moscow, June 1994

Yakubovsky had been discharged from the hospital at the end of May. He still couldn't go out independently, as he suffered from dizziness. On his own, he could hardly move around inside his apartment. Vicky had to return to work, but she continued to look after Vladislav. The tenderness of his beloved woman, her warmness and care, made all the difference, and Vlad began to improve.

Igor and Ann continued to earn money shuttling, but when they were available, they both helped Vicky look after Igor's father. All four of them, as a result, had become close friends. However, each time Vladislav saw Ann, he still felt a disturbing longing. Worse, she had taken to leaving him each time with a kiss. Her lips were so sweet, that Vladislav felt ashamed for his feebleness around Anna.

By the end of the June, with their full support, Yakubovsky recovered. The headaches had gone. He had gained back his weight. And he had gradually begun to exercise in the mornings, and go for walks in the evenings.

During his illness, Igor and Ann had made seven shuttle trips to Poland and Turkey, and one to Odessa's well-known merchandise market called the Seventh Kilometer. Ann had a taste for beautiful but inexpensive things and the Polish-made perfumery and custom jewelry she picked out sold very well; the leather from Turkey virtually flew out of their hands. All of the money they spent they doubled, and sometimes even tripled, giving them a profit of more than three hundred thousand dollars. This made Vlad and Igor think. First, it was unsafe to keep such large amounts of money in an apartment. Second, the time had come to expand the business; both Yakubovsky men had decided that they should try to purchase vodka directly from Poland or Finland. Russia was "the drinking country," so there was no question they could resell it, but they weren't sure how much profit they could make.

Consequently, they decided to legalize their trading activities. Common sense advised that the business be registered simultaneously in Russia and someplace abroad, where they could quickly go, if needed. Such a place, in their opinion, was Cyprus. Russians didn't need a visa to go to Cyprus, there were charter flights from Moscow to Nicosia every day, and that wasn't to mention that the sea was warm and the food inexpensive. Besides, it was a tax paradise.

In Russia, the Yakubovskys registered the company as a limited liability partnership called Owl, LLP. They opened Owl's checking account with Impex Omega, a bank registered in Lithuania. Then on June 22, Vladislav and Igor took a charter flight to Cyprus, planning to visit two small towns, Larnaka and Limassol, on the shore of the warm Mediterranean Sea. Both towns were popular among Russians who were new to the area, and also practically every Russian bank had opened a branch there. In Cyprus, for pennies, it was possible to register any company. And so there, they registered the limited liability company under the name Elephteria, Ltd. Elephteria, in Greek, meant "freedom."

"It is freedom with limited liability," Igor joked.

The Yakubovskys opened the Elephteria, Ltd. checking account through Argentinean Poplar Bank. And, naturally, while they were there, they bought some merchandise, as they say, to compensate for travel expenses. Then father and son returned to Moscow with six bales that were too heavy to lift by hand.

Now, attractive export-import opportunities opened up to them—first, the possibility of tax evasion, and second, the safety of their money from both gangsters and the government (which are basically the same thing when it comes to helping the common citizen).

The technological strategy of such economical activities is simple. Let's assume that the Yakubovskys decide to purchase merchandise. For this purpose, they would have to have a signed contract for the delivery of the merchandise to Owl, LLP, and Elephteria, Ltd., including transportation, liability insurance, and brokers' services. Owl, LLP, could obtain from the bank a short-term loan for the purchase of the merchandise, after which it would wire all credit funds, as a hundred percent advance payment, to Elephteria, Ltd. The contract price of the merchandise would cover the cost of goods, transportation, applicable taxes, customs fee, and brokers' services in Russia. But Elephteria, Ltd. already has a contract for the purchase and delivery of merchandise with a direct supplier for a lower price. Elephteria, Ltd. pays the supplier in full for goods, delivery, insurance, customs duties, and so on. The merchandize still hasn't been delivered yet, but the difference is on the Elephteria, Ltd., account already.

This was the most primitive scheme, though there were much more complex strategies for saving money. In addition, it would be possible to accumulate income from shuttling activity on Elephteria's accounts.

Finally, Vlad and Igor bought a laptop—a Macintosh—as Vladislav had seen Boris Goryanin use a year ago, along with a standard software package and a portable printer. Then all four of them started to learn how to use the computer.

As an experiment, the Yakubovskys decided to buy a truckload of the Polish-made vodka "Viborova." One truckload consisted of forty pallets, and each pallet contained seven hundred sixty-eight one-liter bottles. The total contract was for thirty thousand seven hundred twenty bottles. The contract price for a one-liter bottle of vodka delivered to Moscow was ninety-two cents. After the customs and brokerage fees, and tax, the cost of a one-liter bottle of vodka was a one dollar and forty cents. So they sold vodka to kiosks for three dollars and twenty-five cents a bottle. As a result of this deal alone, within ten days, they made nearly fifty-seven thousand dollars.

In addition, while waiting for the vodka to make its way from Poland to Moscow, Igor and Ana swung by the Seventh Kilometer in Odessa and earned six thousand more.

Yakubovsky returned to work on June 27, but he no longer cared about his job. Instead, all morning long, he thought on the scheme as had the world-famous economist Karl Marx: money-goods-money.

Then right before lunch he was called into his superior's office. Their conversation was short. Either Vlad must submit the application to the medical board for evaluation of his physical ability to continue service, or face dishonorable discharge. Yakubovsky didn't bother to ask why. He was given a twenty-four-hour time limit for his response.

The next day, Yakubovsky submitted the request for a medical examination and for disability pay for the period of one year. His request was granted. For the first six months, Yakubovsky received medical disability based on his medical records alone, without a medical examination. But his next medical examination had to be done no later than December 12, 1994, to determine whether he could continue service for the final six months.

45

California, June 19, 1994

Melissa still had few more days until the big day. With an anxious heart, she had waited for this moment. Dr. Rosner tried to calm her, but the approach of the biggest event in her life had completely captured her, body and soul. Melissa ceased to exercise, as she was afraid of injuring the baby. Her stomach had become heavy, and she could hardly move. She noted, too, that she cried very often. If only Boris was with her, he would take care of her, and everything would be much easier.

It was good that Melissa had the Trunovs. The only thing that distracted her from her worries was her diligence to learn Russian. In that area, her successes were tangible. By now, she was able to freely converse about household matters. She still had a distinguished British accent, but her active vocabulary totaled about five hundred words.

Melissa wanted that George would speak Russian at home, too, because English he would know anyway. So Lyudmila had written down the lyrics to some Russian lullabies and sang them for her. Melissa had learned six of them and, sitting in an armchair, with a hand on her stomach, had sung them to George.

On the morning of June 19, Melissa's father called unexpectedly. It wasn't the normal time. He asked Melissa how she was feeling and how the weather was in California, but, knowing him, Melissa understood that he was making the call for a reason.

As it turned out, the reason was the death of Howard Wiggins, her father's long-time secretary. A car had struck the unfortunate man, speeding into him at no less than seventy-five miles per hour on a normally quiet corner of London. Wiggins flew approximately forty-five feet into the air and then fell, head-first back onto the concrete. He died unconsciousness on the street. The car had not stopped. Melissa's father told her, however, that witnesses had informed the police that a recent London convict appeared to have been driving.

Mr. Howard had served her father for thirty-nine years. He had lost his family as a child, during the bombings in London. In a bomb-shelter at school, he was the only one of his family who survived the bomb that fell on their house. Lonely, Howard Wiggins began to work for Sir Spencer right after completing his education. And now to have such a tragic end!

Melissa was beside herself, knowing she couldn't even consider attending the funeral. Back home, the Trunovs couldn't calm the sobbing Melissa for a long time, but they sincerely empathized with her.

A week later, in London, poor Howard Wiggins was buried. And, in California, Melissa was waiting for Monday to come. It was the day when, at last, she would see her George. Due to the excitement, she couldn't eat anything. She only drank. And then on Sunday, June 26, Melissa began to prepare for the forthcoming surgery.

That night, Melissa didn't sleep. She nodded off by dusk, but then woke up at five o'clock without an alarm. She knelt beside her bed and prayed. Then, hardly able to move, she showered, dressed, and left for the hospital with the Trunovs. When they arrived, Melissa said good-bye to them and, having crossed herself, entered the reception room.

In the pre-op room, she was given a linen dressing gown and warm socks, after which a nurse wheeled in a bed for her. Melissa, supporting her stomach, climbed on it. The nurse covered Melissa with a warm blanket. Lying on her back and with a hand under her head, Melissa whispered a prayer. Some painful minutes passed, and then the nurse wrapped a rubber band around Melissa's wrist and found a thin vein in her hand. She stuck a needle into it, which she covered with several pieces of surgical tape. Then the nurse lifted the bars on both sides of the bed, and wheeled Melissa to the operating room.

The nurse helped Melissa move onto the operating table. She rolled over the metal "hanger" that held a plastic IV bag and, after connecting it to the needle in Melissa's hand, began to measure her blood pressure. Both Dr. Rosen and the anesthesiologist were already there, dressed in their green surgical gowns. When the nurse was finished, Dr. Rosen whispered some encouraging words to Melissa, and then the anesthesiologist administered the anesthesia. Melissa put her hand on her stomach and, smiling, told George, "We shall soon meet, my lovely boy."

Dr. Rosen asked Melissa to count to ten. But at number six, the doctor and the room started to disappear.

Melissa opened her eyes. She didn't know how much time had passed. She looked up at the ceiling and then closed her eyes again. After what seemed like only a few minutes, she reopened them and realized that she had been wheeled into a different room. The bars on either side of the bed were still lifted, and her left hand was on a top the blanket. She felt her stomach. It was much smaller now. Melissa's heart stood still. She wanted to call someone, but she couldn't. Probably, the anesthesia still was working.

Melissa waited, but not for long. Another nurse approached her, smiling, and said, "You have a wonderful boy. But please keep resting, sweetie. He is asleep too. Just wait a little longer, and I will bring him to you just as soon as the anesthesia has worn off."

An about half an hour passed, and Melissa had started moving slowly, and her consciousness had brightened.

The nurse came in with a bundle. "Here is your son. What will you name him?" And she laid the bundle on the bed next to Melissa.

With a gush of love, Melissa closed her eyes and embraced her baby delicately, almost afraid to touch him. Then she began to thank the Supreme for all that he had given her. Little baby George slept serenely all the while.

Dr. Rosen came in then. He congratulated her, and she thanked him for his care and understanding. The doctor told her that all had checked out, and that the baby was perfectly healthy.

Melissa asked when she could feed the baby. Dr. Rosen raised the blanket from her and, having exposed Melissa's breast, he slightly compressed her nipple with his fingers. Some liquid squeezed out, but the doctor explained, that it was not milk yet, and that milk would not appear for another day or two. Now, it was just necessary to wait a little for the anesthesia to wear off. Then it would be possible to start feeding the baby.

Melissa looked at her child with admiration, gently ironing his little fingers, enjoying his presence and not noticing that she was falling asleep again. When she awoke, Melissa saw the nurse holding George. She told Melissa that it was possible to feed the baby now and brought him to Melissa.

When the baby smelled his mom's milk, the sucking reflex kicked in, and for the first time in his life, he started to eat on his own.

After the feeding, the nurse put George on a changing table and fitted a clean diaper on him. And Melissa, resting on an elbow, for the first time really saw her baby. And there, on George's right arm above the elbow, there was a small birthmark, with a form that resembled Australia. It was the very same as Boris's.

47

California, June 27, 1994

Boris often thought of Melissa. Her time to give birth to their son was approaching. How was she? Where was she? He didn't know where to begin to search for her. He called her father, but nobody answered. He didn't want to call Geneva again. But what to do? He could do only one thing: wait.

Goryanin was completely involved in his work. His first project was proceeding swiftly. The framing of the house had been completed. Soon it would be time to install the plumbing and sprinkler system, and then the electric, heating, and air-conditioning.

The plans and drawings of the second project were approaching completion and ready to be sent to the city building department for approval. And now, Boris was ready to start the preliminary architectural design of a third project.

Then, in the middle of July, Boris returned home from work one day to find in his mailbox an envelope without a sender's name and return address. In the envelope, there was a photo of Melissa holding a baby. There was nothing else in the envelope. The inscription on the back of the photo testified that on June 27, 1994, a baby boy had been born, and that she had named him George. In the high-resolution photo, it was clearly visible that above boy's right elbow, there was a small birthmark that resembled Boris's.

Boris looked at the photo for a long time. With what pleasure he would kiss both Melissa and George! And he felt relieved to know they were well. After looking at the photo long enough, Boris began to examine the envelope. On the post-office stamp there was a name of the place of accepting the mail.

It was the city of Santa Anna. And the zip code was 92701. Undoubtedly, this envelope had been sent from California.

The next morning, Boris rushed off to Santa Anna's main post office on Sunflower Street. But the clerk couldn't help Boris determine who had deposited the envelope in the outgoing mailbox. There was, however, one thing he knew for a fact: the envelope had been deposited right in that very post office. If only Boris knew that, right around the corner, on Harbor and Sunflower, there was a law school, and that in this school there was a student named Melissa Spencer. But he did not. So, again, he had only to wait and hope that someday he would see Melissa again—and, even better, become acquainted with his son.

48

Moscow, June 27, 1994

After a rough conversation with the head of his subdivision, Yakubovsky decided to go home—for good. He cleaned out his desk, looked around, and for the last time, walked out of his office. He walked down the long carpeted hallway, descended the main stairway, passed the security checkpoint, and opened the door to leave. And there, on the sidewalk, was Alexander Pushkov.

Yakubovsky's first impulse was to run back inside and stand behind the checkpoint. But by pure willpower, he constrained himself. Furthermore, Pushkov had fallen before him on his knees.

Yakubovsky, not knowing what to think ... He hissed and said, "Get up now. People are looking." And he was telling the truth.

"Forgive me, Vladislav Ivanovich. I won't do it anymore!" Pushkov whimpered in a disgustingly nasal voice behind ostensibly strangled tears. He had rehearsed this scene repeatedly until he could perform it to perfection. The famous Russian stage master "Old Man" Stanislavsky, upon witnessing this performance, definitely would exclaim, "I believe it!"

"Get up, you, idiot! People are looking!" Yakubovsky continued to hiss.

"Let everyone see that I am asking sincerely for your magnanimous forgiveness!" Pushkov pathetically continued to play.

"Get up, at once!" Vlad said.

At last, Pushkov rose from his knees and with a suddenly normal voice, asked where they could sit down, so that he, Pushkov, could convince Mr. Vladislav Yakubovsky of his sincere repentance.

After the conversation with his boss, Yakubovsky's mood wasn't so hot. It was one thing when you were just suspended, but quite another when you were thrown out of service after so many years. So an impromptu meeting with Pushkov surely wasn't improving his day.

Sitting in the Field Camp restaurant across from Pushkov, who had already calmed down, Yakubovsky asked, "And if you had killed me, then what?"

"I would have received sentencing. I would be in prison for a long time."

That Pushkov was lying, Yakubovsky understood. But he also understood that both of them were made of the same cloth. Therefore, he decided to think about how he could use Pushkov to pursue his interests. Yakubovsky told him that he would need to think for a couple of days about how to apply Pushkov's natural talents and unrestrained desire to work for the blessing and prosperity of the motherland.

Pushkov paid for lunch, though it was less than modest, as after his illness, Yakubovsky had gone on a diet and he didn't drink anymore anyway. He hadn't even drunk today after the conversation with his former boss.

They left the restaurant. Outside, it was hot and dry, and the sky and trees were gray. Yakubovsky's soul was somehow gray too.

Pushkov hailed a taxi for them, and took Yakubovsky to the Voikovskaya Metro Station. Yakubovsky had asked to stop there, because he didn't want Pushkov to know where Victoria lived.

Before leaving, Vladislav promised not to submit the claim, regarding Pushkov's attack on him to the prosecutor's office. He told Pushkov to call him in two days, and then they would discuss things further.

49

Moscow, June 29, 1993,

The criminal case regarding an attack by Food Commerce Bank security guard, citizen Pushkov, of Lieutenant Colonel Yakubovsky in Moscow's Central District, was dismissed due to the absence of a written claim from the victim.

By time of their second meeting, Yakubovsky had thought over his plan to use Pushkov. Vladislav knew initially that Pushkov shouldn't be involved in the loan deal. Kravchuk, being always tipsy, was the best candidate for his plan. Unfortunately for Kravchuk, and fortunately for Yakubovsky, Agroprom had gotten rid of almost all it employees, except Kravchuk and Semenov. To boot, both Kravchuk's and Agroprom's reputations had been stained after the failed contractual agreement with Global Oil Research and Sales Corporation.

Kravchuk wasn't capable of making decisions anymore. He could only speak, drink, and sign documents. And as such, these were his tasks. Accordingly, Pushkov would become that worker who would constantly remain in Yakubovsky's shadow, actually fulfilling all of his requests.

For a long time, Semenov had invited Yakubovsky and a bunch of other guys to his sauna, but then Yakubovsky had landed in the hospital. Now, it was time to take advantage of the invitation, and so to reinforce their acquaintance, one might say, Yakubovsky called Semenov and asked if he might also bring along Pushkov to the sauna.

It was unknown whether he rented the sauna just for himself or to lease to others, but it was in a prestigious location at the Dynamo Stadium. The sauna corresponded to the spirit of the time: rather small and dirty, but it was a sauna—something most people didn't even have.

Semenov agreed to let Yakubovsky bring his buddy, and when they arrived, he even suggested "decorating" the company with girls.

"One girl for one guy?" he asked as though it were a question about the beer supply.

Yakubovsky refused. He had beautiful Vicky.

Mr. Kravchuk declared proudly, "I am a drunkard, but not a ladies' man."

Only Pushkov was delighted.

Soon, the "girlfriends" arrived with their pimp. One girl, tall with pimples, introduced herself as Angela. The second girl, with dimples on her cheeks, was rather small and round. She told him that her name was Natasha.

Obviously nicknames, thought Yakubovsky, damning himself in advance. He hadn't come here to participate in a sauna orgy, let alone be the spectator of one.

After a drink and a light snack, Alexander and Alexey—the "Two Stooges," as Kravchuk had named them—joined the others in the sauna. The magnificent four were already at work, as they say, "before of public's eyes." When it was all over, they all amicably left for the showers.

After washing and getting their breath back, the Two Stooges sat down at a table, where Vlad and Gavrila— two Non-Stooges sat silent and stone-motionless, absolutely stunned at what they had just seen. Alexander Pushkov and Alexey Semenov joined them and poured vodka into their own wine glasses, drinking "to the success of our hopeless business." Then they washed down the vodka with cold mineral water, and snacked on pickles and sandwiches with butter and smoked sausage.

"Now it is your turn, gentlemen!" Semenov offered to the still silent and motionless Non-Stooges.

"No, thank you. Let the Lord forgive me!" Gavrila waved his hands and, for persuasiveness, crossed himself and everyone else. Vlad, having drawn his head deep into his shoulders, tossed his hands in the air as if to tell him to forget it.

"Well! In that case, with your permission, gentlemen, we shall continue!" Semenov announced, and then both Pushkov and Semenov amicably lay on their backs on a sofa. And once the girls joined them, it had begun again. As synchronous swimmers, simultaneously, they made inconceivable movements reminiscent of school physics lessons, as if they were figures on an oscillograph. Or synchronous galloping camels, with humps, or breasts, being shaken at their riders. Both girlfriends synchronously closed their eyes and groaned. Apparently, though, Angela was more musical than Natasha, as she churned out noise more quickly and rhythmically, probably because she was skinnier.

Later, having paid off the pimp, Semenov left with Kravchuk. He had acted as Gavrila's wife's lover for a long time already. Usually, Alexey had dinner with them and assisted Mr. Kravchuk in keeping his glass full. And then he assisted Mrs. Kravchuk in dragging her drunken husband into a room where he serenely slept till the next morning. Meanwhile, Alexey and Alevtina would engage in their own carnal joys. It was a blessing that Alexey Semenov was ten years younger than Alevtina.

Pushkov and Yakubovsky took a taxi to the infamous Field Camp.

"What's the matter with you, Alexander?" Yakubovsky asked him. "You are a young, good-looking, healthy guy. Why do you need something like that?"

"Well, Mr. Yakubovsky," Pushkov said. "I hate it. But it is just who I am. I cannot get acquainted with a good girl. Perhaps, there are no more good girls."

They arrived at Field Camp. Silently, they walked in and were seated, and a waitress came and took their order. It was quite visible to Yakubovsky now, that Alexander, as they say, would not suffice for the stars in the sky—but he would, it was certain, do everything he was told.

At last, Yakubovsky interrupted the silence. "Where are you working now, Alexander?"

"Anywhere. I was fired from Food Commerce Bank."

"And what do you want to do?"

"I know what you're getting at."

Vlad smiled. "Would you work for Agroprom?"

"And what would you need me for there?"

"Not too much. But we are working with Agroprom on a contract for the purchase of grain from America. As you probably realize, this is multimillion dollar deal. Reliable executive employees are necessary to us ..." Yakubovsky broke off, enabling the waitress to put their food and drinks on the table.

When she had left, Vladislav had intercepted Pushkov's greedy examination of the waitress with, "Are you really that desperate? Why don't you just get a girlfriend?"

"I know. I had one before, when I was working for KGB."

"Well, that's a problem that easily enough fixed" Yakubovsky said, remember Kravchuk's secretary. "I shall fix you up with one very nice girl. First-class girl. But you shouldn't spoil her. While the grain project is in progress, I will charge you with one very profitable business. Together, you and she will earn good money. But you must promise me to protect her. She could be a very good wife."

After what had happened in Togliatti with Anastasia, Yakubovsky had become somehow warmer in his attitude toward women.

"Yes, I would be happy to meet her," said Pushkov. "My parents will be pleased, too."

Pushkov still did not trust happiness, however. Now, not only had Yakubovsky forgiven him and arranged work for him; he also planned to fix him up with nice girl and allow him the chance to make money. It was suspicious to him.

Leaving Field Camp, Yakubovsky told Pushkov, "Let's meet in the Agroprom office tomorrow at about ten—in Kravchuk's reception area. If I'm late, wait for me. At the same time, you can become acquainted with Valerie."

And all turned out as Yakubovsky had planned. The next morning at ten, Kravchuk wasn't in his office. And convince that Pushkov had already arrived Yakubovsky called Valerie and asked her to call him when Kravchuk came in.

"You, Valerie, would be entertained by that young man," he added.

Yakubovsky was right. As soon as Alexander and Valerie saw each other, they felt the impulse of young deer on a spring run. Both, at the beginning, were at a loss for words, but in a few minutes, Pushkov, being experienced in such affairs, had skillfully started to set a trap. And Valerie, in turn, pretended to be a shy, curious lamb.

When Semenov appeared, horsing around and trying to get involved in their conversation, Valerie cut him off, despite the fact that she usually always just giggled above his lousy jokes.

Then when Kravchuk arrived, Yakubovsky, having been notified by Valerie's phone call, came as well, and they all had a meeting with Pushkov. All of them quickly found common ground for justifying Pushkov's employment.

But having approached the salary question, Kravchuk, threw out a phrase reminiscent of childhood: "I would gladly pay you more, but I can't afford."

"Don't worry about it!" Yakubovsky said, reassuring Pushkov. "You will make in three days more money than you will in a month of working here."

That evening, Alexander Pushkov met Valerie after work. They walked up to the metro, and he escorted her up to her apartment in the Southwest District.

The next morning he registered in the personnel department for work with Agroprom as the project engineer. His lunch break, he took with Valerie.

At the end of the day, both of them left work early to submit applications for travel passports, and in a few days, Yakubovsky had acquainted them with Igor and Anna. Now all four of them could go to Poland and to Odessa's Seventh Kilometer.

Then Yakubovsky loaned Pushkov three thousand dollars to get started.

On the first shuttle trip, Igor, Alexander, and Valerie went to Odessa together. In two days, Yakubovsky would meet them at the Kievsky Railroad Station.

When their train arrived, their sleeping compartments were stuffed with bales. Igor had slept in another compartment, but Alexander and Valerie had stayed to guard the merchandise.

The trip developed successfully. Yakubovsky met them with the truck, and they quickly carried the merchandise to kiosks, where they sold it to retailers. This time, they tripled their money.

That evening, Pushkov Jr. bought flowers for his mom, and then, together with Valerie, went to see his parents. They had to wait a while, as his dad was out picking up his mother from work. But upon entering the apartment and seeing their son with a nice, young girl—something that had never happened before—they understood, and quickly set the table.

Alexander declared that he had brought his parents a daughter. "I am asking you to love her as I love her, and, as they say, to favor her."

Maria, for the sake of the moment, cried a little. Then they spent a good evening together.

Later, when Valerie and her future mother-in-law started to wash dishes, Alexander surprised his father for the second time that evening.

"How much money did you spend redeeming me from the police?" Alexander asked.

"Two thousand dollars," Vasily said, still not sure what Alexander was driving at.

"Here is the money back, Dad. Keep it." And with those words, the younger Pushkov, having taken from his pocket a thick wad of cash, counted out two thousand dollars for his father. "I won't forget your help. Thank you."

"Here it is!" Pushkov Sr. said, accepting the money. "I have lived to see the moment when Alexander has become a grownup."

The following Sunday, the Pushkovs, having collected food and drinks and flowers, went to the Southwest District to get acquainted with the parents of the bride.

50

California, August 1, 1994

It was the hottest season of the year in Southern California. In the following month and a half, the temperature could rise to over a hundred. Baby George had lost a pound. Concerned Melissa took him to the doctor. Dr. Lerner, the pediatrician to whom Melissa has started to go, calmed her down. Furthermore, he has warned her against overfeeding. He advised her to get a special nursery scale and to watch how much milk he consumed at one time. But, as a whole, he was a very good boy. He slept through the night.

Except for her occupation with the baby, when it was possible, Melissa had continued to learn Russian. She fluently read children's books, which Lyudmila had ordered from New York. The Trunovs had completely incurred the housework, preparing food, cleaning, and playing with George. And it was apparent they did it with soul. Melissa had learned a lot from them. She learned how to cook vegetable soup, fish, and pickled meat soups. It was very surprising to Melissa that she liked to fry homemade cutlets. She also liked this taste of food, she experienced in Togliatti, using it to try new recipes with great interest. But it wasn't possible for her to eat a single slice of a herring. Melissa had watched the older couple savor boiled potato with herring every Sunday morning, and each time she remembered how she and Boris had eaten potato with stewed pork.

Sometimes Melissa would take them to a Russian grocery store where she would scan the shelves and recollect Togliatti. Whenever she saw the stewed pork, she would put one can in her basket. And she couldn't be kept away from the pickled cucumbers, milk cream, and dark rye bread.

In addition, Lyudmila had learned from Elena that, just a few blocks from their house, there was a beauty salon owned by a Russian woman named Ruslana. So Lyudmila and Valentin went there to investigate. Lyudmila came out looking ten years younger. Later, they acquainted Melissa with Ruslana, and Melissa began to have her hair done by Ruslana as well. Every time she went for a cut, Melissa tried to speak with her hairdresser in Russian.

Recently, Melissa had also learned from her father, during once of their regular phone calls, that Ms. Doughty had begun to tire more quickly than usual and was going to visit the doctor. Two weeks later, her father told Melissa that Ms. Doughty had been diagnosed with inoperable breast cancer, and had no longer than six months left to live. Now, each time Melissa called London, she talked to Ms. Doughty, who had virtually been both her mother and grandmother, while Melissa was growing up. Melissa, as she could, encouraged the dying old woman. But a trip to London was out of the question. She was still nursing, and George was still too small to be away from his mother or on such a long trip. In a month or two, when Melissa started to feed him infant cereal and other solid foods, then she could leave him for a while in the care of the seniors and go visit her father and Ms. Doughty in London.

But for now, the autumn semester had begun, so Melissa didn't have a spare moment.

51

Moscow, August 4, 1994

Summer had turned to autumn. In northern Kazakhstan, the frost would strike soon. For Victoria, the time had come to resolve the problem of not being able to leave with her parents for Germany. To apply for a travel passport, she needed her birth certificate in her family name, Schmidt, instead of Koval. Of course, she could marry Yakubovsky and become Madam Yakubovsky, but for the passport for permanent residency in Germany, Vicky needed to provide the birth certificate with her true family name.

In early August, Vladislav and Vicky have decided to go to Vicky's native village of Fedorovka. They collected gifts: cognac, instant coffee, underwear, cosmetics, costume jewelry, and cash. From the Moscow airport, Domodedovo, they went to the Siberian city of Omsk. From Omsk, they went to the Northern Kazakhstan city of Pavlograd, where they stayed overnight. And the next morning, they left on a small two-engine plane for the regional center of Kachiri.

The distance between Kachiri and Fedorovka was sixty miles. So they agreed with the driver of a Russian-made off-road car, the GAZ, to take them to Fedorovka for twenty dollars. Vicky and Vlad arrived at Fedorovka before dusk.

Vicky hadn't been back in her village for almost ten years. She remembered it as a clean settlement, with friendly, well-kept people in the streets. What they saw now was awful. Several houses stood empty, their windows broken and covered with crossbars. Everywhere was dirt and dust.

The driver took them to the middle of the village, to the house near the hospital where Vicky had once lived with her parents. Vicky was torn apart looking at the house, seeing what had happened to the home where she had grown up. Now, there were some strangers in the front yard, which apparently lived there. Victoria had no desire to talk to them, and they eventually walked away.

Still sitting in the car, Victoria and Vladislav looked around. Next to the hospital, some drunks sat next to a strange rusted metal construction that reminded Boris of a silo. Near a cracked concrete pedestal on the ground was a semi rotten wooden frame of unknown purpose.

Victoria and Vlad got out of the car, and Vladislav paid the driver. The driver, however, had no phone at home, so they agreed that Vladislav would send him a telegram when they were ready to leave Fedorovka. Then he could pick them up here and take them back to Kachiri.

The driver left and the couple walked to the hospital where Vicky's mother had worked since Victoria had been young. Vicky knocked on the hospital door. She often used to run here, to her mother's working place, with her siblings. The doctor's wife answered. The old lady looked at Vicky, trying to remember something, but couldn't.

Vicky recognized her at once and said, in German, "Frau Martha. I am Victoria Schmidt. Do you not recognize me? I am Vicky, Frieda's daughter."

"Oh, certainly. Certainly. I saw you but I didn't trust my eyes. So it is! Frieda. Young Frieda. And here I was confused."

They embraced and kissed each other.

"Konstantin, come here," the old woman said. "Would you look who is here? It is Vicky. Frieda's daughter."

An old gentleman approached and embraced Vicky. "And you …" he said, looking at Yakubovsky, "forgive me, but you would be?"

Vicky responded. "He is my groom. Vladislav."

"Vladislav Ivanovich Yakubovsky," Vlad introduced himself.

"Konstantin Evdokimovich Murashov," the old man said. "And she is my spouse, Martha. For Germans, it isn't accepted practice to name people with their patronymic names, but we have been Russianized here for a long time."

"Well, what we are standing here for? Please, come in," Martha said.

They entered a registration room in an extension of the building, in which Dr. Konstantin Murashov had lived all his life with Martha. Yakubovsky noticed a large "Titan" water heater. He hadn't seen such a water heater in a long time.

Seeing what Vladislav had become interested in, Konstantin explained, "In the hospital, hot water is always necessary. It was established twenty-five hundred years ago that boiled water is the best disinfectant: simple, accessible, and reliable. Martha, let's feed our guests. These people are tired from a long trip, and now we're exhausting them with famine."

"Yes, yes. You are right," the old woman said, and began to fuss in the kitchen.

Then, while the seniors set the table and warmed some food, Vladislav and Victoria got themselves in order, and brought their gifts into the kitchen.

"These are for you," Vicky said, spreading their wares on the table.

"What for? That is too much for us," the doctor protested. "We are old people. What is necessary for us is health—that's all."

"You've accepted us so warmly, I almost feel we're putting you at an inconvenience," Vladislav noted.

"Vicky is like a close relative to us," Martha said. "Her mother worked with me almost thirty years. A lot happened during those years. I accepted Vicky as a part of the family, and all her little siblings too."

"The earlier village was a German settlement," the doctor explained. "There was order here. And now all the Germans have left for Germany. Vicky's parents and their relatives as well. Martha would like to go, too—we know German in perfection—but where would we go? The Lord hasn't given children to us. So… Here we live as we can."

"And who are those people on the streets?" Vicky asked.

"Immigrants from the southern republics," Konstantin said. "When the authority changed hands there, the local Muslims began to oppress the Russians. Here, they have also moved into our territories. The blessing is that the German houses have remained. But they are drinking! They are heavy drinkers. They all are kicking the bucket from drunkenness. And they aren't working. Nobody comes to the hospital anymore. There is nobody getting ill. And nobody is having babies. Only drinking! I used to do many deliveries here, and wrote out birth certificates. Then I'd to go to the village office to have them stamped and officiated. Now, they say the old Soviet seal is superfluous, but they still haven't obtained a new seal. Anyway, for the last three years, I have accepted only six patients."

The old man appeared to be garrulous, which created a bit of a problem. Yakubovsky had wanted to ask him some questions about Goryanin, but there just never seemed to be a good opening. Vlad decided it would be best not to rush things, though. He would try to get alone with Konstantin tomorrow and ask him about it then.

After supper, Vicky and Vlad went to sleep on the narrow hospital beds in the medical extension.

The next morning, Victoria decided to go for a walk through the settlement to recollect her childhood and to look for her school girlfriends. Yakubovsky stayed back as it was a chance to discuss his case alone with Konstantin.

Yakubovsky began the conversation, looking out the window at the opposite side of the street. He asked Konstantin, "What is the purpose of that peculiar construction?"

"When Khrushchev declared in 1957 that it was necessary to develop virgin soil, they built a cement storage chamber. Cement would drop from that silo onto the platform, and then workers would load the cement onto the dump trucks manually by shovel. That is, until one student built an inclined trench. Then the cement from the silo could slide down into the trucks, and the men didn't have to shovel."

The talkative Konstantin continued. "You know, that same student who built the trench was involved in another story, too. In the village where the students were, a fight broke out between the students' leaders and one lieutenant. They got drunk and began to argue, and the officer was nearly killed. This student saw the wounded man and brought him half-dead to our hospital. He'd be dead if it hadn't been for that student giving him his blood. But he survived."

Konstantin's story coincided with the information that Yakubovsky had received from Peter Grach—about Goryanin. Vlad chose his next words carefully. "And do you remember exactly when all this happened?"

"Sure. I remember perfectly. Exactly one year before Vicky's birth. Oh, her mum Frieda had been so young and beautiful. Vicky looks exactly as her mother did at her age. Many young men were interested in Frieda back then. This particular student was interested too. Those two were hiding from me all the time, clearly engaging in the business of the young!"

"And what was his name?"

"Whose?"

"The student's?"

"Now, please give me a second. There in those books, all was registered."

Konstantin led Yakubovsky to some shelves filled with thick registration books. The books were labeled with dates and organized chronologically by year. Konstantin approached a shelf, and thought for a few moments about something.

Then he asked Vladislav, "And in what year was Vicky born?"

"In 1964."

"You are right. Precisely."

Konstantin retrieved the 1963 registration book and thumbed through the pages. "Here it is. I found it. The officer was Second Lieutenant Kasatkin, Ivan Vladimirovich. And the student's name was Goryanin—Boris Georgievich."

"So you say this student was interested in Vicky's mom?"

"Very interested! Whenever they came to load cement, he always ran in here to get a drink of water. He and Frieda became fast friends, and when he gave the blood, perhaps, it was a dirty needle … Because he almost died from a blood infection. Frieda and another girl had to nurse him back to health. Well, and I treated him as much as I could."

The whole story became clear. Yakubovsky had received proof that Boris Goryanin was Victoria's biological father. But should Victoria know about this? Not necessarily. As they said, the less you know, the happier you are and have a good night sleep.

"It's clear you have seen a lot of things in your lifetime," Yakubovsky said, keeping up the conversation.

"I am a lineal descendant of the Decembrists. One of my great-grandfathers, Lieutenant Murashov, took part in the revolt against Tsar Nicholas I, on the Senatorial Square in St. Petersburg on December 25, 1825. For that, he was banished to Tobolsk. I spent all my life in Siberia. I have been neither to Moscow or St. Petersburg. And now, on an old age, I have become a Kazakh. I am, by heredity, a Russian nobleman, and now I'm not even a Russian citizen. What do you think of that? But it is what it is. What can I do?"

The old man has sighed and continued. "All my life, I've been working. Treating patients, delivering babies, closing the eyes of the deceased. And now, in old age, we have nothing. We shall die and be buried at the public's expense." The old man sighed again and turned away from Vladislav.

"I came with Vicky to get her birth certificate. She needs it to apply for her travel passport."

"So, I shall make one. I still have the forms from the old Soviet times, and of course, the correct stamp. I can make it right now, in fact."

Murashov opened the 1964 registration book and found Victoria Schmidt's birth record. He opened the safe and got out a box of birth certificate forms. Then he found an inkwell and an old-fashioned student's feathered pen. Konstantin dipped the pen into the ink and, with flourishing old-regime handwriting, completed the birth certificate for Victoria Schmidt. When he was finished, he waited a minute to allow the ink to dry. Then he took the seal with the USSR state insignia, breathed on it, and pressed it down on the paper.

Meanwhile, Yakubovsky thumbed through the registration book for 1952. Suddenly, his brain was pierced with an idea. What if he were to become German? Who knew how useful it might be with his future developments?

"Here. It is ready," Konstantin said with pride, handing the certificate to Yakubovsky

Yakubovsky, his hand in his pocket, counted out three one-hundred-dollar bills and then added three more. Then he pulled from his pocket six hundred dollars lay it before Konstantin. "This is for you. As they say, for a rainy day."

The old man had never seen such a large amount of money in his life. Further, he had never seen dollar bills, which were now the basic running currency.

Murashov was ashamed for his poverty. He didn't want to accept this gift, but he couldn't refuse money either.

"What should I do?" Konstantin asked in a monotone voice.

"It is very simple. Write out two more birth certificates. The first certificate must be for precisely the same year, but in the name of Gavrila Petrovich Kravchuk. And, the second one will be for Wolfgang Ottovich Nushke. Here is the record."

"He was Victoria's brother. He died a few days after birth," Murashov uttered, looking down.

"We shall revive him. And as for that adolescent, he will be able to rest in his grave."

"I understand. I understand," the old man said quietly. He understood that he had sold his soul to the devil.

Konstantin wrote out both certificates as Vlad had asked, though he knew it was a shame to do it. Then he took his money and announced that he would be going to his bedroom to take a nap.

Vicky came back excited. After so many years and so many people leaving, she had found her girlfriend Maria Sovenko. Victoria asked Vlad to go with her to meet her girlfriend along with some other people. She asked Frau Martha to please not take offense at their leaving, and then grabbed Yakubovsky's hand. Then, together, arming themselves with souvenirs and cognac, they left.

Vicky's arrival from Moscow, moreover with her groom, was a main event for the remote Fedorovka. About twenty people came to Maria's, and they spread food and booze on the table. Someone had brought an accordion. Vlad tried to speak a little with everyone, but just professionally; he wanted to probe for possibilities, maybe finding a person who could be useful to him. And he found one. An unattractive woman, of average age, appeared to work for the local police. Vladislav hung around her the rest of the evening, and even invited her to dance to the accordion. Her name was Galina Murenko.

Vladislav and Vicky made sure not to return to the hospital too late, as they did not want to disturb the seniors.

The next morning, Vladislav went to the police station to meet Galina Murenko, and Vicky remained at the hospital with the seniors. Both Vlad's charm and his US dollars solved matters quickly. He filled applications for receiving Republic of Kazakhstan passports for Victoria Johannovna Schmidt, Gavrila Petrovich Kravchuk, and Wolfgang Ottovich Nushke. To finalize the registration, however, they needed references and photos. There were no photo centers here, so, they would simply need to bring some from Moscow. But how would they get references?

Yakubovsky returned to the hospital. He asked Vicky to go for a walk with Frau Martha, while he stayed with Konstantin at home.

"Dear Konstantin Evdokimovich," Yakubovsky addressed the doctor. "Think whatever you want, but I need your help again. Please notice, not disinterestedly, that I need statements testifying that Victoria Johannovna Schmidt works in the hospital as a custodian, and that both Gavrila Kravchuk and Wolfgang Nushke work as stokers here. These statements are necessary for me."

With those words, Yakubovsky took out four more one-hundred-dollar bills and gave them to Konstantin. The old man, who had been ill with shame just yesterday, now wrote out the three statements with visible pleasure, and sealed them with the state insignia of the USSR.

When Vicky and Frau Martha returned, both men were sitting in the kitchen. They had unloaded a bottle of French cognac and were washing it down with instant coffee.

By evening, Vlad and Vicky were at the police station, submitting the three statements of information, after which they went to the post office to send a telegram to their driver; they were ready to go back to Kachiri. They agreed to come back with photos.

The next morning, Vicky and Vladislav, having said good-bye to the seniors, left, promising to be back in a month when the passports were ready.

The trip to Vicky's homeland appeared to have been exclusively successful.

52

Moscow, September 6, 1994

When they returned home, Vlad proposed that Vicky become his wife, to which she, naturally, agreed. Thus they discussed the possibility of their moving to Germany. To restore their fluency of the language, Vladislav and Victoria even started to speak among themselves in German. In the beginning they would get confused and just move back to speaking Russian. But in a week or two, it became much easier, and after four weeks, they could speak among themselves in German even in the presence of strangers.

They decided that they would classify their marriage as being between a citizen of Kazakhstan, Victoria Schmidt, and a citizen of the Russian Federation, Vladislav Yakubovsky. After marriage, Yakubovsky would take his wife's last name and become Vladislav Schmidt. This was another reason, aside from picking up their passports, which they would need to return to Kazakhstan.

Before their return trip, Fedorovka Vladislav met an old friend who worked in a special photo laboratory where Yakubovsky used to work. After taking him to lunch at Field Camp and paying him for his service, Yakubovsky obtained from his friend three sets of passport-sized color photos, with a dozen photos in each set. In the first set were Vladislav's photos. In the second, Yakubovsky was disguised as a bald man with a beard and moustache. In the third group, Yakubovsky had been fitted with an extensive head of hair, a moustache, and a beard, and almost resembled Karl Marx.

From Moscow to Kazakhstan, the couple took the familiar route. Vlad had sent a telegram to their old driver before they'd left Moscow, so the driver was already waiting for them in Kachiri. Before going to Fedorovka, however, they stopped at the local grocery store and bought a bunch of nonperishable items: rice, millet, corn, flour, and sugar, a large container of sunflower oil, tea, coffee, and canned beef stew. They also bought vegetable seeds, which were easy to harvest even in the harsh Siberian summer.

With all of these gifts, they arrived at the hospital to see the Murashovs. The seniors were more than happy to receive both their guests and their gifts. And, naturally, Vicky's girlfriends were not forgotten, Galina Murenko in particular.

When Vladislav and Victoria submitted their marriage registration documents, Galina Murenko helped them to accelerate the process by waiving the thirty-day waiting period required by law. To do this, however, she had to make a few trips with Yakubovsky to Kachiri and Pavlograd, where she had connections in the passport office.

In Kazakhstan, it was autumn already. Vladislav hired some men to clean the yard in front the hospital, install a fence around the perimeter, and plant apple trees and bushes with cold-resistant grades of fruit. They also have ploughed and fertilized the backyard, where they planned to plant the vegetable seeds next spring.

Vladislav and Victoria's wedding celebration was such that the whole of Fedorovka remembered the newlyweds for long after, reminiscing about the event during cold winter nights. Thereafter, Ms. Murenko issued travel passports for Victoria and Vladislav Schmidt, and also for citizens of the Republic of Kazakhstan, Gavrila Kravchuk and Wolfgang Nushke.

In Kravchuk's passport picture was Vlad was with an extensive head of hair, a moustache, and a beard. And in Nushke's passport, Vlad was bald with a beard and moustache. Not one of the three passports was registered anywhere, which meant it would be impossible to identify the individuals pictured in them.

From Fedorovka, Vladislav and Victoria went to Kachiri. There, in the general store, they each purchased a set of clothes traditional to the inhabitants of Northern Kazakhstan (the "Louis Vuitton" fashions still hadn't reached them). In these outfits, they couldn't be distinguished from local Germans.

Then, in Kachiri's only hotel, they dressed in their new clothes, took their passport-sized photos, and submitted their applications for immigration to Germany. As their permanent address, they listed the hospital address in Fedorovka, where the Murashovs would be waiting for their documents.

53

California, October 1994

Construction work on the first project went at full speed. The roof had already been covered with waterproof material and tiles. The drywall was in stock and the exterior walls had been treated appropriately. And the framing was ready for final inspection.

Boris's main concern now was to begin on the second project. He had tried to evaluate the risk factor; the first project was not finished yet, but the bank, seeing its progress and Boris's work ethic, was ready to execute the contract for the second loan. Therefore, although he had hesitated at the beginning of the rainy season, after receiving assurance from the contractor that any water damage to the foundation forms would be fixed at no cost to Boris, he made the executive decision to begin the second project. The weather was magnificent. The long-term weather forecast promised rain only at the end of December. And the foundation, including the concrete slabs would be ready by that time.

On the third project, the architect and landscaping designers had finished the plans and drawings. And several subcontractors, having seen Boris's business on the rise, now aspired to work for him. They offered him good prices, and worked well and quickly.

The real estate agent, Robert Hobbs, who had located the construction sites for Boris, also started to appear at the work sites once a week. Robert Hobbs had a breadth of experience, and Boris didn't wave away any opinion from a knowing person, always wishing to make a better product. So Hobbs walked with Boris through the unfinished house and recommended a few changes that would make it more attractive it to a larger bulk of buyers. They discussed people's current tastes, inquiries, and habits.

Hobbs also advised Boris that, even before the completion of construction, he should put the house on the market—in fact, right now. That way, if a willing and able buyer came, it would be great; and if not, there would still be time. Boris could not argue with such reasonable advice, and thus executed an agreement that gave Robert exclusive rights to sell. Robert asked for a six percent broker's commission. In response, Boris offered Robert ten thousand dollars more for his full attention to this job.

Hobbs had not been mistaken. A buyer appeared in two weeks. He probably would have appeared without Hobbs's acceptance of the additional ten thousand, but then nobody really knew. Regardless, it made the process much easier for Boris to have a ready buyer. Now that it was the buyer waiting for the completion of construction, instead of the builder, it was possible to begin on the third project.

Absorbed by work, Boris began to recollect Melissa less often. A year had passed since they had separated, and somehow that past began to grow dim. There was nothing else to be done, and, as the saying went, it was human nature for things that were out of sight to grow out of mind. But sometimes, in rare moments of downtime, Boris wondered whether it was a mistake to have let go of the happiness he'd shared with Melissa. Still, how would he live without Ruslana? And what would he say to Anton? Boris sighed. Anyway, he didn't know where to search for Melissa, and whether they would ever meet again; it was likely just a waste of energy thinking about it.

Little did Boris know that the pretty British young woman who Ruslana had recently told him about becoming her client was the very same Melissa Spencer. As did all husbands, Boris listened to his wife, but didn't really hear what she was saying.

Anton, likewise, had waved away his mother's attempts to acquaint him with the British woman. He was still holding out for his father's promise to introduce him to the Lady whose photo he kept. He was enamored with her, and didn't want to meet anybody else.

And at very this time, in a fifteen-minute drive from their house, small George was growing up. Melissa and the Trunovs surrounded him with care and attention, and George was developing as a healthy child should. He was starting to do things with his hands and to sit up independently, and often when he recognized people close to him, he smiled at the world with his toothless little mouth.

Melissa didn't have a spare minute. She had forgotten that it was even possible just to sit. Her law classes demanded her full feedback, even though she had managed to pull some strings and make some shortcuts. The dean's office had been able to apply some of her credits from the London School of Economy to her current curriculum. And she'd been able to opt out of foreign-language classes due to her judicial translator licenses. Thus, after taking a minimum number of subjects in the autumn semester, Melissa would be able to catch up with her fellow students by the time she was halfway through her program.

Still, Melissa continued to find the time to study Russian. For the last nine months, she had conversed briskly with the seniors, with Elena by phone, and with Ruslana in the beauty salon. She had tried to expand her topics of conversation from household themes, but her vocabulary still wasn't comprehensive enough, so she continued to learn new words. Not ten words a day, as before, but twenty words per week.

Ruslana, semi-joking, had started to tell Melissa about her son, trying to draw her attention to the possibility of Ruslana fixing them up. But having seen that Melissa had no interest in the subject, she decided to leave well enough alone, as Anton had categorically refused to get acquainted with Ruslana's client anyway. Ruslana didn't speak about her husband either, as she thought it would be an unpleasant topic to bring up with the young unmarried woman with a child on her hands. Thus, in her meetings with Melissa, Ruslana never spoke either about her son or her husband. Neither did she show Melissa any photos of them.

54

Moscow, October 1, 1994

At one of their many meetings, Kravchuk told Yakubovsky that in 1991, Goryanin had formed the First Russian Corporation. At that time Boris has sent Kravchuk the power of attorney for opening and managing a bank account in Russia. But Kravchuk was confident that they could use the related documents to also open a bank account in California, from which all payments for the purchase and delivery of wheat could be made. From the same account, Kravchuk, Yakubovsky, and Semenov would also each be paid his fair share of the profit. Such a scheme suited everybody, because the money wouldn't come from Russia, but would remain in the States, which meant nobody would have to pay taxes on it.

For Yakubovsky, as a former employee of the KGB and then the FSB, the problem was that he could visit only countries for which Russians didn't need entry visas. If during the Soviet era, even mice couldn't slip through border security, in the early Nineties, only a travel passport was necessary to get across—except for former employees of those two organizations for which Yakubovsky had worked hard and continuously for the blessings of all mankind. Only in special cases, for example, traveling to Washington for important negotiations, could he obtain such a privilege. So it was a blessing that Yakubovsky had prompted Kravchuk to request a biennial US multi-entry visa. Now such a visa would be useful. On both Yakubovsky's and Kravchuk's travel passports, US visas had been stamped.

And so the men decided to open a checking account in the States through some international bank. To this account, they would wire the funds they received on their wheat purchases.

Yakubovsky carefully thought over each step of the plan that led to their ultimate goal: to steal big money and escape. This phrase had become the motto not only for this project, but also for their entire existence.

Vladislav never alerted Vicky to his plans, although he had no doubt that she would go with him to the edge of the earth, and even beyond. As a matter of fact, he never devoted Kravchuk either. Vladislav believed, not without justification that Kravchuk could bring him down, even without malicious intention. All Kravchuk would need to do is get drunk and start bragging, in which case he would likely be inclined to spill the beans, as it were. But Vlad knew he could, and should, still use Kravchuk to help him reach his goal.

Vladislav started to prepare a trip with Kravchuk to the States. A few days, he studied telephone directories from San Francisco, Reno, and Western Samoa, knowing that, for money to disappear, it would have to cross three borders, change bank accounts, and be converted to three different currencies. San Francisco would act as the money's first stop in the States. The city of Reno, in the state of Nevada, would be the second stop, and an ideal one at that, as companies registered in Nevada, under state law, were not obliged to provide information regarding their owners, even upon the court's request. Besides that, the state required no personal and corporate income taxes. And as a bonus, Vlad knew that, in view of political and economic stability in the United States, as well as state taxation laws, Nevada was one of two states considered the best for offshoring practices—the other state being Delaware.

As for Western Samoa as the third stop, the archipelago of Samoa had been a German colony before WWI. Then, it was divided into two states: Samoa and Western Samoa. The basic language spoke there was English, but due to its roots, German was also used by the locals in everyday speaking. That suited Yakubovsky, as he knew both languages. And as for Wolfgang Nushke, it would be easier for him too.

If a year ago Yakubovsky hadn't had enough money to pay for even a ticket to Washington, now he could purchase tickets for himself and Kravchuk, and also make reservations for them at the inexpensive but convenient Best Western Hotel in downtown San Francisco. For at this time, owing to their shuttle trips and vodka sales, he had saved about five hundred thousand dollars.

They arrived in San Francisco via Frankfurt. Naturally, Vicky saw them off. Shortly before Vlad's departure, Vicky spoke with her parents over the phone. Among other things, they told Vicky that the farm owners were planning to sell it and that it appeared to be an excellent purchase, but they didn't have enough money. If Vicky could assist them, however, the farm would be an excellent place for the whole family to live.

55

Moscow, October 16, 1994

Vlad and Gavrila left for Frankfurt on October 16, 1994, at which point Vlad gave Vicky's parents one hundred thousand US dollars—then the equivalent of approximately three hundred thousand German marks. This was enough to purchase a farm where all of them could live after Vlad and Vicky moved to Germany.

Frieda and Johann, together with a heap of relatives, had arrived at the Frankfurt airport to meet the son-in-law. The noisy company, including both Vladislav and Gavrila, then moved to the Airport Sheraton, across the street from Terminal B.

Soon, however, Yakubovsky left his new relatives at the hotel with Kravchuk, and returned to the airport. He went to the business center near the terminals, where there were, side by side, two German banks—Deutche Bank and Commerce Bank. He opened a personal checking account with the Deutche Bank in the name of Wolfgang Nushke, and a business account with Commerce Bank for Elephteria, Ltd. In each account, he deposited ten thousand dollars.

When Yakubovsky had returned to the hotel restaurant, all of the men were already tipsy, and Kravchuk was absolutely past his limit. Vlad paid special attention to his new mother-in-law. Older than Yakubovsky by only eight years, at fifty, she looked almost the same age as he. Despite getting fat from a German kitchen, she continued to be a woman of natural beauty. She dressed simply but in good taste. Vicky had obviously taken the best qualities from her mother. At the same time, Vicky didn't resemble Johann Schmidt at all. But Yakubovsky's plans didn't include learning from his mother-in-law about the nature of her acquaintance with Boris Goryanin.

Having made a noise until six o'clock, Vicky's relatives finally left. Vladislav then gave some more money to Frieda, and they agreed that, on the way from San Francisco to Moscow, Vladislav and Gavrila would stop over for day or two with Vicky's parents. Then, they could show him the farm they wanted to buy.

After that, Kravchuk went to his room to sleep, but Yakubovsky went to the sauna. Having had a good steam, he then drank a glass of the true German beer and ate German schnitzel with sauerkraut. The next morning, he felt absolutely refreshed, while Gavrila, after all the drinking, did not look the best.

On October 17, around ten a.m., Yakubovsky and Kravchuk left from Frankfurt for San Francisco. The flight around half the globe landed about twelve hours later at San Francisco International Airport. They had no baggage—only carry-ons—so having quickly gone through passport control, they found a taxicab. The driver was Russian-speaking. He and his family had recently arrived from Armenia.

Kravchuk and Yakubovsky went directly to the Pacific Bank of China, where they opened a checking account for The First Russian Corporation. Yakubovsky gave Kravchuk, who didn't know English, all of the inflated cheeks and signed documents, and then translated them for him, modestly keeping to himself select items. Kravchuk had the authorization to manage the account, while Yakubovsky wasn't registered anywhere, which made him rather happy.

Back in the taxi, the driver, who had waited for him while they were in the bank, agreed to their request to work with them over the next few days, and then carted them to the Best Western. Having checked in, Vladislav decided to have a rest, but Gavrila took a tour of the city.

But when Kravchuk left, Vlad jumped out of his room and rushed off to a meeting with his childhood buddy, Michael Lutsky. In school, they were in the same class together for all ten years. But then they parted ways. Michael had left for the States. Of course, it had been impossible for them to keep in touch over fifteen years. But now, Yakubovsky had found his phone number through mutual friends.

Michael lived in the Silicon Valley, near San Francisco. He was working as a programmer for the large company. Still preparing a trip, Vladislav phoned his old buddy. Michael promised Yakubovsky to help.

The friends met at a small restaurant near the hotel. They reminisced about their youth and old schoolmates, and then agreed to become partners in a joint business. As the first step, Lutsky would contact some people who were in the business of registering new companies. Michael assured Yakubovsky that the registration would go through even before Vlad left the States. As for the name of this new endeavor, they came up with the Nevada

Investment Group. The friends agreed to meet in the same place at the same time in three days.

When Kravchuk returned, Yakubovsky was back in his room pretending to sleep. The next morning, Yakubovsky told Kravchuk that he needed to go to Washington for one or two days, then leaving his comrade with one hundred dollars, he went to the airport. He did not take off for Washington, however, but for Western Samoa.

The round trip ticket from San Francisco to Western Samoa, Yakubovsky had purchased in the name of Gavrila Kravchuk back in Moscow. From Moscow he made a reservation in the hotel in the same name. He was planning to buy local visa upon his arrival to Apia, the capital of Western Samoa.

Western Samoa was a group of islands between the Hawaiian archipelago and New Zealand. The population is less than three hundred thousand.

He took a flight to Honolulu, changed planes, boarding a flight by Air New Zealand, and arrived at the airport in Apia at five thirty in the morning. Going through passport control, he presented the passport in the name of Gavrila Kravchuk and paid for the visa. The passport control officer stamped the passport and recorded his arrival to Western Samoa.

Vladislav rented an electric golf cart and drove to the Princess Tiu Inn. Having checked in, he had breakfast, rested in his bungalow awhile, and then went to the city's business district, where all the banks were.

His first stop was the West-Pacific Bank. As a matter of fact, it was just a lawyer's office connected with banks by means of a fax and teletype machine. But at this office, people opened and serviced bank accounts. Speaking German, Yakubovsky asked a bank representative whether he could open a personal account, and having received a positive answer, displayed the passport in which he was pictured with thick hair, a moustache, and a beard. Then Yakubovsky opened the account in the name of Gavrila Kravchuk. He paid the registration fee, deposited two hundred dollars, submitted the remittance forms, selected a password, and left a sample of Kravchuk's signature. In Moscow, Yakubovsky had spent some time learning to fake Kravchuk's signature, studying it to the smallest detail. Now, in the bank, he signed without effort.

After that, Yakubovsky crossed the street and entered into the lobby of the First Bank of Western Samoa, where, having presented the passport in the name of Wolfgang Nushke, he opened another personal account, deposited two hundred dollars, submitted more remittance forms, chose a password, and left a sample of Wolfgang Nushke's signature. Having finished all his business, Yakubovsky returned to the hotel and lay down, waiting for his flight out.

Yakubovsky arrived in San Francisco at about one p.m. On the way back to the hotel, he made a short stop at the Pacific Bank of China, where he filled out some request forms for electronically wiring funds from one bank to another.

By now, Kravchuk was tired of waiting for him. The good part was that the taxi driver was always very talkative on his trips through the city otherwise Gavrila would have become absolutely lonely. He was already fairly tipsy a good portion of the time. Yakubovsky had allowed him to sign some empty request forms for wiring funds from the Pacific Bank of China to Kravchuk's personal account at the West Pacific Bank. Gavrila had signed the documents hesitating to even look at them.

By the time of Yakubovsky's second meeting with Michael Lutsky, Kravchuk was sound asleep. Lutsky gave Yakubovsky a three-ring binder with all of the pertinent registration documents, a Nevada Investment Group, LLC, company seal, and a book of temporary checks for the Bank of America. Yakubovsky also received one hundred sheets of copy-machine paper and one hundred sheets of company letterhead in the US letter sizes.[14] They agreed that Michael would consider what kind of business would be best for them, and then determine how Yakubovsky could receive permanent residency in the States, without requesting political asylum. Both of them understood that it could take a year, even more, before they saw a profit.

Then, on October 21, Yakubovsky and Kravchuk took off for Frankfurt, and arrived the next day. Johann Schmidt met them at the baggage claim. Through an underground tunnel, they went from Terminal A to the railroad station, and purchased tickets to Munich. The train would depart in twenty-five minutes.

Johann Schmidt, by nature a taciturn person, only answered direct questions. He was about fifty-five, physically exceptionally strong, but he couldn't be considered smart. He knew little, so he couldn't talk a lot. Yakubovsky had to visit them to evaluate whether it would be possible for them to live on this farm while their money traveled all over the world.

They reached the farm by the end of the day. And after having gotten acquainted with the present owners and eating a dinner of farm-fresh food, they all turned into bed. Yakubovsky stayed in a small room on the third floor, and Kravchuk stayed on the second.

Early the next morning, Yakubovsky rose from bed and looked out the window. Before his eyes was a view as that of ancient German fairytales: the mountains, covered by a dense black wood, sharply rose up to the sky. Yakubovsky inspected his tiny room. On a wall were some photos. One picture was of a group of people in old-time carriages. In another, to Vlad's sudden surprise, was Frieda, embracing none other than the Lady Melissa.

14 In Europe and Russia the size of papers are different than in the United States.

Yakubovsky was in shock. The past had pursued him. Wherever he was, he came across traces of Goryanin, and now, Melissa had appeared! It definitely demanded investigation, but so reticently that nobody would suspect it, including Kravchuk.

Yakubovsky put his room and himself in order, and then went downstairs to the kitchen. There, the owner, Frau Martha, was making breakfast on the stove. They greeted each other, and to begin a conversation, Vlad asked her where Frau Frieda could be found. Frau Martha smiled. She told Yakubovsky that the rest of the house had risen very early. Frau Frieda had already milked the goats and sheep, and was now preparing butter. Fairly believing that it might be easier to find out from the owner why Melissa Spencer had been here, Yakubovsky then told Frau Martha that he had seen something out the window of his room that he wished to ask her about. With that, he led her upstairs and pointed out to her the tall pine trees he had seen outside.

"What do you call those, in German?" Yakubovsky wasn't proud of coming up with such a primitive line of conversation, but Frau Martha didn't seem bothered by the question, taking it for his weak knowledge of German.

After she answered him, Yakubovsky then asked how they heated the water on the farm and, as if an aside, which the people in the photos were.

"Are they your relatives of yours?"

"No, they are our patients," she answered.

"What do you mean patients?" Vlad asked.

Frau Martha explained that, owing to the magnificent clean mountain air and organic food, they often received patients who were being treated for serious injuries. She pointed out some of them in the photos.

Then Yakubovsky pointed to Melissa. "Who is this young woman embracing Frau Frieda?"

Frau Martha told him what had happened to Lady Melissa and how she had come to their farm for treatment.

Yakubovsky, wanting it to appear that he had asked about Melissa out of sheer curiosity, then asked her a couple more questions concerning two other patients who were pictured. Then he told Frau Martha he would leave her alone now and asked where he could find Frau Frieda.

He had already received exhaustive information about the relationship between Boris and Melissa before they left Russia in October 1993, so this new information meant nothing to him, but somehow it could lead to Boris Goryanin. It would be necessary to be attentive, so that casual imprudence wouldn't bring his new relatives and wife into contact with Goryanin.

Considering the connections between Goryanin and Filimonov, consequences could be unpredictable.

Kravchuk hadn't gotten up yet, so Yakubovsky didn't feel obligated to wait for him. He found Frieda in a small extension adjoining the house, where they processed milk, cream, and butter. Yakubovsky, theatrically outstretching his arms, asked permission to kiss his favorite mother-in-law. Frieda stuck out a cheek. Kissing Frieda, Vladislav was surprised at how elastic and gentle her skin was and how young she smelled. Suddenly he felt his masculine urges provoke him to feel romantic about mother-in-law, but then having recollected his Vicky, who had adopted the best qualities of her mother, Yakubovsky realized there was no need. He was convinced, again, that he loved his young wife. He had really fallen in love, and he loved her. At some point in time, he might even want to live here with her. To live on a farm, far away from the city! This thought surprised him.

Gosh! But it is the truth, he thought. What else do you need, if you have a healthy climate, organic food, and Victoria next to you? Well, besides paradise?

Yet, when his ex-best-half, Natalie, dreamed of raising hens in a village, he had laughed at her. That meant, though, that his negative attitude likely wasn't about the hens.

Yakubovsky suddenly began missing his Vicky. He wanted to be near her, to feel her presence, to hear her voice. He wanted urgently to bring her here.

At this moment, such a metamorphosis had occurred inside the retired lieutenant colonel. He recollected the old gypsy's prophecy: "Through the blood of fornicating with an innocent soul, a disgusting snake will come out from your heart, and you will change. But you will be better. You will quit working for the government, and through your grief, you will clear your soul."

Is my soul clear now? Or it will be more tests? Yakubovsky asked himself. Oh, well …

Yakubovsky went up to Gavrila's room. Yesterday, as usual, he had taken a great interest in the German apple schnapps, and now he couldn't wake up. He was snoring when Yakubovsky woke him up and gave him a half an hour to gather his things. Then he left to go call a taxi.

They two men quickly ate breakfast, and the taxi was already at the front porch when they walked out. Having said good-bye to everybody, Vladislav promised to come back with Vicky soon. That evening, they were back in the Whitestone City of Moscow.

After returning from the trip and realizing that after money was gone an investigation would be requested, in order to have iron-clad alibis, Yakubovsky prepared a written report for him and Kravchuk. Gavrila had no time for that; he was engaged in more serious and pleasant business—celebrating his safe return from the States. Yakubovsky attached all of their tickets, boarding passes, and hotel bills from San Francisco and West Samoa. And in his report, he specified that it was Kravchuk who had flown to West Samoa, and Yakubovsky who had waited for him in the hotel. Having finished the report, Yakubovsky, in behalf of Kravchuk, handed it all over to Agroprom's accounting department. All, of course, except for the financial document that Gavrila Kravchuk had signed in San Francisco.

56

California, November 10, 1994

On Tuesday, November 8, Melissa, as usual, called her father. Ms. Doughty's health had become critical. She kept losing strength in her eyes. With the help of the hospice, Sir Charles had medically equipped a room for Ms. Doughty in the house. They installed a special bed and an IV stand, and employed nurses who applied a painkilling band that allocated a strong, soothing medicine. But the illness didn't let off. Ms. Doughty was dying. In the doctor's opinion, she could live no more than five to six weeks.

George had thoroughly moved onto baby food by now. Except for breast milk, he drank diluted juice and ate kefir with cottage cheese. He liked the canned baby food, too, along with the baby biscuits and crackers. If he liked a meal, then he would start singing and smacking his lips, and if not, then this descendant of Count Spencer wouldn't refrain from spitting at the dinner table—although he did it with a very lovely smile.

After the last conversation with her father, Melissa decided to fly to London for two to three days, just to say good-bye to Ms. Doughty. Lyudmila and Valentin assured her that they would cope with their favorite boy.

So Melissa went to the travel agency that adjoined Ruslana's beauty salon. She purchased a first-class ticket for a round-trip flight via British Airways. She would leave on Thanksgiving, November 23, and return November 27.

Having purchased the tickets, Melissa went to see "Mum Ruslana" as she had begun to call her senior girlfriend. They spoke and wiped eyes. Ruslana immediately offered help with baby. Melissa, naturally, thanked her but politely refused. Though at home she told the Trunovs that, if George became ill, to immediately address either Ruslana or Elena, one of whom could contact the doctor.

Melissa went to London with one carry-on bag. The weather was awful there, as usual. Her father had grown very old, and Ms. Doughty was delighted to see her. When Melissa saw what the cancer had done to the once plum Ms. Doughty, though, she was terrified. The woman was now but a skeleton covered in yellow skin.

Melissa spent all of her time at her father's house, and time went by in an instant. On November 27, Melissa left for the London Airport, taking her father's noble word that, once everything was over, he would fly to California. There, it would be easier for him to grieve. And besides, he needed to get acquainted, at last, with his grandson.

On the plane, Melissa took a sleep-aid pill, and slept the whole flight. But having landed in Los Angeles, she felt absolutely broken. She took a taxi home, and there, after having missed her son for so long, she dragged George's cradle into her room. Then she lulled him to sleep, holding his hand.

57

Moscow, December 12, 1994

Alexander Pushkov and Valerie, Kravchuk's now former secretary, invited only relatives and close friends to their modest wedding. Their honeymoon they successfully combined with a shuttle trip to Turkey. During those shuttletrips, Igor and Alexander had gotten acquainted with several shuttlersfrom Siberia, and now began to bring back goods per clients' requests, making their business even more successful.

After Valerie had left Agroprom, she was admitted into a six-month program at an accounting school. The wise Pushkov seniors had advised the children that if they wanted to have a baby, to do it, so that Val, once she was finished with school, could be hired to work at their eatery as a bookkeeper, and thus become eligible for maternity leave.

The Pushkovs had recently started to look for opportunities to privatize the eatery, which had a dining hall with seating for two hundred; a retail extension, where they sold a bakery and deli products; a huge kitchen; and a warehouse with refrigerating chambers, locker rooms, and storage. The personnel totaled eighty employees. As a matter of fact, it was a combination of a food-processing plant and an eatery. They had discussed the idea of privatization with the current manager, but she was ready for retirement and not in a hurry to make such a decision.

On December 12, Yakubovsky went to the hospital for his medical examination, requested by FSB management. For about a month before this medical commission, he had gone several times to the sauna with Kravchuk, and, for the benefit of business, even got as drunk as the beast.

In the hospital, Yakubovsky took several health tests and even had x-rays of his internal organs examined. And after looking at his dull eyes, probing an enlarged liver, and summarizing all of the test results, the medical-commission chairman told him, "At your age, Lieutenant Colonel, you should take better care of yourself. Considering your present health and the traumas you've received within the last year, I can do nothing for you. You should begin to search for another kind of work. To my regret, you are unsuitable for further service with the armed forces. And, please don't ask me for help. I cannot do anything for you."

The commission chairman signed Yakubovsky's health certificate—which had already been signed by the other doctors participating in the commission—sealed it, and ordered it to be sent to the FSB personnel department.

On Wednesday, December 14, Yakubovsky went to his friend Stanislav Terekhin. The old buddy regretted that his friend could not serve in their "ammunition holder" anymore, but said, "Do you know I am changing my place of service too? While you were ill, there was an order to transfer me to the Office of Attorney General of the Russian Federation as the inspector. They don't have enough qualified people, so they are drawing from the FSB. I have to report to my new job on January 2.

And with that, they agreed to meet at Field Camp to celebrate their new beginnings together and to say good-bye to their comrades.

Somewhere in his heart, however, it was a pity to Yakubovsky to quit. It was a heavy feeling knowing he would have to leave guys who were true friends. Fighting comrades! But then he had set a goal, and, as a crocodile, he was moving stealthily forward to reach it.

58

California, December 1, 1994

In the afternoon, when Melissa arrived home from school to feed George, her father called. He told her that Ms. Doughty was gone. For him, it was a greater loss than even for Melissa. Ms. Doughty had taken care of him for over thirty years. She had started work for Sir Spenser even before he had married Melissa's mother. Ms. Doughty had helped with Melissa just as the Trunovs were helping with George.

Having cried some, Melissa, instead of going back to school, went to church. She lit a candle and said a long prayer for the tranquility of the soul of God's recently departed slave Ms. Doughty. Then she spoke to the priest. After church, Melissa went to the furniture store to buy a new bed for her father's trip to California.

Melissa had completely relocated George to her room. She had asked his permission to move in with her, to which George, a kind boy, presented her with the most radiant smile. He was already trying to sit by himself, and he had learned to turn over. He also liked to throw toys on the floor. Melissa wanted to wean him from breastfeeding because he had started to bite her terribly.

Sir Spenser arrived in California after the funeral. Melissa met him at LAX Airport. They had a little cry on the way home, but entered the house with dry eyes.

The new grandfather met his grandson cautiously. The last child he had dealt with had been Melissa, and he was afraid to take George into his own hands. Having sensed this new person's fear, George burst into tears.

On the other hand, Melissa's father established friendly relations with the Trunovs at once. Grandma Mila, as Melissa had begun to call her, had prepared a full table for his arrival. Sir Spenser was never the boozer, but a shot or two he would put down with pleasure. He loved to test new food, as well, though he never overate. He liked the pies with meat and cabbage, and he was delighted with the potato salad. As a true epicurean, he appreciated the custom of having, after a shot of vodka, a snack—a cracker with red or black caviar. And that's not even to say what he thought about the homemade doughnuts with jam and the house pie "Napoleon" with a cup of tea.

In a few days, grandson and grandfather got used to each other. George had ceased being afraid of sitting on his grandfather's knees, and Grandfather learned to hold George tightly but cautiously. But overall, Sir Spenser preferred Valentin's company. They had even agreed to go fishing together, which this Sir had never done in his life. But he thought it would be possible to give it a try once.

They celebrated Christmas in the amicable company of Mrs. Backinsale and Sharon, and the two women's husbands. Sir Charles remembered Sharon as still being a girl. They put up an elegant Christmas tree and bought gifts for one another. And after, they welcomed in the New Year 1995.

Soon, Melissa was back in school studying for midterms and so became, once again, absorbed by her studies.

Sir Charles left in February. Melissa asked him to think of spending more time with her in California. After all, except for each other and George, neither of them had any other close relatives. Not to mention the California climate couldn't even begin to compare with London's.

59

Moscow, January 2, 1995

Gavrila Kravchuk started an application for a commercial loan through Food Commerce Bank. He gave instructions to the only employee left in his legal department, Mr. Yuri Beloff, to prepare a draft of a contract for delivering wheat in the sum of six million US dollars, adding to the previously agreed-upon amount of five-and-a-half million. The additional five hundred thousand would be a contingency, so the total loan amount needed to be six million. Kravchuk also named a supplier: First Russian, Inc., a California corporation. The chairman of the board of this company was Gavrila Petrovich Kravchuk, and Boris Goryanin was the president. Gavrila found in the company files the extract from the board of directors authorizing him to open the company's account and giving him general power of attorney.

Looking at the document, Gavrila thought, I do not understand. How in the world could Goryanin manage to escape from Cherkizov?

Kravchuk knew perfectly that after he had made an attempt to take the money, which had been wired by Pennington International for the crude-oil delivery in October 1993, Goryanin had closed the bank accounts of both Agroprom-USA and First Russian, Inc., and dissolved both companies. Kravchuk had received statements from the Bank of America regarding the closing of both accounts. Nevertheless, he called Mr. Beloff and gave him the agreement regarding the delivery between Agroprom-USA and Pennington International. Kravchuk then ordered him to construct a similar agreement for Food Commerce Bank for the delivery of wheat between First Russian, Inc. and Agroprom.

"Please, do it as soon as possible," he added. "If there are questions, we shall involve Semenov. He has first-hand experience in the purchase of foodstuff."

In a few days, it became obvious that Semenov should be contacted. Beloff hadn't known where to begin, let alone how to finalize any of the details. Both men spent almost two weeks preparing a rough draft of a contract. And, as usual, in addition to a supplier, they would need to determine a transportation company. After long reflection, they agreed on the Ukrainian company Ukrtransport, which carried loose cargo to the commercial port Ilichyovsk, near Odessa. It was originally planned to purchase high-quality wheat, bring it to Ilichyovsk, and from there, deliver it by railroad to the mill, to process it into flour. Finally, it would go to Russia. But during their discussions, it became clear that, from a financial point of view, it would be more favorable to buy low-quality wheat, deliver it to the port of Rostov, and from there, deliver it by rail to the Moscow Brewery Processing Plant. There it could be processed into alcohol and high-quality vodka, bottled, and then sold. This idea pleased Kravchuk more than anything they had discussed before.

And so to conduct a detailed study of the brewery process, Kravchuk personally, not trusting anybody with this most important step of the business went to Samokatnaya Street, where the Moscow brewery plant was located. He went to the director general, and after short negotiations, he was directed to the testing hall. Clearly, when he was finished there, Mr. Kravchuk's two bodyguards took him straight home.

This new plan that Kravchuk now insisted on was approved by the loan committee at Food Commerce Bank. After all, the plan was recognized as the most financially feasible. Thereafter, Kravchuk went a few more times to the brewery and offered them a significant financial interest in the realization of the final product. Despite the fact that each of his visits to the brewery ended the same, he continued to pursue the work with persistence. He was agreeable with the brewery personnel, but carried out long negotiations, only accepting all of their technological methods after a thorough analysis and a double check of the results—which he did by personally tasting the end product at the factory's testing hall.

Mr. Kravchuk's experiments with his health did not go without consequence. He was admitted into a rehab center with the diagnosis of delirium tremens again. He was connected to an IV and, again, the doctors managed to rehabilitate him from the condition to which he had driven himself. However, this time, Gavrila was in the hospital much longer. His liver and kidneys refused to work. The doctors could not discharge him until the beginning of February.

When Gavrila got back to work, he had a new secretary, Katherine. She had already been working there a long time. Semenov continued to hover around Katherine, as he had around Valerie in the good old days.

"And why is he always near Kat?" Gavrila asked, perplexed. He didn't know that Semenov had already been sleeping with his wife Alevtina for a long time, and that he had always just been horsing around in Kravchuk's reception area because Alevtina's office door was directly opposite the office.

Semenov and Beloff made an agreement with the railroad for transferring the wheat. Considering the decrease of their purchase price from two hundred dollars a ton for first-class wheat to one hundred dollars a ton, they would be able to increase the quantity of transported grain from thirty thousand tons up to sixty thousand. In that case, they would need one thousand bunker cars instead of five hundred. But they couldn't find a carrier in Russia that would allow them such a large capacity. So they found another carrier, again in Odessa. The people in Odessa insisted, however, that the harbor of delivery be Port Ilichyovsk. Their transits across the Ukraine connected with the railroad.

The Russian government had recently adopted a new rule—that all commercial entities operating under hard currency register with an organization called Russian Contract. After the transfer of money, the borrower received one hundred and eighty days to fulfill the contract. In their case, however, as theirs was a transaction dealing with large volumes, this rule was backed by a caveat about "the essential performance of contractual obligations." In other words, they could be allowed additional time, if needed.

The procedure for converting Russian domestic currency into hard currency and then wiring the funds abroad had been simplified since 1993. Still, it was equally necessary to find the organization's quotas on currency transactions and to obtain a license for foreign trade activities.

At the Moscow Brewery Processing Plant, since an immemorial time, there had been an experimental brewery plant funded by the All-Union Scientific Research Institute of Fermentation Products. At this factory, they made the best-quality vodka brands such as Stoli, Posol, and other elite grades, exclusively for members of the Central Committee of the Communist Party, for the government, for members of the joint staff, and so on. In 1992, the experimental brewery plant was privatized, but kept all of its management and, most important, affiliations. The small enterprise actually also received every conceivable and inconceivable sanction, quota, license, and so on. They often acted as intermediaries in financial operations for other companies and private persons. But the most important fact about the company was that Food Commerce Bank was owned by the same group of investors as was the experimental brewery plant.

On Monday, February 13, Gavrila Kravchuk and Alexey Semenov, with drafts of all the documents, met with the manager of the credit department,

Mr. Timur Kagirov, and the deputy chief of the Food Commerce Bank legal department, Mr. Valentin Simakin.

They took the drafts from Kravchuk in order to coordination efforts, and in a couple of days, Simakin called Kravchuk and told him that, basically, everything was in good shape. The bank's management had no objections. The attached business plan allowed them to believe that the return schedule was reliable enough. The bank was quite satisfied with the collateral. All that remained was to add the bank's and borrower's requisites, as well as their addresses, and, from there, as they say, it was onward and upward. But first, they needed to address some details.

The process of addressing "some details" took place on February 19 in the notorious sauna. There were four: Kagirov, Simakin, Kravchuk, and Semenov. It was a clear and frosty Sunday. All properly steamed, some of them had drinks and then all came to a common understanding. They agreed upon the conditions of credit, having not forgotten about the personal interests of Kagirov and Simakin. The amount of credit thus increased to six million five hundred thousand dollars.

The final document necessary for representation to the bank was a personal guarantee of performance under the contract. Here, Kravchuk made a decision that, at that moment, seemed ingenious. As the guarantor, he decided to use Agroprom-USA, a California corporation. Under his instruction, Mr. Beloff prepared and printed out the letter of guarantee. The essence of the letter was that in the case of failing its obligation to deliver wheat under the contract between First Russian, Inc. and Agroprom-USA, Mr. Boris Goryanin would personally undertake the loan and return to Food Commerce Bank the total amount of six million five hundred thousand dollars, plus interest.

Having received from Beloff the letter of guarantee made in English, Kravchuk read the text in depth. Having taken pleasure in imagining Boris's reaction to such an agreement, Kravchuk grinned and took a moment of silence, diligently producing, in half-printed letters, the signature of BORIS GORYANIN.

Kravchuk thought nothing of the forgery. It was an obvious crime, but he didn't care. He only cared about stealing big and escaping.

After a meeting with Kagirov and Simakin, Kravchuk called Yakubovsky and let him know that the loan from Food Commerce Bank should be considered a done deal. Consequently, Kravchuk and Semenov started to prepare a trip to the States to open accounts with Sunshine Bank of Florida, in the city of Miami Beach, for Semenov, Kagirov, and Simakin. Yakubovsky did not go with them to Miami. He had to solve no-less-important problems for himself.

On February 21, Yakubovsky took off for Ural's city of Yekaterinburg, where he went to the US Consulate. There, he completed questionnaires and forms, stood in a long line, and presented the passport of Kazakhstan citizen Gavrila Kravchuk, in which there was his manipulated photo. In those days, the US Consulate could get only lazy people to work for them, and so Kazakh Gavrila Kravchuk received a one-year multi-entrance visa.

From Yekaterinburg, Yakubovsky left for Alma-Ata, then Kazakhstan's capital. In the US Consulate there, he completed questionnaires and forms, stood in a long line, and presented the passport of Kazakhstan citizen Wolfgang Nushke, in which there was his other manipulated photo. In this US Consulate, they used to give tourist visas to everybody, especially Kazakh Germans. And so Wolfgang Nushke also received a multi-entrance visa good for one year.

60

Moscow, March 10, 1995

During the long Moscow winter, it appeared that time had frozen too. Igor, with Ann, who was to graduate that spring, now made twice-monthly shuttle trips. Yakubovsky always met them at the airport, and within a day or two, they would deliver the merchandise to certain buyers, and make a considerable amount of money.

Kravchuk, Semenov, and Yakubovsky were engaged in finalizing the contracts for the purchase, delivery, and processing of grain; the brewery's processing of the grain into vodka; and the bottling, labeling, and, finally, sale of the end product. It was necessary to solve many unexpected problems that had arisen, such as the printing of labels and the manufacturing of corks for the bottles. There were also problems with obtaining certificates of quality, and receiving permits for sale of the alcohol, as well as expert reports. But, gradually all was in place.

By the end of February, Vladislav and Igor decided to purchase a relatively large quantity of vodka on their shuttle trips. By now, their savings account had accrued over eight hundred thousand dollars, all clean. All the taxes had been paid, and every supporting document was in full order. However, such an amount of money, for many reasons, was dangerous to keep in the bank. On the one hand, gangsters could find it. In that instance, the bank could lose money, but the depositors also were not insured. So they would need to perform a simple trading operation, after which they could dump their earnings in the Elephteria, Ltd., account in Cyprus.

Summer was the time of students graduating, the spring army draft returning from service, and families taking vacations. So the sale of vodka shouldn't be any problem. The Yakubovskys thus decided to make a serious transaction. They would buy enough Finnish-made vodka to fill five tractor-trailers. In one forty-foot container, it was possible to load forty pallets, and in one twenty-foot trailer, twenty pallets. Once filled with the boxes, the pallets had to be shrink-wrapped and then densely packed inside the containers. Now, each pallet held sixteen boxes stacked in four rows, totaling sixty-four boxes per pallet. In each box, there were twelve one-liter bottles of "Finlandia." Thus, on each pallet there were seven hundred sixty-eight bottles. The total order made three hundred pallets of seven hundred sixty-eight bottles— altogether, more than two hundred thirty thousand one-liter bottles of vodka.

A bottle of vodka, delivered from the Finnish manufacturer to Moscow, including cost of goods and transportation was one dollar and five cents. The customs duties, other taxes, and a ten percent contingency were fifty-one cents more. The wholesale price for kiosks and grocery stores could be three dollars and twenty-five cents. But the retail price was four dollars in the afternoon and five dollars at night. Thus, in approximately two months, the Yakubovskys could earn more than three hundred sixty thousand dollars.

61

Moscow, March 10, 1995

Yakubovsky received the long-awaited telegram from Kazakhstan: "It's come. Murashovs." Vladislav and Victoria thus took off for Kazakhstan on Sunday, March 12.

Vlad sent a telegram to the driver, who met them in Kachiri. Again, they bought bags of nonperishable food for the Murashovs. Galina Murenko had not been forgotten either. The Murashovs gave them a postcard saying that the applications for their exit visas to Germany for permanent residency had been considered and satisfied, but the Schmidt family should cross the border no later than April 30 of that year. Considering the number of questions they still had to resolve in such a short time, that wouldn't be easy. So having stayed only overnight in Fedorovka, they returned to Kachiri and, the very same day, departed to Moscow.

Vladislav asked Vicky not to sell her apartment. Anything could happen, and they might need it later. They decided to lease her apartment out, but couldn't find a tenant…

It was a mad time. All came at the same point of time: preparation to move to Germany, purchasing of vodka, the shuttle business… Also Vladislav, along with Kravchuk and Semenov, was still in the process of receiving a loan from Food Commerce Bank. In addition, he needed to develop a secret plan for his trip to Western Samoa—yes, and to have an iron-clad alibi.

The delivery of the vodka from Finland was delayed for several reasons, which both Vlad and Igor had to deal with simultaneously. However, Igor did the bulk of the work. He made a trip to Finland, where he observed the pallets being loaded into the containers. He needed to be convinced personally that all of the boxes were shrink-wrapped reliably.

Unfortunately, on some of the cases, the plastic broke due to jolting, and the boxes fell from the container at unloading. Such obvious carelessness, however, wasn't covered by insurance. And, as the result, importers incurred losses.

Igor also remained in constant contact with the transportation company. Due to increase in circulation, they hadn't enough trucks and trailers for everyone. Therefore, for those who were always in contact, cargo was shipped, while the other, less energetic, sorts had to wait.

Passage through the customs office at the city of Vyborg, on the Russian border with Finland, took a lot of time, so Igor decided to send the shipment by ferry, via Latvia's port, Ventspils, on the Baltic Sea. And then from Ventspils, it would go by freeway through the city of Smolensk to Moscow. With this route, the customs inspection could take place in Moscow. But then a fully loaded forty-foot truck and twenty-foot trailer exceeded a hundred thousand pounds, so not every ferry could take all five loads simultaneously. He'd have to wait. And idle time, as it is known, costs money.

The shipment of vodka, therefore, wouldn't arrive in Moscow until May 16, but the Schmidts' exit visa to Germany expired two weeks earlier. So they decided that Vlad and Vicky would go to Alma-Ata, have all of the seals stamped in the German Consulate, and depart from Moscow.

Vlad needed the person on duty at the VIP desk to pass through customs, carrying their travel bag with the six hundred thousand dollars. Then Vicky would need to go through passport control with Yakubovsky's passport and register the departure stamp. Finally, both of them would go through passport control with their Schmidt passports.

Thus, Vladislav Yakubovsky remained a citizen of Russia, and Vladislav and Victoria Schmidt would live in Germany, as German refugees. Of course, only Vladislav, Victoria, and Igor knew about this. They kept it a secret even from Ann.

As for Kravchuk, Semenov, and Pushkov, they couldn't even have guessed Yakubovsky's plans. All they knew was that Vicky left for Germany to vacation with her parents and that Vladislav could not go with her because of the situation with the loan and the delayed shipment of vodka.

The day of their departure was nearing, but the loan documents were all still in the works. Vicky quit her job, and held a going-away party for coworkers at her apartment. Two girlfriends with whom Vicky had worked in VIP came with dates, and Vicky's shift manager brought her husband, a middle-aged man with an uncertain appearance. The VIP Service manager also came with her husband who, like Vladislav, used to work for the FSB, and now was engaged in a private business, naturally connected to the VIP Service.

And so the party began. They drank for the Schmidts' success at their new place, and for their departure, and they drank again and again, as usual. Vlad didn't drink, however, remembering his promise to Vicky a long time ago. He took only a glass of wine, and felt excellently. Vicky didn't drink either. For the last six weeks, she had started to feel sick in the mornings. They suspected she could be pregnant, but Vicky hadn't gone to the doctor. They had resolved that she would receive a check-up in Germany. But just in case, she had stopped drinking wine.

The women started to sob and ran out on the balcony to smoke. The men then began to criticize the new authority and recollected Soviet times. The middle-aged man with an uncertain appearance, having visibly drunk too much, started to stick Vladislav with the request "to send them, from Germany, some rags for promotion." Vladislav spoke with him only out of politeness, but kept his eyes on Vicky. But during their conversation, Vladislav found out that this guy was not so simple. He was working as the shift manager at the cargo customs office. Because of that, Vladislav, continuing to admire Vicky, sharply changed his attitude toward the man. They even agreed that Igor, Vladislav's son, would call him the day after tomorrow to talk about business.

With the snacks that Vicky and Vlad put on the table, nobody was drunk. Vicky turned on some music: the "Argentinian Tango!" Everybody danced, including Vlad, who pressed Vicky firmly into himself. From the sounds of the tango and their affinity toward each other, their bodies became so excited that neither could wait until they were alone.

The party ended at way past midnight. Having closed a door behind them, Vladislav embraced Vicky, kissed her passionately, and then the two withdrew to the bedroom.

62

Moscow, April 26, 1995

On April 26, Igor departed to Helsinki, and on April 28, Vlad and Vicky left for Germany. As they had planned, Vicky went to passport control and had the departure mark stamped on Yakubovsky's passport. Then they checked in two suitcases with things for Vicky's parents and relatives. Then, with a medium-sized travel bag, Vicky's handbag, and Vlad's small briefcase with documents, they proceeded past customs examination and passport control. The VIP-service shift manager personally carried the travel bag. She couldn't have even suspected that she was holding six hundred thousand dollars. Vicky's two girlfriends burst out crying, but after agreeing to stay in touch and visit her in Germany, they calmed down. They said a long good-bye, nestled their cheeks into Vlad's, and left, wiping their slightly swollen eyes with tissue.

Vladislav and Victoria Schmidt took a direct flight to Munich, but upon landing, they "accidentally" were separated. Yakubovsky, with the travel bag, went to the German border guard, having presented his passport for Vladislav Yakubovsky. The passport control officer, having looked at the passport and at Vladislav, negligently awarded him with an arrival stamp.

Victoria went to the other border guard and presented her passport and visa. He took the visa, looked at her, and asked where her husband was. Victoria answered in perfect German, specifying that Vladislav had already passed through passport control and was expecting her. The border guard, having looked around, habitually put a stamp of arrival on her passport. On Vladislav Schmidt's passport, however, an arrival stamp would not appear.

Vladislav and Victoria then met at the baggage claim, retrieved their belongings, and left. There were Victoria's parents already waiting for them. Vladislav, as he had been upon their first meeting, was amazed by Frieda's beautiful blue eyes, and cascading gold ringlets. Frieda appeared too young to be Vicky's mother, but she might pass for an older sister. They kissed each other, and embracing the mother-in-law, Vladislav pressed her against himself. He felt her firm breasts and flat stomach and … at Frieda's age, she still had a waist! Vladislav looked at Vicky and, again, feelings for his wife poured over him.

When they arrived on the farm, it had already started to darken. All of Victoria's relatives, the former farm owners and two Swiss couples came to meet them. They sat around a large table and noisily welcomed the newcomers. Yakubovsky, without problems, communicated in German, astonishing everybody. He sipped at a glass of apple wine. The meal was simple, but so good that they wanted to eat every last bit of it.

The best room was designated to Vicky and her husband. This evening, Vlad and Vicky didn't make love. They simply nestled into each other and fell asleep. When they awoke, the sun had already risen above the tops of the pines. Vladislav rose first. He has quickly shaved and showered, and then left the bathroom to Victoria. She didn't spend a lot of time bathing either, after which they dressed and went outside.

Everyone was already occupied with their usual farm work. Vlad and Vicky walked through the farm, and looked around inside a shed where goats, sheep, and other domestic creatures were kept. Then they went a little into a wooded area and, being overwhelmed by the clean Bavarian air, returned to the house, where a loaf of bread and a jug of milk sat on the table. Two large ceramic cups stood beside. They ate the fresh bread and washed it down with the fresh goat milk. After that, as if on command, but not saying a word, they returned to their room, closed the door, and made love. And afterward, tired, they fell asleep.

When Vlad woke up, he long examined the sleeping Vicky. Then, he put his head on her stomach, and wished that time would stop, and that all of his problems, including the vodka shipments and the loan would be gone forever. In fact, he had everything he wanted here: a farm, a beautiful wife with whom he was in love, fresh bread, and milk; what else was necessary?

As he inhaled the aroma of his favorite body, Victoria stirred, and they started to caress each other. Both of them would be happy if this moment, this life, never came to an end.

Finally, they rose, but reeling in weariness, they somehow lay down and went back asleep. They woke again to a knock at the door. It was Frieda calling them to the table. Enamored as they could be, they went to dinner.

Vlad was given homemade beer, fried goose, homemade bread, organic cheeses, and more. Only now had he understood the pleasure of rural life. He wished he never had to leave, and could just live here and love his Vicky.

The next day, Vlad and Vicky took Vicky's parents' old Soviet-made car to the immigration center in Munich. There, they filled out papers for health services and employment.

Having been convinced that Vladislav and Victoria knew the language, although they had obvious Slavic accents, the social worker decided not to send them to language courses, but to find out where they planned to live and when they could start work. Vladislav said that they would live and work on the farm, after which the social worker left him alone.

When Victoria told him that she used to work for the airport and knew several languages, however, that piqued the social worker's interest. He asked them to wait out in the reception room, and then he made a long phone call somewhere. Then they were asked to come back into his office, where he gave them two thousand German marks for meals and living arrangements. Victoria received a memo for the personnel department of the Munich Airport. Also, in order to get full medical coverage, they received a prescription for a full medical examination, scheduled on May 10.

After visiting the immigration center, they made a little drive across Munich. Vicky had never been abroad, so the trip was a novelty for her. Hungry, they found a small restaurant, parked the car, and went inside. They ordered German dishes, and the meal was excellent.

After lunch, they continued their drive and did not come back to the farm until after dusk. Again, they took pleasure in a German feast, and after supper, walked the farm, enjoying the night's silence and the coolness of the woods, and discussed their future. There was pleasure in rural life, but they had gotten used to the city. Therefore, they decided that, for now, Vicky would work at the airport, and if she was pregnant, they would move back to the farm.

The next morning, Vladislav took Vicky to the Munich Airport, where she passed the interview with an "excellent." The airport had been searching for a person to work in the lounge with passengers riding first-class. Victoria, with her typically German appearance, her knowledge of many languages, and her experience in VIP suited that role. They made her an offer to come to work as soon as possible, to take a two-week training course.

Now they needed to solve two more problems: to rent an apartment close enough that Vicky could get to work by bus, and to register for driving lessons. At the airport personnel department, Victoria received a list of the available apartments close by.

They contacted the listed agent, who showed them three apartments. Not capricious, they chose a one-bedroom furnished apartment with an excellent kitchen for twelve hundred German marks per month. The lease was executed on month-to-month basis.

And what to do next, they would decide after Vicky's medical examination.

With the driving school, they were lucky too. It was located across the street from their future apartment. The school worked around the individual's schedule.

All developed successfully from there. All except for one thing: Yakubovsky did not plan to remain in Germany. After the bank issued the loan and he transferred money to his account, he and Vicky, as well as Igor and Ann, needed to disappear; otherwise, they would be found.

But for a while, it seemed, they would live in Germany. For this reason, he brought Kravchuk to the farm to assure him that this was his plan.

Now, Yakubovsky couldn't imagine his life without Vicky. He loved this smart and beautiful woman, and especially if they were going to have a child. In a drugstore, they purchased a home pregnancy test and conducted the test on their own. The test confirmed that Vicky was pregnant. Now they waited to see what the doctor would say.

They moved into the apartment the very next day, and Vladislav drove Victoria to the airport for her first day of work. On the way back, he stopped at a used car dealer. For three thousand dollars, he purchased a Volkswagen Passat with automatic transmission. This would be easier for Vicky to learn to drive.

And so the routine began. Vicky was occupied in training for six hours daily, while Vlad spent time in the city, in small restaurants and bars, drinking beer, snacking, and thinking, devising various plans of disappearance. Yakubovsky knew that little time remained, but it was also impossible to rush things. He was a true, trained, professional scout, and he would use his knowledge and experience to achieve the plan formulated by Kravchuk back in the winter of 1993: to steal big money and escape.

Yakubovsky also called Igor and Kravchuk daily. It looked as if both of them were progressing as outlined. By now, Yakubovsky needed to fly back to Moscow urgently, but he was waiting for May 10, the day when Vicky would visit the doctor.

On May 10, after Vicky's classes, they went to the doctor. When a smiling Vicky left the office, hanging onto Vlad's neck, embracing and kissing him, all became clear. She only had time to whisper, "The third month. A girl!" And tears of happiness rolled from her eyes.

They rushed off to Victoria's parents to share the news. On the way, they stopped at the flower shop and bought flowers for Vicky and Frieda, and a bottle of true French champagne to celebrate the occasion.

The next day, Thursday, May 11, Vladislav took the travel bag with the money, and they left the farm. The next morning, he would take off for

Moscow. Before his departure, neither of them could sleep all night long. Vladislav didn't want to leave Vicky during such a time, but both of them perfectly understood that it was necessary to earn money. But then she did not remain in Munich alone. Her parents were ready to come on the first call.

Before checking in at the airport, Vladislav went to a branch of Deutche Bank and opened up an account in the name of Wolfgang Nushke, into which he deposited the six hundred thousand dollars. He had left Victoria with five thousand dollars, and, in his pocket, just in case, he had two hundred dollars.

Igor met his father at the Sheremetyevo Airport. As always, Ann was with him. Happy as a child, Vlad told Igor and Ann that his darling Vicky was pregnant with a girl and that she was due in November.

In their turn Igor and Anna told Vladislav that in the morning they submitted a marriage application to the registry office. There was a thirty-day waiting period. So their marriage was scheduled for June 12.

That evening, they celebrated the good news together, and the next morning, Saturday, May 13, Igor drove to Ventspils to meet the cargo.

thought, Anna exploded in the passionate desire granted to her not by Cupid, but by the devil, to be seized, kneaded, unscrewed, and rained on with kisses by the father of her best friend and future husband.

Does he really feel nothing? she thought. *Does he really not feel how, from his casual touch, a shiver runs through my body? Such a wooden block.*

She stood at the door dreaming that Vladislav, having arrived home, would call her. She went to the bedroom and turned down the bed. She changed into a nightgown. She continued to feel Vlad's presence as she mentally named him. Then her languor was interrupted by the phone ringing…

Yakubovsky parked his car in its usual place. Before his eyes was the image of his future daughter-in-law. He continued to hear her laughter and to feel her velvet skin.

I shall not meet with her any more. It is like Middle Eastern sweets—who knows what you may find inside! Think of it. To be hopelessly enamored by my son's wife-to-be! Yakubovsky thought, slowly walking upstairs to his empty apartment. Then he remembered Vicky again. He needed to call her to find out how she was. But in his thoughts was Ann. He felt her presence, smelled her sweet aroma, and heard her voice.

Approaching to the entrance door of the apartment, Yakubovsky heard the telephone ring. But by the time he unlocked the door and got inside, the ringing had stopped.

"That's fine. If someone wants to talk to me, they will call back," he told himself, and began to undress.

Having hung his clothes, he went into the kitchen, put a teapot on the stove, and switched on the TV. Then having flipped through the channel and not finding anything worthy of watching, he switched it back off. Vladislav looked at the clock. It was ten sharp. In the summertime, in Moscow, it did not get dark until very late, and now it was only dusk. Yakubovsky called Ann. Her phone was busy. In Germany, it was eight o'clock, so Vladislav called Vicky. They talked a little about nothing. When he hung up, it was half past ten. Yakubovsky dialed Anna's number again. The phone was still busy.

In fifteen more minutes, Vladislav dialed Ann's number a third time, but her phone was still off the hook. His sixth sense told him that something was wrong. About a half-an-hour passed and Vladislav called again, only to receive another busy signal. It was impossible to wait any longer. He dressed, and put on a holster with his Makarov pistol, which they had also found in Igor's current apartment. Out of habit, he always kept the weapon on him.

Igor's apartment was about a twenty-minute drive. Vladislav parked and took the stairs up to the upper floor. He stopped there and listened. All was silent. Vladislav came down to Igor's floor. At the entry door, he stopped and listened. All was silent. He got out his pistol and rang the doorbell. But Ann didn't answer. He rang again…

Yakubovsky opened the door with his keys. In the entryway, the light was on, but there was silence in the apartment. The light was on in the bedroom, but the bedroom door was closed. Yakubovsky very cautiously opened the bedroom door. What he saw startled him. Anna was sitting on the floor next to the bed. Her right leg was bent under her and she was sitting on it. It was unnaturally white. The left leg was straight. Anna was pressing the telephone receiver to her chest. Her eyes and mouth were open. Her eyes were vacant and she feverishly shivered. Her face was white, and her forehead was cold. She obviously was in shock. But what had happened to put her in such a condition?

Yakubovsky cautiously examined the apartment. All of the windows and the back door were still closed and locked. He checked the kitchen and the bathroom. There were no signs that someone else was, or had been, in the apartment. That meant she was in shock from something she had heard over the phone.

Vladislav put his pistol back in its holster. "All right. That, we will find out later. Now, it is most important just to get her out of shock."

Yakubovsky went back into the bedroom and took the telephone from Ann's hands. Then, with tenderness, he lifted the young woman and put her on the bed. Ann's right leg was congealed. Vladislav rubbed her temples, but she continued to look straight ahead at nothing and kept shivering. Yakubovsky felt both her feet. The right foot was colder than the other. Apparently, it was simply numbed. Vladislav cautiously started to massage her right leg, starting a little above knee and then moving down to her shin and her toes. Gradually, trying not to make any sharp movements, he then started to straighten her leg. In a few minutes, the circulation was restored, and her foot began to grow warmer.

Yakubovsky found some clean socks in the dresser and put them on her feet. Then he laid a pillow under them and covered her with a blanket.

Vladislav left her in the bed and went to the kitchen. He put a teapot on the stove and found a first-aid kit. He needed some ammonia, but there was none in the kit. He went to the living room and got a bottle of cognac from the bar, and returned to the kitchen. He poured some cognac into a glass and drank it in one gulp. He poured another shot. The teapot whistled. Vladislav got a tea cup from the cabinet, dropped in a teabag, and filled it three-quarters of the way with hot water. Then he filled the rest of it with cognac. He carried the mixture into the bedroom.

Yakubovsky put the teacup on the floor and gently raised Ann's head.

He brought the cup to her lips, and as the smell of the cognac struck her nose, she slightly started. From her throat, a groan similar to a sob escaped. Yakubovsky allowed her to smell the cognac again. She twisted in a grimace. Now she started to sob.

"What happened to you, girl? What has happened?" Vladislav asked. But instead of giving an answer, she only sucked air through her lips, and shivered. Obviously, she couldn't speak.

Yakubovsky put the tea to her lips to give her a taste. It had slightly cooled and would be possible to drink in small sips. He filled a teaspoon with tea, raised Anna's head, and put the spoon into the girl's mouth. She did not swallow. The tea mixture dissolved in her mouth by itself. Yakubovsky filled her mouth with some drops of tea again. Then again and again. Gradually, warmth began to spread through her body and she started to return to consciousness.

Choking on a sob, she uttered, "Igor … Igor … Igor is no longer around!" Then she emitted a lingering moaned, grabbed Vladislav with both hands, and pulled him down to her.

He tried to pull her hands off of him and get her to relax. "What do you mean, he is no longer around? Where is he? Did you hear something by phone? What happened to him? What happened to you?"

Anna didn't answer, so Yakubovsky continued to have Anna drink until she had finished the whole cup. Meanwhile, he drank pure cognac from a glass. Then, though not trusting what she tried to explain next, Yakubovsky through her convulsive sobbing, gleaned the following: someone had informed her that Igor, driving on the Minsk Highway, had collided head-on with a bus. Igor was pronounced dead at the scene of the accident.

Anna never drank hard liquor. So the cognac quickly did its business, and she started to calm down.

To come to his senses, Vladislav got up and went to the kitchen. Two-thirds of the cognac bottle was empty. He took the bottle and drank the rest. He frowned, and, sighing hard, returned to the bedroom. Anna was curled up on the bed and lay without moving. It looked as if she was asleep.

Yakubovsky went to the telephone in the entryway. He sat down on the chair next to it and dialed the FSB officer-on-duty in the Moscow regional office.

"Assistant to the officer-on-duty, Captain Bodrov," a voice answered.

"Lieutenant colonel of the Service of External Intelligence Vladislav Ivanovich Yakubovsky is speaking. Please, do me a favor, captain. Please, check the operative report on Igor Vladislavovich Yakubovsky. It looks as if he was involved in a car accident on the Minsk Highway."

"Just a minute."

After a few minutes, which seemed years to Yakubovsky, there was a click, and the voice returned.

"Forgive me, Comrade Lieutenant Colonel. How is Igor Vladislavovich related to you?"

"He is my son."

"Unfortunately, Igor Vladislavovich is registered among the victims of traffic accidents on the Minsk Highway. The accident was located across from the Scientific Research Institute of Agriculture, two kilometers from the Moscow Circle Road. The car was a Zhiguli, the fifth model, with state license plate number 45-17 MOH. The police had it towed to the Moscow Circle Road mile marker on the Minsk Highway. Igor Vladislavovich was delivered to the Odintsovo City Hospital and declared DOA. It was not possible to save him. Comrade Lieutenant Colonel, please accept our condolences. What can I do for you?"

But Yakubovsky did not hear him anymore. He silently hung up the phone. Vladislav rose from the chair and, with lowered head and shoulders, went to the bedroom. He kneeled before the bed. Ann was now on her back, covered up to the throat with a blanket. Her eyes were opened.

Yakubovsky put his head on her stomach to calm down. He did not cry. Men do not cry. He simply stayed put, having hardened from the burning pain. Anna put both her hands on his head, having no energy left to cope with such tragedy.

Yakubovsky stood, went to the living room, opened a bottle of vodka, and went to the kitchen. The kitchen was in half darkness. Only the moon shone through the window. Not turning on the lights, he took two glasses from the cabinet. Yakubovsky sat at the table and poured the vodka into both glasses. He got a loaf of bread and cut off two chunks. Then he covered one glass with one piece and slightly salted the second one. Silently, he drank the full glass of vodka in one swig and bit off some bread. He rested his head against his opened palms on the table, and his shoulders began to shake.

There, Ann found him. She couldn't be alone anymore, and had come to the kitchen in her nightgown. She approached Vladislav and nestled up to him.

"I want to drink for the tranquility of Igor's soul. He was the closest friend of mine."

Vladislav pulled out a chair for Ann and turned on the lights. He then got one more glass. He poured vodka to its rim and then poured a little glass for Ann. They silently drank, not having clinked[15] their glasses.

"How shall we live without our Igor?" Yakubovsky asked, addressing

15 This is another Russian tradition—when people are drinking for tranquility of the souls of departed folks, they do not clink their glasses.

himself. "How good everything was, and now we are in grief. What have you done, son? What?"

His shoulders began to shake. He then calmed down and, not knowing what else to do, arose and said flatly, "Well, all right. I shall go."

"No, no, don't leave me! Vladislav, you shall never leave me behind!" Anna said, addressing Vladislav for the first time since he'd seen her. Anna rushed to him. "Don't leave me behind, please!" She bitterly began to cry. "Igor has left me, and now you want to, too! I so love you. Please!"

"Then I shall stay and drink some more," Yakubovsky said, and, not understanding what he was doing, walked to the bar and took out the last bottle. Then, still standing at the bar, he opened it and drank directly from the bottle. Going back to the kitchen, he handed the bottle to Anna and told her, "Take it. You have to drink too."

Poor Ann, absolutely heartbroken, and never having had a sip of alcohol in her life, poured a full glass for both herself and Vladislav. Together, they drank to the bottom of the bottle and took bites from the same small slice of bread. Yakubovsky, who hadn't drunk for almost three years, felt as if the ground had left from underneath his feet. Somehow, Anna dragged him to the bed and took off his shoes. Too embarrassed to pull down his trousers and take off his shirt, she put him on the side of the bed facing the room. And not completely understanding why, she climbed over the unconscious Yakubovsky, lay on the other side of the bed, and passed out too.

It was already dawn when Yakubovsky woke up with an unpleasant sensation in his throat. He hardly had time to reach the toilet and kneel before he was throwing up as never before. With loud howling and shuddering, he vomited endlessly, until finally, he stopped and his body filled with the chills. He could barely force himself up off his knees. He turned the faucet on and, for some time, rinsed out his mouth. Then, he drug his legs into the kitchen, where he found a jar of pickles in the refrigerator. He opened it and had some drinks of the cold brine. Now he felt a little better.

Yakubovsky returned to the bathroom and to quell the heavy odor coming from his mouth, he squeezed toothpaste from the tube directly into his mouth and rinsed it. Then he returned to the bedroom, took off his holster with the pistol and his trousers, and climbed under the blanket in only his shirt. He nestled up to the warm Ann, embraced her, and fell asleep.

Ann woke up when the sun was shining strong. Having seen Yakubovsky in the bed next to her, she felt warmth rise to her head, and only then recollected the terrible events of the previous night. The heavy smell of alcohol came from Yakubovsky's mouth. She had a disgusting taste in her mouth, too, and in her stomach there was a terrible weight. She felt sick. Then she had a terrible thought: "Oh, what will I tell Igor?" But having remembered that she never would be able to tell him anything again, she wanted not to wake up. Anna closed her eyes, but after lying down for a minute, she realized that she couldn't fall asleep, and she thought it would be better to get up while Vladislav was still asleep.

Silently, trying to not wake Yakubovsky, she climbed over him. On tiptoe, she has made her way into the bathroom. Suddenly, she got sick and rushed to the toilet. Once relieved, she brushed her teeth and took a hot shower. She stood under the jets of water and cried. It was too much for her. Anna was ashamed that she had slept with Vladislav in the same bed. She was ashamed about her dreams of Vladislav, about her foolish imagination. The shame forced her not to think of Igor for a while. But the recollecting in detail the events of the last night, she was convinced that nothing had happened between her and Vladislav, and she started to feel better.

Anna stepped out of the bathtub and dried herself with a towel. Her nightgown appeared to have gotten dirty when she threw up, so she wrapped herself in the towel, partially opened the bathroom door, and peeked out. It was silent in the apartment, and Vladislav was still asleep. So very quietly, Anna entered the bedroom to find some clothes. When she began to open the dresser drawer, it squeaked. Yakubovsky woke up and saw Ann in the nude, looking for her clothes. Vladislav, blinking, was stricken with the sight. To say that she was beautiful would have been an understatement. She was gorgeous. As gorgeous as only a twenty-two-year-old beauty could be. Vladislav was frightened that he had seen what he shouldn't, and closed his eyes, pretending to still be asleep.

Anna, frightened of waking Vlad, had noticed nothing. She put on a dark dress. Then, having looked at her reflection in the mirror, she remembered that it would be necessary to cover all of the mirrors in the apartment. She took out a bed sheet and threw it over the mirrored closet door. Then she took another bed sheet and went to cover the entryway mirror too. Then she went to the kitchen and cleaned off the table.

The wall clock showed six twenty-five. Having waited for a while so as not to confuse Ann, Yakubovsky silently got up and went into the bathroom. He undressed, brushed his teeth, shaved, and took a shower. Now he felt much better. His head didn't hurt anymore. Only his stomach felt slightly uneasy. He returned to the bedroom, dressed, and went to the kitchen, which had been restored to full order. The utensils that had been left on the table last night were washed and put away, the table was clean, and the teapot was ready on the stove.

Anna, having seen Vladislav, sighed hard. Her eyes were pouring with tears. She leaned her head against his shoulder and began to shake from the crying. Vladislav took her hand and kissed it. Then he embraced her and, having pressed her into himself, kissed her head. They stood for a few minutes. Then Anna pulled free, went to the stove, and turned on the gas burner under the teapot.

"I need to go," Vladislav told Ann. "You don't need to go with me. It will be too heavy for you. I need to call Pushkov."

"No. No. I shall go with you. Don't you remember? You've promised never to leave me. I cannot remain alone. It is too terrible for me. I shall go with you. You will not abandon me, promise?"

"What are you talking about? Of course I won't. But you cannot go with me now."

"Where are you going?"

"To the hospital."

"All right. I will do as you say," Ann conceded.

Vladislav left, closing the kitchen door behind him, and went to the entryway to dial Pushkov. Having heard what had happened, Alexander reacted with shock.

Vladislav told him, "Now, I am going to the Odintsovo Hospital. Igor's body is in the mortuary there. After that, I will go get the death certificate, and then to a cemetery. But I need your help. Please, you and your father, in police uniforms, go to the mile marker on Minsk Highway at the Moscow Circle Road. As soon as possible. Igor's car will be there. The briefcase with all of documents concerning the vodka shipment should be in the car. I need to get that briefcase as soon as possible. Otherwise, there could be problems."

Pushkov reacted instantly. "Understood. I am calling my father now."

Vlad thanked Pushkov, hung up, and returned to the kitchen. Ann was sitting on a chair in the middle of the kitchen, her legs spread out, resting her elbows on her knees, and supporting her face with palms. Her eyes looked somewhere distant, and she didn't move.

Yakubovsky squatted in front of her. "Dear, please take care of yourself. You and I have to be strong for each other. You must be strong for me."

"I will be strong. But it happened so fast. I already had to go through all this once, when I lost both my parents. And then it happened very fast, too. I am guilty. I am bringing these misfortunes."

"Please stop it!" Vladislav commanded, raising his voice. "We shall be together. It will be easier to go through this misfortune together."

From his resolute tone, Anna's head dropped from the pull of grief, as she took Vladislav's outstretched hand, and, tightening her grip, slowly rose. Her figure had become limp and her shoulders stooped.

Then leading her into the entryway, Yakubovsky left her for a minute to go back to the bedroom and hid his pistol in the closet. Then, together, they left.

"We shall go to my apartment first," Vlad told her. "We need to get some money."

64

Moscow, May 17, 1995

Alexander Pushkov dialed his father. Vasily Pushkov had just gotten back home from taking his wife to work. Having heard about Igor, he became very upset, but kept calm. A tow truck would soon be sent to get Igor's car, and everything in it would be destroyed. So they'd need to hurry. He quickly changed into his police uniform and went outside where his son was waiting.

This early in the morning, there was no traffic, so the Pushkovs quickly reached the mile marker. They arrived just in time; the tow truck was just raising the front part of the totaled car. Alexander jumped out and ran up to the tow truck.

The tow-truck driver bellowed, "What do you need?" But, having seen the elderly police major approach behind him, he changed his tune. "I was ordered to pick up the damaged car. So I am doing my job. And if I am doing something wrong, there's the commander."

The car looked terrible. The driver's side was totally smashed. The windshield was gone. The front door was hanging on only by the lower hinge. The steering wheel and driver's seat were scattered about on the ground. But the right side of the car was practically untouched. The passenger's side door was still closed. The combined speed of the bus and the car coming at each other was probably so high, that the car was virtually cut in half.

Having seen what was happening one of the traffic cops on duty, a second lieutenant in a bulletproof vest and an automatic machine gun came over. He saluted the senior officer and has asked, "What can I do for you, Comrade Major?"

The Pushkov Sr. saluted the second lieutenant and answered, "This car belongs to our friend. The guy was lost last night in the traffic accident. We want to look to make sure there weren't any personal belongings to pass onto his father."

"Certainly. I don't see any problem. Take everything you find."

The tow-truck driver lowered the lift. Alexander easily opened the right door and was terrified. Everywhere were splashed of caked-on blood. On the floor, right under the glove compartment, was Igor's briefcase. On top of the briefcase, there were several crumpled newspapers, so the case had been only slightly splashed in blood. On the passenger's backseat was scattered a bouquet of faded flowers, also covered in blood.

Alexander got a piece of clean cloth from the trunk of his car. Then he returned to the totaled car, and, trying not to touch any blood, took the briefcase out and carefully wiped it with the cloth.

"Dad!" Alexander addressed his father. "Have you seen? He purchased those flowers for Anna. Maybe we should get them for her?"

Vasily shook his head. "It is not necessary. It wouldn't change anything. It would only upset her more."

Except for the flowers and Igor's briefcase, there was nothing left in the car. They examined the trunk, but it was also empty. It was clear that those who had dragged over the car the night before simply had not noticed the briefcase under the newspapers.

Alexander took some money from his pocket. He handed the driver five dollars and the second lieutenant twenty. "Drink, guys, for the tranquility of Igor's soul. He was a good man."

There was nothing more to do after that, so the Pushkovs left.

Meanwhile, Vladislav and Anna were at Odintsovo—the town in suburb of Moscow. The mortuary was in a separate small building behind the main hospital. They silently stood at the entrance to the mortuary and waited for the doctor to bring them an official death certificate. The doctor had been called already, and should be there at any time. On the way to the hospital, they had stopped at a drugstore, and Vladislav had bought a small bottle of liquid ammonia.

The doctor arrived in about ten minutes. He greeted Anna and Vladislav.

He looked attentively at both of them and asked, "What is your relation to the deceased?"

"I am the father," Yakubovsky deafly responded.

"I am Igor's bride," a now sobered Anna answered.

"If you are the bride, I cannot allow you in. Only the father. Wait for us here, dear." The elderly man looked at the girl with sympathy. "It is not necessary for you to go. Please, forgive me."

The doctor took a key from huge hook, opened the door, and, together with Vladislav, went inside.

Already in a hallway, the doctor turned and locked the bolt on the entry door. "There is no need for her to see this. And even for you it will not be easy. Have you been to a mortuary before?"

"To tell you the truth, not often."

"Then it will be hard for you."

They went down some steps into a dark, gloomy hallway that smelled of mold and medicine. The doctor found the light switch and turned on the lights. There were two doors beside them. On one door was a sign that read "Laboratory." On the other door, the word "Freezer" was painted on.

"We will enter only for one minute. And then, I shall execute the job with formality. Would you be able to identify the body by looking at only the feet?"

"I hope so," Yakubovsky answered with a squalled voice.

"Are you ready?" the man asked. Then he opened the door with the painted label and stepped in.

Vladislav stayed in the hall while the man switched on the lights has and retrieved some thin rubber gloves from a box on a small stainless-steel table.

He put on the gloves and then gestured Vlad forward. "Please."

Yakubovsky took a deep breath and walked inside. On some wooden plank beds, bodies were covered by short gray bed sheets from under which naked feet peeked, each large toe attached to a tag.

"And here is how we finish our terrestrial way," the man philosophically murmured, lifting the bed sheet from the first body. It was a woman. Or, more accurately, what once had been a woman—a skeleton covered in thin yellow skin.

"Forty-two years old. Cancer." The man commented. "And here, apparently, is yours."

The doctor raised the second bed sheet, and what Vladislav saw would force anyone to shudder. For where there should have been a face was something wrapped in plaster and duct tape. Duct tape was also repeatedly wrapped around the chest, and a large heap of plaster lay on the bottom part of the stomach. Only the legs appeared untouched.

At that instant, he recollected the time his first wife, Igor's mother, happily smiling, handed him the small lump wrapped in a blanket; the time Igor began to walk alone; the first time Vlad had picked him up from kindergarten. And now, before Vlad's eyes, is all that remained of his son.

"He died instantly, on impact. Even if he survived for a little while, he felt nothing," the doctor sympathetically told Vladislav. "It will be necessary to bury him in a closed coffin. It is not necessary for your son to be remembered as such."

But Yakubovsky couldn't hear the man anymore. He began to settle on the floor. The doctor put his hand firmly in Vlad's underarms and pulled him up, helping him into the hallway. Then the man took his gloves off, got a pack of cigarettes from his pocket, and handed one to Vladislav. With non-bending fingers, Vladislav took it. The doctor then took one for himself, clicked open a lighter, and having taken a puff, stretched the light out to Vladislav.

Back at the entrance, the doctor looked at Vlad and said, "You should stay here with the girl. I will go sign the certificate and be back shortly."

Ann looked at Vladislav. It was as if his face had melted. A cigarette shook in his hand. Two years ago, under Vicky's insistence, Yakubovsky had quit smoking, and now his head began to spin from the nicotine. He recoiled from Ann and rushed to some nearby bushes, hiding behind them and heaving. Convulsions proceeded for a few minutes after. By that time, the doctor was back. Having seen what had happened to Yakubovsky, he gave the death certificate to Anna and rushed back into the mortuary. He came back out a couple of seconds later with a glass of water and a clean cloth. Vladislav began coming back to his senses. He rinsed his mouth, spit, and rinsed again. Then he dabbed his hand into the water and rubbed some of the cool liquid across his face. Then not drying it, he stood before the two of them, wet and pale.

Eventually he recovered enough to speak. "Thank you, doctor," Vladislav sputtered. Then he turned and walked away on bended legs.

Ann ran behind him, gripping the piece of paper, until she caught up with him. They stopped. Vladislav embraced Anna, and nestled up to her. And so they stood for at least five minutes. Motionless. Silent. Only sometimes slightly shuddering, with tears escaping their eyes.

"We have to go to the priest." Yakubovsky said, having taken a breath.

"Are you able to drive?" Ann said.

"I have to. Now we need to be strong and do things for ourselves."

They walked silently to the car. Yakubovsky didn't think at all. He looked at the road, letting his thoughts be carried as if by leapfrogs in his head. He couldn't concentrate on anything.

Finally they reached the church that, in the winter of 1994, they had come to with Igor to ask the young priest to consecrate their apartment. The priest, Father Theofil, was there. He recognized Vladislav and Anna. When they told him what king of grief brought them, the priest read a prayer. Then they approached the saints and lit candles. Clearly, the Father agreed to perform the burial service for Igor. However, having found out that the coffin would be closed, he was distressed.

"But there's nothing that could be done," Father Theofil concluded. "This is the way the Lord decided to call to his court the soul of his recently departed, Igor."

The three of them went to the Vagankovsky Cemetery to plan the funeral. They decided to bury Igor on Saturday, May 20. That would give them time to call everybody, and as a bonus, no one would have to go to work the next day, after what would inarguably be a long, sorrowful reception. Then Vladislav and Ann took Father Theofil back to the church, and returned to the apartment.

They didn't want to eat. Anna, after suffering and being totally exhausted, went to bed. Vladislav spent some time on the phone. He called to the husband of Vicky's former colleague who worked at customs and told him about what had happened. After the usual condolences, they agreed that the trucks would deliver the vodka to the customs warehouse, where they would be processed gradually, though customs fees and other charges would apply.

Then Vladislav called Pushkov Jr. He had been back for a long time and had been waiting for Vlad's call. They decided that both Pushkov men would transport the vodka to the various kiosks, tents, and stores, take payment for the goods on a cash-on-delivery basis, and then deposit the money into the Owl bank account daily. Yakubovsky would pay all expenses, fees, and taxes, and offer them ten percent of the sales price for their services.

Then Vladislav asked Alexander to put his mother on the phone. He asked Maria whether it would be possible to hold the sorrowful reception at the Pushkovs' dining hall. The number of people attending would be known by tomorrow evening. Maria told him that the price would be determined by the menu and setup. And so they have agreed to speak the following evening.

Then Vladislav called Vicky, and spoke for a long time. Vicky wished to come, but she still didn't have the necessary German documents. Therefore, they decided that it would be better for her not to go.

Having hung up with Vicky, Vladislav called his first wife, Irene, Igor's mother, and filled her in. He decided not to call Natalie. Why should he?

After the conversation with Igor's mother, Vladislav went to the kitchen to make some tea. He set the table with cheese and sausage, while he waited for the water to heat. Then he switched off the gas burner, and left the kitchen. He went into the bedroom, knelt beside Ann, and has put his head on the blanket. Anna wasn't sleep. She put her hand on his shoulder. They kept silent, and then both sighed and went to the kitchen to have tea.

Those few days before the funeral flew by as if in a dream. The Pushkov men took care of the vodka sales. Maria took care of the reception preparations. Yakubovsky called all of the relatives, his friend Stanislav Terekhin, and his former chief to tell them all what had happened. Vladislav's former boss sympathized, and promised to call back tomorrow and let him know how many people would attend the funeral service. Ann called her girlfriends from the university, and all of them who were still in Moscow said they would come. So, gradually, they tallied about a hundred and fifty guests.

The simplest way to provide drinks for the reception was to use vodka shipments, and they decided that a one-liter bottle for every two people would be just right. The food would be simple but tasty.

And as they say, when trouble comes, open up the gate. For the night before the funeral, Frieda called and told Vladislav that Vicky had had a miscarriage. She had been operated on last evening.

The story was that Vicky had come back from work feeling funny, so called an ambulance. Frieda received an emergency call from the hospital, and went there immediately with her husband. The doctor told them that Vicky had had miscarriage and needed to have "cleaning" surgery. She would stay in the hospital for no less than three days. Her life was not in danger, but the child had been lost.

Frieda tried to console Vladislav, but it didn't help. Later, having found out what had happened to Vicky, Anna had a long sob. It was a pity to her that such tragedy had befallen all of them—Vicky, Igor, Vlad, and her.

Vlad and Ann didn't go to bed until it was already almost daybreak, nestling up to each other.

65

Moscow, May 20, 1995

The day of the funeral, neither of them remembered how they got out of bed and got ready for the day. Vladislav tried to call Victoria in the Munich hospital, but it was too early with the two-hour difference.

They left the apartment and took a taxi to the cemetery. After that, everything passed in a fog. People delivered speeches. Father Theofil prayed. Guests brought flowers and wreaths. Everything seemed mixed up: the closed coffin with Igor's body, the news about Victoria. Ann stayed next to Vladislav, feeling his support. Irene, Igor's mother, fainted, nearly falling into the open grave. Somebody delivered more speeches. All of it flashed before them as if someone were twirling a huge kaleidoscope, churning out varying images in constant motion. And it was impossible to understand the meaning of it all.

They partly came back to their senses upon driving to the dining hall. Ann had to be dragged from the car by two girlfriends, and Vladislav was leaning on Stanislav Terekhin on one side, and Gavrila Kravchuk on the other. At the entrance to the dining room, on a small table, was Igor's enlarged photo. In front of the photo a candle was burning. Father Theofil had set out a box for donations to his church.

Vladislav sat down with Ann, and they poured themselves drinks. Irene's father, a retired colonel but still not an old man, said some words in Igor's memory, and all drank. Three minutes had not passed when Kravchuk asked for permission to speak. Gavrila spoke long about Russia losing its best sons, about the Soviet Union, and about the revival of Russian national ideas. All drank again. When Vladislav had drunk to Gavrila's words, his glass had been full, but he hadn't felt the alcohol. Anna's glass had been full too, and she drank it all in one gulp. They started to spill their third drinks.

Yakubovsky then took the bottle to pour some more for himself, but his glass was already full to the rim. Once of his comrades must have poured it for him. But when, after Igor's mother's words, they all drank again, Vladislav realized that his glass had actually been filled with water.

He looked around and leaned over, whispering to Ann, "Is that you pouring water in my glass?"

"Please, do not drink any more, my darling," she said. "Do you remember how sick you have been recently? Forgive me, please."

And with these words, she lifted her glass and stood, and then, as though it were unintentional, stumbled and leaned her elbow on Vladislav's shoulder. He felt her shivering. At that point, Ann told people that she and everyone there had lost a really good friend, a man who was always ready to come to the aid of someone in need. She was absolutely right. Igor really was a good guy.

The vodka was finished quickly, so Pushkov brought in another twenty-bottle box. Soon, the young officers of Federal Service of External Intelligence were becoming acquainted with Anna's girlfriends, and they began to feel that it was time to leave the relatives alone with one another. Kravchuk was carted away by Alevtina and his bodyguards, as usual. Irene's parents left with her. Finally, Vladislav and Anna being exhausted and depressed, but absolutely sober, slipped out the door together, without saying good-bye to anybody. Vasily Pushkov having seen them slowly heading toward the exit, caught up with them. And not saying a word, he led them to his car, opened up the doors, and motioned for them to get in.

66

Moscow, May 28, 1995

Eight days had passed since Igor's funeral. Vladislav and Ann had spent them silently. The Pushkovs continued to distribute vodka. They worked exclusively in the subdivision where Vasily Pushkov had been the neighborhood policeman, and so knew every business there. Vladislav went to customs daily, where he legalized papers and paid the duties and taxes. He also went to the bank daily, where he deposited the proceeds, and wrote checks for fees and taxes. Everything was reconciled up to the last penny. By the time every bottle had been sold, he had collected six hundred thousand dollars.

Ann was constantly with him. She wouldn't depart a step from Vladislav. They had a strange relationship. They hardly spoke to each other, only occasionally exchanging single, short phrases. They avoided even looking at each other. And at the same time, they were constantly with each other.

In the mornings, Yakubovsky got up earlier, shaved, showered, and made breakfast. Anna got up after he'd left the bathroom, and by the time she got in the kitchen, breakfast was ready and already set out on her side of the table. They ate breakfast silently, but together. After breakfast, Anna cleaned up the kitchen and washed dishes. Yakubovsky waited for her, and together they left the apartment and together went around doing errands and such. Every day, it was the same routine: they had lunch in the same small restaurant, and in the evening had supper at the apartment. After supper, having not even turned on the lights, they wished each other good night, took showers, and went to bed in their separate rooms.

During the night, each often woke, listening to see what might be happening in the next room. Both thought about each other, but both were afraid even to hint about their feelings, and whether anything was possible … at all.

On Sunday, May 28, the ninth day after Igor's funeral, Vladislav and Ann got up early, picked up Father Theofil, and went to the cemetery to see Igor's tomb. The Father prayed, after which they put vodka into small glasses, and then from one glass, poured vodka onto the ground, before drinking their own and having a small snack. They were just beginning to pour a second round when Vladislav's first wife, Irene, showed up. Ann rushed to her, but somehow slid on a piece of gravel and twisted her right ankle. She screamed, and her ankle began to swell. She couldn't walk.

Vladislav carried Ann to his car. Pressed up to her, he shivered from his affinity to Ann. Anna shivered also. They dropped Father Theofil off at the church, and went home. Anna managed to half-walk into the bathroom and took a shower, while Yakubovsky made her some hot tea.

A thunderstorm had started to gather. A real Moscow thunderstorm! Everything had become stuffy. The clouds had lowered almost onto the rooftops. Feeling overheated, Vladislav unbuttoned his shirt. He poured Anna's tea and took it into her room.

There Anna lay covered with a sheet, her foot resting on a pillow. Vladislav set the cup on a nearby chair and helped her adjust the pillow.

Outside the window, a bolt of lightning cut the sky in half and a thunderclap resounded. Startled, Anna screamed and hopped up, embracing Vladislav and nestling into him. The sheet slipped partially off of her, exposing a breast, and neither had the energy to constrain their mutual feelings any longer. They threw themselves against each other and began to kiss each other's faces, eyes, mouths. Kissing Ann, Vladislav began to pull off his shirt, feeling Ann help him. He kissed her neck, breasts, and kept going down, simultaneously removing his trousers and flinging them away. By this time, he had already flung the bed sheet from the girl and had seen her absolutely nude.

Yakubovsky, kissing her stomach, was now completely undressed too. Ann bent her knees and pressed them to her chest, exposing herself for love. At this time, another loud thunderclap resounded, announcing to the whole world their affinity for each other.

"Love me! Love me, darling," the young woman repeated, having sunk down onto the floor from happiness. Time had tested her passion for Vladislav, but, like he, she never had expressed her feelings. Now both of them spilled their passion.

And so the gypsy's prediction came true: "The grief will be. Through the great grief you will incorporate with her. During a roar of thunder you learn your wife. During a roar of thunder you will conceive your child"

After that moment, Vladislav and Ann spent four days in bed, occasionally eating but then rushing again into each other's embraces. Once Ann whispered to Vladislav, "We shall name our baby Igor so that he will always be with us."

Those four days, Vladislav never called Victoria in Germany, but that didn't mean he did not think about her. In fact, nearly all his time thought about this complex and difficult situation into which they had appeared at the will of destiny. But how to resolve it, he didn't know. Yakubovsky absolutely, sincerely respected—moreover, loved—Victoria. Even as he knew she loved him.

But with Ann! He didn't simply love her. It was a passion, surprising in its furious strength. He breathed this woman. He touched her with trembling hands and trembled at her touches. Ann, in turn, felt the same for Vladislav. The difference in their age didn't hinder them. For a long time, they had loved each other. Only now had this gathering energy been released overtly.

But how to deal with Vicky, Vladislav did not know. All he could think of was that, yes, sometimes things happened in life; there were situations that were neither fair nor rational. However, he knew that all of them, in time, were resolved.

67

Moscow, June 3, 1995

Vladislav finally got the courage to call Victoria in Germany. But when he heard Vicky's voice, her tender words touched him, and he couldn't bring himself to tell her about Ann. He couldn't hurt her. He hadn't enough cruelty. What they spoke about instead was absolutely unimportant.

On Monday, June 5, Vladislav and Ann, who still hadn't left each other for a minute, went to the registry office to pick up Igor's official death certificate. The very same day, Kravchuk called. He told Vladislav that he had received loan approval from the bank and that all of the credit documents were ready for execution; the money could be transferred the very next day.

That night, Vladislav and his young girlfriend barely closed their eyes. For the first time in his life, Yakubovsky couldn't make a decision independently. The situation had become critical. If the credit documents were signed, thus keeping him in the game, he could not remain in Moscow for more than thirty-six hours after transferring the money. Leaving without Ann, however, wasn't an option. Yakubovsky's and Kravchuk's America visas would expire July 30, and Anna didn't have an American visa at all.

Yakubovsky's marriage with Victoria in Kazakhstan had, for all current intents and purposes, been fictitious—due to the fact that it had been concluded under a false name. In Yakubovsky's internal Russian passport, there were only stamps of registration and his divorce with Natalie, and in his travel passport, information regarding his marital status was absent. The marriage certificate from Kazakhstan and the passport issued to him in the name of Vladislav Schmidt were in Germany at Victoria's apartment.

So using the paper he'd received from his friend and partner Michael Lutsky in the States, Vladislav put together a contract for supplying airline companies with vodka packaged in small bottles of fifty milliliters. Such bottles usually sold on international flights. Under this contract between the Russian company Owl and the American company Nevada Marketing Group, the supplier would supply twenty million bottles in two years. The total amount on the contract was seven million dollars. Yakubovsky prepared the contract, as required, in two languages: Russian and English. He signed the contracts on behalf of himself, as an authorized person of Owl, and on behalf of Michael Lutsky, as an authorized person of Nevada Marketing Group. For greater effect, he added both companies' seals. The well-known firm, Elephteria, Ltd., was also listed as a participant in the contract. This project took Vlad two days

Before applying for visas at the US embassy, Yakubovsky also registered the contract for supplying airline companies with vodka with Russian government organization Roscontrac and made business cards for himself, as the general partner; for Ann, as the interpreter; and for Gavrila Kravchuk, as the business consultant.

Vladislav and Ann, with Kravchuk's passport, were at the US Embassy on Thursday, June 8, by eight o'clock and got in the line. A long line had formed out on the street. A policeman checked people's documents and kept the order. The same policeman distributed questionnaires and application forms. For that, he collected a small tribute of three dollars per set of documents.

For the interview with the US embassy Yakubovsky had brought along a folder with photos for all three of them, the original contract for the delivery of vodka from Finland, the contract for the purchase of grain, and registration form for his apartment and two cars. The line had about one hundred people and moved slowly. Between standing in line, one uncertain individual, uninhibited in the presence of the policeman (it was obvious they were in collusion), rushed around offering intermediary services for fifty dollars each. He extended the offer to Yakubovsky, as well, but Vladislav refused even to speak with him.

By lunchtime, their turn approached. An employee of the consulate, speaking broken Russian, checked their passports, while a strict-looking Marine waved some piece of iron across them, possibly checking for demolition bombs or weaponry.

When they finally appeared before the vice consul, who was sitting behind a bulletproof window, they were relieved to learn their preparations weren't all for naught. Having pretended that he didn't know English, Yakubovsky simply presented his and Kravchuk's passports, with the biennial multi-entrance visas, for the vice consul's observation. Ann's knowledge of English wasn't too bad at all. Besides having lessons in school and at the university, she attended the city's language college and attended a thirty-day immersion class, taught in the professor Lozanov's method, at Moscow State. She acted as the interpreter. After being tortured in line for about twenty more minutes, their visas were issued.

Now they had only one last thing to do—register for marriage. Ann and the late Igor had submitted their application to the registry office on May 11, and their wedding had been scheduled for June 12. So directly from the US embassy, they went to the local medical clinic and located the women's office. Both money and natural charm assisted, and they left the medical center a certificate stating that Ann was pregnant.

The next day, on June 9, Vladislav and Ann went to the registry office, where Yakubovsky went to the managing director's office. There, he presented his FSB certificate with the state insignia, his internal passports, the certificate of Igor's death, and the certificate of Ann's pregnancy. Presenting these documents, along with personal charm and the envelope with ten Franklin portraits did the job, and thus their wedding was scheduled for Monday, June 12.

On June 12, Vladislav and Anna, elegantly dressed, and with a bouquet of red roses, appeared before an employee of the registry office. Yakubovsky had purchased wedding rings for both of them. In addition, he had purchased for Ann a diamond set consisting of gentle, good-quality earrings, a pendant on a gold chain, and a ring. In front of the registry office, as always, a few professional witnesses turned around. Two of them, without special negotiation and for a reasonable payment, agreed to participate in their wedding.

After signing the marriage documents and hearing the parting speech of the employee, they received the marriage certificate, put stamps on their internal passports, and went to the Indian restaurant where they had seen each other for the first time. They sat at the table, looking into each other's eyes, drank a glass of champagne to their happiness, and remembered Igor. Then they left for home to prepare for their departure.

By this time, the Pushkovs had earned sixty-five thousand dollars and redeemed from the former manager of the dining room her shares, becoming the rightful owners. The first step that Vasily Pushkov then made was to go the regional police department and suggest they use the premise, free of charge, as a stronghold for the neighborhood police division. So, the dining room had serious support. Second, they started to remodel the large, empty hall on the second floor into a dancing hall, with a bar and slot machines. In the huge kitchen, they looked into adding equipment for the manufacturing of sausage products. And while all this was in the works, the Pushkovs released a new line of culinary products, which began to be carried in kiosks, delis, and grocery stores. And their business increased.

68

California, June 7, 1995

In the morning, Melissa, as usual, had breakfast and left for school. The Trunovs were in the kitchen watching TV, expecting George to wake up at any time. Yesterday, they had sent their daughter thirty thousand dollars that she could use toward an apartment, and were very happy.

On her break between morning classes, Melissa called home to check in, and everything was in order. When she arrived back home around one o'clock, however, she found Lyudmila in confusion.

"Valentin is behaving strange. He is lying down and doesn't feel so good. Maybe he is ill?"

Melissa found Valentin lying on the living room sofa. Having seen Melissa, he tried to get up, but didn't have enough energy. Melissa, without hesitation, called an ambulance.

The paramedics arrived in ten minutes and took Valentin's blood pressure. It was eighty over sixty. They decided to take him to the hospital. Melissa followed them in her car and Lyudmila remained with George at home.

Valentin was carried into the emergency room and connected to several medical devices. In a short time, the doctor approached Melissa and asked her what relationship she had with the patient and whether he was married.

"Doctor, what is wrong with him?" she asked.

"Cardiac arrest. We are powerless at this point. We will try to support him until his wife's arrival, but after that—it will last just as long as he will hold on."

Melissa rushed back home. She fastened George into his car seat, seated Lyudmila, and returned to the hospital. By this time, a tube had been inserted into Valentin's throat and he was under anesthesia. The doctor silently told Melissa that one of his lungs had failed. Lyudmila took her husband's hand,

and at that very moment the heart monitor, instead of displaying the curvy heart beats, showed a straight line.

They buried Valentin Trunov in California ground, and it became silent in Melisa's house. Even little George, somehow understanding that grief was occurring, was unusually quiet and well-behaved.

69

Moscow, June 14, 1995

The signing of the credit documents was scheduled for Wednesday, June 14, at nine o'clock in the Food Commerce Bank. The money should leave the bank the next day, Thursday, June 15. Naturally, Yakubovsky wasn't present at the signing, having been deferred by his vodka-delivery business, but he agreed to call Kravchuk at the bank to congratulate him on such a significant event.

In actuality, Yakubovsky was at the travel agency, from where, at ten o'clock, he called Kravchuk. And having been convinced that the loan contract had been signed, he purchased all of his necessary airline tickets and made all of the necessary hotel reservations.

Then Vladislav went to the Impex Omega Bank, where he presented the contract for vodka delivery to airline companies. He had requested that all of the money in the Owl account be converted into dollars, and then wired the money to the Elephteria, Ltd., account in Cyprus. He wired eight hundred fifty thousand dollars. The remaining balance of twenty six thousand Yakubovsky took in cash.

In 1995, all Russian banks had corresponding accounts in the Bank of New York, and all were coordinated by a woman named Natalie. She had begun her work at the bank as a teller, but was quickly promoted. When the Soviet Union collapsed, Natalie got busy. She persuaded the management of the Bank of New York to open an office in Moscow. On behalf of the bank, she then offered contracts for corresponding services to the newly formed Russian private banks. Natalie was a real workaholic, hustling day and night, and gradually, not one or two but practically all Russian banks, had corresponding accounts with the Bank of New York between which accounts wire transfers could be made.

One conditions of the wire transfer was that all of the funds coming from the sender during the day accumulated in its corresponding account, but didn't officially process until midnight. So only the next day money could be sent to a beneficiary's bank. And again, in the beneficiary's accounts, the funds would not be recognized until twelve midnight. Thus, it took two business days for money to arrive in the beneficiary's account.

In this case, money was wired from Food Commerce Bank on Thursday, June 15. So, Vladislav would need to send a request signed by Kravchuk to wire the money on Monday, June 19. Thus, June 19 was their first "milestone date."

The second milestone date would be one hundred and eighty days from the date the money was wired out of Food Commerce Bank. According to Russian legislation enacted in spring of 1995 concerning state control over the usage of funds, in case the conditions of a contract were not followed through on, all hard currency funds were subject to be returned within a hundred and eighty days. And this rule was enforced strictly.

Yakubovsky had been planning this operation for a long time, and at last the time had come for him to take action. He called Stanislav Terekhin.

"Let's get together," Vladislav suggested after engaging in the usual small talk. "We haven't met for a while."

Terekhin invited Yakubovsky to his summer cottage on Sunday, June 18. "There will be some old friends joining us as well. We can all hang out for a while, just like we used to."

So, on June 18 Vladislav arrived at Terekhin's summer house. He hadn't shaven for a few days, and his clothes were slightly wrinkled. The slight smell of vodka hovered around him, owing to the fact that, just before his arrival, Yakubovsky had slightly irrigated his shirt with the substance. Being among old friends, he was silent, and didn't try to climb into conversations. He treated everybody with cigarettes and smoked some as well. Then he left early, saying warm good-byes to everybody, but feeling slightly uneasy. Before his departure, however, Yakubovsky pulled Terekhin aside and asked to meet him the next Sunday. Terekhin said he looked forward to it.

The next morning, Monday, June 19, at nine sharp, Yakubovsky arrived at Agroprom. Anna, with a travel bag, was waiting for him in a cab. From Kravchuk's office, Yakubovsky sent two faxes. The first, signed by Kravchuk, was a request to transfer all of the money from the First Russian Corporation account at the Pacific Bank of China to Gavrila's personal account at the West Pacific Bank in Western Samoa. The second fax, again signed by Kravchuk, was to the West Pacific Bank. It was a request to prepare six-and-a-half-million dollars in cash, in vacuum-sealed packages of five hundred thousand dollars each.

After both faxes left, Yakubovsky took copies of them to Agroprom's accounting department and filed them for registration. Then, having said good-bye to Kravchuk's Secretary, Katie, he headed to the elevator. In the hallway, Yakubovsky met Alevtina, and walked her to her office, where he said good-bye. Before leaving her office, however, Yakubovsky had a thought. He took out of his pocket the key to the Igor and Ann's former apartment and gave it to her. He asked her to look after the place and to contact him should anything go wrong. Then having left, he rode the elevator down the main floor and joined Ann in the cab for their ride to the Sheremetyevo Airport.

In the very complicated chain of embezzlement that Yakubovsky had developed, Sheremetyevo was the weakest link. Mr. Wolfgang Nushke, the Kazakh German, might be recognized by Victoria's former coworkers or his own. But there wasn't any one around it. He'd only be able to make the connecting flight if he flew from Moscow. And then he had to be back in Moscow on Saturday evening in time to meet Terekhin on Sunday, June 25.

They reached Sheremetyevo by noon. Vladislav said good-bye to Anna in the car, and they agreed that she wouldn't leave the apartment under any circumstances.

"There is enough food," he assured her. "Please, don't meet me on Saturday. I will go directly home. Already missing you."

Then at 2:40 that afternoon, Yakubovsky, or, to be exact, Kazakh citizen Mr. Wolfgang Nushke made it out of Moscow on a Transaero flight. The plane landed at Los Angeles International Airport at 4:50 Pacific Time, on Monday, June 19. Having been in the air for thirteen hours, he had barely lost any time.

Wolfgang Nushke made it through passport control and customs and eventually out of the terminal. Then having wandered through the airport and being convinced that nobody was following him, Yakubovsky-Nushke went to Terminal 3, where he found a restroom, changed his clothes, and donned a wig. As Vladislav hadn't shaven for a few days, he now looked almost like the man specified as Gavrila Kravchuk on his passport.

Satisfied with his new appearance in the mirror, Yakubovsky-Kravchuk returned to the International Terminal. He checked in on Flight 1 to Auckland, where he was to arrive at New Zealand's main airport. Having had a bite at McDonald's, Yakubovsky-Kravchuk proceeded to board. He left at 9:30 p.m. It was still Monday, June 19. On its flight to Auckland, the plane crossed Zero Meridian and landed at five twenty-five a.m., Wednesday, June 21 the New Zealand time.

There, Yakubovsky-Kravchuk checked into a hotel and slept until noon.

He then left from Auckland for Western Samoa at two twenty p.m. After several hours, the plane crossed Zero Meridian in the opposite direction, and landed at the Apia Airport at seven fifteen p.m., Samoa's time, but on Tuesday, June 20. It was not an error: the day had really turned back. And it was not a miracle, after crossing Zero Meridian twice.

At passport control, Yakubovsky presented Mr. Gavrila Kravchuk's passport and paid a few dollars for the local visa. A board guard stamped the passport and recorded Kravchuk's arrival time in Western Samoa.

As before, Yakubovsky checked in at the Princess Tiu Inn. He got a bite to eat and took a shower. He was really tired, but didn't want to sleep. The evening was damp and stuffy. Yakubovsky walked out onto the small balcony attached to his room. The darkness was as it can only be in the tropics. Cicadas roared like motorcycles. Then from the darkness, two voices sounded—a man and a woman. They talked among themselves in Russian. As was Vladislav, they were on the balcony attached to their room. They would not have expected that, in this part of the universe, so remote from the motherland, that someone else would understand them. Yakubovsky couldn't see them, but if he didn't know any better, he might have thought that they were rehearsing the final scene from "A Fairytale about Fisherman and the Gold Fish," by Russian poet Pushkin.

"Well, and what is enough for you?" the man said sternly. "Nothing. Nothing is good enough. I stole two million greens, and that is still not enough for you! Have you forgotten how you used to mix stucco at the construction site? And now you are rich! And at what risk to me? Have you thought about what would happen if they found us? No? Well, you'd better. Just put that in that clever little head of yours. I swear, if they were to unscrew your head, there would be nothing inside of it."

The woman hissed something in reply, but Yakubovsky couldn't make it out.

"Who needs you? Oh, except me—the fool," the man continued to bristle.

"Sh … sh … sh … sh," went her hissing again.

"Well, so go! Go now! You can leave this island directly by foot."

More hissing.

"Then shut up and go, and don't ever come back. Understand? Tell me that you understand!"

"Sh … sh … sh … sh."

It seemed to Yakubovsky that the guy had tried to embezzle two million dollars. It seemed half the country was occupied with this idea, and the other half—oh well, they just kept drinking.

Vladislav continued standing on the balcony for a while, thinking about the sad destiny of his people. Then growing sleepy, he went inside, undressed, took sleeping pills, and went to bed. Tomorrow would be a difficult day for him.

In a minute, he had already forgotten about what he had just involuntarily witnessed, and fell asleep. All night, he dreamed about what was happening in the now "united" country called Russia.

But life went on. The next morning, Vladislav awoke at nine, put himself into order—not forgetting the wig—and left his room. He bought a cup of coffee and a doughnut for breakfast, and went to the store in the hotel, where he purchased three huge suitcases. Then he approached the customer service desk and asked where he might employ two bodyguards. The customer service agent called a private security agency called Willy Wong Security. In twenty minutes, two hefty good fellows were sitting with Yakubovsky in a hybrid car. In general, all Samoans were known to be large, but Yakubovsky hadn't seen such big guys in his life, even in the Special Operation Forces.

Together, they went to West Pacific Bank. Yakubovsky presented the passport for Gavrila Kravchuk, a citizen of Kazakhstan. Then Yakubovsky-Kravchuk, without a problem, walked into the vault with his empty suitcases, and loaded them with twenty-six vacuum-packed bundles of two hundred fifty thousand dollars each. The bodyguards took the filled suitcases back to the car.

About five minutes later, they arrived at the National Bank of Western Samoa. Yakubovsky-Kravchuk sent the bodyguards to wait for him on the street, and when they had gone, he handed over the cash-stuffed suitcases, without presenting his passport, and in exchange received a cashier's check for the sum of six-and-a-half-million dollars, made out to the bearer. Check in hand, Yakubovsky-Kravchuk called back his bodyguards, and together they returned to the hotel. Having paid them off, he then released the Samoan fighters, tipped them with an empty suitcase, and went up to his room.

In his room, he removed the wig and changed clothes, but didn't shave. Then he went back to the First Bank of Western Samoa. There, Yakubovsky-Nushke deposited the cashier's check from the National Bank of Western Samoa into Wolfgang Nushke's personal account.

Back at the hotel, finally finished with his day's work, Vladislav was spent. Today's performance had demanded endurance and nerves of steel, and had put an enormous pressure on him, and now he required serious rest. So he had a good dinner, took two sleeping pills, and retired to his bed.

The next day, June 22, Yakubovsky-Nushke returned to the First Bank of Western Samoa, and having ensured that all six-and-a-half million had been processed into the account and were now available, he completed a request to wire all of the money to Wolfgang Nushke's account at the Deutche Bank at Frankfurt's airport branch.

Yakubovsky-Kravchuk left Western Samoa at three p.m., Thursday, June 22, and arrived in Auckland at six p.m. on Friday, June 23. After a three-hour layover, he then flew to Los Angeles, where he arrived at two thirty Standard Pacific Time on the same day.

Another long layover at the Los Angeles Airport, and Yakubovsky-Kravchuk took off for Moscow, arriving at shortly after six p.m., Moscow Time, on Saturday, June 24.

Ann had been impatiently awaiting his return. She hadn't been filled in on all of the details of his trip, but knew one thing: that what he was doing would support their future. She hadn't even considered the moral side of the issue, as only unmaterialistic people thought about morality. All the same, she knew that she and Vlad passionately loved each other and that Yakubovsky would never betray her…

… But then, quite possibly, Victoria Schmidt thought the same.

The first thing that Vladislav did upon arriving home was to burn the fake Kravchuk passport, dump the ashes into the toilet, and flush two times. Then he called Terekhin to specify the time of the next day's meeting. Having pretended that the connection kept being interrupted, Vladislav asked Terekhin to call him back at his home phone number.

Terekhin's call back provided Vlad with an iron-clad alibi who could testify that Yakubovsky was, indeed, at home in Moscow both on Sunday, June 18, and on Saturday, June 24, for a total of six days.

Likely a year would pass before the office of the Attorney General would initiate an investigation regarding the embezzlement of six-and-a-half-million dollars from Food Commerce Bank. Yakubovsky, naturally, would be among the suspects. And, naturally, the investigations team would consider all of the possibilities, including Yakubovsky's flight from Moscow to Western Samoa and back. They would also consider that fact that the money was in the account at twelve o'clock midnight. But there was one thing investigators would not consider: while the day is just beginning in Auckland, New Zealand, the day in Samoa has still not ended. And rationally, investigators would conclude that the number of money transfers and flights that Vlad would have to carry out to succeed at such a feat would take a minimum of eight days—but, due to his meetings and phone conversations with Terekhin, it would be apparent that he could have only been absent from Moscow for six days Thus, Yakubovsky would be excluded from the list of suspects in the embezzlement case.

On Sunday, June 25, Yakubovsky met with Terekhin. He hadn't shaved for many days. He put on the same outfit he'd worn at his visit nearly a week ago, again moistening his shirt with vodka. So when Vladislav, in worn shoes and crumpled trousers, appeared in front of Terekhin, he received a long lecture from his friend about how he was still young and how it was still necessary to behave professionally and not let himself go. Now Yakubovsky's alibis were iron-clad.

Vladislav told Stanislav that he understood and that in the next day or two, he would shave and fix himself up for a business trip to Germany. How it would fare, he promised to tell Stanislav upon his return.

70

Moscow, June 26, 1995

Vladislav and Anna left from Moscow for Frankfurt on June 26. In Frankfurt, they stayed at the Airport Sheraton, where they had a good time together in their room and ate supper in the dining room.

The next day, Yakubovsky left Ann at the hotel, and went to the business center in Terminal A, where the Deutche Bank branch was located. There, he presented the passport in the name of Mr. Wolfgang Nushke and received a cashier's check for the full amount of the account. Besides the six-and-a-half-million dollars, there was the ten thousand that Yakubovsky had deposited upon opening the account. In addition, there was one hundred and forty thousand dollars that hadn't been used for the vodka delivery from Finland. So the total amount of money equaled six million, six hundred fifty thousand dollars. Convinced that all of that money was available, Vladislav had it all wired to the Nevada Marketing Group account with the Bank of America in the States.

Then he left Terminal A, went to the subway station, and purchased a ticket for the next train going to Munich. A very heavy conversation with Victoria would ensue.

71

Munich, Germany, June 27, 1995

Since Vladislav and Anna had begun to live together, he had often thought about how to reconcile with Victoria. If Igor were still alive, he wouldn't even be in a relationship with Ann, but then the gypsy's prediction would not have come true either. Vladislav couldn't find an appropriate solution, or, for that matter, an inappropriate one. All he could do was to tell Victoria the truth warmly, respectfully, and with love.

Still not having found the right words, Yakubovsky arrived at the Munich Airport where Vicky worked. On the way to the VIP center, he stopped in a restroom, brushed his teeth, and shaved for the second time. Then, feeling refreshed, he purchased a bouquet of roses for Vicky. But his legs almost refused to go.

Vicky, having seen Vlad, threw her arms around his neck, but he only slightly touched his face to her cheek. Vicky instantly knew something was different. Wise with experience, however, she decided to wait until a more appropriate time to ask. She would be finished at work in an hour and a half. Looking at Vladislav with her huge blue-blue eyes, Vicky asked him to wait for her in the hall near the VIP center. He sat in an armchair and then had a good idea. He should go to the bank and to wire to Cyprus the six hundred thousand dollars that he and Victoria had brought to Germany.

When Vicky returned, Yakubovsky, in the soft armchair, after a sleepless night with Anna and being infinitely on the move had fallen asleep. Vicky touched his cheek, and he instantly woke up. He took her hand and brought it to his lips. Together they went to the parking garage and took Victoria's Volkswagen Passat home.

Victoria recently have received German driver's license. She was very proud about that, but Vlad didn't even pay attention to the fact that she was driving…

On the way, Victoria chattered ceaselessly. She had been missing Vladislav for so long, and was now trying to make up for lost time. She asked questions and then answered them. Suddenly, she said something that forced Yakubovsky to forget about his weariness.

"Do you know …" Victoria told him, "Do you remember when you came to Sheremetyevo the first time and begun to ask questions about Boris Goryanin? He is here, in Munich, with his wife. Today, they return from a cruise on the **Romantische Straße** and they have invited us to dinner this evening."

"Who?" Yakubovsky asked, not hiding his shock. "Who invited us to dinner this evening?"

"Boris Goryanin and his wife. What's the big deal?" Victoria answered, dragging out each word.

Meeting Goryanin had not been included in any way into Vladislav's plans. Especially now that Goryanin's name was listed as the guarantor of the return of the funds and after Kravchuk had forged his signature. Yakubovsky had seen Kravchuk's Letter of Guarantee. The forgery had been badly done. And though Kravchuk hadn't told him where he had taken the letter, anybody except for Kravchuk could have made it. Their meeting could be extremely dangerous for Yakubovsky. He had done so much work to build up this chain of events in which money could just disappear, and now the whole operation could be destroyed.

"I hope that you have not told him about me," Yakubovsky said. "I hope … you didn't tell him we are married?"

"And why is that such a big deal? We've known each other for a long time. Are you ashamed of me?" Vicky asked, sounding insulted. "No. I didn't tell him."

She sensed in his question that something big had changed. Her Vlad was different than before. Tears rolled from her eyes.

Yakubovsky was silent too. He closed eyes. In his head instantly ripened the plan. He distinctly imagined them walking into the apartment. Victoria would get out a vase and put her bouquet in it. Then, yearning for his caresses, she would throw the coverlet off the bed, hurriedly undress, and run into the bathroom to draw a bubble bath. About five minutes later, she would call him.

"Vlad, Vlad! Come here, darling!"

He would enter into the bathroom, remove the towel from the holder, and with a playful voice, asked, "And whose beautiful small feet with such tasty toes are these?"

Victoria would lift her foot from the water and stretch it out to him for a kiss. He would take her foot with his right hand, cover it with the towel, and grip it firmly. At that time, he would cup his left hand under her knee and jerk the bottom part of her body upward. Unexpectedly to her, Victoria's head would sink under the water, and she would founder, trying to escape, inhaling, and only swallowing water.

In a minute, it would be all over. He would slowly lower her leg and rest it on the edge of the tub, with her head and trunk remaining under the water. Victoria's parents would find her in a few days and call the police. And by that time, any traces of struggling would be gone, as her body would be swelled with water. It would be classified as a typical accident …

Vlad woke up to Vicky rubbing his shoulder. They had arrived at her apartment and were already parked. Victoria got the impression that he hadn't slept for few days. They took the elevator to the second floor and went in.

Vicky got a vase out of the kitchen and put her bouquet in it. Then she went to the bedroom, threw the cover from the bed, and undressed. Naked, she escaped to the bathroom and turned on the water in the tub on. She brushed her teeth while the water collected and then added some bubble bath. Then about three minutes later, she was calling to her Yakubovsky: "Vlad, Vlad! Come here, darling!"

72

Miami, Florida, June 15, 1995

Gavrila Kravchuk left Moscow for Miami right after signing the loan documents. Then he would wait for Semenov and Yakubovsky. From Miami, they would send the request for wiring money from the First Russian Corporation account at the Pacific Bank of China to his personal account in Miami. In accordance to their plan, Vladislav would be stopping for a day or two in Munich before taking off for Miami.

Yakubovsky suggested that Kravchuk, to save a few dollars, should stay in a Motel-6 near the ocean, and demanded that Gavrila strictly observe total abstinence from drinking. Kravchuk swore to remain sober.

"Why would I drink?" he'd asked. "I have to wire money." He had forgotten that he had signed all of the wiring instructions a long time ago.

Besides, Kravchuk was largely lucky. First, Yakubovsky had lent him two thousand dollars to add to the one thousand he already had on him. Second, he had managed to dissuade Alevtina from flying with him, as she had to take care of the business in Moscow. And then as unique an inconvenience as it was, he would need to buy round-trip tickets rather than those for one-way only, even though Gavrila didn't plan to return to Moscow for three or four years.

Upon arriving in Miami, he was lucky again; his taxi driver spoke Russian. Originally from the city of Sukhumi, he had fled the war zone between Georgia and Abkhazia, and had come to Miami.

"There is a lot of work here," the driver told Gavrila. "A lot. As there never was at home. And I am happy."

As Kravchuk listened to him, he dreamed of how he would soon be lying on the beach with some young ladies. Reaching the hotel, the driver made a telephone call to one of the local Russian-speaking ladies. She came to the hotel in a heartbeat. The driver introduced Kravchuk to a young Ukrainian girl, who worked in "the service industry." The girl was a true beauty. She became quickly accustomed with Gavrila Petrovich, and even stayed with him in his hotel room.

Yakubovsky didn't show up within the agreed-upon three days. He didn't show on the fourth, either, or even the fifth. Kravchuk tried to call him in Germany and even contacted his relatives, but for some reason, he could get nowhere. Money was melting before his eyes. Angela, Gavrila's new so-called girlfriend, left on her first full day with him to "run to the grocery store," but apparently forgot to come back. And, incidentally, one thousand dollars had run out with her. Gavrila somehow managed to get to the grocery store on his own, however. He purchased six bottles of whisky, a bottle of Coca-Cola, and a few snacks.

By his tenth day in Miami, and still no Vladislav, Kravchuk was able to track down the cab driver who had taken him to his hotel and acquainted him with Angela. The driver took care of Kravchuk, who, by now, had lost all human form. At least he had a return ticket to Moscow.

The driver took Agroprom's blue-faced president to the airport free of charge, and dragged him on a luggage cart to the Russian airline company "Aeroflot" check-in counter.

"Please accept your passenger," he told the airline representative. Then handing over Kravchuk like a piece of luggage, he left.

The airline rep called a doctor. It was, by far, not the first incident of its kind in his experience. After being approved for flight, Kravchuk boarded, but upon his arrival in Moscow, he was picked up by an ambulance, which then drove him to the narcological clinic where he had become a regular. Kravchuk spent three months there, qualifying for physical disability leave, without the right to work.

By this time, Alevtina had moved in with Semenov. Together with the Kravchuk's teenage daughter, they moved into a two-bedroom apartment. But, to Alevtina's honor, she did not throw Gavrila out. Once a week, she went to visit him in the clinic. And after his discharge from the clinic, Alevtina moved Gavrila into Yakubovsky's former apartment, to which she still had the key.

Kravchuk quickly went downhill after that, drinking on the streets and picking fights with other alcoholics.

"A bad apartment," said the three eternally present old women, camped out in front of the building.

73

Munich, Germany, June 27, 1995

While Vicky was in the bathroom, Vladislav rummaged through the desk in the living room. He found the passport in the name of Vladislav Schmidt, the marriage certificate from Kazakhstan, the car purchase agreement and registration, a spare car key, and a second set of keys to the apartment in Munich. Yakubovsky put the passport and marriage certificate in the internal pocket of his jacket, and pulled out a sheet of notepaper. On it, he wrote the following:

> *My darling!*
> *The soldier is always the soldier.*
> *Always yours…*

Vladislav put the car key and in his pocket, and attached his note to the set of apartment keys. Having thought for a second, he took from his pocket his set of keys from Victoria's apartments in Moscow, and attached them to the note too. Then he took his briefcase and, silently tip-toeing, left the apartment.

Yakubovsky took Victoria's car to the airport and parked in her designated employee stall. The branch where he had deposited the six hundred thousand dollars that they had brought to Germany was still open. Vladislav was completing a form to request that the money be transferred to the Nevada Marketing Group account at the Bank of America, when he suddenly remembered his second meeting with the old gypsy. He heard her voice saying, "Always be generous with whom you are in love and who loves you."

Thinking for a few seconds, he tore up the form he was working on and started another. On it, he wrote wiring instructions for the transfer of one hundred thousand dollars to the Nevada Marketing Group account. Then he requested a cashier's check made out to Victoria Schmidt in the amount of five hundred thousand dollars.

Vladislav asked the bank employee for an envelope and a piece of paper and write a note:

> *Darling, forgive me, but this is the order of thing.*
> *I wish you happiness!*
> *He enclosed the note and the check in an envelope and sealed it. On the envelope, instead of an address, he wrote, simply, "For Victoria Schmidt." He returned to Victoria's car, opened the driver's door, and put the envelope on the front seat. He laid the car key on top of it. Then holding the door handle in the closed position, he shut the door, and it locked.*

From the parking garage, Yakubovsky went to the Kempinsky Hotel near the airport. He checked in, proceeded to his room, and slept for fifteen hours.

Awaking in the middle of day, on June 28, Yakubovsky showered, shaved, had lunch at the hotel restaurant, and checked out. After lunch he went to the bank to check the balance on his account. A hundred thousand had left to Cyprus, but the rest was still available. He cautiously approached the parking garage, careful to avoid any chance meeting with Victoria. The car was there, but in a slightly different position than he had left it yesterday. Both the envelope and the key were gone. Vladislav went to the railway station and left for Frankfurt.

There, Vladislav and Ann spent one more night in the Sheraton. The next day, Yakubovsky checked in for a flight to Cyprus, Larnaka, alone. There would be no return flight from Larnaka until Saturday, July 1.

In Larnaka, Yakubovsky stayed at the hotel where he'd been with Igor, and in the morning, he went to Poplar Bank. In the Elephteria, Ltd., account was available eight hundred fifty thousand dollars. He wired all of it to the Nevada Marketing Group account at the Bank of America. By Vladislav's calculations, he had now wired to the United States a grand total of seven million six hundred thousand dollars.

Yakubovsky had to stay in Larnaka until Saturday, so he called Ann every couple of hours, just to hear her voice, to enjoy her breath. Vladislav could not wait until the moment he would see Ann again. In the meantime, he slept and ate off his exhaustion, and bathed in the sea. Yet, for some reason the water was always cold. And Victoria's voice was always calling him: "Vlad, Vlad! Come here, darling!"

Finally back in Frankfurt on Saturday, July 1, he and Ann spent two more nights in the Sheraton. On Monday, July 3, at 10:45 a.m. they departed to San Francisco.

Michael Lutsky met them at the San Francisco airport with a bouquet of red carnations for Ann. Michael wouldn't allow them even to think of checking in at a hotel. The Lutskys lived about an hour from the airport in a city called Sunnyvale.

To get there, they took the Central Expressway through Silicon Valley. Michael told them some of the silly names of companies there, and Vladislav listened and smiled. Today, he was looking upon America with new eyes, and it was a pity to him that he had spent so many years in vain. It was a pity to him that Igor would never get to see this. For Ann, everything in America was a surprise.

The Lutskys lived in a rather small house; nonetheless, it was in a gated community and it was their own. There, they had dinner and took a small tour around the neighborhood. And when Vlad and Ann lay on the wide king-sized bed in the guest room, she quietly giggled and whispered, "Vlad, I want such a house—and such a bed, too!"

A shocking experience for Yakubovsky was to observe the Lutskys' neighbors' without a request from the authorities displaying the national colors, and, further, to watch as they, without prompting, truly celebrated the Fourth of July. To celebrate the holiday, the Lutskys bought some good cuts of steak, which they marinated and grilled.

On Wednesday, Vlad and Ann made their first purchase in America. In the name of the Nevada Marketing Group, they bought a pickup truck—a Ford F-150. Vladislav had decided that they should break tradition and live as Americans: their car should be made in the USA. The truck had a very comfortable five-seat cabin, with a powerful motor. It could pull a boat or a trailer. But, most important, it was safe, which was a requirement for Ann, who had, since Igor's accident, started to cautiously regard motor vehicles.

In a few days, when they had started to feel more acclimated, they began the search for an apartment. They found a very good complex in a small town called Santa Clara. It was located just several blocks from the Lutskys. With Michael's help, they purchased only the most necessary furniture, linens, and kitchen items.

Now the priority was to become legal residents of the States. Again, with Michael's help, they found a lawyer, who specialized in the legalization of immigrants. His name was Jerry Hernandez. Having talked to the Yakubovskys, he advised them, first of all, to register for marriage in the USA, and, as soon as possible, have a child. This idea, even without the legal advice, had been imposed on them anyway, as Ann's monthly cycle was late.

At the doctor's, a simple test confirmed that she was pregnant. And on that next Friday, together with the Lutskys, they went to a city called Reno, in Nevada, and registered their marriage under laws of the state. They celebrated their wedding at a very good restaurant.

Gradually, Vladislav and Anna Yakubovsky grew more accustomed to America, remembering their past life less and less often. And a few weeks later, their lawyer Jerry Hernandez brought them their first American documents—their Social Security cards.

74

Munich, Germany, June 26, 1995

Vicky called for Vlad again, but he didn't come. Vicky rinsed the soap off, dried herself, and left the bathroom. She thought he had fallen asleep again, and wanted to tease him about it. But he wasn't in the bedroom. She looked through the apartment. Yakubovsky wasn't anywhere. He had mysteriously disappeared.

Victoria noted that her vase of flowers had been moved to the desk, and then something next to it caught her eye. Approaching the desk, she saw keys and a note. She was dumbstruck, frozen in place. Further, Vladislav's passport and the marriage certificate were gone. Now Victoria understood that she would never see her Vlad again.

Growing weak from what was happening, she lowered herself onto the chair and burst out crying. This was bitter and insulting. She knew for a fact that she had done nothing to change his feelings for her. She had always given only the best for her Vlad. She has washed and ironed his clothes, and kept the apartment in order. And to look at another man wasn't possible.

Maybe he had received a special order. Perhaps he was under cover. Or perhaps he had to disappear—maybe the police were searching for him. In fact, he had slept so much, maybe her Vlad was risking his health, even life, carrying out this difficult task.

Victoria, ever the Soviet, didn't suspect that a miracle had happened—that she was still alive! That, instead of being in her current position, as painful as it was, her body could be lying at the bottom of the tub. And she remained alive only because Yakubovsky hadn't remained the Soviet person. Moreover, he had been converted because of her.

So many things she had been about to tell Vlad! Three days ago, Konstantin Murashov, with his wife Martha, had arrived from Fedorovka. Refugees from

Tajikistan had begun to live in the hospital without permission. Although they could understand the victims' position, it made it impossible for them to live normally. Because of that, the Murashovs had submitted documents for their departure. They were released from the village within three weeks. The old couple hadn't even had time to get their things together before the permission came, so the doctor had burnt everything that remained. Konstantin burnt all the hospital records—none of those people were still there anyway. He burnt all of the birth and death records stamped with the USSR insignia. Even the seal he threw into the flames. The old man cried. His whole life had burned in an old cast-iron heater "Titan."

Vicky had also planned to tell Vladislav about Boris Goryanin and his wife. Both of them had looked at her strangely, and it was visible that they were trying to remember something.

Then suddenly Ruslana, Boris's wife, had asked her, "Is your mum, casually, called Frieda?"

How could she have known that? She had wanted to ask the Goryanins how they knew her mom's name, and had planned to at their dinner that evening.

But till late that evening, Victoria kept sobbing and talking to the invisible Vlad, and didn't make it to dinner. How could she go anywhere with her eyes so swollen with tears? And even if they did meet, what would they say? And what would it change? And so Victoria would never have the chance to know that her biological father was Boris Goryanin.

In the morning, after a sleepless night, Vicky left for work with puffy eyes. She hadn't drunk even a drop of tea. There was no desire. She went outside, but her car wasn't there.

"He even stole my car, the snake!"

Indignant, Vicky took the bus to work. Maybe he had no choice, though, she mused. Maybe he is risking his life carrying out an important task, and here I am abusing him! Yet, Victoria continued to doubt.

Having arrived outside the airport, she walked in through the parking garage and noticed that her car was in its usually spot.

"Vlad is back!" she squealed, but when she approached the vehicle and saw the key and envelope on the front seat, something poked at her insides.

Victoria opened the door with her key. She picked up the spare key and put it in her purse, and then opened the envelope and read the note. She then looked at the check and gasped.

"Here I am abusing him, but Vlad loves me. If he didn't, he wouldn't have left so much money."

In that, Vicky was right. Vlad really wanted, under the complex circumstances, to make things the best he could for her.

That afternoon, having escaped from work, Vicky went to the bank and opened an account in her name.

That weekend, Victoria met with her parents and told them what had happened. Mom will be Mom, however, and so, together with Frieda, Vicky had a little cry. But then they resolved that life should move forward, and they had to live with what they had.

Time is healing. In a few months, Victoria had all but forgotten her Vlad.

Then, shortly before Christmas, a group of Russian officers came to the VIP Service Center. They were experts from the Joint Staff of Russia, commissioned to communicate with NATO's military organization. Among them, a youngish general, having seen Vicky, fell paralyzed with astonishment, and Vicky couldn't take her eyes off of him either.

That day, he departed with his group to Moscow, and had only had time to exchange phone numbers with Victoria. But the next morning, Yuri, as he was called, called Vicky and told her that he had submitted a request for a five-day vacation.

The general returned to Munich three days later. He came to see her at the VIP Service center, in full general regalia, with a huge bouquet of flowers.

After Vicky left work, they spent the rest of the day together. They talked and talked, and unable to resist her feelings for him, Vicky spent the night with him. And the next morning, they went to her parents' together, where Yuri asked for the hand of their daughter.

They never left each other after that. In fact, Yakubovsky had said once, that women such as Vicky become generals' wives.

... Even on a horse, one cannot outride his own destiny.

75

California, August 8, 1995

Boris and Ruslana woke up to the sharp repeated ringing of the phone. They had just returned from a trip across Europe and still were not back on a normal sleeping schedule.

As soon as the half-sleeping Boris said hello, the voice on the other end started to reproach him in a rapid speech.

"I was in the hospital with Kravchuk, and he advised me to call you. He is asking when you will begin the deliveries of the wheat. What should I tell Mr. Kravchuk?"

"And are you sure that you are not calling from the hospital? How did you manage to dial my number while in a strait jacket?" Boris tried to laugh off the matter. "And, in general, it usually is a good idea to introduce yourself first."

"Yes. Certainly. My name is Alexey Semenov. I am an employee of Agroprom."

"I don't know you from George Washington's white horse, who crossed the Potomac river. Please, tell Mr. Kravchuk that he needs to ease up on the drinking. By the way, young man, that goes for you too."

"This is not a joke. It is a very serious matter. Agroprom has taken the credit from Food Commerce Bank for the delivery of wheat, for six-and-a-half million dollars. We have a Letter of Guarantee signed by you."

"Who signed the guarantee?"

"You."

"Me?" Only now did Boris fully wake up. "Excuse me? Could you please send me a copy of this Letter of Guarantee, and a copy of the bank-wiring instructions? Such a contract isn't even necessary to me. I shall examine the documents, though, and if I have to pay, I will."

"How I can send them to you?"

"By fax is fine."

"Will you give me your fax number, please?"

Boris dictated to embarrassed Semenov his fax number.

"I will send it there."

"Please, I would rather grateful," Boris said, and hung up the phone.

Then, not having given any value to the conversation, Boris went right back to sleep. He regarded the call as a sign that Kravchuk needed something from him.

In the morning, Boris found on his fax machine copies of the Letter of Guarantee and the wiring instructions.

The problem was that nobody, including Semenov, knew that Kravchuk had forged Goryanin's signature. But he had forged it so carelessly—so ineptly and roughly—that when Goryanin looked at the so-called Letter of Guarantee, he burst out laughing. This piece of junk wouldn't cost him any lost sleep. And that wasn't to mention the wiring instructions for multiple transfers, all typed on various typewriters in different fonts. A cursory examination of the presentability of this document would put to rest even the most aggressive assumption in any court.

Food Commerce Bank, though registered duly, was run by the owners of the Moscow Experimental Brewery Plant, which was used for doubtful operations. (In fact, all of the operations of Food Commerce Bank had a rather doubtful character, as did its owners. It was not mafia money, in the full sense of the word, but something rather similar.)

The wiring instructions from Food Commerce Bank reflected a chain of events regarding the transfer of six million, five hundred thousand dollars from the Agroprom account at Food Commerce Bank to the Moscow Business Bank and then to the Bank of New York— and only then to the First Russian Corporation account at the Pacific Bank of China in San Francisco. Each transfer contained addresses, phone numbers, and the account numbers for every beneficiary.

Goryanin knew that he had never opened any account for the First Russian Corporation. Further, the corporation had been dissolved in 1993. He waited until nine o'clock and called the Pacific Bank of China in San Francisco. His conversation with the bank representative was very simple.

"My name is Boris Goryanin. Would you mind providing me with the balance on this corporate account number?" Boris read the number on the bank's wiring instructions.

After a minute, the bank rep returned on the line. "Sorry, sir, but your name is not on the list of people having the right to receive such private information."

That was quite enough for Goryanin. He asked to be connected to the bank's chief of Internal Security. The chief wasn't available, however, so Boris left a voice mail saying that he had information regarding fraudulent activity in which Pacific Bank of China was involved.

Then he found, in the telephone book, the number for the Orange County FBI. His conversation with them was even simpler. After Boris introduced himself and said that he had information regarding financial fraud, the agent-on-duty told him that they were not engaged in those types of investigations. Still, Boris wrote down the phone number, date, and time he had called, along with the name and personnel number of the agent with whom he spoke.

The chief of Internal Security at the Pacific Bank of China, Mr. Bill Hall, called him back a week later. During their conversation, Boris faxed him a copy of the false Letter of Guarantee, a copy of the certificate that he had received from the Department of Corporations of California in regards to closing the First Russian Corporation in 1993, and a copy of Food Commerce Bank's wiring instructions reflecting a chain of transfers for a total amount of six million five hundred thousand dollars.

To Boris's remark that he assumed the money had left the bank the very same day as they came, Bill Hall answered positively. Moreover, he told Boris that the money had just arrived in the account on Friday, June, 16, and then was transferred out again on Monday, June, 19, to Gavrila Kravchuk's personal account at the West Pacific Bank in Western Samoa. Since Food Commerce Bank was closed on the weekends, the two transactions had taken place one day after another. And after that, the money seemed to disappear. For further investigation, a special international decision would be required, he said, but then no information could be gathered from Western Samoa, because Samoan legislation guaranteed client confidentiality in regard to the deposit and transfer of financial assets. At the end of their conversation, Boris again recorded the phone number, date, time, and contact person, Mr. Bill Hall.

Goryanin knew that, under Russian law, hard currency payments for commercial contracts, if deficient, were subject to return within a hundred and eighty days. And in Russia, there was strict control over the use of hard currency funds. Therefore, he expected more to come from this, but not until probably early January 1996.

To protect himself, he combined all of his notes and copies in a manila folder. He labeled it and put in the metal safe in his office.

In a week, Goryanin had already ceased to think about the issue. Doing daily business on his construction sites, working with the architect, tending to marketing and accounting, checking invoices, and sending reports to the bank occupied all of his time. Moreover, he and Ruslana had recently returned from their trip through Europe—and catching up after vacation takes twice as long as the vacation itself.

Boris still couldn't understand why Victoria Koval hadn't come to dinner with them. They had met so warmly. It was a pity that he hadn't asked Vicky when she was born. Ruslana agreed that Vicky very much reminded her of Frieda, from the Kazakh village. It was a pity that Vicky hadn't come.

76

California, September 1995

Autumn had come, and George was now fifteen months old and running already. He hadn't begun to speak yet, though he understood much and tried to show everyone his own character. He was at that age when kids investigate the world around them. Melissa and Lyudmila had to cover all the electrical sockets and put stoppers on the cabinet doors.

Melissa was beginning her second academic year. Considering the intensity of her studies, she had no spare time. Her father came to visit them a second time. Together with Lyudmila, he puttered with George. On weekends, when Melissa was busy doing homework, they would take George to the beach. It was remarkable that he, not knowing Russian, and Lyudmila, practically without English, were able to communicate so freely. Sir Charles liked Lyudmila's cooking too—and, in particular, the pies and pastries.

Only several blocks from Melissa's house, the Goryanins lived. Both Boris and Ruslana owned businesses, and both worked from sunrise to sunset through the week. And if something couldn't be finished then, they would complete it on the weekends.

Boris had sold his first house at a profit. He had paid off the construction loan, the suppliers, and the subs. With the money that remained, he purchased another lot, and deposited ten percent into a special savings account. He had planned to one day give all of the money saved in this account to Melissa.

Boris's large profit was due to one simple factor—he minimized his expenses. He didn't have any salaried employees; he had no office or warehouse. He didn't need to pay for a watchman or utilities. He was the general contractor, the superintendent, and the bookkeeper. He personally placed all of the orders with small companies, where he communicated only with those who had the power and ability to make decisions on the spot. His efficiency outweighed that of all the competition. And by the end of the year, Boris began putting together the projects for the fourth and fifth sites.

Ruslana rendered essential help toward the family budget. She worked seven days a week, acting as a hairdresser for six, and, on Sunday mornings, cleaning her salon.

77

California, February 8, 1996

Goryanin's assumptions regarding Kravchuk's loan proved to be true. In early February 1996, Goryanin's telephone, once again, rang out in the dead of night.

Knowing that it could only be a Russian calling, he answered rather originally. "Who is not sleeping in the middle of the night?"

"Did we wake you? I'm sorry. We have to discuss a very important issue with Mr. Goryanin. But if it isn't convenient, we can call later."

"You have wakened me already. Goryanin is speaking."

"Is this Mr. Goryanin? How are you?"

"And how are you?"

"Excuse us. We are calling from Food Commerce Bank. This is the chief of the loan department, Timur Kagirov, and right next to me is the deputy chief of the legal department, Valentin Simakin."

"What kind of damage could I have caused your bank that you would go to this much trouble to find me?"

"You, Mr. Goryanin, need to return six-and-a-half-million dollars."

"To whom?"

"To our bank."

"What? Did I steal money from you? Or did you lend me the money?"

"You are the guarantor of a loan for the delivery of wheat. A large sum—"

"And how to be with a key from the volt in the bank, where this money is?

"Don't interrupt me; otherwise we will meet in the other place!"

Obviously, Kagirov and Simakin hadn't liked Boris's joke. "Well then, going forward please be more specific," Boris replied. This conversation was beginning to bother him.

"A large sum of money was stolen from our bank, and you, Mr. Goryanin, were a participant in this criminal activity. You are a direct accomplice of this crime."

"Let's approach this question from the other side," Boris countered. "And don't answer me, but just think about it. When was the last time you saw me at your bank? When I signed something there? And, in general, if I were to suddenly walk into your reception area, is there one person there who would recognize me?"

This final bit of rationale seemed to work on them, but the fact remained that they still needed the money back, and no amount of rationale would achieve that.

Before saying good-bye, Boris said, "Listen to me. A half a year ago, I had similar conversation with Alexey Semenov from Agroprom. I have informed the FBI about this conversation. Similarly, I will advise the FBI of our present conversation; therefore you, gentlemen, should think twice before sending your gangsters my way."

"We are not gangsters ..." Kagirov stated flatly, obviously taking offence.

"I didn't know," Boris concluded.

The phone call ended with notification that Food Commerce Bank would submit a claim to the Attorney General, who would then make any further decisions on the matter. And on that, they said good-bye.

Now Boris knew that, in a year or two, he would be called somewhere for an interview or even a deposition in the presence of lawyers. So he got out the manila folder labeled "Kravchuk's Bank Fraud," and recorded the date and time of the phone call from Food Commerce Bank and the essence of their conversation. Then he called the FBI.

After listening to Boris's story about financial fraud, the agent on duty told him that they weren't engaged in such investigations. But Boris, knowing full well what he was doing, again wrote down the specifics of the phone call: the phone number, date, and time, and the name and personal number of the agent he had spoken to.

This very same day, Mrs. Anna Yakubovsky gave birth to a boy. The happy parents named him Igor. By this time, they had received the so-called L-1 (the visa of millionaires). Vlad was a legalized citizen, and he and Ann had received green cards for permanent residency in the States. So next on their list was to start up their business. But what kind?

After considering various possibilities, Vladislav, with Michael's help, decided that the simplest and most profitable route would be to purchase a residential apartment building and rent out units. They found a ninety-one-apartment complex. Each unit had two bedrooms and two baths, two carports, and access to the swimming pool and gym. The complex was in Santa Clara, next to a large shopping center and close to the Lawrence Expressway. After negotiations, they purchased it for five million in cash. The complex already had eighty-three-percent occupancy.

Their gross income ended up being a hundred and forty thousand dollars a month. In view of all their expenses, the net profit remained fifty-six thousand dollars per month.

Also, Yakubovsky purchased two homes for his family and for Michael's. Both houses were in a nice gated community and cost about a million dollars each.

Ann decorated their home, and they began to live as people. In another year, their second child was born—a nice little girl. And so the gypsy's prediction had come true. How could he not have trusted her after all?

78

California, May 25, 1996

More than two years had passed since Melissa had moved to California, and today, wearing a violet doctorate gown and a cap with gold embroidery, she proudly proceeded to the podium where she would be presented with graduation certificate from law school and a doctorate of law diploma. At the ceremony were Melissa's father, Lyudmila, and George. The whole thing was very solemn.

Afterward, Melissa was photographed holding the diploma, surrounded by her relatives, and then they left for home, where, that evening, they would celebrate. Some girlfriends from school, Mrs. Backinsale, Sharon, and Elena were among the guests to amicably celebrate the significant event.

The next morning, on Sunday, the doctor of law woke up to see that her son had somehow managed to get out of his bed and into hers. As he slept, Melissa stretched and went to the bathroom. She looked at herself in the mirror. Two and a half years had passed since she had parted with Boris, and soon, she would be thirty. Her face had no wrinkles and her figure was still that of a twenty-five-year-old. But sad eyes gave away her secret thoughts. After a minute or two, Melissa stepped into the shower and let the jets of water wash away all of these unpleasant meditations.

When Melissa came out of the bathroom, George was awake, standing on the bed and trying to jump on the mattress. He wasn't too successful. Melissa changed his diaper, washed his smiling face and little hands, and then, together, they went down to the kitchen. There were "Grandpa Chailz" and "Aunt Milya," as George now called them, already fussing over breakfast. They didn't hide their mutual interest anymore. George, who had a healthy appetite, first ate porridge and then washed it down with a cup of apple juice.

After breakfast, elegantly dressed, they all went to church. Lyudmila was an atheist, but she went to church with them anyway. It was so nice there. Everyone politely greeted each other and the pastor spoke beautifully.

The next day, Melissa went to the library to begin preparations for the California Bar exam. The Bar was usually scheduled only two times a year, and the next exam would be October 27. In order to participate in the examination, Melissa had to fill out registration forms, and Mrs. Backinsale promised to send them out at the first opportunity.

Again, there had come long days for Melissa. She was engaged in her studies twelve hours a day, only able to give George an hour of uninterrupted time. And she needed nine hours of sleep in order to be mentally competent for her studies.

The California Bar Exam is a three-day exam. Days one and three consist of essay exams (three essay questions in each morning section) and an afternoon session testing performance skills. The questions covered seventeen basic areas of lawyer activity. Written answers to questions would be forty percent of the final grade. Yet, the most challenging part would be on the second day, when she would have to answer two hundred questions covering relations between the states of the union. Considering the complexity of the examination, statistically, only about thirty-five to fifty-five percent of those examined successfully passed the exam.

Melissa prepared most carefully, but on the day of the exam, she was worried. Melissa had had time to answer all of the questions, but, unfortunately, her name did not appear among those who had successfully passed. She would need to continue to study and take the next available Bar, this time scheduled in February 1997.

79

California, February 25, 1997

By now, George was almost two years old, and he had turned into a real prankster. This mischievous toddler spoke, without stop, in both Russian and English. If he could, he would watch cartoons for hours.

For the second time, Melissa Spencer was ready to take the California Bar, and she successfully passed it. Afterward, totally exhausted, Melissa required a good rest. So, all four of them went to Hawaii. Two weeks of the caressing ocean and plenty of sleep did the job.

Back home, Melissa started searching for work. She wouldn't even consider the possibility of moving elsewhere, however. She still hoped that one day she would meet Boris and that he would participate in George's life.

Melissa had some essential advantages over other beginning lawyers. First: her attendance at the London School of Economy and Political Sciences. And, second, her knowledge of several languages. After a short search, she was hired as an assistant at the United States Attorney's Office, representing the US government. The US Attorney's office was in Los Angeles, so Melissa had to spend a lot of time on the road. Her duties included handling any business connected to Europe, including Russia. She already knew Russian rather well; she could read and write it practically without a dictionary, and could speak it fluently, though with a British accent.

Then, in early 1998, she received on her desk an inquiry from the State Office of the Attorney General of Russia: Boris Goryanin had been called as a witness before a grand jury in a case related to the embezzlement of six and a half million dollars from a Russian bank. Five-year-old memories gushed over Melissa: Kravchuk, Yakubovsky, and … Boris.

80

California, April-May, 1998

In mid-April, pulling up to his house after work, Boris saw a young man standing at the entryway to his front-yard gate.

He stopped and rolled down the window. "May I help you?"

"I am looking for Mr. Boris Goryanin."

"That's me."

"There is certified federal mail for you. Please, sign."

Boris signed the receipt, and the young man left. He has turned around the large envelope and studied it. There was the emblem of the US Attorney on it. Inside the envelope, there was a federal subpoena requesting he appear in court on May 15, 1998, to testify under the oath before a grand jury.

So on Friday, May 15, instead of his usual working clothes— jeans, a light shirt, and walking shoes—Boris put on black trousers, a shirt and tie, and dress shoes. He left the house at his normal time of seven o'clock, and drove to the Federal Building in Los Angeles.

A half-hour before nine, Goryanin was parking. Then he grabbed the manila folder he had been composing and walked into the building. He presented his driver's license to the security guard, walked through the metal detector, and took the elevator to the ninth floor. The door to the room specified in the judge's order was still locked, so Boris waited in the hallway. After a few minutes, a huge, clumsy security guard came down the hall holding a plastic cup that gave off the aroma of coffee. The guard affably greeted Boris, and suggested he go in the next room, and get a cup of coffee.

When Boris returned, the security guard, who was apparently the court marshal, was already standing at the opened door, holding a list of the participants for that morning's session.

By nine, the courtroom was filled with people, and an average-aged gentleman entered the room. The court marshal locked the door and loudly announced the beginning of the session. The gentleman, who happened to be the deputy to the United States attorney, asked the court marshal to check who was present. The court marshal called the name of each participant, followed by his or her role in the session. Boris Goryanin was classified as a witness.

In front of Boris's table was a table at which a man and a woman sat. The man turned out to be the investigator for the Attorney General of the Russian Federation, Mr. Stanislav Terekhin. The woman, whose name Boris couldn't remember, was the federal court interpreter. One more assistant to the United States Attorney settled down next to the deputy of the United States attorney, right behind Boris. On the left side of this assistant there was a public defender who could come to the aid of Boris if he asked for legal advice. On Boris's table, there were a few sheets of paper, a ballpoint pen, and Boris's manila folder.

The deputy to United States Attorney, Mr. Robert Blitts, addressed Boris. "Mr. Goryanin, do you need an interpreter?"

"Thank you. I do not think so."

"Then let's begin. Mr. Goryanin, please stand up and raise your right hand."

When Boris had done what he was told, Mr. Robert Blitts said, "Now repeat after me," and proceeded with the words of the oath.

"I, Boris Goryanin,"

"I, Boris Goryanin,"

"In front of a grand jury,"

"In front of a grand jury,"

"Promise to speak the truth, and nothing but the truth, so help me, God."

After Boris had finished repeated the oath, Mr. Robert Blitts told Boris to be seated. Then he turned and addressed Terekhin.

"Mr. Boris Goryanin is yours. You may proceed with questioning."

So far, Terekhin had kept silent. Now he fidgeted in his chair and then addressed Boris in Russian. The interpreter translated his statement into English.

"Mr. Goryanin. My name is Stanislav Ivanovich Terekhin. I am a senior investigator for the Attorney General of the Russian Federation. We are here to ask you some questions. But before we start, for the record, please state your name."

"Boris Goryanin."

"What is your address?"

"314 Pacific Avenue, Huntington Beach, California." Boris Goryanin answered in English, which the interpreter then translated, for Terekhin, into Russian. And so went each question.

"What is your date of birth?"

"April 25, 1945."

"Where you were born?"

"In the city of Moscow, in the USSR."

The questioning proceeded in this way for half an hour, after which point the attorney had established Goryanin's biography, but had not yet started to ask him anything of essence.

Then, suddenly, his tune changed. "Does the name Gavrila Petrovich Kravchuk mean something to you?" the attorney asked.

"Yes. We used to be, I thought, friends and business associates."

"What do you mean?"

"Please, be more specific."

"When you said friends, for how long did you know each other?"

"Since 1990."

"How would you describe your personal relationship with Kravchuk?"

"Please ask me direct questions and I will give you straight answers."

"What did you do as friends?"

"We used to meet and speak on the phone on a regular basis. We made plans for the future. We made plans to develop a business together."

"What kind of business?"

"Agroprom once worked on a program called the Revitalization of Russia. This program had support in the Kremlin. Kravchuk was the brains behind the program. My role was to design high-quality townhomes for reasonable prices by using progressive technology in their construction. The idea was that the houses would be attractive to military personnel and young families from small towns. The business was able to generate a lot of job opportunities and was a key in solving the demographic problem. Kravchuk had connections in the Kremlin. On his desk was even a red, all government direct-line telephone, which he called 'vertushka.' You know what it means."

"And then what happened?"

"He started drinking. He was drinking a lot. Finally, he lost his humanity."

"Being a friend, why did you not help him?"

"Are you serious?"

"Yes, I am."

"Let's go to the next question."

"What do you know about the purchase of grain?"

"I have nothing to do with it."

"Why?"

"Because, we are not business partners anymore."

"But you signed a Letter of Guarantee for six and a half million dollars."

"Do you mean this?" Boris opened the manila folder, took out the faxed copy of the letter, and held it in the air.

"Yes." Terekhin nodded.

"This is not my signature," Boris proceeded.

"So whose signature is it?"

"I do not know. That's your job to find out."

"That is precisely what we are doing here," Terekhin said, smirking.

Boris reached into his shirt pocket, took out his American passport, and handed it to the marshal to give to Terekhin. "This is what my signature looks like."

The attorney looked at Goryanin's passport signature and compared it to the signature on the letter. Then, without saying a word, he returned it to the marshal.

"This too." Boris took his wallet out of his back pants pocket and retrieved his driver's license. Again, he handed it to the federal marshal.

After inspecting this second piece of evidence, Terekhin asked, "Would you please make several samples of your signature in front of us?"

"Easy," Boris said with a smile.

On a sheet of a paper in front of him, Boris signed his name several times and then handed the sheet to the federal marshal. "I hope that this will eliminate at least one name from your list of suspects."

Terekhin ignored Boris's remark and continued questioning. "What do you know about the letter? How did you get a copy of it?"

"On August 8, 1995, Mr. Alexey Semenov called from Moscow. He asked me to return six and a half million dollars. I thought it was a joke, until he supported his request by faxing me a copy of the letter along with the wiring instructions from Food Commerce Bank."

"Have you discussed this matter with anyone since that time?"

"Yes. I contacted the FBI," Boris answered. "And I called the Pacific Bank of China, and spoke to the head of security, Mr. Bill Hall. As a matter of fact, Mr. Hall told me that the money you are looking for was wired to Kravchuk's personal account with the West Pacific Bank in West Samoa just one day after it had been wired from the Bank of New York. Furthermore, in one day, the money had been cashed and taken out of the bank."

"Have you been contacted by anyone else?"

"Yes. On February 8, 1996, Mr. Kagirov and Mr. Simakin from Food Commerce Bank called me."

"And then what?"

"I contacted the FBI and let them know."

"What did the FBI do?"

"They did nothing. But on the bright side, they are constantly guarding me. Not only me, but all American citizens." No one in the room seemed to appreciate Boris's joke.

"With your permission, may I change the subject and ask you several questions on another case?"

"Sure."

"I have a record of your confession that you killed four citizens of the Russian Federation. Is that correct?"

"Yes, but they were not citizens. Citizens are humans. They were subhuman. They were animals. And I killed them in self-defense. In fact, I killed them defending not only my life, but also the life of my dearest friend. Her honor, her dignity, and her life."

"Those are your words. Is there anyone else who can support that statement?"

"I can support that statement," a voice came from behind Boris.

He could have recognized that voice out of a million others. It was the voice of Melissa Spencer.

81

California, May 15, 1998

Boris's head rotated back toward her voice. There was Melissa rising from her seat located next to the deputy of United States Attorney Mr. Robert Blitts. Boris was in shock. He could not take his wide eyes off of her, let alone muster the wherewithal to say something. But the sight of him said more than any words could. A few seconds had passed before he realized that Melissa has said it in Russian.

Against instruction, Boris rose from his chair. He saw only Melissa and nobody else.

Melissa, seeing Boris look at her, turned to Mr. Blitts and in a begging voice, said, "Robert, please call a recess."

"The session of this hearing is in recess for ten minutes," the deputy proclaimed over the confused whispers of those present.

All rose, and Boris and Melissa, paying no attention to anybody, rushed toward each other. They embraced and stood there frozen in each other's arms, while everyone left the courtroom. When they were alone, Boris, not able to constrain his feelings, kissed Melissa on the eyes, lips, and cheeks. Melissa replied in kind. Then, at last, their impulsive feelings passed, releasing them to pull apart and examine each other joyfully.

Both of them had been silent until this moment, but now started to speak simultaneously. They weren't interrupting each other, but one would ask a question right on the heels of the other's question, neither waiting for a reply. Then realizing how absurd they must appear, they stopped, laughed, and Boris, immediately serious again, asked, "Melissa, is that you? My mila, how are you? How is George? How are you here?"

"Boris, darling, I shall tell you everything, but we'll have to wait till the end of the session. I will not go anywhere. Do you believe me?"

"I trust you. Let's get something to drink. I am so excited that my throat has dried up.

"Mine too."

Holding hands, they left the courtroom and went to the cafeteria.

When Boris and Melissa, each holding a plastic coffee cup, returned to the courtroom, the court marshal, on the order of the deputy to the United States attorney, proclaimed that court was back in session.

The deputy to the United States attorney asked Mr. Stanislav Terekhin whether he had more questions for the witness Mr. Goryanin or for Ms. Spencer. Mr. Terekhin, through the translator, said that he was completely satisfied with Mr. Goryanin's answers and that he had never intended to question Ms. Spencer.

Carrying out the decision of the federal judge, the deputy then asked Boris Goryanin to provide his signature thirty times on a special form. Boris executed this simple task with excitement, but not from the task—from Melissa's presence. All his thoughts were now about Melissa. In a fog, he could hardly wait for the conclusion of the interrogation. But finally, he was asked to undersign each page of the court report, after which the session of the grand jury ended.

Boris approached Melissa, smiling with the pleasure that, at last, he was seeing her again. Looking at her eyes full of tears, he waited while she said good-bye to the deputy and the foreman of the grand jury. Then Melissa turned and told him in Russian, with a light British accent, "Boris, please wait for me here. I need to get my briefcase. Then we can go."

Having Melissa beside him and, moreover, speaking to him in Russian, Boris had lost not only the ability to speak, but also to think, slowly. This was not something familiar to Boris. While Melissa was getting her briefcase, Boris continued to shake his head and repeat to himself in whispers, "Melissa, Melissa. Darling!"

Then as Melissa approached him with her briefcase, he took her into his arms and asked in a serious tone, "How did you get involved in this case? What are you doing? Where do you live? Where is George?"

"Boris, talk to me in Russian. I know Russian now. We speak it at home. George knows both languages."

"Did you say you speak Russian at home? Are you married?"

"No, Boris. I haven't married. After you, I haven't been involved with anybody. We have a Russian nanny, and George and I are learning from her. We live in Orange County, near you, Boris."

They were in the parking lot, and approaching to Boris's car. It was a

Toyota 4-Runner, like Melissa's, but in silver. He helped her into the front passenger's seat and closed the door behind her.

Then after seating himself, Boris turned to Melissa and gave her a long look. Unable to constrain his pleasure at seeing her, he leaned over and embraced her, and again started to kiss her face. Melissa didn't hide her feelings either. Finally, having satisfied the gush of feelings, they stopped and sat back in their seats.

Suddenly, Boris felt a strong pain in his solar plexus, like it was in Novomatushkino. The pain was so strong, as he had received gunshot wounds. A grimace crossed his face, and he put his hand on his solar plexus.

"What's wrong?" Melissa asked.

"A terrible pain. As I had then! Do you remember?"

"Yes, dear. I do remember. I remember everything! Let's lie down a bit and the pain will go away."

And so they joined hands, reclined their seats, and closed their eyes. From the sudden rush of emotions cause by this long-awaited but unexpected meeting, both of them had grown weak.

Melissa woke up first. Still holding Boris's hand, she leaned over and nestled her lips into Boris's cheek. He awoke from her touch. The pain was gone. They smiled each other.

The Boris put his seat back up and turned the key in the ignition. "Where is your car?" he asked.

"In employee parking. But I'm afraid that if I drive today, I won't be able to make it home. My legs are weak. I am so glad to see you. At last, we have met! So … I was hoping you could bring me back here on Monday, and after work, I will take my car home."

"It is so strange to hear you speak Russian. You are doing it so well. And your accent is charming. You are so marvelous. If I could, I would eat you."

"Please don't even think about it. I don't want to be chewed. I am only bones anyway!"

"Do you want me to tell you, you are bony? No. You look remarkable. Great."

"Hey, we'd better stop joking around and go. It is a long drive to my house."

And with that, Boris put the car into drive.

"You should meet George," she told him as they pulled out of the parking lot. "You will like each other."

"Who does he look like? I hope he looks like his mom."

"But he looks like his daddy. And he talks a lot too, like his daddy!"

"Well, since we have a long drive, why don't you start from the beginning?

Tell me everything that has happened to you since that moment we parted in Frankfurt."

And so they slowly made their way down the I-5 Freeway. It was Friday, and the southbound traffic to Orange County was packed bumper to bumper. At times, it seemed they were hardly moving. Yet the time seemed to pass quickly as Melissa told Boris the story of her life for those years. He listened to her without interruption, as she jumped from one thing to another. She didn't concentrate on the bad moments, however, and told him the good things in detail.

Only once, when Melissa told him what had happened to her in Geneva, did he react, as he couldn't restrain himself; in fact, he nearly screamed.

Melissa had ended her story by the time they were nearing the 605-Freeway. And only then did Boris jump in.

"But why? Why did you just disappear from me like that? Keep hiding our son from me? Why? I was searching for you, but it was like you were just gone."

"I know you were searching for me. And, yes, I was hiding from you. But, meanwhile, I made everything possible to be close to you." She paused, thinking, and then continued to speak almost without pausing. "Boris, how do you see our relationship continuing? If you were to ask me whether I love you, I would say, 'Without a doubt.' I love you very much. But I love you as a true, dear friend. All these years, I have never been with another man. And I never will be. But I will never be involved in a romantic relationship with you either, because as much as I am in love with you, I respect your wife. I cannot. And you cannot … yet, at the same time, George needs a father. And I also respect myself and my needs. But what else can we do? If I knew the answer, I would have called you a long time ago."

Finally, Melissa stopped and took a breath. Boris was silent. He could tell that she had been suffering, desperate to talk to him about all of it.

After a couple minutes, he broke the silence. "My story is much simpler. All these years I was working, building houses. I am simultaneously the builder, the bookkeeper, and the superintendent, and as a result, I doubled the money you gave me. One million dollars is back in the account in Germany, and then there is another million, which I shall not touch without your consent."

"Boris, will you? I trust you just as much now as I did then. I know that you are intelligent and fair. George is smart too! You wouldn't believe it. We had his IQ checked, and the psychologist told me it was no less than one hundred and fifty!"

They left the freeway at Beach Boulevard, and Boris drove south toward the ocean. He went two blocks and turned left into a shopping center.

Boris and Melissa got out and Boris led her into a toy store. As they walked beside each other, Boris was once again struck with the non-believability of the current situation.

Melissa, seeing him suddenly smile at his thoughts, asked, "What are you smiling for?"

"Because you are beside me. And I know that we will be beside each other always."

"Yes, that's true. I shall be your best friend."

They entered the store, and Boris scanned the shelves a while. Then he asked Melissa, "What do you think—the fire truck or the building crane?"

"The construction set." Melissa smiled.

Boris purchased the large construction set made of wooden blocks and then led Melissa next door to the flower shop.

"Please, make me three bouquets," he told the woman at the counter. "Two with roses and one of carnations."

While the woman prepared the bouquets, Melissa patiently waited, staying silent. But when they left the shop, she asked, "For who did you purchase the bouquets?"

"Red roses for you. They are so lovely, like you are, and I have never gotten you flowers. The other rose bouquet is for your Russian nanny. And the carnations are for Ruslana."

"Ruslana? Is that your wife? Boris, do you know … we are friends with a Ruslana. She owns a salon. Is that … your wife?"

Boris stopped mid-step and looked at her. "Yes. But … how is that possible?"

"She does my hair, and we are friends. Sometimes we even have lunch together."

"And you haven't told her our story?"

"No. I didn't realize the connection until now, when you just called her by name."

"But what about her last name?"

"We have known each other for three years, but I never knew her last name. She knows mine, but only because I am her client."

"Unbelievable!"

After that, they were silent, both absorbing this new revelation. They got into the car and, in ten minutes, were pulling onto Melissa's street. Anxious about meeting George, Boris's knees shook, and his mouth dried up again. This was nothing to take lightly. He was going to see his son for the first time!

They entered the house, and upon hearing the door open in the living room, a little fellow rushed in toward them. Boris looked at him. He was Anton's exact copy when he had been four years old. Having seen the stranger, the boy stopped for an instant and then ran to his mother. He embraced her legs and hid behind them, peeking out at Boris.

Boris, in turn, observed his child and smiled. Then not knowing what better to do, Boris stretched his right hand out to the boy and said, "Let's get acquainted, son. My name is Boris."

The little fellow, having suddenly recovered from his first impression, suddenly began to chatter. "I know you. You are my grandfather. You used to be my daddy, but now you are old and became my grandfather."

George escaped to somewhere, but, in a minute, returned. In his hands, he held an enlarged copy of the photo that Boris had enclosed in Melissa's handbag in Togliatti. And, sure enough, there was Boris in the photo, only six years younger. In the photo, he looked almost like Anton did now.

"It is my daddy, when you were still young. But now you are my grandfather." He ran up to Boris.

Boris lifted the child and pressed the little body to his own. They stood for a while embracing each other.

Lyudmila walked in, and seeing Boris with George in his arm, understood everything: Melissa, at last, had met with Boris.

"George," Lyudmila said, "climb down, darling. It is heavy for a grandfather to hold such a big boy."

To that, George quite reasonably answered, "Grandfather is not holding me. We are holding each other."

The old woman began to fuss, addressing to Boris and Melissa. "Well, what are we all standing around for? Let's go to the kitchen, and I will feed you something."

"But we haven't been acquainted yet," Boris said. "Wait, just a minute."

Boris returned to the car and retrieved the two rose bouquets and the construction set. He took them back inside and handed one of the bouquets to the senior.

"Here. These flowers are for you. And this is for you, George."

Boris gave the child the huge box. George took it exuberantly and dragged it over to a spot on the floor to open.

Melissa stood at the door, the other bouquet in her hands. She hadn't known how George and Boris would react upon meeting each other. But what she saw had amazed her. If Boris, the grown up, had coped well with the excitement of their first meeting, then George had flat-out amazed her with his child's simplicity and spontaneity. Now Melissa felt the assurance that all would be good. All of her worry had been in vain.

From the excitement of the day's event, Boris's insides shook and he felt weak. However, he accepted Melissa's invitation for a tour of the house. Everything was cozy, simple, and clean. George's room was on the second floor, and Melissa had hung up pictures of characters and scenes from Disney cartoons. There was a child's bed with a handrail, and the floor was covered in toys. In Melissa's bedroom, there was a narrow single bed, a large desk with a computer and printer, and a shelf filled with books in different languages. A TV was suspended on the wall. In the third room, there was another single bed.

"It's my father's room, when he comes to see us," Melissa told him. "He is in London now. He is selling his house and then he will come and live with us."

"I remember Sir Charles," said Boris. "We spoke when we were in Togliatti."

"Please, come down to the kitchen!" Lyudmila's voice rang out from downstairs. "I have a meal on the table!"

But suddenly, Boris didn't feel hungry. He was shaking from weariness. "Melissa, please forgive me, but I need to go now. Let me come back tomorrow morning. I had a very difficult day today, and I should have a rest. And you, probably, should too."

It was true. Melissa also felt she could hardly move. She led the way downstairs and toward the front door. But before telling him good-bye, she stopped at the small entryway table, reached into her briefcase, which she had left on the floor, and took out her business card and a pen. On the back of the card, she wrote her home address and phone.

Boris embraced and kissed George. The boy was upset that his grandfather was leaving, but Boris told him that tomorrow morning, they would build a house together with his new blocks. George calmed down. Then Boris called out a good-bye to Lyudmila, and, together with Melissa, walked to his car.

"You cannot imagine how happy I am," Boris told her, "that you and George live so close. You are the smartest lady in the world to have made all this happen."

"I am the happiest lady in the world, too," Melissa told him, tears rolling out of her eyes.

Boris cupped Melissa's face in his hands, and, with kisses, dried up her tears. "Everything will be okay, Mila. Right? You are still my Mila?"

"Absolutely. And you are my Mila, too." Melissa kissed Boris on the cheek. "Please come see us tomorrow. We will be expecting you."

It was about six o'clock when Boris pulled out of the driveway, and it was only a few minutes' drive to his house. Pushing the garage-door opener on his car visor, suddenly, Boris felt a sharp pain shoot through his chest, back, and left hand. He put the car into park, and, pushing through the pain, he slowly left the car and dragged himself into the house and fell on the sofa.

What if he was dying and would never see Ruslana, Anton, Melissa, and George again? He was still gripping Melissa's business card in his hand. Then coldness flashed all over him, and Boris fell into semi consciousness.

Lord, wagging his tail, approached his master on the sofa, and sensing something was wrong, began making short, sharp barks. But Boris did not move. Lord began to bark louder.

Hearing Lord, Anton came downstairs to see what was wrong. He had just returned from the hospital, where he worked as a shift doctor in the intensive care unit. Anton tried to wake his father, but Boris only moaned. Seeing the business card in his hand, Anton took it and put it in his pocket. Boris moaned again. Anton knew that his father was not all right. He checked Boris's pulse. It was weak and faltering. He picked up his cell phone and dialed 911.

After hanging up, he took off his father's wristwatch and grabbed the wallet from his back pants' pocket. He elevated his feet and head with a pillow, and took off his shoes. Then Anton went to the garage and got his medical suitcase from his car. He measured Boris's blood pressure. It was low. He opened a plastic container with nitroglycerine and put one of the pills under Boris's tongue. Then he put on his stethoscope and listened to Boris's heart. In his opinion, Boris's condition was critical, but stable. Anton took the plaid blanket from off the back of the couch and covered Boris with it.

The ambulance would be there any minute, so Anton removed Lord to the kitchen and locked the kitchen door. The he heard the siren. A police car pulled up to the house first, and an officer knocked. After ensuring this wasn't a false alarm, the officer went outside to provide free entrance to the paramedics.

Another siren was heard. This time, it was the ambulance. Two paramedics, one with a medical bag, got out and ran into the house. They saw Anton putting a needle into Boris's right hand. Both of them had worked with Anton before, in the emergency room.

"Hi, Tony. How did you get here before us?" one asked briskly.

"This is my dad. I just got back from my shift and found him here."

"I am sorry. But you seem to be handling it okay."

"Thanks. I think so."

The paramedics secured an oxygen mask over Boris's nose and mouth, and connected it to a tank. In a few breaths, it became easier for him to breathe.

Boris's face went from white to pink, and he regained consciousness. He stirred, acting somewhat confused.

"Dad, it's Anton. Stay quiet and don't move. They are taking you to the hospital now. I shall go with you."

"Anton … I had Mel … issa's business … card," Boris sputtered between breaths. "Remember her? I promised I … would go see her and … George." As he spoke, Boris seemed to regain some strength, and then began to talk more fluidly. "Please, call her. Promise … do everything you can to see them. Love them. Help George. And … tell Mother that I always loved her. All of you be happy and do … not quarrel. Protect each other."

"Who is George?" Anton asked.

"Later, son. Later."

The paramedics carried in a stretcher and lay Boris on it.

"Tony, where do you want to take your dad?"

"To Fountain Valley Regional, where I am. I am going with you guys."

Anton checked to make sure Melissa's business card was in his chest pocket. Then he locked the front door and has left for the hospital in the ambulance, together with Boris.

82

California, May 15, 1998

In the ambulance, Boris was connected to IV, and Anton kept speaking to him, to be sure that Boris stayed conscious. After Boris was brought to the emergency room, he was transferred to the intensive care unit where Anton worked.

Anton told his father, "We're here now, so just relax and save your energy. I will be with you the whole time."

"You should rest," Boris whispered. He knew that Anton had just come off a twenty-four-hour shift.

"I'm used to long hours."

Anton worked independently for three years. Before that, he was an intern, working alternating shifts—a thirty-six-hour shift twice a week, and a twenty-four-hour shift twice a week.

It had been about a half an hour since Boris had crawled onto the sofa. Anton knew he needed to call his mother.

"Mum, listen. Please, don't worry. Dad had a heart attack. He is in the hospital, and I am right here with him. You don't need to come. In fact, it would be better if you waited until morning."

"Oh! What?" Ruslana lamented. "Is he in your hospital?"

"Mum, I told you—don't worry."

"That's easy for you to say. Don't worry. Too late. I'll be there shortly."

Then Anton called for a couple of the senior doctors. When Doctors Strom and Patel had learned that Dr. Goryanin was asking for them about a consultation regarding his father, both responded that they would come immediately.

While Anton waited for them to arrive, he carried out a special request for his father. He called Melissa.

"Hello?"

"Good evening. May I speak to Lady Melissa, please?"

"This is she."

Anton noted the pleasant timbre of her voice. "My name is Tony. I am Boris's son. I am calling you from the hospital. My father suffered a massive heart attack and will be unable to come visit you tomorrow."

"What? What did you say? Oh, my Lord. Please, please tell me that you are kidding me. This is not a funny joke," Melissa said.

"Well, unfortunately, I am not kidding you."

"Where are you? In what hospital? May I come see him?" Melissa asked in an alarming tone.

"Please don't," Anton said. "First of all, considering his condition, he is doing fine. Secondly, you would not be able to come to the ICU. And finally, I will be staying with him until I consider his condition stable."

"But how can you get into the ICU. Why would they let you stay with Boris?"

"I am a doctor, and work in this ICU."

"Please. Please. Let me see him. If he would go, I would never forgive myself."

"Okay, let's agree to this: tomorrow morning, I will come see you straight from the hospital and let you know how he is doing. If something should go wrong before then, I will call you and get you here. I know that your car is in LA. We will get it back for you by Sunday. Agreed?"

"What are you talking about? I will get a cab."

"Let's talk more tomorrow, okay? Are you all right? Please, don't cry. I will not let my father go."

"Do you promise me?"

"I do."

"What is your cell number?"

"I will give it to later. I have to go now. My colleagues are here. We will evaluate Dad's condition, and I will call you in about forty minutes."

"Please. I will be waiting."

Anton and the other two doctors closely examined Boris. Anton drew blood for analysis, and then all three traced indications on the monitor. When the results of the analysis were ready, they agreed that Boris had had a heart attack. The good thing was that it had happened at home, and that Anton had been there. Otherwise the result might have been worse. The doctors wished Anton good luck and left.

"Dad, you should lay quiet and not worry about it. Think positively. I know your diagnosis and I know precisely how to treat you. I spoke with Melissa and I am going to call her again to keep her updated. But before that, I will call Mom." Anton sat wearily on a chair next to the bed.

He dialed their home number. Ruslana picked up instantly. "What did you and the doctors decide? How is Boris?"

"I'll give the telephone to Dad first, and then I'll tell you about my talk with the doctors." He put the phone up to Boris's ear.

"Ruslana," Boris said weakly. "Don't worry. I am just fine. Toni is looking after me well. It is only cold here and boring."

"You just get better and don't bother giving me orders. I know Toni knows what to do. But do you remember in Kazakhstan when I was with you and you recovered? I will come see you tomorrow and then you will be fine again."

"They don't let strangers into the ICU. Employees only."

"I am not a stranger. They will let me in. I know how to talk to people; they will let me in. But don't worry about that right now. You just need to have a good night's rest. You probably were stressed about the whole court ordeal yesterday, and this is the result. Anyway, good night."

"Good night. You don't worry about me either, and get some rest."

Anton hung up the phone, then looked at his dad and asked, "How long you have been involved with Melissa?"

"That's just the point. We met again only today. She works as the assistant to US Attorney in Los Angeles."

"All right, well that explains a lot. You got a decent dose of adrenaline in the courtroom, and then you saw her. And you probably met the baby. Am I right?"

"So? Yeah. But they are not guilty. And what do you want? That I wouldn't see them?"

"Yes. You're right. They are not guilty. But you, when you leave from here, you should take care of your health if you want to continue to be with us."

"So, morals begin. You ordered me not to worry, and now you are exciting me."

"Daddy, what is it with this woman?"

"She is the best in the world … after your mother, of course."

"And what will you tell Mum?"

"It is you who will tell Mum. You will tell her that you have met your destiny."

"I don't understand?"

"There is nothing to understand. I love Ruslana. Besides, I am as old as a grandfather. But you are brothers. So you should be the daddy to our boy. And then you can have more kids together. And I will look at you and be pleased. Call her, son. Go to her. And then I shall rest easily."

With that, Boris sunk into his pillow and closed his eyes. Anton covered him with two blankets. Then he left and went to the doctor's lounge to call Melissa. She was waiting and picked up the phone at once. Anton told her about Boris's condition, and then they agreed that Anton would come see them in the morning.

Anton needed some sleep. He thought about going to his office, which adjoined a small room with a bed and a private restroom, which included a sink, a toilet, and a shower. This room had been provided to him for those night shifts on which he was the doctor on duty, so that he could rest and put himself into order if possible.

But tonight, it turned out, Anton wouldn't rest. The emergency room doctor on duty had gotten ill, and later that evening the ambulance had brought in a motorcyclist. The young guy had fallen off his bike and then gotten run over by the car on the road behind him. The ER nurse called Anton. He didn't have a choice but to order a nurse to remain with Boris so that he could leave to tend to the patient. Then the policemen brought in a Latino, who, during an arrest, pulled a gun on the officer. The teenager received eight bullet wounds in response, two of them in the chest. Then, at about seven in the morning, a pregnant woman was brought in, already in labor. Her roommate had called 911.

By morning, Boris's condition was stabilized, and Ruslana arrived. Anton had brought his mother a gown to wear, so that she wouldn't be expelled, left instructions to the nurse on duty to keep him posted, and provided the doctor on duty with all of Boris's information. Then he shaved, gave his mother the key to his office, and took Ruslana's car to go see Melissa.

Naturally, Melissa was prepared for her first meeting with Boris's son. She was dressed in a short white dress with bright flowers and shoulder straps, which complemented her long neck, round shoulders, and firm breasts. The color of the dress only enhanced her slightly tanned skin. Red high heels accentuated the beauty of her long legs, and the red coral necklace around Melissa's gentle neckline made her appear five years younger than she was.

When Melissa answered the door, and Anton saw her for the first time, he, just as his father once had, felt something inside him that he could only liken to the impact of lightning. Anton stopped dead. For the first few seconds, he had practically lost his ability to speak.

"How are you, Anton?" the young woman asked in Russian, but with an obvious British accent, and stretched out her right hand for a kiss. Then she slightly tipped her head to one side, making her simply charming.

"How do you do?" Anton murmured in English, and didn't kiss, but slightly shook, the outstretched hand.

At this time little George appeared. Hesitating to approach Anton, he again clasped Melissa's legs and, with a child's spontaneity, loudly declared in Russian, "Mum! You have mixed up everything again. You told me that I would be seeing my brother, but Daddy has come. Yesterday, I thought Daddy was coming, but it was Grandfather. You are always mixing things up."

Anton, having still been mesmerized with Melissa, just now realized that they were speaking Russian among themselves.

"How do you know Russian?" he asked, amazed.

"And why is that surprising?" Melissa asked, her eyes sparkling. "If you speak English, why can't we speak Russian? And why are you still standing at the door? Please, come in. How is Boris doing?"

"Dad's condition, I'm estimating, is stable. But he needs constant supervision. Last night, unfortunately, I couldn't be with him the whole time, but I hope to be able to take him home by tomorrow evening."

And then Anton told Melissa how his previous night had passed. George listened to his story with an open mouth. Melissa, in turn, took an interest in Anton. She was in love with Boris, and Anton was his exact copy—just twenty years younger. Gradually, both Anton and George warmed up to each other.

Watching the clever little fellow, Anton told Melissa, "I was exactly like George when I was his age."

"What do you mean?"

"Everything. His appearance. And his mannerisms."

"I behave myself. I obey grown-ups." George had decided to join the conversation. "Did the boy on the motorcycle get hurt?" George asked, remembering Anton's story.

"I can take you for a motorcycle ride," Anton said, trying to change the subject.

"Are you serious?" Melissa said. "Don't frighten me."

"Here, look." Anton sat on the sofa as if he were mounting a bike, throwing over one leg and then the other. Once seated, he held his arms out and spread his hands apart as if he were holding onto bike handles.

"Young man, please have a seat on the motorcycle," he told George.

George instantly was accepting the game. Smiled all mouth he jumped on Anton's knees and seized his hands.

Anton imitated the sound of a motorcycle has revving up and then taking off.

George was beside himself with pleasure. "Where are we going?"

Anton, now realizing that he might be riding this motorcycle for quite some time, told him that they were only learning to ride the motorcycle, and, for now, were practicing in the backyard.

To that, George declared that he already knew how to ride, and that he needed to go to the grocery store to buy some food.

Melissa, wanting to get more closely acquainted with Anton, then asked him whether he really could take her to the grocery store, as her car was still in Los Angeles.

George, having heard that Anton might leave with his mum, began to cry. "We haven't even played and you, mum, are already taking my daddy away."

Anton wondered why George kept calling him "Daddy," but didn't protest. He liked Melissa. He had liked her since the moment he saw her photo in the newspaper. And now, with each minute, he was falling deeper in love with her.

Anton, too, liked George. He saw himself in the boy. In fact, the idea of becoming this boy's daddy didn't really bother him. Really, that role seemed to suit him just right.

"It's not necessary to make a kid cry over trifles. Take my car, and I will stay here and play with him. Will you return soon? I should get home and get some to sleep. I haven't slept for almost forty hours straight."

"Then don't worry about it. You sleep, and tomorrow, if Boris is better, you can take me to Los Angeles to get my car."

"Melissa, I think you misunderstood me. I didn't mean to give you the car just so that you would leave. I just didn't want the boy to cry."

"Oh, that's even better. So now he will be spoiled and begin to give the orders."

"But we just met," George whined. "Mum, please let us play a little."

"Don't go too far on your motorcycle," Melissa said, reconciling. "I'll be back soon." And with that, Melissa took the keys from Anton and left.

When she returned a half-hour later, she was amazed. Anton and George, in an embrace, were asleep on the sofa. Anton was sitting, leaning on the back of the sofa, and George lay on Anton's lap, with one hand under his head like a pillow, and the other wrapped around Anton's neck. Looking at them, Melissa suddenly realized how tired she was of being the mom and the dad simultaneously. She suddenly felt like she would like to quit her job and stay at home and manage the household.

She took off her shoes and, trying not to wake them, brought the shopping bags into the house. She tiptoed through the kitchen, putting away the groceries, and then put on an apron and started to fix salad and pelmeny. She wanted to make a big meal for Anton, but in truth, she still didn't know how to cook very much.

Anton and George continued to sleep, despite the smell of toast, pelmeny, and coffee emanating from the kitchen. Then, suddenly, Melissa heard a cry. George had probably been in such a deep sleep that he hadn't been able to wake up to go to the toilet.

Sure enough, to his shame, the boy had had an accident. Naturally, Anton had gotten wet too. When he woke up and realized what had happened, he didn't know what to do—to be angry or laugh.

George stopped crying and then, still sitting on Anton, declared, "Don't worry. I'm just sweaty."

Having heard him, Melissa became ridiculous with laughter. Anton burst out laughing too.

Hearing the uproar, Lyudmila came in, and after discovering what had happened, she carried away George to go change him, while poor Anton remained in wet trousers. He wanted to go—to change his clothes, to walk Lord, to sleep, but Melissa wouldn't him until he'd had lunch.

After lunch, Anton left, having promised that that evening, on the way to the hospital, he would bring Lord over to meet them.

George, dreaming of a dog, requested to go with Anton, but Melissa was relentless. "Anton needs to change," she told him, picking him up. And so Anton, over George's sobbing, at last, said good-bye and left.

Sitting in the car, he remembered George's joke about sweating and thought of Melissa's reaction, and he burst out laughing. Anton felt good being with them. To tell the truth, he hadn't wanted to leave.

Anton walked Lord for five minutes, gave him some food, and then, not having enough energy to even take a shower, he set the alarm clock for five. Then he called his mother and told her that he would be in the hospital by seven.

83

California, May 16, 1998

At six o'clock, Anton was driving his Jeep to Melissa's house, the huge figure of Lord towering behind him. When he got there, he parked, and ordered to Lord to sit and stay. He rang the doorbell. After about a minute, there was no answer.

Then he heard George's shout: "Mum, mum! Fast! Daddy's here!"

Melissa opened the door, and the smiling Anton held out a bouquet of red roses. Melissa politely thanked him and invited him in.

Anton asked George, "So, do you want to meet Lord?"

George's eyes began to shine.

"Please, don't worry," Anton told Melissa. "I will keep the situation under control. Lord is very gentle dog, but he will need to warm up first. And you, young man," he said, looking at George. "Jump on."

George jumped, and Anton hoisted him up and carried him out to the car. When he opened the door, Lord jumped out. George, noting his size, narrowed his eyes and whimpered a little.

"Inside!" Anton ordered, and Lord, following Anton, walked into the house.

Melissa was slightly frightened too, when the huge dog buried his head into her chest and started to sniff her.

"Could we feed something, for a treat, for example, pelmeny?" Anton asked Melissa.

"Mum, give the dog pelmeny," George whispered, continuing to squint. Then he ordered Lord, "Sit!"

Melissa, trying not to show that she was afraid, quietly took from a saucepan a single piece of food and held it out to Lord.

The dog looked at Anton. "Permissible!" the master said, and Lord, having opened wide his huge mouth, stuck out his tongue and delicately took the treat.

"I … I … I want to do it," George whispered, growing a little bit bolder.

"Okay," his mum said.

George fled from Anton's hands, and then changed his mind. He lifted both hands upward, wanting Anton to lift him again.

Anton lifted George up and then George said, "Maybe we can feed him from here?"

Anton took a piece of pelmeny out of the pan and called Lord.

"Well?" he asked George. "Do you want to try to give him a piece?"

"I'll look from here," George said smartly, unwilling to take the risk.

But when Anton dangled the piece of food, Lord drew nearer and his head ended up right next to George's. Anton felt something warm spread across his trousers. George had again had an accident, but this time out of fear.

Melissa tried to hold in her laugh, until her shoulders, chest, and stomach began to shake. Anton could hardly constrain himself either. But in a moment, they both burst out laughing simultaneously. Melissa had to rush for a napkin to wipe the tears from her eyes, and Anton began to shake in hysterical laughter.

And the originator of all this laughter, having taken hold of Anton's cheeks like handles, asked, "Are you are laughing over me?"

With that, Melissa and Anton burst into a second round of laughter.

Finally, looking at his wristwatch, Anton, still holding George, walked outside, called Lord, and opened the car door. The dog jumped in.

George, seeing Melissa following them out the door, jumped down out of Anton's hands and asked her, "Where is Daddy going?"

"To change his trousers," Anton answered, and he and Melissa, again, broke out in moans of laughter.

"Yes, Daddy needs to change trousers and go to the hospital to see Grandfather," Melissa told George. "And you need to change your trousers as well."

"Will you come back?" George asked Anton.

"Do you want me to?"

"I love you very much. And Lord too. But he loves pelmeny."

"And you?" Anton asked Melissa.

"Call me from the hospital and let me know how your father is. I will be waiting," Melissa told him, slightly touching Anton's hand.

Although she wouldn't admit it yet, Melissa had already made up her mind. And Anton had made up his. He had made up his mind within the first fifteen seconds of meeting Melissa, as she had stood at the threshold of her house, inviting him in. Yes, his father was right. This woman was his destiny.

Anton went back home and changed his trousers. He put two more pairs of trousers in his car, just in case. Then having left Lord at home, Anton drove to the hospital, thinking all the while about Melissa and George, the small pissing boy.

When he arrived in his father room in ICU, Ruslana was still there, but Anton decided not to speak with her about Melissa yet. He examined his father's lungs and heart, checked the indications on the monitor, and made a cardiogram. Boris's condition was stable. The rest of his healing would be up to him.

"It would be best for you to be at home," Anton told him. "Tomorrow evening, I and a couple of guys will take a bed and all of the necessary equipment to the house. Then we'll come back to get you, and I'll stay with you at home."

Ruslana supported her son's decision. She was very proud that her boy had matured so much and was beginning to accept and make very serious decisions. Now, if only he would get married and have kids!

84

California, May 17, 1998

That night in the hospital, all was quiet. Most of the personnel had left for home, and Boris and Anton both had an opportunity to rest.

The next morning, Ruslana brought Boris breakfast. She didn't trust hospital food. Anton, having left Mother with Father, took his mother's car home. He had breakfast, took care of Lord, cleaned himself up, and called Melissa. He asked her to meet him outside, and they would go pick up her car.

As he approached Melissa's house, he wondered if that "prankster-pissing boy" as Anton mentally called George, was crying that he wanted to go with Daddy and Mummy too. He was. The fact that Anton's car didn't have a car seat didn't help matters. But eventually the youth won, and so George, having arranged himself just right on Mum's lap, promised to calm down. He even agreed to wear a diaper just in case. They stopped at Sears, where Anton purchased a car seat for George. And after they had put it in and buckled George into it, the boy dropped quickly off to sleep.

As Anton with Melissa drove together, their eyes sometimes met and they smiled each other.

Then, at one point, Anton asked, "Why do you think George persistently calls me Daddy?"

"I think because I have Boris's photo in my room. You now look almost like your father did in that picture. George has seen it many times. I very much loved your father. But, when we met again two days ago, after so long a separation, I told him that I couldn't see myself as 'the mistress.' And I would never want to ruin what Boris has in his life now. And he would never want that either, because he loves Ruslana very much."

"So what is my role in this whole drama?" Anton asked with bitterness.

"Let's not rush things. We have only known each other for two days. But if you're asking me what I think of you, I will tell you, in all fairness, that I like you very much. I find it pleasant to be with you. And George likes you, which is very important to me. But please don't hurry things. I haven't dated anyone since I returned from Russia, and not because I am hypocrite; I just respect myself."

"All these years?"

"Except for your father, I had only one other man in my life, and he got ahold of me using date-rape drugs. If you're interested, I will tell you the story—but later. Anyway, I didn't know how horrible he was back then, and I almost married him.

"Oh, yeah. I saw the engagement photo you sent to Father."

They were already driving into the Federal Building's parking garage, when Melissa asked Anton, "Would you like to spend this evening with me, or do you need to be with your father?"

"No, I have taken one week of vacation," Anton said. "Mother will be with him. I would very much like to be with you this evening. Let's have dinner together. We'll go somewhere and make a night of it."

As a token of consent, Melissa nodded and put her hand on Anton's. He brought her hand to his lips and kissed it.

Melissa got out of the car and woke George. She began to pull him from his seat so that she could put him in her car for the ride home. Through tears, George said that he wanted to stay with Daddy.

Anton asked Melissa if she would allow him to take the boy home. "I shall drive carefully," he assured her.

Well, what else could he tell him—no?

Lulled by the moving car, George slept all the way home. When they reached Melissa's house, Anton took out George and carried him to his room.

Melissa went back outside with Anton. They said good-bye, agreeing to meet at seven o'clock. But Anton would not come into the house to get her; otherwise, George would start to sob again.

From Melissa's, Anton went to the hospital. He hastily ate lunch in the cafeteria and then walked to the ICU, where he loaded onto a hospital bed an oxygen tank, a set of attachments, and some heart medication. The hospital attendant rolled the hospital bed out to the ambulance, and asked the driver to take the equipment to Dr. Goryanin's house. He said it should take no more than thirty minutes.

Once the driver was back, Anton and the attendant rolled Boris out to the ambulance. Anton rode with his father, and Ruslana went home in Anton's car. Having seen the car seat, she wondered what it meant.

It was half past five when Boris got home. They situated him in the medical bed, and then Anton quickly connected all of the devices before dashing away to shower. He shaved longer than usual, and dressed better than usual, and at ten minutes to seven, was out the door.

"Don't bug him with your inquiries, Ruslana," Boris told her. "It seems now is a crucial time in our son's life. When the time comes, he will tell all."

After coming home that evening, Anton examined his father. Boris was much better, but Anton ordered him to stay in bed, except to go to the toilet. In the bedroom where Boris was, the deck door was wide open. And through the screen door, the air smelled clean with a hint of flowers.

In the morning, secretly from his mother, Anton told his father that he had met Melissa and George. When he told him the story about George peeing on him—twice—Boris laughed so loudly that it sent Ruslana running from the kitchen. She accused Anton of not sparing his father.

"On the contrary," Anton argued. "Laughter is medicine too." Still, she banished him from the room.

Over the next few days, Anton continued to monitor Boris's condition, providing medication as needed, listening to his heart, and making cardiograms. Gradually, all was back to normal. Anton told his parents that if Boris kept improving at this pace, in couple of days, the hospital bed could be taken away. The main thing now was to keep resting.

Ruslana had taken off work to be with Boris, and she was with him all the time, except when she had to run to the kitchen to prepare meals or snacks for him.

85

California, May 31, 1998

Two weeks later, Boris's condition had improved substantially. He was walking around the house, and sitting in the backyard. Anton and Melissa had met several times already, and they spoke over the phone every day.

That Sunday evening, Melissa was waiting for Anton. She was dressed and watching for him out the window. She had told Lyudmila that she would be with Anton all evening.

Melissa was wearing the small black dress that she had purchased for a special party at the US Attorney's office. She wore it with black pumps and soft pearls. And with her small evening bag, she looked highly sophisticated. Anton was struck in the heart upon seeing her.

They went to the John Dominick restaurant in Newport Beach. Anton had reserved a window table with a view of the gulf for eight o'clock. They ordered a bottle of Italian Chianti Classic, Caesar salad, and halibut. Anton, able to wipe the smile from his face, kept looking at Melissa.

Melissa lifted her glass and they toasted. Then she asked about Boris's condition. He told her that she could visit him after the meeting with Ruslana. She then suggested drinking for Boris's prompt recovery. Anton was amazed at how well she understood Russian tradition.

"I had a good teacher," Melissa told him, not hiding her favor toward Boris.

Waiting for the salad, Melissa rested both her hands on the table, and Anton instantly covered her hands with his. She didn't recoil. Anton's carrying on was pleasant to her.

All evening long, they joked. Anton told her some funny stories from his medical practice. Melissa shared stories from her life, too. After dinner, they went for a walk on the embankment. Anton took Melissa's hand, but she pulled it away. Then she took Anton's hand with both of hers and snuggled into him. Soon, though, she grew tired.

"Excuse me, Toni, but it is time for me to go home. I have to go to work tomorrow," Melissa told him.

He took her home, and opened her car door. As she stood to get out, he couldn't constrain his feelings any longer. He embraced her and started to kiss her face and lips. Melissa embraced his neck and answered him with a long kiss.

Anton asked, "Will we meet again tomorrow?"

"I cannot wait. But only if Boris feels well. By the way, if you wish, and you have the time, please come over and take George for a walk. He would love that," Melissa said.

The next day, Anton told his mother that he was taking Lord for a walk. But instead, he put the dog in the car and went to see George.

Having seen Anton, George was delighted. But when he saw Lord, he deflated and asked Anton to hold him. He wanted to play with the dog, but was afraid of Lord's imposing size. Finally, having gotten a little more used to the dog, he sat on Anton's shoulders, and, having narrowed his eyes, touched the dog's head. Being convinced that Lord wouldn't bark and growl, George, having grown bolder, lowered himself down Anton and even offered Lord some food. After that, George couldn't be torn away from the dog. He started to run with Lord in the house, to throw him a ball, and even to pet him. George was proud that he had overcome his fear.

"My friend, Lord," he said.

After two hours of playing with George at Melissa's house, Anton and Lord, over George's roars about his Daddy going, left. At their parting, Anton promised to come back that evening.

When he arrived that night, Melissa was just getting home from work. But having seen Anton, her weariness was instantly gone. George, climbing up into Anton's arms, told his mother that he had made friends with Lord. Anton and Melissa decided to go eat at Clam Jumpers on Brookhurst Street, known for their generous portions of food. They ordered the all-you-can-eat salad bar, and two glasses of red wine.

They felt easy and good with each other and in the air was that electricity that develops between people when they are at the beginning of a relationship. Anton admired Melissa. He liked her each movement, her each word, and the sound of her voice.

Anton, as the vast majority of young doctors in America, was so loaded down with studies and training that, to tell the truth, he had not had the time to experience women. At the university, he had had a girlfriend whom he had moved in with. She was a whimsical person with unpredictable behavior. Her things were always scattered around the apartment, and her dishes stayed dirty until Anton washed them. His other connections with women were casual and, except for causing regret the morning after, didn't create any other feelings in him.

With Melissa it was different. Yes, he had seen her photo earlier, and had dreamed of her. But dreams were like fairytales. Now it was for real. Anton was amazed that she had only a single bed in her room. But the most amazing to him was her fidelity to Boris. This woman had done everything to be close to Boris, and, at the same time, for all those years, hadn't made any attempt to contact him, understanding that it could destroy his relationship with Ruslana.

But some questions remained for Anton. What was his place in this difficult and confusing situation? What would his relationship with his father be after this? How would Ruslana behave when she found out about Melissa and George? And still, despite everything, he wanted to be serious with Melissa, and he really would like to become a true father to his half-brother.

And for Melissa, the situation was uneasy too. How could she look to this person with whom she had fallen in love at first sight? Melissa has realized that her love for Anton was a continuation of her love for Boris. Anton inherently replaced Boris, only he was young and free. That Boris whom she had loved madly was still there in Russia, but here he had been converted into Anton. But, how could she make Anton believe that? What would her relationship with Anton become? How would Ruslana react to all this? And what if George became attached to Anton, but then she never developed a relationship with him? And where would Boris fit into their life? But, at the same time, she felt that her unconditional love to Boris had changed; it flashed with new force and had passed onto Anton. Melissa felt again the same feelings she had had for Boris—a boundless desire to be beside him, to feel with each cell of her body her affinity for this person whom she had known for only three weeks.

Certainly, Melissa sensed Anton's affinity toward her as well. She was glad to know him, but most of all, Melissa was afraid to lose him.

Having finished dinner, they left the restaurant. Anton touched Melissa's hand, and she immediately took his hand. And so they reached the car parked under a sprawling magnolia tree. Anton opened the door for Melissa, seated, and began to kiss her. In turn, she embraced Anton and answered his caresses.

"Melissa, darling. Let's go somewhere. I am dying to make love to you. I want you," he whispered, hoarse from excitement.

"Me too," Melissa whispered. Then she suddenly discharged him and became serious. "Toni. Please. Don't. If you want to know whether I love you, I am. Very much! And for this reason I am afraid to lose you. And what about you? If you find, in time, that you don't like something about me, will you lose interest in me? You have never told me whether you are involved with anybody else. I know nothing about you, and you know little about me. Believe me. I am very interested in you. But for how long will this proceed? How long will you love me? And, I am not free. Please, do not forget, that I have George."

Anton embraced Melissa and whispered in her ear, mixing words and kisses. "Darling! Melissa! I remember that I have a half-brother-son. And we shall make him a sister. Do you want that George should have a little sister?"

"Very much. I even know what we should call her. Mila, or Milana. I very much want that we should have a girl. I would quit work and look after all of you. You still won't know that my pelmeny is actually from the Russian deli!" Melissa laughed quietly, as only a woman who felt favored could.

Anton nestled harder into Melissa, and she felt his physical desire to make George's sister right now. She understood his feelings and shared them. But she was still nervous.

"And if you left us suddenly? What would I do with two children?"

"With three. You just told me that you are ready to give up your job and to look after us. And then what if we have more kids? Then what?"

"You are kidding me! Yes, and then what would I do? Please give me more time, and you, too." Melissa embraced Anton again and started to kiss him. "You know my feeling for you. We still have time to have a good long talk. And I have to go to work tomorrow. And George should be put to bed. I know that he is waiting for me."

And so they left. But when they pulled up to her house, Melissa turned her whole body toward him, hugged his neck, and said, "I don't want you to leave. I feel so secure with you. You are necessary to me, Toni. I need you as a man, and as the father of my children, and as a friend."

"You are so beautiful!"

"It is to you that I am beautiful, and you are beautiful to me too," she whispered. "Come tomorrow at the same time. Only don't come into the house. Wait for me on the street. George is upset that we are leaving without him. And, please, send our regards to your father."

Melissa fluttered out of the car. At the door, she turned and waved to Anton, continuing to look as she walked inside. When Melissa had closed the door behind her, Anton could still taste her charming lips. Then he smiled with the smile of a man who feels in love.

86

California, June 1, 1998

Boris had practically recovered and no longer required attention. Certainly, he required regular care, but for the most part, he could take care of himself. After walking Lord, Anton had fixed Boris and himself a light breakfast, and afterward, he washed the dishes and fed Lord. But somehow Anton had let Lord into Boris's room. After seeing his master, whom he had been missing all this time, he got excited and started licking Boris on his chest and his head. The dog wanted to climb on the bed but knew he was not allowed.

Having pet Lord for a while, Boris washed his hands and returned to bed. Anton came in and sat in a chair near the bed and suddenly asked his father to tell him how he had gotten acquainted with his mother.

Boris, not one to rush through the details, told Anton everything about the train ride to virgin soil in Kazakhstan. As Boris told his story, he recollected small details of their first meetings. He remembered the village in which they had lived. The barrack. Trips to Fedorovka to get cement. He told Anton all about Frieda, about the wounded officer, and about his illness. Boris told, and memories came back to him as though they were happening not to him, but to someone else he knew.

Before, it was as if he hadn't really realized what was going on. But now, having seen his past more objectively, it was an alarm sounded, and it suddenly dawned on him that he could have gotten Frieda pregnant. Boris wanted to find her and talk to her. But it had been so many years.

At that moment, Boris understood that he was getting old. He broke off, tired from the story and the memories, and then drifted off to sleep.

Anton went down to the kitchen and made himself some lunch. He couldn't concentrate on a single subject. He loafed around the house, waiting for Boris to wake up, or for evening to come, so that he could see Melissa again. He wanted something to happen.

Mother came home at six o'clock, and Anton fed her. Ruslana was surprised, and sensed this act of generosity was not "just because." Then when Anton, dressed up, had dashed away, she realized that the time for those life changes that she had been wanting for him had apparently come.

Another two weeks flew by. Every evening, Anton met Melissa. Their "days off," they spent with George.

On June 14, Melissa called and made an appointment with Ruslana for Friday, June 19, at five o'clock. She would be her last client of the day.

That Friday, in due time, Melissa arrived at Ruslana's beauty salon. Her eyes shone with youth and happiness. Ruslana wasn't surprised when Melissa embraced her, but she became surprised when Melissa, instead of sitting in the barber chair, invited her to go have a talk somewhere. Ruslana suggested walking to Greek restaurant in the shopping center.

They were seated at a table for two in the corner. The waiter brought the menu and then left. Ruslana was silent, expecting an explanation from Melissa about what this all meant. Melissa could not get her thoughts together. She put her hand on Ruslana's, and, looking into her eyes, smiled.

At last, Ruslana couldn't wait any longer, and understanding that Melissa was unable to speak, tactfully asked, "Did something happen that you want to talk to me about?"

"Happen?" Melissa whispered, her eyes radiant. "Mum Ruslana, I am enamored."

"Are you in love? I had wished you could meet my son, but he didn't even want to hear about it. So, who is this lucky man?"

"Your son. Toni."

"Toni? How did you meet? Where? I cannot believe it! I am so happy. Why didn't he tell me? I love both of you, and I was ignored! The same as my Boris! He had a heart attack because he holds everything inside. He only tells me when he has problems. Well, so, and how does Anton feel about you?"

"He says that he is in love … but, Ruslana … that's still not everything," Melissa said, turning almost abruptly serious.

At this time the waiter was bringing them their order: gyros, rice, grilled vegetables, and sauce. Besides, he brought warm pita bread. Melissa asked the waiter if there was any Russian vodka in the restaurant. Then she asked him to bring two glasses, with a double shot in each, and ordered pickled cucumbers. Then while the waiter left to get the additional order, both of them were silent.

Ruslana still felt insulted that nobody had told her anything, but, at the same time, she was glad that Anton, at last, would grow into his life.

The waiter brought the vodka and pickled cucumbers. They lifted their glasses, and Ruslana said, "For your happiness!" and drank the full glass in one gulp. Melissa did the same. Then both had a piece of pickled cucumber.

"Wow! Melissa! Where did you learn to drink vodka? Only Russians drink like that."

"In Togliatti."

"Where? Where … did you say?"

"In Togliatti."

"When were you in Togliatti? You never told me about that."

"I didn't tell you because this conversation had never come up. I never even knew your surname. I didn't know your husband's name. You never called your son's Russian name. And I never saw their photos. Can you believe that?"

"No. But that's the truth."

"Ruslana? How about seconds?"

"Go for it, daughter. I have feeling that we will have fun tonight!"

Melissa called the waiter and asked him to bring a repeat of the last order. Momentarily, he brought them each two more double shots of vodka.

Now Melissa lifted her glass. "Let's to drink for you and your husband, that both of you always will be happy with each other."

They clinked their glasses, took a sip, and had a snack.

"You should eat. Otherwise, we might have a problem," Ruslana said.

"I'll be all right."

They ate a little, but Ruslana and Melissa both were already slightly tipsy.

Melissa called the waiter again. She addressed Ruslana in Russian and then the waiter in English, "As they say, God loves a trinity. Please, bring two more glasses."

Ruslana didn't object. She sensed that Melissa's story was only beginning. When the waiter left, Ruslana repeated her question. "So, when were you in Togliatti?"

"In September of 1993. At the time the civil war was beginning there."

The waiter brought their third round of vodka, and Melissa lifted her glass. "I would like to drink, that you, Ruslana, will constantly have love, peace, and mutual respect in your family and in your life with Boris. That both of you will lived together long and happy."

Ruslana noticed that Melissa had called her husband by name. They clinked glasses, drank, and had a snack.

The vodka was doing its business already, so Ruslana said, "It looks like we are going to have a long conversation. Let's call Toni and ask him to come and pick us up here later."

Melissa took out her cell phone and speed-dialed Anton. At that time, he was at home with his father.

When he saw Melissa's number, he answered immediately.

"Toni! It is Melissa," she uttered with a slightly braided tongue.

"I know. Have you already left your office?"

"I left early today. I'm with Mum Ruslana in the Greek restaurant by her salon. How is your father is doing?"

"What you are doing there? You sound like you're drinking."

"We are conversing about life."

"While drinking?"

"We are having a very serious conversation. Yes. We are drinking. Otherwise, this conversation will not happen."

"Why didn't you invite me? I would like to talk with you."

"Toni. If you can leave your father, please come and take us home."

"Certainly. Dad feels well. When?"

"In an hour."

"I love you. Please, don't compete with Mum. She can drink a lot."

"Me too. In an hour."

It was strange to Ruslana, sitting and listening to this woman talking to her son. Her son. It became sad to her. She understood in her mind that that was life, and that her son was already grown. But he was her son—her child.

Ruslana called the waiter and asked him to, yet again, repeat the order. He returned with two more glasses. "For you and Anton. That all would turn out well for both of you!" Ruslana lifted her glass. "You, daughter, look after him. It is you who will be the master of the home."

"Thank you, Mum Ruslana. May I call you simply Mum, for fun?" Melissa asked with a braided tongue.

"Yes, daughter," Ruslana said and wiped her eyes with a napkin. "So. Please, continue your story about Togliatti."

"Well …" and Melissa, deeply moved from the vodka and the situation, told Ruslana, in detail, everything that had happened to her in Russia. Only she didn't name the person who had been there with her. Sometimes, a sob would interject Melissa's storytelling, but she would just wipe her eyes with napkins and continue. Ruslana sobbed too. It was awful to learn what had happened to Melissa.

They ate, but continued to call over the waiter. And after some time, Ruslana started remembering some of what Boris had told her about his last trip to Russia. And internal alarm began to sound subtly in her soul. But she continued to let Melissa speak and to have a good cry.

When Melissa has started to tell about what had happened to her in

Geneva, Ruslana cried almost in a full voice. Then finally, Melissa reached the point in the story where she, in a wheelchair, was hiding from her former lover in Frankfurt.

"So, you haven't seen him since then?" Ruslana asked.

"No."

"And you didn't write to him?"

"No. Only twice, I sent photos. Once when I was in the hospital with the marriage announcement, and the second time when George was born."

"And that's all?"

"Yes. That was all. I never made an attempt to destroy his family. In fact, he loves his wife. And she loves him."

"And you? And your son? Hasn't he seen his son?"

"He saw his son once," Melissa answered, now absolutely drunk. And for persuasiveness, she nodded her head.

"Where? When?"

"On Friday."

"Today?"

"No. On Friday, May 15."

"So. And then what happened? He doesn't love you?"

"No, he doesn't. And I cannot love him. He has a family. A wife and a son."

"So what about you?"

"I have fallen in love with his son."

"So it was Boris!"

"You hadn't figured that out yet?" Melissa asked.

"Well, you're no good either—you never told me!"

"What? Well, what did you expect me to say? That I was nearly raped by gangsters in Russia and that your husband saved both of us from death, while my groom behaved like a mad animal?"

Ruslana moved her chair closer to Melissa, and, having embraced, they began to sob in full voices. The restaurant host and the waiter were about ready to show them to the door when Anton entered.

He saw Mother and Melissa absolutely drunk. What should he do? He paid the bill, walked Ruslana to the car and seated her, and then went back and gently picked up the totally drunk Melissa and carried her out. She clasped his head with her hands and started kissing him.

When they walked into Melissa's front door, George came running with a shout: "Daddy's here!" Then he saw the unfamiliar woman and became shy.

Having seen George, Ruslana was dumbstruck at how much the child resembled Anton at his age. And at the moment, with her eyes and mind still altered from the vodka, she still somehow hadn't understood that the boy's father was not Anton, but Boris.

Attentively looking at George and opening up her arms for a hug, she said, "And you don't want to get acquainted with your grandmother?"

George looked at Ruslana and asked, "Who are you?"

"She is your grandmother, Ruslana," Melissa told him, dragging out every word and nodding her head.

While they were getting acquainted, Lyudmila came in. She quickly figured out what was going on and embarked to the kitchen to set the table. Anton called his father and asked how he was doing there, and if he needed anything. Boris answered that he was fine and that there was no need to worry about him. Boris knew from Anton that Melissa and Ruslana were meeting, and he understood it would be better for him to stay out of this festivity.

The next morning, on Saturday, Melissa couldn't lift her head. The "absence of training" had affected her. She didn't come to her senses until the middle of the day. Anton had come over to help her. Nanny Lyudmila, seeing the situation, went for a walk with George, leaving Melissa and Anton alone. She told them that they would be back in two hours.

When Lyudmila and George returned from their walk, Anton and Melissa were dragging the single-sized bed from Melissa's bedroom into George's room.

Melissa said. "He is already a big boy, and he can sleep on an adult bed."

"He is already a big boy," Lyudmila affirmed.

They disassembled George's cradle and stored it away just in case, then they left to the nearest furniture store to buy a new, larger bed.

"There is a big sale going on right now," they had explained to Lyudmila before leaving.

"Yes, there is a big sale," Lyudmila echoed.

Ruslana wasn't able to go to work either. She had to reschedule a few of her clients' appointments. But she quickly came to her senses. She didn't go to work anyway, having decided to have a serious talk with Boris. Then, she had a second thought: the past cannot be changed. She had liked Melissa for a long time. And Toni and Melissa were in love with each other, and seemed to be good for each other. So she decided to put on the brakes.

Still, Ruslana approached Boris and brought a tight fist up to his nose. "You should be happy that I knew nothing about it and that you are ill at the moment. If it were not for that, I would beat you to a pulp!"

Boris, assuming Ruslana and Melissa had already straightened things out, decided not to add to this delicate topic. Then deferring his weakness, he closed his eyes, and went to sleep.

When Boris woke up, he saw Ruslana sitting on the chair and looking at him. She had calmed down. Ruslana was convinced that nothing would threaten her family. Her son was getting married. After all, little George was his half-brother.

The little fellow looked exactly like Anton when he was small. She remembered the small Anton, and then she remembered the small George, and she wanted to see the boy again.

She asked Boris, "Why don't we take Lord and go see how George is doing?"

With that, Boris got out of bed, put himself in order, and, together with his wife, went to see Melissa. When they pulled into the driveway, they saw Anton's car with new mattress strapped to the roof. Anton and Melissa, who were taking bags and packages of sleeping accessories out of his car, cordially greeted them.

Lord, pushing away his masters, flew into the house first, waiting for someone to give him a bit of pelmeny. George was delighted that Lord, not to mention his grandfather and grandmother, had come to play with him.

Ruslana, seeing the children haul in the new queen-sized mattress, rushed to the kitchen to help Lyudmila set the table. Boris couldn't calm down the naughty George and Lord.

Anton and Melissa got the mattress upstairs, assembled a bed frame, and put on a base followed by the new mattress, periodically distracted by kisses. Then Anton went downstairs "to put things in order," and Melissa started to dress the bed with new linens. While they were away, she had given her word to Anton that both of them would stop drinking.

"We shall have a healthy child," she told him.

When they had all gathered around the table to celebrate the purchase, Ruslana summarized it all. And she wasn't mistaken. This night Anton wouldn't come back home. He had moved in with Melissa.

87

California, June 21, 1998

Anton showed up at home the next afternoon. He looked exactly how he should: a little confused with a silly smile. Anton told his parents that he had proposed to Melissa, and that she had accepted it, and that he had purchased her an engagement ring. And with those words, he showed them a red velvet box. Inside was the beautiful white-gold ring with a two-carat diamond.

His parents, naturally, congratulated him and Ruslana asked, "So where's the bride?"

"They're coming."

Ruslana and Boris rushed to change. In a few minutes, their house was filled with George's squeals, as he rushed after Lord. The huge dog was rushing through the house knocking down everything in his path. Melissa kissed Ruslana and cautiously substituted a forehead for Boris, who kissed her under Ruslana's steadfast sight.

Then Melissa told them that she and Lyudmila had to go to the airport to meet her father, and asked if they'd mind George staying with them. Then Melissa told George that he would be staying with Grandma and Grandpa. But being excited by the bustle, he misunderstood Melissa. George thought that Melissa said that he wouldn't be left alone with them. George burst into tears, having told her that he wished to remain with Grandma and Grandpa. And as soon as he understood that he was wrong, he calmed down, and with a burst of energy, resumed chasing after Lord.

While Melissa was gone, Ruslana and Anton set a celebratory table. Boris, as the recoveree, shirked off doing any work. Instead, he observed George playing. Sitting in an armchair and looking at this little fellow, Boris just now realized how much he loved his son-grandson. And though all's well that ends well, he still very much regretted that circumstances had not allowed him to communicate with little George since his birth.

By the time Melissa and Lyudmila arrived with Sir Charles, three hours had passed, and Boris had put George down on Anton's bed for a nap. Lord had calmed down also.

After they were all seated around the table, Anton officially lowered on one knee and asked Sir Charles Spencer for the hand of his daughter, Lady Melissa Spencer. Having received consent, he put the engagement ring on Melissa's finger. Everyone kissed each other and congratulated the couple. After dinner, Anton took George home, and Melissa's father temporarily lodged with Boris and Ruslana in Anton's room.

Anton and Melissa's wedding was scheduled for the beginning of December. And per Melissa's very special request, they decided to get married in a church. Anton, understanding how important it was for Melissa, quickly agreed, though it didn't matter to him either way. He was an atheist.

Amicably, already a big family, they celebrated George's fourth birthday, and right after the event, they began preparations for the wedding. To start, they all took dance lessons. Then the men withdrew, but the women actively worked, searching out a reception venue, picking the menu, ordering flowers and invitations, and choosing the dresses and suits to be worn.

Anton and Melissa decided to take their honeymoon on the cruise ship to Alaska, after which the other family members expressed the desire to go to Alaska too. Because the Alaska tour was available only in the summertime, the decision was simple: in the middle of August everybody would go to Alaska, and, after the wedding, Anton and Melissa would take an official honeymoon on a cruise around the Hawaiian archipelago.

Boris started practicing the violin again, which he hadn't done in a long time. By now, he had finally totally recovered after his heart attack and had resumed work. As before, he took Lord to the construction site daily. Sometimes Grandfather Charles and George joined them too. Sir Charles had started to consider investing the money he'd received from the sale of his place in London. Prices for real estate kept growing; therefore, such an investment seemed promising. So, believing he would be successful, and with the help of Boris who became his business partner, they made a joint investment in four construction sites.

The trip to Alaska was outstanding. Early in August, the Goryanins and Sir Spencer with Lyudmila boarded the cruise ship *Harmony*. The white giant squeezed under the Golden Gate Bridge and sailed into the ocean. Impudent seagulls saw them off, as some of the passengers had mistakenly begun to feed them. Flying around the stern and shouting, the seagulls constantly demanded more, and, in return, left "presents" on some of the sea goers observing their flight. But at last, the bread, rolls, and other common seagull fare was terminated, and convinced they wouldn't get anything more, the seagulls returned to harbor, as the *Harmony*, at full speed, headed for Alaska.

Stewards delivered their luggage to their cabins. The ship's safety crew met with the passengers and provided instructions on the use of life jackets. And only after that did the passengers rush to the dining room and ate as they had never eaten before. And so life on the cruise ship began.

The next day, the *Harmony* continued her way along the West Coast, and having recovered from gastronomic shock and being convinced that the volume of the stomach is limited, everyone gradually cooled down at the buffet. Hoping to see whales, some folks observed shoals of dolphins through their binoculars.

While they were eating in the restaurant on the fifth deck, Anton saw two colleagues; Diana Stoner and Alice Hodzhaev had just recently completed their internships and started work at the same hospital as Anton. Now, the two young doctors, with their husbands, were celebrating in the restaurant. He introduced them and their husbands—attorney Timothy Stoner and private detective Rustam Hodzhaev—to his family, and all of them decided to join tables together. Timothy and Rustam were both private investigators and business partners in Irvine, California.

Having connected all their tables, the noisy companions continued to celebrate this wonderful trip to Alaska.

Of course, they were all sad to see the cruise come to an end, but everyone returned home with priceless memories.

88

California, December 1998

Seven months had passed since Boris had met Melissa. December, and, at last, the day of the wedding had come.

The marriage bustle began in the early morning. In both houses, everyone was rushing around. The phones were ringing nonstop. Nobody would sit down for fear of crumpling a suit or dress. Sir Charles Spencer was dressed as only a London dandy could be.

As the service began, Melissa was accompanied by Sir Charles down the aisle. The Lady carried herself as she had learned in Swiss boarding school. Anton stood at the altar beside his parents. He leaned over to his father and whispered, "Finally, I am marrying her, Daddy."

"Be happy, son," Boris answered, his voice shivering from excitement.

"Stop it. Shame on both of you!" Ruslana hissed.

When it was over, the newlyweds loaded into the limousine, and the visitors filled their cars and two buses. They all went to the Ritz Carlton in Laguna Niguel for the reception. Out-of-town guests had checked in at the hotel a day before.

The whole time, Ruslana kept tabs on Boris, making sure he sat quietly and wasn't overactive. Sir Spencer supervised and made sure the evening flowed smoothly. And when the couple opened their gifts, Melissa's father presented Anton and Melissa with the key to a special house built by Boris. Both Boris and Charles, in advance, agreed to go in on such an expensive gift.

Then in a moment of calm, Boris walked into the middle of the room, took his violin, and played. First, he played Mendelssohn's "Wedding March," and then Fritz Kreisler's "Tournaments of Love." Next, he played Schubert's "Night Serenade." Melissa understood all. Memories gushed over her and she, for no reason apparent to anyone else, embraced her new husband.

The dances then began. Boris danced with Ruslana. Sir Charles didn't cease to dance with Lyudmila, whose large downstairs bedroom he had already moved into.

When the "White Waltz" was announced, Melissa approached Boris.

"How do you do?" Melissa said with an exaggerated British accent and eyes full of tears. Then she stretched out her hand to him, and not for handshake but for a kiss. Then she slightly tilted her head to one side, making her simply charming.

"How do you do?" Boris replied with an exaggerated Russian accent. And then he kissed her hand with the gallantry of which only a real English Lord was capable.

They started to dance.

"All these years, I thought of you. Every day. I remember every moment," Boris told her, holding her around the waist.

"Me too," Melissa answered, looking into his eyes.

"I love you today, the same as I loved you then."

"Me too. I love you the same as before. But now I love you even more. I love you for our mutual past. I love you in the present, in your son and my husband. I love you in the future, in our son, and I shall love you up to the end of my days. And now I am carrying your granddaughter, the daughter of your son. Our daughter, I shall name Mila, in honor of my dearest Mila of all."

"Are you pregnant?" Boris asked.

"Yes." She smiled. "What happiness it is to carry a child!"

The song ended, and Melissa curtsied. She stretched out her hand, and he touched with his lips her eternally cold fingers.

Melissa found Anton and, embracing his neck, whispered, "Hi, darling. Let's go for a little walk."

They went out onto the hotel balcony. Before them, up to the horizon, crept the smooth surface of the light-blue ocean. Foamy waves were rolling onto the sandy shore. The huge, fiery red sun was slowly falling into the ocean, hiding halfway behind the Catalina Islands.

Melissa and Anton embraced, looked at the sunset. Ahead of them was a long life full of winning and losing, rainy and sunny days, meetings and partings. They could only hope that God would continue to send them the happiness to enjoy, as now, watching the sunrises and sunsets that would test their love for many years to come.

89

Moscow, January 12, 2009

In the Kremlin on the celebration of the Prosecutor's Day, prosecutors, inspectors, and veterans of law enforcement gathered. Among them were the general major of justice, Stanislav Terekhin, and the general lieutenant of justice, Ivan Filimonov. Having known each other for many years, they sat next to each other for the ceremony. After listening to speeches and a celebration concert, they decided to find a silent, cozy restaurant.
They sat at a booth and placed modest orders. In the beginning, they talked about the past, and at some point, Filimonov casually remembered the service record that Lieutenant Colonel Terekhin had sent Filimonov, in response to his inquiry about the Office of the Attorney General regarding Lieutenant Colonel Yakubovsky's business trip to the States in 1993.

Terekhin kept silent, recollecting something, and then asked, "Comrade General, did you ever hear about our agent, Mr. X.?"

"And who was he?"

"That means you haven't heard. Now, I can tell you, but only on one condition: when we leave here, you will forget this story. I didn't tell you anything."

"Agreed."

"We were friends with Vladislav Yakubovsky in military school. He was fairly fluent in several languages. That which I couldn't learn for a week, he picked up instantly."

The officers fell silent when the waiter showed up with their order. When he left, they clinked their glasses, and drank.

General Terekhin continued. "I should admit, I don't often see information in our literature about one of the most active agents in the USA—Mr. X. Though his name has been undeservedly forgotten, at one time, he occupied a high position in US counterintelligence. Mr. X. was recruited as our agent in 1981. The information he gathered was so valuable that, after his first contact, he was paid fifty thousand dollars. At that time, that was quite good money. But we had a good enough budget to pay for the information of our agents.

"Mr. X. was super active. He collected and transmitted information from his very first day of work for us. But he was arrested on February 21, 1994, and sentenced to life by the federal court, without the possibility of parole. Now he is in one of the confidential federal prisons. We don't have any information on his status. Our last contact with Mr. X. took place in the summer of 1993 in Washington.

"During that time, Agroprom employees were negotiating a contract with Global Oil for the delivery of crude oil. Nothing happened with this oil adventure. But if contract would have been fulfilled, it's anyone's guess which the Russian oil oligarch might be— Gavrila Kravchuk or somebody else.

"I had an opportunity to meet and interview Boris Goryanin in Los Angeles in 1998. Could you believe, during his interrogation under oath before the grand jury, he ran into the English Lady whom he had rescued in Russia. She was the assistant to the US attorney in California."

Terekhin broke off. They drank their shot and had a snack.

He continued. "Contacts with Mr. X. were maintained by the ranking officer of the Service of External Intelligence, who was working under the pseudonym 'Vlad.' Usually 'Vlad' met with Mr. X. at different locations through the world. At these meetings, Vlad would transmit to Mr. X. anywhere from twenty to fifty thousand dollars. As I said earlier, Mr. X. was so active, and obtained information that was so valuable, that from 1985 to 1989, he was paid almost two million dollars.

"After 1989, we didn't have any personal contact with Mr. X., until, in the beginning of 1993, he sent a note demanding payment for his services. This contact took place in July of 1993. Our officer, 'Vlad' met Mr. X. As a result of this contact, there was an exchange of information for money. It was the last contact.

"Mr. X. was extremely professional. He was able to avoid all any suspicion. But according to one of several existing versions of the story, a psychic was connected to the group conducting the investigation of this information leakage. This psychic specified that the leakage was coming from inside the CIA, and named six suspects. Among them was Mr. X. So surveillance was started on all of them. In another version of the story, Mr. X. was 'handed over' by one of the officers of the KGB. The rest was simple business.

"Anyhow, as I said before, Mr. X. was arrested in February 1994, when he checked in on a flight to Europe. The investigations group had established that, for eight years of his work, Mr. X. had transmitted almost fifty thousand pages of classified documents. Based on this data in the USSR, and later in Russia and in countries in East Europe, more than one hundred CIA agents were arrested in connection with these transmissions."

General Terekhin broke off again, so General Filimonov took the opportunity to ask, "So, that Lieutenant Colonel Vladislav Yakubovsky … is he this 'Vlad'?"

"I didn't say that," Terekhin answered sharply, waving his hand. Thus, he had let Filimonov know that it was time to change the subject.

"By the way, where is Yakubovsky now? If I am not mistaken, he was one of the suspects in a case of embezzlement of six-and-a-half million dollars," General Filimonov said.

"Yakubovsky lives in the USA now. He is in full order. Married. Three children. I personally conducted an investigation of some case. In 1998, I was in the USA as a representative of the attorney general. We interrogated Boris Goryanin as a witness. There was a counterfeit Letter of Guarantee specifying that Boris Goryanin would be financially responsible, returning six-and-a-half million dollars in case of a default on the contract."

"And what happened?"

"He easily proved that his signature was forged. He was totally innocent."

"And Kravchuk?"

"He couldn't steal that much money. He was too deep into hard drinking."

"Then who? Yakubovsky?"

"That's just the point. He couldn't have done it either. It all happened at the same time that his son died in a traffic accident. He was in Moscow the whole time, and drinking a lot too, overcoming the grief. I personally met him at my summer cottage and had phone contact with him during the time that, ostensibly, Kravchuk was in Western Samoa and cashed the money out. So really, it all converges on Kravchuk. But Kravchuk couldn't have done it. Couldn't by definition even—he's an alcoholic. And to do that, the sober calculation was necessary."

"Then who is he?"

"The only one person it could be is Yakubovsky."

"But you just told me that he had iron-clad alibis."

"Yes. But now I am confirming that: he did. But out of all suspects in this case, only Yakubovsky and Goryanin have money. If Goryanin earned his money through hard work and brains—by building houses in the US and selling them for a profit, but Yakubovsky … he suddenly grew rich. Although … after he left the service, he had begun to shuttle. But even shuttling couldn't yield such results so suddenly, especially in those times.

"In order to develop a plan and carry out the embezzlement of several million dollars, a person has to be a professional, as Yakubovsky was. We used to have high qualified professionals," General Terekhin finished with a smile, and raised his glass.